# OUTSTANDING PRAISE FOR
# HAYWOOD SMITH:

### Secrets in Satin

"Haywood Smith always provides her fans with an exciting, extremely powerful historical romance . . . filled with two wonderful lead protagonists and several famous historical persons. Her latest epic masterpiece work, *Secrets in Satin*, will cement her audience belief that she is a winner in a genre known for its great writers."

—*Affaire de Coeur*

### Shadows in Velvet

"Haywood Smith's debut novel stimulates fans of this genre . . . this tale is an exciting, fast reading experience that readers simply must purchase for their collections."

—*Affaire de Coeur*

"A rich, warm, engrossing tale filled with wonderful characters and detail. I enjoyed it tremendously."

—Heather Graham

"A superb romance as rich in history as it is in passion. *Shadows in Velvet* will not only fascinate but enthrall readers. Splendid . . . a wonderful debut."

—*Romantic Times*

# SECRETS IN SATIN

# Haywood Smith

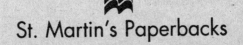

St. Martin's Paperbacks

This book is dedicated to life's real heroines
(especially Betsy, Charlotte, and Susan)
women strong enough to survive the pain,
wise enough to change,
and brave enough to love, and laugh, again.
And to life's real heroes
(like Herschel, my brother Jim, and Ron)
men with the courage to commit.

# Acknowledgments

I'd never have been able to write this book without the wonderful critique and impeccable editorial instincts of a brilliant young author, D. Evelyn King. Thanks, Diane. I'm looking forward to seeing your name on a book cover, and soon.

I also extend warmest appreciation to Christopher Clare, M.D. (the world's best neurosurgeon and a gem of a human being), and David Adams, P.A. (the world's best physician's assistant, kind enough to care and wise enough to really *listen*). Thanks, guys, for putting this middle-aged Humpty Dumpty back together during the writing of this book. Thanks, too, to the staff at Atlanta's Piedmont Hospital, my home away from home now that I'm a "crumbly."

To my editor, Jennifer Enderlin: What a pleasure it is to work with such a talented, understanding professional. You really are an angel.

And to my agent Damaris Rowland: You're the best. Let's just hope we don't end up drinking too much lemonade on the next one.

My gratitude, as well, to Southeast News for giving a new author a chance—and for being patient with my enthusiasm.

# ❄ CHAPTER 1 ❄

*A*s the sole male survivor of the Creighton bloodline, Edward Garrett, Viscount Creighton, had learned more than most men about women. Yet when it came to the fairer sex, he was certain of only one thing: He liked them.

He not only liked women, he enjoyed them.

He reveled in the enfolding resilience of the fat ones and savored the litheness of the thin ones. He relished the way the short ones looked up at him and the tall ones matched against his own substantial height. He appreciated the elegance of the noble ones and the down-to-earth practicality of the common ones.

With rare exceptions, he found something likable in almost every woman he met. The only females who failed to stir his blood or his sympathy were self-righteous courtiers of a certain high-born ilk—cold, unnatural creatures whose judgmental haughtiness snuffed out any hope of honest emotion. Those, he avoided as studiously as he pursued the rest.

And he did enjoy pursuing the rest—at least he had until two months ago, when he'd accepted a commission as lieutenant in King Charles's Cavaliers. Since then, female companionship had been limited to the harlots who plied their age-old trade from canvas brothels in the army's wake.

On this unseasonably cold October night in the year of Our Lord sixteen-hundred-forty-two, the threat of civil war was about to become a reality. Tomorrow Garrett and his fellow Royal Cavaliers would do battle against their own countrymen. That was why he chose to spend what might be his last night among the living in the arms of a whore. Making love had always been a confirmation of life to him—even more so now, in the face of death.

After an hour of vigorous, creative coupling, Garrett was interrupted by the earl of Ravenwold's drink-slurred voice from outside Maeve's tent. "Creighton, this is your commander! You've had your turn. Withdraw and give the rest of us a chance!" A murmur of ribald discontent affirmed the presence of his fellow officers outside.

Garrett sighed. His fingertip traced one of the brows above Maeve's worn, florid features. "You have lovely eyebrows, sweet Maeve. They're arched as delicately as the wings of a gull." His brief farewell squeeze released a whiff of cheap perfume that almost masked the odors of the camp.

He disentangled himself and stood, the heat of his naked body giving off a faint vapor in the cold air. Garrett covered Maeve with the soiled bedclothes. "Much as I have enjoyed this, I must go. It wouldn't do to anger my fellow Cavaliers on the eve of our first battle."

"Stay a little longer. No extra charge." Maeve's fingers ruffled the tawny curls on his calf. "The others can wait. You're worth the lot of 'em, and then some."

"I am humbled by your generous offer, my precious, but I must decline." Garrett pulled on his breeches resolutely. He had no intention of letting mere pleasure put him at cross-purposes with Ravenwold only hours before their first battle. Though he'd reveled from London to Warwick with the moody commander, Garrett knew better than to presume upon Ravenwold's patience. The man had none.

"Withdrawing as ordered, your lordship," Garrett called through the canvas, prompting another spate of coarse jests from outside. He sat on the edge of the bed and retrieved his boots. The secret pocket inside one yielded two shillings and a gold sovereign—all that Dame Fortune had left him after tonight's gambling. The shillings weren't quite enough, but the sovereign was far too much.

After only a moment's hesitation, he shrugged and pressed all three coins into Maeve's palm.

She stared at him in elated disbelief. "A sovereign? Milord, surely you don't mean to . . . I mean, the shillings are good enough." Even as she spoke, her fist clenched tightly to secure her prize.

Garrett pulled on his shirt over his head. "Keep it all." He tugged his thick, wavy hair free of the neckhole. "If I live through tomorrow, there'll be more where that came from. If I don't, the gold will do me little good." He pulled his supple buff leather boots up over his knees, then rose to leave. "Don't spend it all in one place. Farewell, Maeve." His last glimpse of her, she was clutching the coins to her bare breast in amazement.

Ten hours later, Maeve lay dead in the shattered remnants of her tent, killed by errant cannon fire. A thousand yards away at the base of Edgehill, Garrett and Ravenwold were back-to-back, surrounded by rebels and battling for their very lives.

Sixty miles away in London, Elizabeth, Countess of Ravenwold, decided that she could not remain abed any longer. She rose, though every motion set loose a nauseating tide of pain and every breath felt as if a knife were stabbing her in the ribs.

She needed help. And she needed a friend, one who could be trusted not to betray her agonizing secret. She must go to Anne Murray.

Unfortunately, this time there could be no pretending she'd fallen down the stairs.

As she limped painfully to her dressing table, Elizabeth tried to prepare herself for what she would see in the looking glass. But when she finally eased herself down in front of the mirror, she barely recognized the bruised, swollen face that looked back at her. A ragged gasp escaped her puffed, broken lips when she confronted the evidence of her husband's rage.

She had promised herself never to let this happen again, but all her precautions had been useless. Ravenwold had given no warning of his visit. Three days ago she had returned from shopping to find him waiting in her bedroom—drunk, angry, and determined that this time, the seed he brutally planted in her would bear fruit.

Elizabeth's efforts to escape had only further inflamed him, as had her stubborn refusal to pretend enjoyment of his rough advances. But Ravenwold was as clever as he was cruel. Even while he cursed her barrenness, he knew how to punish her without damaging her chances for conception.

He'd struck her in the face, twisted her arm until she thought it would break, kicked her ribs, ripped the clothes from her body, pinned her down, and bitten her breasts until they bled, then knocked her half-senseless so he could spread her legs and slam into her again and again until she was raw. But he never struck her abdomen or threw her down hard enough to stir her womb.

Then, without a word, he had left her to rejoin the king's forces at Warwick. He hadn't bid her good-bye, just announced to the servants that he was off to battle.

Battle. Elizabeth couldn't let herself think of that, for fear she'd wish him killed a thousand times.

She crossed herself, trying to focus on the blessed fact of his absence, then bowed her head and murmured, "Holy Mary, Mother of God, and blessed Saint Anne, hear my petition and bear it to the Father. Please, let me be with child this time." As she prayed, her swollen eyelids leaked tears that she was powerless to stop. "Have mercy, dear Lord. If I don't conceive soon, I know he'll kill me and answer to no one for it."

Why did she bother to ask for mercy? In all her life, she had gotten precious little, except from her sister, Charlotte. And Anne Murray. Now that Charlotte was attending the exiled queen in Paris, Anne was Elizabeth's only friend.

Maybe it's better, Charlotte's not being here, Elizabeth thought. Charlotte wasn't strong like Anne. It would break her heart to see what Ravenwold had done.

Elizabeth sighed, wincing at the resulting stab to her ribs. Then she summoned up her strength and rang for her maid.

Gwynneth responded in record time. "Milady?"

The open pity on her maid's face prompted a fresh wave of shame in Elizabeth. She turned aside and dropped her chin, hiding her black eyes and split lips behind the tangled blond curtain of her hair. "Send a messenger to Miss Murray's. Ask her to meet me at the usual place. If she says yes, order the coach brought round."

Gwynneth gasped. "But, milady isn't strong enough. Surely—"

Elizabeth forced a firmness she did not feel into her voice. "I know you mean well, Gwynneth, but I haven't the strength to argue with you. Please. We'll handle this the way we did last time. I dare not send for a doctor. You know they all peddle gossip for a price here in London. The earl would be furious if anyone found out." She sank weakly against the chair. "Run along, now, so you can come back and help me dress."

Gwynneth returned in fifteen minutes. "The messenger ran all the way to Miss Murray's and back. Miss Murray said she'd meet you at the usual place within the hour."

"Thanks be to God," Elizabeth murmured, grateful that Anne understood the need for discretion. "I only hope I'll be ready by then."

Even with Gwynneth's gentle help, it took Elizabeth more than half an hour to dress. Every movement was agony, and she kept having to lie down to keep from swooning.

At last she was decently attired and standing. Gwynneth settled Elizabeth's cloak about her shoulders, then raised its hood to conceal her mistress's injured face from prying eyes. She offered a steadying arm. "I wish milady would let me ask Miss Murray to come here. I know she would."

"No. It's safer this way." Elizabeth concentrated on putting one foot in front of the other. She could make it one step at a time, with the same determination that enabled her to survive one day at a time. "My husband might cause trouble for her if he found out she'd helped me. You know how the other servants talk."

Gwynneth scowled. "Aye, milady. But I'll not betray milady's trust."

Elizabeth leaned heavily on her arm. "I know you won't, Gwynneth, and I thank God for that."

Twenty minutes later, it took all Elizabeth's strength to dismount from the carriage and walk without limping into the milliner's shop. Gwynneth helped her inside, then waited in the foyer as Elizabeth had instructed her to do. By the time Elizabeth reached the milliner's display salon, she could barely stand up; she swayed in the arched opening, her hand gripping the molding for support.

Inside the salon, Anne Murray sat with her back to Elizabeth, her pretty face smiling into a large looking glass as she tried on an outrageous broad-brimmed hat with white ostrich feathers. The moment Anne saw Elizabeth's stooped, wavering reflection in the glass, she paled. "Milady! What has happened?" She shoved the hat at the clerk and rushed to support her friend.

Elizabeth couldn't help flinching with pain when Anne grasped her forearms. She murmured, "I'm all right, really. I just need to sit down for a moment."

The milliner, her expression more curious than sympathetic,

quickly provided a sturdy chair for Elizabeth to sit in.

Anne reached into her purse, extracted several coins, and pressed them into the milliner's hand. "I'll take that hat, and the other one I tried on. Now, please see that we are not disturbed. I wish to speak to this lady in private."

The milliner nodded. Without a word, she locked the door to her shop, closed the draperies of her display window, then disappeared into the workroom. Only then did Anne carefully fold back the hood that concealed Elizabeth's ruined face.

"No," Elizabeth protested miserably, too weak to stop her.

"Dear God." Anne's hand flew to her mouth, her eyes brimming with tears. In an instant, her anguish shifted to fury. "I vow, what I wouldn't give for one clear pistol shot at that husband of yours!"

"Oh, Anne, don't." Elizabeth cast a worried look at the door to the workroom. "Such idle talk won't help."

"Maybe not." Anne's dark eyes blazed with indignation. "But don't try telling me you fell down the stairs. I didn't believe it the last time, and I certainly don't believe it now." She gingerly wiped away a stray tear from the corner of Elizabeth's swollen eye. "Don't worry. Anne will take care of you." She took Elizabeth's arm and tried to help her to her feet. "Come. You're going home with me. Father was a tutor to the royal family before he became a provost at Eaton, and Mother's still undergoverness to Prince Henry and Princess Elizabeth. My parents have some powerful friends at Court who can see to it Lord Ravenwold doesn't do this again."

"No! You mustn't tell them. My husband will kill me for certain if he finds out I told anyone!" Elizabeth shrank back in panic. The motion released a wave of white-hot pain in her ribs. She saw stars, then everything went black.

She awoke, choking, to the stench of spirits of ammonia. "Tinkers and tacks!" She shoved the offending vial out of her face. "Take that away!" Opening her eyes, she found Gwynneth chafing her wrist and Anne kneeling before her, vial in hand.

Elizabeth fanned weakly at the lingering ammonia fumes. "Forgive me, but those spirits make me cough, and every time I do, it feels like someone's stabbing me in the ribs."

Anne groaned. "Dear heaven, he's broken your ribs." Capping the vial of ammonia, she shot a meaningful look at Gwynneth. "No wonder she fainted when I tried to pull her up."

She hovered over her friend. "Oh, Lady Elizabeth, I'm so sorry. I didn't mean to hurt you further."

Elizabeth managed an unconvincing smile. "It's not your fault. I shouldn't have tried to pull away."

All business now, Anne motioned to Gwynneth. "Come. Help me with your mistress. She needs medical attention." The two women took Elizabeth's forearms and began to ease her from her chair.

"No doctor," Elizabeth objected. "They dispense more gossip than medicine."

"We can trust this one." Anne's tone was soothing. "He's a friend. Lives in the mews just behind this shop. We'll use the back way, so no one will know you went there." She helped Gwynneth guide Elizabeth toward the rear door of the shop. "Remember those fertility potions I brought you? Well, Dr. Low is the one who ordered them for me. He supplies me with all my herbs and medicines, and he's a very good surgeon." Anne paused to raise Elizabeth's deep hood, concealing her face. "I just want him to take a look at you."

The three women moved slowly into the crowded mews. At the end of the courtyard stood a well-maintained town house bearing a sign that proclaimed, DR. LOW, SURGEON.

"Come on, now," Anne coaxed. "Only a few steps farther."

The doctor, himself, met them at the door. He was a thin, elderly man with white hair and kind eyes. "Come in, come in. Put her on the examining couch in my study, but be gentle."

As she helped Elizabeth onto the examining table, Anne told the doctor, "This lady wishes to remain anonymous. I know I can rely upon your discretion, Dr. Low." She exchanged a meaningful glance with the doctor. "I fear that in addition to her other injuries, she may have some broken ribs."

Dr. Low turned a concerned expression toward Elizabeth. "Does milady feel well enough to allow an examination?"

Elizabeth couldn't have gotten up and left if she'd wanted to. She was too sore, and too weak. "I suppose so."

"Very well." He closed the heavy draperies of the examining room, then handed Gwynneth a pressed, neatly folded sheet that smelled of starch. "I shall wait outside while you help your lady disrobe. Cover her well with this, then summon me when she is ready." He ushered Anne back into the foyer.

Undressing was every bit as painful as dressing had been, but took less time. Fifteen minutes later, Elizabeth had stripped down to her chemise. Gwynneth lowered her gently back onto the leather upholstery of the examining couch, then covered her from chin to toe with the clean linen sheet. Once she was satisfied her mistress's modesty was intact, she called in the doctor, then sat nearby, her eyes averted.

Elizabeth steeled herself for the humiliation of a strange doctor's hands and eyes on her body.

"Try to relax, milady. I'll be as brief as possible." After listening to her breathing with the aid of a long metal funnel, he folded the sheet down to her hips, then gently palpated her abdomen through the thin fabric of her shift. When she winced, he looked down on her with sympathy. He covered her. "Due to the nature of milady's injuries, I must make a more intimate examination."

"Very well," Elizabeth consented numbly.

Dr. Low pulled up the bottom of the sheet, exposing her legs. "Milady will please raise her knees."

As he began his examination, she closed her eyes and thought of the many doctors and charlatans she had seen in the last four years. Every time, she had hoped that at last someone would be able to cure her barrenness. The remedies were always expensive, sometimes even absurd, but she had tried them all. Nothing worked.

That was what had caused the trouble between her and Ravenwold.

Her husband hadn't always been so brutal. When they were first married six years ago, he had treated her decently enough. But with every passing year of childlessness, he had grown more sullen, more angry, more violent. Now he was desperate for an heir, and vicious.

"Milady may lower her legs now," the doctor instructed, covering her again. He rinsed his hands in a basin, then dried them.

Elizabeth watched him. This doctor seemed different. Something in his manner made her think he saw her as more than just a potential fee or a collection of injuries and symptoms.

He returned to the examining table. "Now, let's see about those ribs." His hands were gentle as they felt along her ribs through the sheet, but Elizabeth couldn't suppress a cry of pain when he touched where Ravenwold had kicked her. "Aagh!"

"Forgive me for hurting milady," he murmured. The surgeon closed his eyes and felt the broken bones again, then shook his head. "I fear Miss Murray was right. Milady has at least two broken ribs. Possibly three, but fortunately, there doesn't seem to be any damage to the lungs." Dr. Low turned to Gwynneth. "Help your lady dress while I prepare a potion for the pain." He laid a reassuring hand on Elizabeth's forearm. "Hold on for just a little longer. I'll be right back with something to ease milady."

When he started away, Elizabeth clutched at his sleeve. "Doctor, you examined my . . . womb." She flushed with shame at the open reference to her most intimate parts. "Did you see any cause for my barrenness?" She let go and looked away, too embarrassed to face him.

"Everything appears to be perfectly normal." He asked, "Are milady's moon cycles regular?"

Elizabeth nodded in confirmation.

"Well, then. Perhaps it is just God's own good timing." He added with forced cheerfulness, "I have known of several women who had no children until they were approaching the change of life. Be patient, milady. God's timing is often not our own."

Elizabeth tried to hide her disappointment. She did not dare tell him that if God took much longer to grant her children, she would be dead by her own husband's hand. "Anne told me you deal in medicines, fertility potions. Perhaps you've heard of something new . . ."

"As a matter of fact," he offered, "I have just received a shipment from the Orient that includes several rare powders and herbs purported to improve fertility. If milady wishes—"

"Please. I'll buy all you have." Elizabeth faltered. "That is, if you can extend me credit for a few days." She hadn't thought to bring along what little money she had left.

"Do not concern yourself, good lady," he assured her. "Of course, you may have them."

Now if Ravenwold should somehow discover she had been to the doctor, she could tell him she had gone seeking a fertility cure.

Dr. Low bowed. "My apothecary is upstairs. If milady will excuse me . . ."

"Of course."

He hastened away, closing the door behind him.

Elizabeth forced herself upright. "If I can survive getting dressed again, I can survive anything," she grumbled.

"That's the spirit, milady," Gwynneth said, fetching her clothes.

Elizabeth had just finished dressing when she heard a knock and the sound of Anne Murray's voice from the entry hall. "Is everything all right, milady?"

"Admit Miss Murray," she instructed Gwynneth.

When Gwynneth obliged, Anne swept past her to Elizabeth's side. "It got so quiet in here, I thought you'd died."

"Not quite dead yet," Elizabeth observed. "Gwynneth, help me onto that chaise." Perhaps she could breathe easier propped up.

Once she was settled, Anne sat at the foot of the chaise. "I'm sorry I lost my temper earlier and blurted everything out like that." Her big brown eyes leveled. "But I couldn't bear to see what he'd done to you. It isn't right."

"No, it isn't right, but it *is* permitted." Elizabeth's voice was flat. She realized it was futile to pretend any longer, especially with Anne. "My husband thinks he has his reasons. He's the last of his line, with no other relatives, and I have been unable to give him the heir he wants so desperately. If he dies childless, the titles and holdings transfer to me."

Anne's eyebrows shot up.

"Yes. I know it's unusual, but the title has distaff rights of inheritance." Elizabeth patted gingerly at her swollen lip. "I had no idea until he told me, himself. Then he turned right around and accused me of deliberately . . . interfering with nature to prevent conception, just so I could have the last laugh when he died."

Anne's outraged expression spoke more eloquently than words.

"Of course, there is no truth to his suspicions," Elizabeth murmured, grateful for her friend's loyalty. "He wasn't like that when we married. I've always wanted children as much as my husband wants them. I think he believed that, at first. But as time passed, he grew more and more hostile and suspicious."

She could not admit that in six years of marriage, her husband had never touched her in private—not so much as taken her hand—except in anger or as required to exercise his marital prerogative. Lately, he hardly came home at all, seeking her out only when he was frenzied with drink and rage.

Elizabeth looked into Anne's kind face and realized she could no longer bear the burden of Ravenwold's accusations alone. She confessed, "Now he's convinced . . . that I *did* conceive, but I did something to . . . it's too horrible to repeat, what he thinks."

Anne's eyes brimmed with tears. "The man's mad, and madmen are dangerous. You mustn't go back, Lady Elizabeth. If you do—"

Elizabeth finished for her. "He'll kill me. Maybe not the next time, but if I don't conceive, he'll do it eventually—beat me to death, bury me, and marry someone who can give him what he wants." The prospect loomed too real to think of.

Anne took her hand. "Please come home with me. Just for a few days, until you're better. Ravenwold would never have to know."

"He'd find out somehow. He always does." Elizabeth sighed in resignation. "He'd ruin anyone who knew the truth." Unable to remain in any one position for long without excruciating pain, she forced herself upright, then sat on the edge of the chaise until her head stopped swimming. "I dare not think what Ravenwold would do if he should find out you'd given me shelter. He's a powerful man and could cause terrible trouble for you and your parents." With England on the brink of civil war, the slightest unfavorable rumor could cost Dame Murray her position as undergoverness. Ravenwold would not hesitate to destroy anyone who knew his dirty secret. "No. I cannot risk going home with you."

She managed to stand with Anne's help, saying, "But I won't stay in London. When my husband left, he ordered the servants to pack and take me back to Cornwall as soon as I was able to travel. He said the civil war will break out any day now."

Anne's frown deepened. "Dangerous times, for a gentlewoman to venture abroad."

"More dangerous, here, I should think, if Mr. Cromwell and his wretched Puritans have their way." In the three years since she and Anne had struck up an acquaintance in the milliner's shop, Elizabeth had grown very fond of her friend. "I worry for your safety."

Dr. Low's return put an end to the conversation. "Ah. Milady is up." He paused on the threshold and held out a basket containing two bottles and a brown parcel. "Everything milady requested is here, plus the written instructions."

"I'll carry them, sir," Gwynneth offered.

"Quite." Dr. Low turned and handed her the basket. "It wouldn't do for milady to lift anything for a while."

Anne pulled a small purse from her pocket. "What do we owe you, Dr. Low?"

"Three pounds, ten. That includes the medicines. And the basket."

"Why don't we call it four?" Anne offered. She emptied a dozen gold and silver coins into her palm, then counted out what they owed.

"Anne, no," Elizabeth protested. "Our agents will pay."

"Nonsense." Anne leveled a trenchant stare at her. "Why bother your husband's agents with a bill? You know it will only annoy his lordship."

"Oh," Elizabeth said. "I see what you mean." Anne was protecting her, making certain Ravenwold didn't find out.

"Milady can repay me the next time she's in London." Anne handed Dr. Low four silver coins, then dropped the rest back into her purse and pocketed it. She gingerly took hold of Elizabeth's elbow. "Come. I'll help you to the door."

The doctor followed, instructing Gwynneth as he went. "The brown elixir dulls pain; it will help milady sleep. Give her two spoonfuls every six hours, but no more. The green liquid promotes healing. She's to have one teaspoon of that with every meal. The wax-sealed bundle contains those special herbs from the Orient, to be taken as a tea, once a day." As they neared the door, he stepped past the women to open it.

Dr. Low frowned at Elizabeth's unsteady progress. "Although milady's broken ribs do not appear to have damaged her lungs, I recommend complete bed rest for at least three weeks." His frown deepened. "Is milady certain she's well enough to travel?"

She had little choice. Elizabeth deflected his question with, "Thank you for your concern, Doctor. And for your help." Raising the hood of her cloak, she added, "I pray the herbs will work. If not, we may not meet again this side of Heaven." Impulsively, she gave Anne a brief, awkward hug. "I think it would be safer for you if Gwynneth and I went back to the coach alone. Farewell, my friend. Remember me in your prayers."

She left as she had come, one painful step at a time.

# ❧ CHAPTER 2 ❧

### Two Years Later—Cornwall

*G*arrett's mount crested yet another bleak, rain-soaked Cornish hill to bring him within sight of his destination at last. Just ahead, Castle Ravenwold's black stone walls loomed stark and forbidding atop a steep coastal promontory. He raised his hand in the driving rain and ordered, "Detail, halt."

Behind him, ten mounted guards and the wagon bearing the earl of Ravenwold's coffin halted on the muddy track. The eerie silence that followed was broken only by the spatter of raindrops and distant, muffled pounding of a stormy sea.

He motioned the nearest guard. "Rogers, ride ahead and notify Countess Ravenwold that we will be arriving within the hour." He didn't relish spending one minute more than necessary in this wretched weather, but good manners required giving the earl's widow sufficient warning of their arrival. "The rest of you may stand at ease and rest your horses."

As he watched the man gallop away, Garrett tightened his fur-lined cloak against the westerly wind. The cold drizzle pouring from the brim of his hat, he drew a flask of brandy from his saddlebags, savored a warming swig, then passed the rest to his grateful men. "Take only enough to warm yourselves, lads. We wouldn't want to upset the countess by arriving in our cups."

The rain didn't stop until they rode across the drawbridge of Castle Ravenwold. As they passed through the stone entry tower, Garrett looked up at the spiked portcullis and hoped the chains securing the ancient gate were in better repair than the rest of the place.

Lowering his gaze, he directed his mount across the bailey toward the living quarters. Garrett hardly noticed the waiting ranks of black-clad servants lined up beneath the arches. His attention was drawn, instead, to a single, erect figure standing alone at the forefront.

The countess; it had to be.

She was tall for a woman, austerely dressed in black, her hair completely covered by a black cap and snood. Yet she wore no veil.

In spite of himself, Garrett shivered. Castle Ravenwold's mistress matched this dreary place, the white oval of her face as cold and still as a winter's moon reflected in the bottom of a well.

He rode forward, dismounted, approached to a respectful distance, then bowed to his hostess. "Countess Ravenwold?"

She nodded.

"Allow me to present myself, milady. I am Colonel Creighton, Viscount of Chestwick. Your late husband was my friend." Rarely at a loss for words in even the most difficult of circumstances, Garrett hesitated. There was something acutely unsettling about the intensity with which the countess's blue eyes bored into him.

Surely, she couldn't suspect the truth. . . . Only Garrett and the soldiers who had gone with him to claim the body knew that Ravenwold had died in a brothel, his throat cut as cleanly as the whore's beneath him.

His eye was drawn to a slight motion from Countess Ravenwold's right hand, the only betrayal of tension beneath her icy exterior. Garrett saw her thumb rubbing compulsively against the first joint of her index finger.

Instantly, the hand disappeared into the folds of her skirt.

He continued smoothly, "If milady will direct her servants to show them where, my men will place the earl's body in state."

"No. Take . . . the body directly to the chapel." Her voice was as tight and pinched as the rest of her. "The grave has been prepared, and the priest is ready."

Garrett was hardly one to stand on ceremony, but this breach of common decency caught him completely off-guard. "But surely there are relatives, friends, who will wish to pay their respects, to—"

The countess interrupted tersely. "There are no relatives. And no friends." She eyed him suspiciously. "Present company excepted, of course."

Faith, she was a cold one! Ravenwold might have had his faults, but no more than most men Garrett knew. The earl had been generous with his money and never cheated at cards or dice. And he was as brave and loyal a soldier as Garrett had ever known. The man deserved better than this.

Still, etiquette demanded that Garrett honor the widow's wishes. "Very well, milady." He nodded to the men, who began loosing the coffin from the wagon bed.

"Come." The countess turned abruptly and led the way inside.

As Garrett followed, he marveled at her lack of womanly motion. Back rigid and head held high, she seemed to float ahead of him across the cold stone floors.

Inside the great hall, tattered banners hung limply overhead, each bearing the faded silhouette of a black raven on what had probably once been a dark blue background. The place was clean but threadbare and drafty, in worse shape than the crumbling exterior.

Garrett quickened his pace to keep up with the countess. At the far side of the great hall, she entered a passage that led to a small chapel. Just inside the chapel, she abruptly stepped to the right to avoid the gaping hole in the center of the floor.

A papist priest stood at the head of the grave, his back to the ornately carved altar where a life-sized Christ writhed convincingly on his cross. Garrett's staunchly Protestant soul shuddered at the sight of the crucifix. He scanned the idolatrous imagery that cluttered the tiny chapel's stained glass windows and statued niches, then turned his attention to the grave.

On one side of the raw opening was a steep pile of dirt. On the other, a freshly hewn gravestone lay across two timbers. Garrett read the inscription:

Here lieth
Robert William, XVIII[th] Earl of Ravenwold
N. Anno Domini 1610
M. Anno Domini 1645, the last of his line
Who gave little mercy in this worlde
But shalle require much in accounting to Almightie
God

Garrett looked up in amazement to the countess's pale, emotionless face. He could hardly imagine the depth of spite that would prompt such an epitaph. No wonder Ravenwold hadn't gone home once since the civil war had started!

Still, there were formalities to be observed. He asked the rigid countess, "Would you like to see him before he's laid to rest? I could have my men open the—"

"No!" Her blue eyes flared angrily, then narrowed with what he read to be fear. "You saw him, didn't you?" she demanded. "It *was* Ravenwold? You're certain?"

Garrett nodded. "Aye."

The fear left her, replaced by blank aloofness. "Then there is no need to open the coffin. I have seen more than enough of my husband."

The priest rolled his eyes and crossed himself, a worried frown creasing his well-fed features.

Garrett made up his mind then and there to leave for Bristol before another dawn. Even the jealousies and infighting of headquarters seemed preferable to this dour place and its eerie mistress. Bitterness permeated Castle Ravenwold so thoroughly Garrett could almost taste it.

Behind him, he heard the heavy shuffle of his men bearing the rope-bound coffin. Garrett stepped into the hall and motioned them silently into the chapel. The men struggled through the doorway, then placed the casket atop the gravestone, untied the ropes, and lowered the earl of Ravenwold's mortal remains into the ground. After they settled the coffin, the honor guard stood to attention and waited for the service to begin.

But before the priest commenced, the countess addressed Garrett's men imperiously. "This will be a private ceremony. You are dismissed."

Garrett bristled. Hostess or no hostess, she had no right to command his men. His voice tense, he said, "Milady, they're only doing as I ordered. The earl of Ravenwold's rank and stature merit an honor guard, at the very least."

She turned the full, wintry force of her cold blue eyes on Garrett. "This is my house, sirrah, and my husband. The funeral shall be as I wish it." She paused, glaring at the men, who looked from her to Garrett and back in confusion. Then she added, almost as if granting some great favor, "The viscount may remain, of course." She looked at Garrett with the faintest hint of contempt. "In deference to the *friendship* you bore the earl."

Garrett had never in his life wanted so much to slap a woman. By thunder, she was a soulless, sarcastic witch! He nodded tersely to his men. "As the lady wishes. You are dismissed, but be ready to leave an hour before dawn." He bowed to the countess and offered an acerbic, "We do not wish to impose upon the countess's grief one moment longer than necessary."

If she took offense, she gave no indication. Instead, Countess Ravenwold merely turned to the priest, who hastily began mumbling the sacrament in Latin.

At the conclusion of the rite, the countess scooped up a handful of earth and hurled it atop the coffin. Then she stood motionless, looking down as if to memorize every detail of her husband's grave.

Garrett waited a long time before breaking the silence. "If it pleases milady, I shall see that my men are fed and provisioned. Then I would like to retire. We need to make an early start in the morning."

The countess started briefly, like someone coming out of a trance, then turned to Garrett, her eyes glazed with unshed tears. "Of course."

Garrett had rarely seen such stifled torment. He was about to decide he'd judged her too harshly, when she turned away from his scrutiny, her voice hardening. "Thank you for bringing him home. I know the journey was difficult and dangerous." She pivoted back, her face once more cold and unreadable. "I am in your debt, sir."

Garrett bowed. "Think nothing of it, milady."

That was one debt he hoped never to have need of collecting.

# Chapter 3

Garrett wasn't certain of the hour, but deep in the night, he sat up abruptly in the darkness, the hair standing on the back of his neck.

For a brief instant, he didn't know where he was. Then he inhaled the musty odor of the bed curtains and remembered.

Castle Ravenwold.

He could hear the storm howling outside, forcing its way through the ancient castle's chinks and crannies. The heavy damask bed hangings billowed rhythmically in and out, as if some giant creature of the night were breathing just beyond them. Garrett pulled the curtains open and saw the shadowed images of his stone bedchamber.

He settled back into the musty featherbed and pulled the bedclothes up under his chin, wondering what had wakened him.

Across the room, the fire ebbed and flared unnaturally with every gust of wind. But that wouldn't have wakened him. The bedcurtains had been drawn, shutting out all but the faintest light. Even if they hadn't been, Garrett had grown accustomed to the flicker of the campfire and the cold, shrieking storms of Cornwall during the long journey here. Now he was dry and warm, at least.

Probably just a nightmare. He lay back and silently repeated his prayers. That usually put him right to sleep, but this time, he remained edgy and alert.

After what seemed like more than an hour, he gave up and rose. The sooner he got out of here, the better. The storm would offer perfect cover for their leaving, should any Roundhead spies be watching. This place made his skin crawl, as did its mistress.

His men had bedded down in the kitchen near the warmth of the huge fireplaces. They could be ready to travel in less than a half hour. Garrett dressed as quickly and quietly as he could, then headed for the main stairway.

But just as he reached the top of the open stairway, he looked down into the great hall and saw a vision that stopped him in midstride. A woman with gloriously unbound blond hair walked unsteadily on bare feet across the cold stone floor below, her hand holding a chimneyed lantern aloft. Garrett couldn't see her face, but her fur-lined robe had slipped seductively from her shoulder, revealing her sheer nightgown and a tantalizing suggestion of feminine nakedness underneath. Then she stumbled and turned slightly, showing enough of her face to cause Garrett to catch his breath.

By thunder, it was Countess Ravenwold!

He leaned away from the light, afraid that she would see him. But the countess didn't seem to notice him. She pulled her robe closed against the hall's cold drafts and continued toward the chapel.

Garrett felt as if someone had landed an unexpected blow to his chest. He would never have guessed that Countess Ravenwold's widow's cap hid such lush, golden tresses. Nor that her stiff, somber mourning gown concealed such generous curves.

It had been a long time since a woman had so surprised him.

Goaded by curiosity, he descended the stairway and headed for the chapel instead of the kitchen. He knew he shouldn't, but he felt oddly compelled to follow her. Garrett trod softly, keeping far enough back so the countess would not hear him. When she entered the chapel, he waited fully a minute before creeping up behind the half-opened doors. Ashamed at himself for doing it, he peered through the wide crack near the hinges. What he saw shamed him, indeed.

Ravenwold's grave had already been filled in and covered by the slab. The countess had dropped to her hands and knees upon the gravestone, her body shaking silently. The fluttering lantern threw stark shadows across the little chapel.

Garrett turned aside and closed his eyes, deeply sorry to have intruded upon her private suffering. He had judged the woman most harshly, without knowing anything. Now, confronted by the evidence of her grief, he wished he'd gone straight to the kitchen instead of following her.

With agonizing slowness, he turned and made his way down the darkened hallway. But no sooner had he reached the great hall, than he heard a sound from the chapel that sent a chill straight through him.

A lyrical soprano voice—clear and lucid as sunlight on a running brook—echoed from the shadowed stone vaulting high above. The words were slightly slurred, but the cheerful melody flawless:

> My wedding cup was bitter gall that poisoned love's illusions, all,
> But death cruel destiny did cheat, and now my lord is maggot's meat.
> The taste of solitude is sweet. The taste of solitude is sweet.

Garrett's mouth dropped open.

As the song repeated, he turned and carefully retraced his steps, peering through the crack to find Countess Ravenwold, her robe askew and her back to him, singing and dancing with fluid abandon on her husband's grave!

After one particularly unsteady pirouette, she collapsed into a heap, one long, well-shaped leg exposed to the thigh. And a very nice thigh it was, her skin as fair and fine as ivory. Then she let out a thick, inebriated giggle.

Drunk!

Garrett wrestled down a strong urge to laugh aloud.

So she *hadn't* been grieving before. She'd been laughing!

Garrett was mystified and fascinated in equal measure. This golden, wanton creature couldn't be the same rigid, bitter harridan he had met, but she was.

Countess Ravenwold rolled onto her stomach and spread-eagled flat against the marble slab. Her long, elegant fingers lovingly caressed the words etched into the marble. "Well, Robert, it seems you were right after all. I *shall* have the last laugh. And the title, the holdings, whatever's left. It's mine now. All mine." Her voice edged upward. "Mine. Mine." Then she burst into tears, sobbing as her fists flailed the hard, cold stone.

Garrett watched, spellbound, his emotions alternating between horror, amazement, and a disturbing stab of lust.

Despite her secret excesses, the woman was too hard to be believed. Gloating, even *dancing* on her husband's grave! Garrett thought of Ravenwold and shook his head. Then he turned and made straight for the kitchen.

Elizabeth wept for all she had suffered. She had lived the past two years in mortal fear that Ravenwold would return and kill her for her barrenness, but now he was dead, really dead, leaving her free to release the anger that had poisoned her for so long.

At last, her secret hope had become a reality, and it was safe to vent her rage. She pounded her fists until they lost sensation; she cried until her body chilled from the cold slab beneath her. But just as her tears began to subside, she heard a distant footstep.

Instantly silent, she struggled to her feet and stumbled into the hallway. Across the great hall, Colonel Creighton strode rapidly toward the kitchen, his tall, blond figure plainly identifiable even at a distance.

Elizabeth shrank back into the shadows, her heart skipping a beat.

Had he heard? Had he seen . . . ?

Creighton paused when he reached the kitchen and shot a withering look in her direction. Though she knew he couldn't see her hiding in the shadows, she tingled with shame as if she stood, stripped naked, before him.

He *had* seen and heard, the bounder! Spying, like some Peeping Tom!

Elizabeth shook with embarrassment and rage. Creighton couldn't leave soon enough to suit her. She thanked the Blessed Virgin that she would never have to see him again.

She only prayed he'd be gentleman enough to keep what he'd seen to himself. But if Ravenwold was the kind of man Creighton called friend, she was doomed. Everyone at Court would hear of what she'd done.

Her tears starting afresh, Elizabeth crept back into the chapel. There, on her knees before the altar, she vowed never to leave Cornwall again.

\*      \*      \*

Garrett found his men already half-dressed in the kitchen. They had heard the distant song and mistaken it for the cries of a ghost.

Glad for their haste, he did not tell them otherwise. He wanted to get as far away from Countess Ravenwold as he could, as fast as he could.

Twenty minutes later, he led the last of his men past Castle Ravenwold's grumbling gatekeeper. Garrett didn't look back until they were well away, and when he did, it was only to ask God's help for the next poor, unsuspecting wretch who had the misfortune to wed the Countess Ravenwold.

# ❧ CHAPTER 4 ❧

### March 24, 1648 (Three years later)

*E*lizabeth checked the contents of the heavy basket Gwynneth was holding, then climbed out of the coach unassisted. Her last pair of good boots sank into the mud, forcing her to hold her heavy widow's weeds indecently aloft until she found surer footing. Once she made it to the grassy verge, she shielded her eyes from the bright sunlight and called to the driver, "Pull ahead a bit, Terrell. The road's still amuck here."

The old man colored. "Beg pardon, milady."

When the carriage rolled to a stop on drier ground, Gwynneth dismounted, scowling, and joined her mistress. "I don't know why you keep him on, milady. He can barely find his way past the bed curtains. I do believe he's half-blind."

"Hush, Gwynneth. He'll hear you." Elizabeth set out down the grassy slope toward a humble stone cottage that overlooked the sea. When they were out of earshot of the coach, she said, "Terrell has served two generations of Ravenwolds well and faithfully. Would you have me repay such loyalty with dismissal?" She shook her head. "You know he'd never find work elsewhere. Why else do you think I've kept him on, when I had to let so many others go?"

"I'm sorry, milady." Gwynneth had the decency to look ashamed. She stammered, "I didn't mean to . . . that is, I . . . About the money . . . You won't be sendin' *me* away, will you? Even if milady couldn't pay me, I'd want to stay."

"Thank you, Gwynneth, but let's hope it never comes to that." Elizabeth had given up so much already in an effort to keep her tenants from starving. "The rebellion complicates matters. I pray that it will end soon, but prudence forces me to think otherwise." The truth was, she didn't know how much longer she could manage on what little Ravenwold had left her. Every month the Crown needed more: more young men for the army, more taxes to pay them, more provisions to feed them. Soon there would be no tenants left but women, children, and old men to fish or work the fields. And then what would she do? What would they all do, the hundreds of families who looked to her for protection and guidance?

The question loomed, huge and unanswerable, in her thoughts. In spite of the March sunshine and unseasonably warm wind, she shivered, then crossed herself.

"Is milady all right? Perhaps we should turn back . . ."

Elizabeth kept up her pace down the steep fallow field that lay between them and the farmhouse. "No. A cat just ran across my grave." To counter the ill omen, she said "cat hairs" three times, kissed the crucifix that hung from her necklace, then silently repeated three "Our Fathers."

The wind caught her heavy black skirts and sent them billowing, making it difficult to see where she was stepping, but Elizabeth didn't mind. She was glad for the rare sunshine and grateful for the fair breeze that would dry up most of the mud and offal. The fresh smell of the sea scrubbed the air and held the promise of warmer days.

At the stacked-stone wall that surrounded the barnyard, she opened the wicket gate and called back to Gwynneth, "Be sure to fasten the gate well, or the sheep will get out." Once inside, she headed for the long, low stone cottage that had sheltered generations of Edmunsons. The farmhouse was still several yards away when its door burst open and a disorderly tide of children poured forth.

"It's milady, Mum! Milady's here!"

As always, Elizabeth and Gwynneth found themselves surrounded. Ignoring the little goat that nibbled at her hem, Elizabeth smoothed three-year-old William's tangled dirty curls. She said solemnly, "Hello, William." Like his brothers and sisters, the child had lice and needed a good scrubbing. Elizabeth turned to the eldest, Lona, a shy girl of ten who held a bare-breeched infant on her hip. "How is your mother today, Lona?"

Lona's blush was evident even through the grime that streaked her face. She averted her eyes and said, "A bit stronger, milady, thanks to that stew ye brought, but still helt to 'er bed."

The other children stared intently at the basket on Gwynneth's arm, but were too shy to speak. Knowing how hungry they must be, Elizabeth reached in and extracted several apples. She gave the first to eight-year-old Tannie. "Here you are, Tannie."

Delighted by the sweet treasure, the boy bowed awkwardly. "Thank ye, milady."

As she distributed apples to the others, Elizabeth said, "Tannie, please run tell my driver that I shall stay longer than expected. Then come back inside. You'll all be needing baths."

At the prospect of a bath, Tannie's expression of heartfelt gratitude shifted to one of dread, then settled into resignation. "Aye, milady. I'll tell 'im." He hung his head dejectedly and set out across the yard at a snail's pace.

Elizabeth almost smiled. She called after him, "Don't take too long, Tannie. I have dried figs and cheese for everyone who bathes without complaint." The children had shown a particular fondness for figs, even dried ones. "If you dawdle, there might not be any figs left when you get back."

Six grubby little faces brightened, Tannie's among them. He let out a whoop, then sprinted for the coach.

Gwynneth, though, frowned in disapproval. "Those were for milady's lunch. What will milady—"

Elizabeth took the basket from Gwynneth, silencing her protests with a quiet, "I'd rather have an empty belly and bathe seven *willing* children, than a full belly and bathe seven *unwilling* ones."

Gwynneth's frown shifted to a wry smile. "Milady has a point." She turned to the children. "All right, wee ones, run fetch the water. I'll go inside and stoke the fire to heat yer bath." Her voice dropped to a good-natured grumble. "Assumin' there's anything to stoke the fire *with*."

"If not," Elizabeth offered, "I'm sure the children can always find some dried offal for the fire." At Gwynneth's squinch-faced reaction to the smelly prospect of burning sheep shite, Elizabeth admonished, "You needn't wrinkle your nose up. If things at Ravenwold don't change soon, we might be forced to burn offal instead of sea-coal, ourselves." She pushed aside the oily sheepskins that covered the doorway. Inside at the far end of the dim interior, Ada Edmunson struggled to sit up in her sagging bed. "God bless ye, milady. I knew ye'd come ere the food ran out," she said weakly.

Elizabeth crossed to Ada's bed and gently urged the fevered woman back onto the straw mattress. "Save your strength, Mistress Edmunson." Once Ada was settled, Elizabeth drew up a three-legged stool and sat close by. "Has there been any word of Mister Edmunson? I've written his regiment several times, but received no reply."

"No, milady." Ada's eyes closed, her sallow, gaunt face bleak. "I'm sore afeared 'e's slain, but Lona says we mustn't give up 'ope."

Like so many of the families who wrenched a living from Cornwall's harsh hills and harsher seas, the Edmunsons had fared poorly since the civil war had taken their menfolk. When Ada's illness had struck, the effect on her family was devastating. Without help, they would have perished months ago.

"Lona's right, Mistress Edmunson." Elizabeth patted Ada's dry, callused hand. "We must all keep praying and hoping for Mr. Edmunson's safe return. I pray for that daily, as I do for an end to this terrible war."

Several of the children entered, bearing leather buckets of water from the cistern. Gwynneth followed, her arms laden with driftwood, and proceeded to stoke the embers in the fireplace beside Ada's bed.

Elizabeth shifted the conversation to a more positive subject. "I wrote Dr. Low in London about your illness—the fevers, the sweats, and trembling—and he sent me a miraculous new remedy made of cinchona bark powder." She drew a corked bottle of dark brown liquid from the basket and handed it to Ada. "I've prepared it as an elixir. See that each of the children gets one teaspoonful every day. You are to have three teaspoons a day—one on waking, one at midday, and one at eventide. Dr. Low swears it will make you well in no time and prevent the children from falling ill."

Ada frowned miserably, a tear coursing from the side of her eye.

"What's wrong, Mistress Edmunson?"

Ada barely got the words out. "We 'aven't a teaspoon, milady."

A surge of sympathy and embarrassment warmed Elizabeth's neck. She rummaged in the basket until she found the silver utensils packed for her own use. "But of course, the teaspoon is part of the cure. It must be silver, and I've brought one with the medicine.''

Gwynneth cleared her throat loudly with disapproval at her mistress's latest extravagance.

Elizabeth shot her a warning look, then handed the spoon to Ada. "Now Gwynneth and I are going to tidy the house, bathe the children, then start a pot of soup before we leave.''

Ada clutched the silver spoon in one hand. With the other, she reached for Elizabeth's hem, drew it to her cracked lips and kissed it, then looked up at her benefactor. "I can never repay milady's kindness, but the good Lord will reward ye for helpin' the likes of us, and us not even papist.''

Embarrassed, Elizabeth gently pulled her hem free of Ada's grip. "None of that, now. Hunger and sickness know nothing of Catholic or Protestant. The same God commands us all to help each other. And we're all loyal subjects of the Crown.'' She forced a smile for Ada's sake. "Rest easy now, so Gwynneth and I may see to what needs doing.''

The sun had long been set by the time Elizabeth's coach returned to Castle Ravenwold. Stiff and weary inside her damp, bath-splashed clothes, she shook Gwynneth awake. "We're home.'' But before she could gather the strength to climb down from the coach, an elegantly clad courier approached from the stables.

The short, thick-set messenger bowed, his satin livery gleaming dully in the torchlight. "Milady. I bring urgent message for Madame la Comtesse Ravenwold.''

At the sound of his heavy French accent, Elizabeth's breath caught in her throat. Something must have happened to Charlotte in Paris! A surge of dread tingled through her as she stepped down to the cobblestones. "I am the Countess Ravenwold.'' Elizabeth confirmed the words by revealing the Ravenwold family ring that covered her middle finger from knuckle to knuckle. "Give me the message.''

The courier bowed again, then drew a folded letter from his pouch.

The torchlight illuminated the queen's distinctive seal as Elizabeth accepted the missal. Her mouth went so dry she could barely speak. "Thank you.'' Only the direst of circumstances merited the risk and expense of sending a courier from France during these uncertain times.

*Please, dear Lord, let Charlotte be all right.*

As motherless children, the two sisters had helped each other survive their father's cold, unrelenting discipline and abuse. Since their father had died, Charlotte was Elizabeth's only close relative. If anything happened to her, Elizabeth would be truly alone in the world.

She tried to keep the fear from her voice. "Gwynneth, see that the messenger is fed and provided with a place to sleep. I'll sup in my chambers."

"Very well, milady."

Fifteen minutes later when Gwynneth brought a tray bearing bread, cheese, dried figs, and wine into her sitting room, Elizabeth was still staring at the unopened letter in her hand.

"Is it bad news, milady?"

"I fear so. The letter bears the queen's seal." Dangerously close to tears, she looked to her maid's kind face for strength. "I haven't had the courage to open it."

Gwynneth set the tray on the table. "I'll open it, milady."

"Dear Gwynneth." Elizabeth managed a wan smile. "But you can't read."

"Well, at least it would be opened. Wouldn't that help?"

"Thank you, but no." Nor would waiting change what was inside. As always, Elizabeth forced herself to do what must be done. She opened the letter and read:

Her majesty Queen Henrietta Maria extends felicitations to her servant and vassal, the countess of Ravenwold. This message is sent at the request of Lady Markham—

Charlotte, Elizabeth thought. Oh, please, dear Lord, don't let anything have happened to Charlotte.

—Lady Markham, our valued and faithful lady-in-waiting, requesting with the utmost urgency that the countess attend her sister, who has fallen gravely ill. All necessary arrangements have been made. The courier who delivers this message will serve as escort to the countess. Regretting the unhappy circumstances which necessitate this communication,

Henrietta Maria, Regina Brittanium

Elizabeth moaned. She had spent the day ministering to Ada Edmunson, a woman she barely knew, while her only sister lay ill—perhaps dying. And she'd given away all of Dr. Low's medicine! If only she'd kept some, she could have taken it to Charlotte.

Perhaps it wasn't too late to help her sister; Charlotte might yet be alive. But for how long? How long had it taken for the courier to reach her? Elizabeth rose. "Where is the messenger? I must speak with him at once."

"In the kitchen, milady. I'll fetch him right—"

"No." She waved Gwynneth back. "I'll go to him. You stay here and pack. We're leaving for France tonight."

"Tonight! But milady is exhausted. And travel is so dangerous these days. Surely milady can wait—"

"We cannot wait." Elizabeth left Gwynneth to her protests. She called back, "I'll explain later. Just start packing."

She found the messenger wolfing down a bowl of stew at the long kitchen table. He stopped eating abruptly and rose to attention when she approached him. Elizabeth motioned for him to sit down. "Please, go on with your meal." When he hesitated, glancing hungrily at the bowl of stew, she added, "You must eat, for I'd like to leave as soon as possible."

The man nodded and sat, but did not resume eating, waiting for the questions that were sure to come.

Elizabeth needed only the essentials. There would be time for the rest later. "How long did it take you to reach me?"

In heavily accented English, he replied, "Ten days, madame la comtesse."

So long! She smothered a groan. Charlotte could be dead already. Or recovered. "The letter says that arrangements have been made for my passage. What are they?"

"A sheep, she waits at Grah-vzend."

"A sheep?" Elizabeth's brows drew together in confusion.

"*Oui.* Sheep." The messenger frowned at her failure to comprehend. "Zees is ze word for *vaisseu, non?*" He made a rocking motion with his hands.

"Oh, a ship." Then the rest of what he had said sank in. Elizabeth gasped. "Gravesend!" Gravesend was on the other side of England!

He gave a Gallic shrug. "Ze blockade."

"But Gravesend is more than a week's coach ride away. Even on horseback, it will take at least five days to get there.

Couldn't we sail from a closer port?''

The messenger frowned, clearly baffled by her rapid speech.

Elizabeth searched her memory for the few French words Charlotte had been able to teach her. She said haltingly, *"Nous pouvons pas departer plus pres d'ici?"* hoping that she was asking if they couldn't leave from a closer port.

The messenger's frown deepened. Apparently, he found her French as indecipherable as her English. Then his face cleared. *"Ah, je comprend."* He shook his head matter-of-factly. "No, madame la comtesse. Eet must be Grah-vzend."

"But the roads are so muddy," Elizabeth thought aloud. Then she remembered her late husband's stallions. There were still three of his magnificent warhorses in the stable. She and Gwynneth could ride two, leaving one for the messenger. She had enough gold stashed away to cover travel expenses. Elizabeth looked hopefully to the Frenchman. *"Les cheveux . . . un pour moi et un pour vous. C'est plus rapide, non?"*

He tucked his chin in consternation. *"Cheveux?"*

Reviewing what she had said, she realized why he seemed so confused. "Tinkers and tacks! *Cheveux* is *hair.* I meant *cheval*—horse."

Relieved, he nodded. "Ah, *oui, cheval.*" But as before, his smile was short-lived. *"Non.* Very *dangereuse,* madame la comtesse. We mus' take ze coach. Ze rebellion. *C'est trop dangereuse* to ride in ze open."

He was right of course. Not to mention the fact that although Elizabeth was an expert horsewoman, Gwynneth could barely sit a saddle. She would never be able to keep up. And Elizabeth couldn't very well go tearing off unchaperoned in the company of a strange man.

They would have to take the coach. She consoled herself that the coach would at least provide shelter from the elements and privacy from prying eyes. "Very well. I'll have the groom ready the coach and fresh horses. Please finish your supper."

As she rose, Elizabeth realized the route to Gravesend would take them near London. A fresh spark of hope lightened her spirits. When they neared the capital, she could send word ahead to Dr. Low that she needed more cinchona bark powder, and some willow bark powder, as well. If Dr. Low had them, and if he could get them to Gravesend before she sailed . . .

So many ifs. And what good would anything do if Charlotte were beyond help?

Elizabeth pushed away the horrible thought, clinging to the conviction that Charlotte was still alive. She would know if her sister were dead. She would have felt *something*.

Turning her attention to immediate matters, she sent the scullery maid to notify the groom of their departure, then she addressed the cook. "How soon can you prepare provisions for myself, Gwynneth, and the messenger—enough for at least a week?"

The cook pursed her lips. "Two hours, if milady doesn't mind eating mostly dried chine and cold biscuits. There's plenty of wine and cheese, but the dried fruit is almost gone."

"Do the best you can and see that it's packed into the coach. But be sure to leave enough food for the rest of you. I don't know when I'll be returning. Until then, Mr. Goodshire will be in charge." Her bailiff was an honest and reliable man. "Oh, and Cook, don't forget to send food to the Edmunsons while I'm gone."

"Aye, milady."

"I'll be upstairs packing with Gwynneth, should you need me." She started for the stairs, then paused and turned back to the messenger. "You must be exhausted from your journey, sir. Will you need more than a few hours sleep?"

The man shook his head. "*Mais non,* madame la comtesse. I 'ave slept zis afternoon many hours, awaiting ze comtesse return."

Hours? And she had wasted more time, afraid to open the letter. Elizabeth resolved not to delay their departure one minute longer than necessary. "I shall see you at the stable in two hours, then."

Eight dangerous, grueling days later, the coach reached Gravesend. As she had planned, Elizabeth had sent a courier to London from Kingston-on-Thames. Now as she disembarked at dockside in Gravesend, she searched the faces in the milling crowd for someone who might be looking for her. She was about to give up when a familiar feminine voice accosted her from behind.

"Milady? It *is* you! Thanks be to God."

Elizabeth would have known that voice anywhere. "Anne!" She spun around to find Anne Murray's face almost hidden by the deep hood of her cloak. "What are you doing here?"

Anne grinned, producing a substantial bundle bound in oilcloth and tied with string. "Dr. Low got your message, but he was tending a patient and couldn't deliver it himself. He was afraid to trust anyone else, so he sent for me, and here I am." She handed Elizabeth the precious bundle. "He put in the cinchona bark powder and willow bark you asked for. He even added a few new herbs that might be of help to your sister. There's a note inside explaining everything."

In spite of the beating she'd taken from their journey, Elizabeth felt her discouragement ease. "What would I ever do without you and dear Dr. Low? You're always coming to my rescue." She took the package and gratefully counted out as much cash as she could spare. "I'll have my agent send you the rest."

Anne shook her head and pushed Elizabeth's black-gloved hand away. "I'll not take your traveling money. You can pay me when you return." As always, she understood Elizabeth's predicament.

"Are you certain?" Anne's mother had died the preceding August, and Elizabeth wasn't certain how the Murrays were managing on just Anne's father's stipend. "Since your mother passed away, I wasn't sure . . ."

"Father and I are fine. We can afford a small loan for a friend."

"Bless you, Anne. I'll send a note to my agent in London before I leave. He'll see that you're paid." Elizabeth closed her fist on the money and smiled. "My escort has gone to check on our ship. Do you have time to visit?"

Anne glanced about with uncharacteristic nervousness. "Yes, but let's do our chatting in the coach. It might be safer for you if we weren't seen together."

After eight days on the road, the coach was the last place Elizabeth wanted to be, but something in Anne's manner made her agree. "As you wish." She opened the door and said, "Gwynneth, would you like to stretch your legs while I visit with Miss Murray?" She handed her maid some of the money, then dropped the rest back into her bag. "Here. I'm sure you'd like some warm food, too." They hadn't had a hot meal since stopping to change horses in Hampton Court. "There's an inn down the block. After you eat, bring some stew back for Monsieur Galleaux and me."

Gwynneth happily set out to accomplish her errand, leaving the two women alone in the coach. As usual, Anne didn't mince words. "How did you know I wanted to speak to you alone?"

"I sensed it. You seem preoccupied. Wary."

Anne glanced out the window again, then nodded. "I am. I don't think I was followed, but one can never be too sure."

"Followed? Anne, what's happened?"

"I've grown up, that's all." Her friend pushed back the hood of her heavy cloak to reveal a mischievous grin. "Being a good, obedient daughter has brought me nothing but heartbreak, so I've decided not to be good any longer. It's wonderfully liberating, I can tell you."

Elizabeth knew from their correspondence that Anne and Thomas Howard had fallen deeply in love, only to have his suit rejected by her mother, owing to his poverty. Brokenhearted, Anne had obediently watched her prospects for marriage fade over the next three years. Now that her mother was dead, she had rebelled at last.

Anne's eyes sparkled. "I've met the most fascinating man— a Colonel Bampfield, a friend of my brother's. Father disapproves of him completely, but at this stage in my life, I do not care. I have no proper suitors and will doubtless die an old maid." She straightened defiantly. "But I shall not die of boredom, thanks to Colonel Bampfield. He is a most attentive lover."

"Anne!" Elizabeth was shocked to hear such talk from devout, pious Anne.

"As I said, I have grown up." Anne glanced out the window, then addressed Elizabeth with gravity. "I have gladly brought your medicine, but in return, I must ask a great boon of you. It's a matter of life and death."

Elizabeth asked warily, "Does it concern Colonel Bampfield?" Much as she owed her friend, she respected Anne's father and did not wish to deceive him.

Anne shrugged. "Only indirectly. He entrusted me with the delivery of a most urgent message for his highness, the Prince of Wales. I tried to book passage to France, but there is none to be had for love or money. Then Dr. Low told me of your message. It had to be Divine Providence." She drew the letter from her cloak. "Would you take this to his highness?"

Elizabeth felt the blood drain from her face. "The Prince of Wales?"

Always ready with the latest servants' gossip, Gwynneth

had told Elizabeth of the Prince of Wales's flight to Europe. Creighton had gone with him. Elizabeth had been glad, relieved that Creighton had left the country. As far as she knew, the knave still served at the prince's right hand. Now Anne was asking her to risk the humiliation of seeing that scoundrel again. "I couldn't . . . I mean, I could take the letter, but someone else would have to deliver it."

Anne shook her head. "Forgive me, milady, but this concerns a matter of such import that I dare not trust the letter to anyone else. Only his highness, from your hand to his. It must be, or all is lost." She placed the letter into Elizabeth's hands and closed her own around them. "I would not ask it if there were any other way."

Elizabeth had never seen Anne so desperate or so serious.

How could she explain? She couldn't tell Anne about Creighton and what happened that night in the chapel three years ago. Even thinking of it sent a hot tide of humiliation coursing through her. If she were to see him again . . . Elizabeth cringed, knowing better than to rely on Creighton's discretion. Everyone at Court knew the rogue was no gentleman; his high living and romantic escapades had been favorite topics of gossip among courtiers and servants alike.

She couldn't face that sneaky, spying scoundrel again. "But you don't understand. There are things . . . That is, I . . ."

Anne withdrew her hands, grave disappointment evident in her expression. Obviously, this was, indeed, a most serious matter.

Elizabeth realized that her dignity was the only thing standing in the way of helping her friend. Or was it her pride? "Oh, Anne. I want to help you, but there's someone with the prince, someone I cannot bear to see again."

Anne's eyes narrowed. "Who?" Seeing Elizabeth color, she guessed, "Creighton? Don't tell me *you*—"

Elizabeth blanched. Had the blackguard told everyone in England that she'd danced on her husband's grave?

"It *is* Creighton!" Anne peered at Elizabeth as if seeing her for the first time. "I never would have dreamed . . . I mean, you don't seem to be his type. But then again, he's always saying that *every* woman is his type."

"Don't be absurd." Both outraged and relieved by Anne's insinuation, Elizabeth dared to hope that perhaps Creighton hadn't told everyone what she'd done, after all. But she couldn't have Anne thinking she and Creighton . . . "I assure you, there is nothing that even vaguely resembles a romantic attachment between Viscount Creighton and me. Nor has there ever been."

Anne grinned. "Good. Because if anything should ever happen to Colonel Bampfield, I just might want to sample Viscount Creighton's legendary talents, myself, although I suspect that his reputation, like most legendary lovers', is more myth than fact."

"Well, I am *not* one of his conquests. The man's a blackguard."

"More's the pity," Anne commented, undaunted.

Elizabeth couldn't help but smile. "Anne, you have become the most scandalous woman . . ."

Her friend chuckled. "We're opposite sides of the coin now, milady. You follow all the rules, and I follow none. You obey, I rebel. You are good, and I am as bad as I have the opportunity to be."

"You're not bad, Anne. You're the kindest, bravest, most honest woman in the world." Elizabeth looked at the letter in her hand. Ever since her own mother's death, she had tried to be invisible so she would be safe. She'd taken no risks and broken no rules, but earned only heartache and abuse. Maybe it was time to stop being invisible.

Hang Viscount Creighton!

She tucked the letter into her pouch. "I'll deliver your letter to the Prince of Wales, my hand to his as you asked. You have my solemn vow."

The admiration in Anne's eyes said far more than words. "I knew I could count on you."

"One question, though. What if someone tries to take it from me?"

Anne shrugged. "Burn it or eat it—whichever you can manage."

"Eat it? Surely you're joking."

"Nay, milady. I'm as serious as the plague." Anne raised the hood of her cloak and slid forward on the seat. "But should milady find it necessary to eat the letter, it will go down easier in small pieces. Trust me, I speak from experience." She scanned the street before disembarking, then gave Elizabeth's hand an impulsive squeeze. "Godspeed, Lady Elizabeth. And

God save the king.'' Then she left, closing the coach door behind her.

Elizabeth felt a strange sense of loss as she watched her friend disappear into the milling sailors, vendors, and merchants who crowded the docks. Never, in all her twenty-eight years, had she left her native England. Nor had she ever set foot on a ship. Rattling off a prayer for traveling mercies, she turned her eyes to the gray, choppy waters where the Thames met the channel.

Though she'd never sailed the sea, she knew its signs, and what she saw did not bode well. A cold wind had kicked up, bringing low clouds that now obscured the sun. Elizabeth shivered, suddenly feeling as if winter had doubled back to devil their crossing. For once, she was glad of her heavy widow's weeds.

What was the date? She'd almost lost track during the endless jolting days and nights on the road.

When she calculated, she realized it was April first.

Fool's Day.

Hardly an auspicious time to make the crossing . . . or to undertake an adventure, but that was what she had vowed to do.

# ❧ CHAPTER 5 ❧

*F*our hours later, Elizabeth leaned over the edge of her narrow berth in the tiny ship's cabin and retched into the basin Gwynneth was holding. When the spasm subsided, she felt Gwynneth wipe her forehead with a cloth soaked in cold sea water.

"There, there, milady. I know it's terrible rockity, but the storm's drivin' us to France at record speed. We'll soon have milady back on dry land and feeling better."

"Not if I die first," Elizabeth muttered grimly. The smell of pitch and unwashed bodies fouled the air below decks, making her nausea even worse. She struggled to sit up. "Perhaps some fresh air—"

Gwynneth cut her off. "Nay, milady. The captain's ordered all passengers to stay below." The maid looked askance at the other women wedged into the tiny cabin, then whispered, "The cabin boy told me that two seamen have been washed overboard already."

Elizabeth sank back onto the tightly stretched canvas that served as a mattress. "I almost envy them, the way I'm feeling now. Better to drown quickly than die by miserable degrees."

"Here now," Gwynneth scolded. "Such talk. As far as I know, no one's ever died of seasickness, and milady's unlikely to be the first." She wrung out a fresh compress and laid it across Elizabeth's neck, her tone once again soothing. "Try to rest. We can't be far from France. Once milady is back on dry land, she'll feel fit as a thistle. And tomorrow's Easter. Perhaps we can find a church along the way and attend Mass."

Elizabeth shook her head. "No. If we make landfall, we mustn't stop for anything. I must reach Charlotte." A dis-

jointed fact swam into her consciousness. "Anyway, they keep
a different calendar in France. Charlotte told me. I don't know
if it's Easter there or not."

Gwynneth was undaunted. "Well, it'll be Easter to us, and
Mass or no Mass, milady will live to celebrate Resurrection
Day. That's a promise."

Elizabeth wished she could believe Gwynneth's reassur-
ances, but she had never felt so deathly ill, not even when
she'd almost succumbed to Gypsy Fever as a child. Her head
swimming, she decided that her devoted servant must be lying
to protect her from the truth. But what did it matter? In this
terrible storm, the ship might not make it to France, anyway.
Elizabeth crossed her fingers for luck, kissed her crucifix, and
said three "Hail Marys" before another surge of nausea stole
her concentration.

She didn't know which was worse, opening her eyes to the
lurching shadows thrown by the swaying lantern overhead, or
closing her eyes to be tossed in darkness against the bulkhead.
Deciding that darkness was preferable, she gripped the rails
that held her canvas cot and tried to maintain some shred of
dignity in her final moments.

She was dying. She had to be.

Charlotte might be dying, too. Elizabeth was twenty-eight,
but Charlotte was only twenty. So young. So sweet.

*So unlike me.*

Charlotte was soft and gentle, never stubborn or distant.
Despite the harshness of their lives, Elizabeth's younger sister
found something to love in everyone and everything—even in
Elizabeth.

Elizabeth turned on her side and curled into a miserable ball.
Charlotte couldn't die. Not yet. *Dear Father, if it will spare
her, take me. Please, take me instead of her.* The heartfelt
prayer was interrupted by another wave of nausea. When it
eased enough for her to go on, she prayed with conviction,
*But if you do decide to take me, Lord, please do it soon.*

She wouldn't mind dying, really, especially if it would save
Charlotte. The truth was, Elizabeth had felt like an old woman
ever since their mother had died trying to give birth to a stillborn son sixteen years ago. Father had forbidden them to cry,
and Elizabeth had obeyed, as always, but she had comforted
four-year-old Charlotte's secret sobs. Since then, life had been
hard work and endurance. Perhaps it wouldn't be so bad to

die, if she could just do it and be done.

Elizabeth's lids snapped open at Gwynneth's unexpected touch.

"I'm sorry, milady. Didn't mean to wake you. Just changing the compress." She drew the now-warm compress from Elizabeth's throat and replaced it with a cool one. Blessedly, the ship seemed to have stabilized somewhat.

"I wasn't asleep," Elizabeth murmured grimly, "I was thinking." She stared into Gwynneth's broad, freckled face. Then she grabbed the basin and heaved up what little substance was left within her.

Garrett sat in silence beside Lady Charlotte's bed at the Louvre, wondering if he'd made a mistake in coming. He knew the look of death and saw it now in her sunken cheeks and graying skin. She was so thin, probably no more than three stones, her substance devoured by the malignant disease that grew inside her.

Such a contrast to the pleasing roundness she had enjoyed only months ago.

Lady Charlotte's eyelids fluttered open. Her pupils were huge, giving her eyes a spectral appearance. "Viscount." She licked her cracked lips. "So sweet, coming to see me, all the way from St. Germain."

"Don't feel you must talk, Lady Charlotte. Save your strength." Garrett took her hand and kissed it. It felt as thin and insubstantial as a ten-year-old's, but Lady Wyndham's face was that of an old, old woman. Only twenty, she had aged generations in a few short weeks of suffering. Death would be a release now, Garrett knew, but he grieved at the thought. Their paths had crossed often in the tight-knit community of exiles, and he had developed a genuine fondness for the shy, gentle young widow who served the queen so faithfully.

"Thank you for coming, old man," she murmured, quietly teasing him the way she used to about the ten-year difference in their ages.

"Are you calling me old?" he responded, as he always did.

"You are old. Older than I shall ever be." Her hand tightened briefly in his. "You're twenty-eight now, and still a bachelor. Shame on you, sir. I was married at twelve, my sister at eighteen. How have you managed to escape?"

Garrett shrugged, grinning. "Lucky, I guess."

"You came to see me." Her lids drifted shut. "Most of the others have stopped coming, for I fear it grieves them to see me like this, but not you." She looked up at him, her bleak expression softened by affection. "You are the truest of friends, dear man, to see past my sickness." A wracking cough gurgled up her throat.

Garrett watched in frustration as agony briefly distorted her face. "May I get you something? Have the doctors—"

Struggling to recover herself, she gasped out, "They've given me drugs. Eases the pain, but I sleep too much. Sleep the time away." She shifted uncomfortably on her pillows.

"Here. Let me help you." Garrett rose and gently lifted her frail shoulders, fluffing the pillows behind her. He detected the all-too-familiar, sickly sweet smell of necrotic flesh on her breath. Just like his father. It wouldn't be long now.

She eased, her head rolling against his chest. "Mmm. Feels so good, with your arm around me that way. Like my mother used to hold me when I was small."

Garrett's throat tightened. So little, this gentle soul asked of anyone. On impulse, he carefully slid into the bed next to her and cradled her gently to his side. "Then I shall hold you for as long as you want." He stroked a lusterless tendril at her temple. "Are you comfortable, precious girl?"

"Much better." Lady Charlotte sighed, easing into his embrace.

Garrett kissed the top of her head, thinking of his own sisters and praying that God would spare them such torment. "Then go to sleep, precious girl, and dream of angel's wings."

Four muddy, travel-weary days later, Elizabeth was ushered into the forbidding medieval structure that housed England's exiled queen and her retinue. Her bundle of precious medicines clutched in her hand, she addressed the ornately clad servant inside. "Please inform her majesty that Countess Ravenwold has arrived. I would like to see my sister, Lady Markham, at once."

The servant's expression wrinkled with sympathy. "Please to follow me, madame la comtesse. I 'ave orders."

As she obliged, it became evident that the news of her arrival preceded her progress through the Louvre's ancient hallways. From the lowest footman to the highest-ranking courtier, almost everyone she passed glanced at her in sympathy, then looked away. Though every pitying expression fed the fear that clawed at her heart, she still hoped against hope that Charlotte might be alive. She followed the servant through a crowded room full of petitioners and, to her surprise, was led not into her sister's room, but the queen's bedchamber.

"Countess Ravenwold." Bedridden, Henrietta Maria acknowledged Elizabeth's curtsy with outstretched hands. "Come closer, my dear." Her hands dropped weakly to the coverlet. "Forgive my not receiving you properly, but I have suffered a relapse of the rheum that has plagued me since the birth of my precious little Henriette Anne."

Elizabeth stood at the bedside. She barely recognized this haggard woman as the once-vivacious, beautiful queen who had presided over Britain's Court in happier times. Now the French-born queen was a mere shadow of herself, the life gone from everything but her eyes—eyes that held a message Elizabeth did not want to face.

The queen spoke softly. "Please sit. I wish to speak with you privately." A footman appeared with a chair and placed it just behind Elizabeth. The queen nodded to her ladies. "Leave us. All of you." At her command the servants and attendants retreated, closing the door behind them.

Elizabeth sank numbly into the chair, glad for its support. Though she prayed otherwise, she knew what the queen was going to say.

Henrietta Maria did her best to cushion the blow. "*Chère* countess, I fear I must be the bearer of tragic news. Your sister, who was as dear to me as my own, did not survive the night."

Charlotte was gone. The one person Elizabeth really loved. The only one who had ever loved *her* since their mother's death. Charlotte, who had shared the pain of their childhood, yet somehow managed to find a quiet joy that eluded Elizabeth.

Gone. Dead.

Elizabeth sat very straight, staring ahead as she waited for the pain to come. But it didn't come. Instead, numbness crept through her, robbing her of even the release of tears. She heard herself ask, "May I see her?"

The queen nodded. "But of course. She has been prepared for burial and is lying in state in her chamber." She hesitated, then added, "After you have rested, we shall talk again. There are certain arrangements to be discussed. For now, go to your sister.''

Elizabeth nodded and rose, her eyes barely seeing.

Tears spilled from the queen's eyes. ''Lady Charlotte's quiet joy was a blessing to all who knew her, especially to her queen. Such devotion. She sustained us when we were forced to flee England. It was so difficult to leave our beloved husband and children, and we were so ill, yet she never let us give up.'' She sighed, then granted Elizabeth a look of exquisite sympathy. ''Your sister was a candle in the darkness, madame la comtesse. The world will never be as bright without her.'' The queen rang for a servant, and Elizabeth heard someone enter and whisk away the chair. Henrietta Maria, tears still flowing down her cheeks, directed the unseen servant, ''Summon a page to take madame la comtesse to Lady Markham's room.''

Elizabeth stood there, her only emotion muted shame that she could not share the queen's tears. She wondered abstractly if the last of her feelings had died with Charlotte. If so, she would never be able to properly grieve her sister's loss.

The page appeared and said, ''Madame will please to follow me.''

She curtsied to the queen. ''Thank you, your majesty.'' Then she backed away and followed the page into the outer chamber. All conversation ceased when she entered the salon. The waiting courtiers stared at her in silence, some with pity, some with open curiosity. Elizabeth kept her posture rigid. Feeling like a character in one of her own dreams, she passed among them without looking left or right. She kept her eyes on the uniformed boy who led her through this unfamiliar place.

Maybe when she was alone with Charlotte, she could begin to mourn.

The page took her up a flight of stairs and down a long hall to a doorway flanked by tall candlesticks. Atop them burned candles as thick as Elizabeth's arm.

His tone properly sober, the boy suggested, ''Per'aps madame la comtesse prefers to eat and rest a bit before—''

''No.'' Elizabeth dreaded seeing her sister dead, but at the same time hoped the sight would free her to grieve. ''I wish to be alone with my sister. And I do not wish to be disturbed.'' Her voice took on a strange harshness. ''Is that clear?''

"As madame la comtesse wishes." The page opened the door, then retreated.

Garrett Creighton was on his way to pay his last respects to Lady Markham when he turned the corner and saw Countess Ravenwold standing before the open door at the far end of the hall. He halted abruptly, unwilling to intrude upon her grief. After she had gone inside, he would turn and leave unnoticed. But she did not go inside. Long seconds passed, yet she remained motionless in the hallway, her back ramrod straight.

What was she doing? Garrett peered at the distant figure. She looked like a person in a trance, her eyes staring sightlessly ahead, a wad of black skirt clenched in her fist, her hair obscured by a mourning cap and veil.

That glorious hair, covered. At the memory of the countess's long blond tresses, Garrett shivered with the same odd mixture of desire and revulsion he had felt that night three years ago.

He should leave. He turned to go, but felt compelled to look back.

She hadn't seen him. She was still frozen outside her only sister's death chamber. Garrett saw no shred of emotion in her.

How could she be so cold?

Lady Markham had loved her sister dearly, speaking of her so often, in such glowing terms, that Garrett had begun to wonder if he hadn't misjudged the countess three years ago. But seeing her now, so emotionless in the face of her only sister's death, he renewed his original assessment. The woman had to be as hard and blackhearted as sea-coal. Shaking his head, he quietly left her to her privacy.

Elizabeth stared into the darkened chamber, unable to lower her eyes to the still figure laid out on the bier in the center of the room. She barely noticed the black drapings that festooned the walls and covered the mirrors and windows, or the Markham heraldic banner on the wall. Instead, she focused on overcoming the paralysis that seemed to have locked her joints. It took all her strength to put one foot in front of the other and pass beneath the hatchment that hung over the door.

Once inside the candlelit chamber, she lowered her eyes to gaze on the body of her sister. Charlotte was barely recognizable, shrunken, her gray skin stretched tight across her skull. But it was Charlotte . . . motherless at four, married to an old man at twelve, widowed and impoverished at thirteen, dead at twenty. Elizabeth stood beside the bier and looked down at the features so altered by disease and death. "Oh, Charlotte."

Yesterday, her sister was still alive. Only yesterday. Elizabeth remembered every delay in her journey and wished with all her soul that she could live the trip over, push harder, get here sooner with the medicine. It did not matter that the medicine might not have worked. At least she would have been able to try. And to say good-bye.

Now it was too late. *Too late . . . Too late . . . Too late.* Over and over, the words shuddered through her.

Elizabeth reached out and covered her sister's hand, then recoiled. Charlotte's flesh was almost as cold and stiff as the silver crucifix wedged between her lifeless fingers. Yet still she could not cry, could not feel anything but guilt. Her heart as dead as Charlotte's cold, rigid flesh, Elizabeth locked the door, then sank to the kneeling rail beside the bier and began to intercede for her sister's soul.

Elizabeth didn't know if it was day or night when she heard Gwynneth's voice calling from the hallway.

"Milady, it's me, Gwynneth. Please come out. You must eat something, drink something. It's been more than a day. And the queen wants to see milady . . . about the funeral and all."

Elizabeth lifted her forehead from the velvet hangings of the bier. Surely it hadn't been that long. She'd dozed off several times while praying beside Charlotte's body, but . . .

Her muddled thoughts were interrupted by a loud growl from her belly. Maybe it had been more than a day. She struggled to her feet. Her joints were stiff as an old woman's. She crossed the room, unbolted the door, and opened it.

At the sight of her, Gwynneth burst into tears. "Oh, my poor lady! Look at you." Her plump arm circled Elizabeth's waist, providing warmth and welcome support.

Elizabeth hadn't realized how weak she was until she had someone to lean against. She murmured absently, "Don't cry, Gwynneth. I'm all right."

Gwynneth was unconvinced. She sniffed loudly, then spoke as if she were addressing a sick child. "Come along, now. We'll get some nice hot food into milady, and some mulled wine. And then, after milady's had a nap, I'll help her dress to see the queen."

The queen. "Certain arrangements," her majesty had said. The funeral. Elizabeth must see that Charlotte was properly buried. She straightened. "Home. I want to take Charlotte back to England."

Gwynneth guided her toward her bedchamber. "Aye, milady. We'll take her home."

But the queen had other plans.

Her majesty was sympathetic when she spoke with Elizabeth, but there was no mistaking the firmness in her manner. "Would that we could grant madame's request, but we cannot. Because of the blockade, our resources are strained to the limit. We can barely arrange to transport the living back and forth to England; we cannot ship Lady Wyndham's coffin home for burial. She must be buried here . . . with all proper ceremony, of course, in a place of honor that befits the lady's station."

Elizabeth heard what the queen said, but she could not accept it. "But surely there must be some way . . ." Why was it suddenly so hard to think, to express her thoughts? Ever since she'd learned of Charlotte's death, Elizabeth had felt fragmented, almost as if she'd been drugged. Now in the face of this unexpected complication, she could barely manage to speak a coherent sentence. "If it's a question of money," she offered, "I will guarantee the cost, your majesty, even if I must sell everything I own."

The queen shook her head sadly. "*Chère* comtesse, it is not a matter of money, although money counts for a great deal in this dreadful rebellion." She motioned to the sparse furnishings and threadbare hangings of her bedchamber. "If madame will but look about her, she will see that we are barely managing here, entirely dependent upon the charity of our sister queen, who has rebellions of her own to deal with."

France, too, was struggling with insurrection. Accustomed to Castle Ravenwold, Elizabeth had failed to notice the Louvre's drafty disrepair. Now as she looked about, she realized that this ancient fortress's stone corridors and chambers had been constructed for security, not comfort, and were anything but luxurious.

The queen continued, "Every sou we can spare is directed to helping our beloved sovereign defend his throne." She shifted against the pillows, her eyes feverish. "His majesty needs every bullet and every keg of powder we can send him. We cannot spare the cargo space to transport the dead back to England." Her face softened. "Think of the loyal lives that could be lost. Lady Wyndham's coffin would take up enough space to provision at least ten musketeers. Surely you would not wish those men to die for lack of powder."

Elizabeth shook her head. "I hadn't thought of it that way, your majesty, but—"

The queen's interruption was gentle. "Lady Charlotte was always most generous with our cause. Ever since we left England, she refused to accept her stipend, telling me to put the money toward armaments and ammunition for our cause. I do not think she would have wanted to deprive our loyal soldiers."

Elizabeth could not deny the queen's logic, and she knew better than to argue. Even in ill health, Henrietta Maria possessed a formidable will, as inalterable as her determination to preserve the monarchy. Suddenly weary, she accepted the inevitable. "Very well. I bow to your majesty's wishes."

"I knew madame would understand." The queen sank back. "Because of our affection for Lady Wyndham, we have commissioned a suitable marble tomb." She cast an approving eye at Elizabeth's black damask dress, the only decent mourning gown she had left. "I see madame already has the proper mourning attire."

"Yes, majesty. Since the death of my husband, three years past."

"And now this. Dear comtesse, how bravely you endure." Visibly showing the strain of her illness, Henrietta Maria hastened to settle the matter. "Would two o'clock tomorrow be convenient for the funeral? At our request, Cardinal Retz has agreed to officiate."

A cardinal! Obviously a gesture on the queen's part to make up for burying Charlotte on foreign soil.

Elizabeth nodded. "Yes, majesty. Tomorrow." Once she saw Charlotte laid to rest, she could go home. Elizabeth had nothing left but her place as Countess of Ravenwold. At least in Cornwall she could be useful, live out her life alone. But the thought of returning to England stirred the memory of Anne Murray's face, and Elizabeth's rash promise. "*. . . from my hand to the prince's. You have my vow.*"

The letter! She had almost forgotten. She looked up to see

the queen studying her with a puzzled expression.

"Something is troubling madame?"

"I . . ." How much could she safely say? Should she ask for the queen's help in obtaining an audience with Prince Charles? Elizabeth hesitated, uncertain.

Everyone at Court knew of the strain between the queen and her eldest son. Gwynneth had been brimming with stories of how Prince Charles barely spoke to his mother. When he had fled England, the crown prince had refused his mother's insistent demands that he join her in Paris, going instead to his sister's elegant palace at the Hague. Only an outbreak of typhoid convinced him to leave. With nowhere else to go, he had accepted the queen's offer and moved to nearby St. Germain. Now the prince made no secret of his resentment for his mother's interference.

If the queen were to ask her son to grant Elizabeth an audience, he might refuse to see her, simply out of spite.

No. Help from the queen would be worse than no help at all.

Henrietta Maria's patience was obviously fading with her limited strength. She prompted, "Madame?"

Elizabeth stammered, "I . . . I was wondering if I might impose upon your majesty's hospitality a bit longer . . . a business matter. Here. I don't know how long it will take . . . perhaps several weeks."

The queen's expression cleared. "But of course. Madame is welcome for as long as necessary." She motioned for her ladies. "And now, if madame will excuse us, we must rest."

"Forgive me. I have overtaxed your majesty." Elizabeth curtsied, then backed away.

The queen called after her, "Until tomorrow, madame."

Garrett exited his coach the next afternoon and climbed the stairs of Notre Dame to the tolling of the death knell. He hesitated only a moment before entering the cathedral.

As a man—and a Protestant at that—his presence at a lady's Requiem Mass was hardly customary. Yet he'd felt compelled to come, telling himself it was because of the affection he held for Lady Charlotte.

Inside, the exquisite harmonies of the choir filled the cathedral. Despite his Protestant sensibilities, Garrett looked up and marveled at the soaring stone vaults and magnificent stained glass windows. If God should ever have need of a house, surely it would be one as splendid as this.

Garrett followed the procession of black-clad noblewomen and their maids toward several rows of chairs arranged at the front of the cathedral.

Lady Charlotte's coffin lay just inside the altar rail, flanked by two banks of votive candles. One by one, the women genuflected, approached the rail, lit a candle, then knelt in prayer before taking a seat.

Garrett stepped aside, uncomfortable with the Roman rituals. Until he had come to Paris with the prince, he had never darkened the door of a papist church. Since then, protocol had required the prince's presence at several papist ceremonies, and Garrett's along with him. But this was the first time Garrett had ever gone alone, of his own accord, to a Roman service.

Selecting a spot in the shadowed side loggia, he took up a discreet position at the rear of the gathering. Owing to the queen's poor health, attendance was restricted to members of the Court, with the mob kept outside for a change.

Though he was glad to be free of the usual leering crowds, Garrett couldn't help thinking the assembled mourners looked lost and pitifully small in the great cathedral—an oddly fitting circumstance for the funeral of a woman as shy as Lady Charlotte.

Then one of the queen's ladies stepped aside, giving him a view of Countess Ravenwold's back. Garrett would have known that back anywhere. As always, the countess bore herself straight as a pike. He couldn't see her face, and told himself he did not want to. He was here because of his respect for Lady Charlotte, not to see the countess.

From the gallery above, trumpets signaled the queen's arrival, prompting the little congregation to rise as one. But instead of turning with the others to face the approaching royal entourage, Garrett's gaze was drawn to the tall, elegant countess who had come to lay her only sister to rest.

For one fleeting moment, her features crumpled, ravaged by loss. Then her eyes closed. When she opened them again, her expression was as emotionless as the carved stone saints above the altar.

Three days later, Elizabeth was no closer to seeing Prince Charles than when she'd started. She knew nothing of the mechanisms governing such matters—who to bribe, who to threaten, who to flatter. What was worse, the exiled British Court seemed to have taken on the inexplicable complexities of its French counterpart.

Viscount Creighton was the only person she knew close to the prince, and he was the *last* man she would ask for a favor.

Elizabeth was beginning to despair of delivering Anne's letter at all.

Then an outrageous idea occurred to her. There *was* a way she could speak to the prince.

No, she told herself. You would never have the nerve.

But desperate situations called for desperate measures. Elizabeth feared she would lose her mind if she couldn't go home soon. She was almost out of money and ashamed to impose on the beleaguered queen's hospitality any longer. And when she tried to use her wretched French, the natives acted as if she were spouting Greek. Never in her life had she felt so lonely and out of place.

She *had* to go home.

Elizabeth made up her mind. She would speak to Prince Charles, tell him about the letter, even if she had to break every rule of decent behavior to do it.

# ❈ CHAPTER 6 ❈

### April 9—St. Germain

*I*gnoring the reproachful looks of those around her, Elizabeth scanned the circle of waiting courtiers at the royal levee. Her mere presence at a social gathering so soon after her sister's death flouted the most basic rules of decency, but this was her only chance to speak to Prince Charles. Though she dared not deliver the letter publicly, she was determined to tell the prince about it, despite the fact that protocol allowed him, alone, to set the topic of conversation.

Somehow she would find the courage. Hidden in the folds of her skirt, her right thumb compulsively rubbed nervous circles against the side of her index finger.

The plump matron next to Elizabeth nudged her companion and said, "Look. It's James the White. The prince's entourage has arrived."

Elizabeth turned to see the marquis of Ormonde—nicknamed for his pale complexion and white-blond hair—waiting to be announced. If Ormonde was here, then the rest of the prince's entourage was not far behind. She crossed her fingers for luck and recited silently, "Cat hairs, cat hairs, cat hairs," wishing with all her might that Viscount Creighton would not be among the men who gathered around Ormonde. Then she saw a familiar, tawny mane half a head taller than the rest of the prince's attendants.

If she could have felt anything, Elizabeth would have been humiliated. As it was, she dully acknowledged that she would have to shame herself under Creighton's mocking gaze. "Damn." The soft utterance prompted a look of shocked disapproval from the round little matron beside her.

Across the room, the herald rapped his staff and called out,

"Lord Jermyn . . . Master of the Rolls, Lord Culpeper . . . Viscount Creighton . . . the earl of Berkshire . . . the earl of Brentford . . . the marquis of Ormonde."

One by one, the prince's attendants and advisors stepped into the ballroom and lined up on either side of the doorway. Then the trumpets sounded, and all eyes turned to the entrance. The herald announced, "His Royal Highness, the Prince of Wales."

Everyone bowed or curtsied as Prince Charles strode into the room, his attendants and advisors trailing behind him. The last time Elizabeth had seen the prince, he'd been a lanky, engaging ten-year-old. Now at almost eighteen, he was taller than most grown men and wore the shadow of the crown with a maturity far beyond his years. As always, he began the levee by addressing the highest-ranking guest present, then worked his way around the circle, down the ranks one by one.

Elizabeth had waited until the last minute to slip into the lower echelons. Now all she could do was wait for her turn and pray that no one asked to see her nonexistent invitation. She watched as the prince, prompted with names and information by his attendants, acknowledged each guest's bow or curtsy with a nod and a murmured inanity.

She tried hard not to look at Creighton, but she—along with most of the other women in the room—found her gaze drawn to the tall, tanned soldier whose height, golden coloring, and powerful size testified to his Saxon heritage. His infectious smile was that of a rake, not a warrior. The man was obviously a bounder.

It didn't matter what Creighton thought about her or said about her, she told herself. She would do what she must, then go back to Cornwall and stay there. Forcing her eyes from him, she stared straight ahead and mentally rehearsed what she would say when the prince finally reached her.

Then the crown prince was standing before her, his olive complexion even darker close-up and a look of supreme boredom in his heavy-lidded eyes. Elizabeth dropped into a curtsy and murmured, "Forgive me for speaking so boldly, your royal highness, but my friend Anne Murray has entrusted me with an urgent message for your highness." Heart pounding as she rose, she saw a spark of interest flare in the prince's eyes, but nothing else changed in his languid expression. He acted as if she hadn't said a word.

Creighton cocked his brows in surprise, his cheeky grin as insulting as a slap in the face. Berkshire and Culpeper exchanged scowls, and the marquis of Ormonde grew even paler—if that was possible. Prince Charles merely murmured, "Madame has suffered a great loss in the death of her sister. Please accept our condolences."

Elizabeth wished the floor would open up and swallow her. She'd shamed herself, and all for nothing. Worse. Now, thanks to her presumption, Prince Charles would probably keep her waiting forever for a private audience.

As the group moved on, Creighton shot her an amused glance. He probably couldn't wait to tell everyone what a fool she'd made of herself—not just today, but that night three years ago at Castle Ravenwold. Elizabeth knew she ought to care, but she didn't: The only thing she cared about was getting back to Cornwall.

After the prince had finished the levee and departed, Elizabeth marched numbly through the milling, gossiping courtiers, her presence prompting whispers and glances. As she reached the outer hallway, a young page approached and bowed, proffering a folded message.

Elizabeth took it from him. The wax seal bore the Prince of Wales's imprint. With shaking hand, she stuffed it into her pocket and crossed to the exit. "Footman, I am the Countess Ravenwold. Fetch my maid and see that my coach is brought round."

Gwynneth arrived with her cloak only moments later, just as the hired coach drew up to the curb outside. The maid frowned with concern. "Is everything all right? Milady is pale as porridge."

"I'm fine, Gwynneth," Elizabeth snapped. "I simply wish to return to the Louvre as quickly as possible."

Once they were settled in the coach and on their way, she opened the prince's note and read:

His Royal Highness the Prince of Wales commands the presence of Countess Ravenwold for a private audience at ten o'clock in the morning upon the morrow, April 10, anno domini 1648 at St. Germain.

A private audience. Tomorrow! She would finally be able to deliver Anne's letter. "Thanks be to God." She refolded the note and clasped it to her chest.

"Gwynneth, I've been granted a private audience with the prince tomorrow morning. Then we can go home." Home, where she could properly grieve her sister's loss, safely away from prying eyes and listening ears.

That was all she wanted, really—to be left alone at last.

The next morning she arrived in a rented coach at St. Germain precisely on the stroke of ten. As a footman ushered her through the palace to the long passageway that served as Prince Charles's waiting room, she felt as if everyone were staring at the pocket where she clutched Anne's message.

Elizabeth followed the servant across the waiting room to a heavy, drawn drapery. The footman pulled back the curtain to reveal a furnished alcove, where an open window provided a lovely vista to the gardens below. "Madame la comtesse will please wait here." After she glided past him, he closed the curtain, shutting her away from curious eyes.

She perched on the edge of the upholstered settee and waited to be summoned.

And waited. And waited. And waited.

Was the prince always so tardy with his appointments?

Lulled by the murmuring voices beyond the curtain, she slid back into the settee and yawned. Last night she'd hardly slept a wink. Now, with the midday sun warming the sweet April breeze that wafted through the open window, she could barely keep her eyes open. The next thing she knew, she woke abruptly to the horrifying notion that she'd been snoring. Surely, she hadn't allowed herself to fall asleep—worse, yet, awakened herself with her own snoring. . . . But her mouth *was* dry, and her ears still echoed with the rasping sound.

She straightened and looked through the window to see that the shadows of the sun had shifted completely, now casting long, dark fingers from the west. The day was almost gone. Her stomach growled noisily; she had eaten nothing since dawn.

Elizabeth rose and peeked through the curtains into the waiting room. Only a few petitioners remained, among whom was a slack-jawed, portly gentleman who snored sporadically in his chair.

*Must have been him,* she thought, relieved. Then she saw the marquis of Ormonde enter from the audience chamber.

The pale diplomat announced to the remaining visitors,

"Ladies and gentlemen, I beg your indulgence. His royal highness will grant no more audiences today. Please come back tomorrow."

Elizabeth drew back, disappointment awakening a twist of feeling inside her. She needed only a few seconds to hand the prince Anne's letter. But she dared not give him the letter in front of just anyone. Who could say what trouble that might cause for Anne, or for the prince?

Or for herself.

No, she had to do it privately. And she had to do it today. She would go mad if she couldn't leave Paris soon.

She peeked through the curtains again. Lord Jermyn, the prince's tutor, was shepherding the last of the disgruntled petitioners out. Then he crossed back through the sunlit passageway and opened the double doors to the prince's audience chamber. "Everyone has gone, your highness."

Had they forgotten about her?

Elizabeth's mind churned. Why couldn't she pretend she'd just awakened and emerge as the prince was leaving? She could hand him the letter and be on her way.

She heard Prince Charles bellow, "Ormonde! Culpeper! Jermyn! Leave us! I would speak with Creighton alone."

Ormonde's voice interjected, "Of course, your highness, but perhaps this matter would be better dealt with after speaking with the lady in question. I'm certain this is just a misunderstanding, easily—"

The Prince of Wales seemed in no mood for interference. He shouted, "I said leave us! This is between Creighton and me." She heard footsteps approaching. "And take the guards with you! I will not have this, or the lady, discussed in the kitchens tonight!"

*The lady?* Elizabeth's ears tingled. Surely they hadn't been talking about *her?*

No. Of course not. Unless Creighton had dared to tell the prince about that night three years ago . . .

Elizabeth's thoughts were interrupted by the sound of Jermyn, Culpeper, Ormonde, and the guards exiting the waiting room. After they had gone, she looked out to see that the passageway was empty. The double doors to the audience chamber stood open, blocking the alcove from view. If she was careful, she could wait behind the door without being seen and intercept the prince on his way out. Elizabeth eased from behind the curtain. Five cautious steps took her to a safe spot beside the open door, where she waited for the prince to come out.

She quickly regretted her decision to leave the alcove. Charles and Creighton couldn't see her, but she could hear them, and she realized immediately that she did not want to.

Charles's voice shook with rage. "Is this how you repay me, Creighton, the thanks I get for making you my friend and confidante? Betrayal, of the basest sort!"

"Never have I betrayed your highness!" Creighton's voice was grim. "Who makes this charge? Bring the coward here, to speak his baseless accusations to my face."

Charles's tone dropped to a chilling growl. "He *is* here." The crown prince, himself, was accusing Creighton!

Elizabeth realized she was definitely in the wrong place at the wrong time. Much as she hated Creighton, she did not want to be caught in the middle of this. She took a step back toward the alcove, but halted when the floor groaned beneath her.

"Don't play innocent with me, Creighton!" Charles ranted. "I've seen the way you toy with women. I cannot fault the lady in this. After all, the duchesse de Chataillon is only a woman, and women are weak, suggestible. But you should know better, flirting behind my back!"

The duchesse de Chataillon.

Elizabeth had met the duchesse de Chataillon, and the lady was anything but weak. Hard, ambitious, unscrupulous, and shameless—but not weak or suggestible. Still, the woman would have to be a fool to jeopardize her position as the prince's favorite by flirting with one of his own retainers.

"Nay, sire!" Creighton protested. "The lady is like a sister to me! My conversations with her, as well as my actions, have always been completely chaste."

Charles hooted. "Chaste? There's not a nit's worth of chastity in your whole body, Creighton, and you know it!"

Elizabeth could almost hear the insolent smile that accompanied Creighton's response. "Would your highness have me ignore the lady? That would hardly be polite."

"This isn't about politeness, and you know it!"

"If my presence discomfits your highness in any way," Creighton offered smoothly, "I will be happy to tender my resignation and rejoin my regiment." The prince snorted in derision, but Creighton continued, "Think what you will of me, sir, but your doubts do the duchesse de Chataillon a great injustice. Her devotion to your highness is beyond question.'' He paused. ''Sire, the lady barely knows I exist. You are a future king; I am but one of the nameless subjects privileged to serve in your shadow. Why should the duchesse notice the shadow, when she has the sun itself?''

What offal Creighton was spouting! Prince Charles's suspicions were probably well-founded, if the gossip she had heard about Creighton was true. Elizabeth ventured another tiptoed step, only to hear the floor creak again. Wincing, she stilled, afraid to move farther.

Beyond the open door, the prince said, ''Pretty words, Creighton, but we've been wenching together long enough for me to know how all the women flock to you, highborn or low. Well, this is one woman you can't have.''

So Prince Charles wasn't always the levelheaded adult, Elizabeth mused. Jealousy had him acting like an overgrown adolescent with his older, more accomplished retainer.

Creighton actually had the brass to chuckle, but the words that followed were deadly earnest. ''My loyalty to your highness does not permit even the thought of any impropriety with *any* of your highness's . . . friends.''

Freshly aware that she needed to escape this embarrassing situation, Elizabeth hit upon the idea of sliding her feet across the polished wood floor. When she tried it, her soft leather slippers carried her soundlessly toward the alcove. She had almost reached safety when she heard rapid footsteps approaching behind her.

''Who goes there?'' Creighton called to her. ''Halt!''

She froze. How could he have seen her through the narrow crack?

The prince stormed past him to confront her with, ''What are you doing here? How did you get in?''

Almost too terrified to move, she turned slowly and stammered, ''Y-Your highness sent for me.'' She dropped a deep curtsy. ''I was here at ten, as requested.'' Rising, she gestured to the alcove. ''The footman put me in there, and I waited all day. When no one came to get me, I fell asleep—''

Creighton, his golden complexion ruddy with anger, approached her and demanded, ''How long have you been listening? What did you hear?''

Charles swatted Creighton's arm. ''I'll ask the questions!''

He turned back to Elizabeth. "Were you eavesdropping? What did you hear?"

Six years of Ravenwold's abuse had taught Elizabeth to lie with conviction when her safety was at stake. She looked the prince squarely in the eye and declared, "I heard nothing, sir, only mumbled voices in the distance." She lifted her chin. "When I came out and saw that everyone else had gone, I wasn't sure whether to go back to the alcove or leave."

Charles seemed to accept her explanation, but Creighton was not so easily fooled. He glared at her, prompting a guilty, sidelong glance that betrayed her lie. But before they could question her further, Elizabeth remembered the reason she was here. She dropped to her knees before the prince and pulled the letter from her pocket. "Your highness, here is the letter I told you about. Please take it. I have sworn to put it into your hand, and yours alone."

Charles's manner changed abruptly. He took the letter and uttered a clipped, "Hold her."

Creighton's hand closed tightly on her upper arm, lifting her none too gently to her feet. Suddenly she was conscious of his size and strength. Huge and fair as a Viking warrior, he towered over her. Elizabeth tried vainly to pull away. "You needn't break my arm. I'm not going anywhere."

Blue eyes as cold as a winter sky glared down at her. "His highness said to hold you, and hold you I shall."

Charles asked her, "How long have you had this letter?"

"Since April first." Elizabeth straightened. "When our mutual friend discovered I was bound for Paris, she asked me to deliver the message into your highness's hand, and yours alone. I've tried for days to obtain a private audience, but—"

The prince cut her off, pointing to the letter. "Did you read this?"

Elizabeth was genuinely taken aback. "Nay, sire! I am neither meddlesome nor foolish enough to do such a thing." She glanced at the carefully scripted gibberish covering the page. "Anyway, it's obviously in code."

Charles scowled.

Elizabeth risked saying, "I beg your highness's forgiveness for this intrusion, but I couldn't leave until I gave you the letter, and I was desperate to go home." Her voice trailed to a whisper. "I must go home."

"Be grateful that you can, madame," the prince snapped.

"Some of us cannot." He nodded to Creighton. "Release her. Fetch Culpeper and Ormonde, but be discreet."

Creighton let go of Elizabeth's arm, bowed, then turned and left.

"You"—Prince Charles motioned to Elizabeth—"follow me." He led her into the audience chamber. "Close the doors." As she obeyed, he settled at a cluttered desk. Charles drew out a tiny book that hung from a golden chain about his neck, then used it to begin deciphering the coded letter.

Elizabeth stood waiting for a full ten minutes before her growling stomach attracted the prince's attention. He looked up to see her swaying slightly. "Are you ill?"

"Nay, sire." Feeling more than a little lightheaded, she ventured, "I beg your highness's pardon, but I've had nothing to eat or drink all day. If I do not sit down soon, I fear I shall fall down."

"Sit, then." The prince motioned to a chair. "But don't go anywhere." He returned to his decoding.

Thirty more minutes passed before Creighton thrust the doors open for Ormonde and Culpeper. Two armed guards stopped in the hallway behind them and closed the doors as the prince's attendants entered, bowed, and awaited his highness's instructions.

"Well, gentlemen." The Prince of Wales looked up, his face clearing. "Your timing is excellent. I've just finished decoding this message. It seems our disreputable friend in London is ready to deliver the small package we ordered."

Ormonde glanced pointedly at Elizabeth. "Sire, perhaps this matter is best discussed in private."

The prince shrugged. "She brought me the letter, and I saw no evidence it had been tampered with. But perhaps you're right."

"It might be wise for one of us to keep an eye on her," the marquis suggested. He arched an eyebrow at Creighton. "I think the viscount would be an excellent choice."

The prince exchanged a meaningful glance with Ormonde. "Good idea." Wales nodded to Creighton. "Take her outside and see that she speaks to no one. We'll decide what to do with her later."

Creighton frowned, obviously unhappy to be dismissed. He turned and bowed with insulting brevity to Elizabeth. "The countess will please accompany me.''

Elizabeth rose and preceded him into the hallway.

Ormonde watched the guards pull the doors shut behind the countess. In discussing the king's revenues with Chancellor Hyde, Ormonde had learned quite a bit about Countess Ravenwold's finances, but almost nothing of her political sympathies. She'd answered the king's call for men and provisions, but had pleaded poverty and sent no gold for the cause. He couldn't help wondering if she were telling the truth about the gold, or holding back.

And what was she doing here, mixed up in this? Was she acting as an agent for the Irish? Or the Scots?

Or the queen.

Ormonde tipped his head toward the door. ''How does she fit into all of this?''

''Ravenwold's widow?'' The prince shrugged. ''Says she knows Mistress Murray, our contact to Bampfield in London.''

Culpeper chuckled. ''Bampfield's doxy and the countess? Now there's an odd pairing.''

Charles was not amused. ''Odd, but perhaps fortunate for us. We know our regular channels of communication have been compromised. There's a chance no one else has seen this message.''

Despite the countess's explanation for her role in this matter, Ormonde was more than a little suspicious. If only Ravenwold's widow wasn't such an unknown quantity. In all the years Ormonde and Ravenwold were acquainted, the earl had never once mentioned his wife. As far as Ormonde knew, Ravenwold hadn't gone home from the first shot of the civil war until his unfortunate demise in Bristol. ''Ravenwold's loyalty was beyond question, but what do we know about the countess?''

Culpeper spread his hands. ''I knew her father, Lord Compton. Bit of a plank, Compton, but decent enough. Devout papist. Bloodlines go all the way back to the Normans. His wife had two daughters, then died giving birth to a stillborn son. He dowered the elder girl most generously to Ravenwold. Married the younger one off to Sir Thomas Markham eight years ago.''

Ormonde looked up in surprise. ''Markham must have been ninety. How old was the countess's sister?''

"Twelve." Culpeper's disapproval showed in his face. "Lord Markham didn't make it to their first anniversary, and the girl's father died shortly after that." He mused, "Countess Ravenwold inherited her father's lands, but widowhood left Lady Markham almost destitute. For some reason the countess didn't take her sister in, so the queen offered Lady Markham a position in her retinue. Her majesty grew quite fond of her."

"Lady Charlotte was one of the few Englishwomen here who could speak decent French," Culpeper volunteered. "Came in handy more than a few times, I can tell you. Bit of a bother that she died."

Charles made no pretense of patience at Culpeper's ramblings. "And what, pray tell, does all this have to do with the countess?"

As usual, it fell to Ormonde to summarize things for the prince. "First, the countess had a legitimate reason to come here. Second, she is obligated to the queen for taking in her sister, so she may be in league with her majesty. Third, the countess is a papist, probably devout. We needn't discuss the implications of *that*. Last—and most importantly—as Ravenwold's widow, the countess presently controls enormous holdings in Cornwall, not to mention the lands in Devon she inherited from her father."

Culpeper's brows knitted. "Ravenwold's been dead for years. How is it the king hasn't married his widow off to someone we can trust?" He regarded the prince. "Zounds! The woman's as dangerous as a mule's hind foot!"

Prince Charles glared back at him. "I think it's safe to say that my father has had more pressing matters to occupy his time."

"True, your highness," Ormonde injected, "but Lord Culpeper has a point. How can we be sure of the countess's loyalties?"

The Prince of Wales frowned. "A disturbing question."

As Ormonde considered the matter, a beautifully ironic idea began to shape itself in his mind. He'd known for some time that Wales was jealous of Creighton's success with women. Though Creighton dismissed the prince's growing antagonism, Ormonde was worried for his friend the viscount. This inspiration might just put Creighton back in the prince's good graces and solve the problem of the countess, as well.

Ormonde regarded the prince. Young Wales was as stubborn

as he was impulsive. Somehow, he had to make the boy think this was all his own idea. He extended his hand. "Might I read Bampfield's message, your highness?"

Garrett kept his long legs relaxed as he lounged on the opposite end of the bench from the countess. He glanced at the two armed guards standing at attention on either side of the closed audience chamber doors. They could have kept an eye on the woman. Why had Ormonde suggested Garrett for the chore? Garrett had a bad feeling about this, but he'd be damned if he'd let the countess know how worried he was.

He looked her up and down, curious. The woman was made of ice. She'd barely batted an eyelash when she'd been caught lurking about like a chambermaid gathering gossip for the highest bidder. Now she was sitting there as stiff and proper as a bishop's wife. Well, she was no bishop's wife. Garrett knew her veneer of propriety was only an act. Three years ago he had seen what lay behind that veneer. The woman was a consummate hypocrite.

A fresh wave of anger rose inside him. She probably couldn't wait to tell her friends how Charles had scolded him like a schoolboy, and without cause.

As if responding to Garrett's hidden surge of emotion, the countess turned her pale face toward his.

Garrett wondered how he could ever have thought those cold, rigid features attractive. Then he remembered the sight of her stumbling through the darkened castle, her glorious golden hair unbound. Maybe it had been her hair.

He forced his mouth into an insolent smile, glad to see her answering flash of annoyance. Lucky for her she wasn't a man, or he'd have challenged her to a duel for what she'd heard through the keyhole. As it was, he could only hope that the prince would come up with a suitably unpleasant consequence for her eavesdropping.

Back inside the audience chamber, Ormonde read the hastily scribbled translation of Bampfield's message. "Delicious. I only wish I could be there to see it."

Colonel Bampfield was a scurrilous fellow, an ambitious professional spy, but he had devised a clever plan to smuggle Prince Charles's younger brother James, the Duke of York, out of England. Only when Prince James was safely on the Continent would the succession be assured. Ormonde smiled.

"If all goes well, our package will be safely out of England within the fortnight."

Culpeper glanced over the message, then handed it back to the prince. "God save the king, and God save your highness and the Duke of York."

Ormonde sobered. Time to put his thumb into the pie. He only hoped Creighton would have the good sense to thank him when it was all over. "I'd feel better about all this if we had one of our own people there."

"Aye," Culpeper agreed. "Someone whose loyalty to your highness is beyond question. It wouldn't do for your highness's brother to fall under the influence of anyone who might cause . . . friction between your highness and himself. I fear the monarchy would not survive a dispute about the succession."

"True." Ormonde planted another seed. "And concerning the countess . . . Didn't his majesty grant your highness permission to settle a match for Viscount Creighton?" The king had resisted at first, but thanks to Creighton's wealth and unquestioned loyalty, Ormonde had managed to convince the king to provide a blank marriage contract so Prince Charles could settle a match for his retainer. "Perhaps your highness might have an idea that would solve all our problems at once?"

At first the crown prince seemed confused by the change of subject, then a look of comprehension dawned. "The marriage contract!" Wales smiled with wicked delight. "I'd forgotten all about that." He opened the desk drawer and rummaged around until he found the document. He unrolled it. "Creighton and the countess . . . but of course! It's so simple." He grinned up at his two advisors. "If Creighton were to marry the countess, he'd have a perfect excuse to return to England. Then he could oversee the shipping of our little package."

Ormonde had known the prince would catch on. Young Wales was sharp; one day he might make a great king. The marquis pretended to consider the matter, thinking aloud. "Interesting. And if the ceremony were to take place immediately, the newlyweds could depart straightaway. Of course, that would mean the countess wouldn't have a chance to say good-bye—or anything else—to the queen."

The prince instantly grasped his meaning. "Yes. They could leave tonight."

Culpeper chuckled. "Tidy. Very tidy."

"Still, I wonder," the crown prince mused. "I doubt my father intended to allow me such latitude in selecting a bride for Creighton." He unrolled and scanned the marriage contract. "Creighton is immensely rich, but his great-grandparents were commoners. Made their money in shipping. The countess's bloodlines are most impressive, as are her holdings. My father might prefer to ally the lady elsewhere."

"Perhaps," Ormonde conceded. "But according to Mr. Hyde's tax rolls, Countess Ravenwold is land poor. She claims her late husband ran through his own fortune and most of hers." They all knew firsthand of Ravenwold's gambling. "Creighton, on the other hand, has one of the few fortunes capable of supporting the countess's estates. His wealth should more than make up for his inferior rank. The match makes perfect sense."

"We could always ask his majesty to make Creighton earl of Ravenwold," Culpeper volunteered. "That would even things up nicely."

Knowing the prince's jealousy of Creighton, Ormonde smiled at the irony of Culpeper's suggestion. But the idea had its merits. "Parliament has made inroads in the north, and Creighton's holdings are in a key location. We need his loyalty now more than ever. An elevation in rank would make the marriage far more acceptable from his perspective."

Culpeper's brows drew together. "Do you think the king will cooperate?"

Ormonde nodded. "Under the circumstances, I'm almost certain he will. Especially if we are unanimous in our support."

Prince Charles pinched his full lower lip, deliberating.

"What about the countess?" Culpeper fretted. "Technically, she has the right to refuse remarriage."

"Technically, yes," Ormonde agreed. "But she hasn't the money to pay the necessary fines." He recalled a recent discussion with Hyde. "As a matter of fact, I don't think she's paid any fines at all. We *could* argue that she owes the Crown three years' ransom for her single status."

Culpeper smiled smugly. "So much for the countess."

Ormonde said smoothly, "Considering her financial problems, I should think the lady would be most grateful for such a match."

"Oh, you do, do you?" The prince considered the matter at length. Then he inhaled deeply, inked a quill, and wrote the countess's name into the blank space on the marriage contract. While he blotted and sanded it, he said, "From what I know of women, I rather doubt the lady will appreciate our intervention." He looked up, his expression serious. "But she will obey, as will Creighton, or they'll both face charges for treason."

Ormonde's heart contracted. He genuinely liked Creighton and intended him no harm. "Treason, sire? Such a harsh word."

Charles's olive complexion darkened, confirming the dangerous edge to his next words. "These are harsh times, sir, and refusal to obey a direct order from the sovereign is treason, pure and simple." His features eased. "But I am not an unreasonable man. I shall make it perfectly clear to the viscount and countess that this will stand as a test of their loyalty. That should settle the matter." An unexpected grin lit the prince's face. "This will infuriate my mother." Obviously, the prospect pleased him immensely.

He turned to Culpeper. "The wedding must take place tonight, as soon as possible. Otherwise, the queen is sure to get involved and ruin everything."

"I agree, your highness," Culpeper responded. "The ceremony should take place immediately."

"There's just one other thing . . ." Ormonde added.

The prince and Culpeper looked at him expectantly. Ormonde was counting on the fact that once Wales made up his mind, no obstacle could dissuade him. This obstacle was substantial. "The countess is papist, but Creighton's a staunch Anglican. He'll never agree to a Roman ceremony."

"Blast. That complicates things," Wales grumbled. But after several silent, pensive moments, he declared, "No Roman priests, then. We'll have an Anglican ceremony."

"But your highness," Culpeper protested, "the countess is a devout Catholic. She'll never agree to such a thing. Rome won't recognize the union. She'd be—"

Wales cut the objection short with a harsh, "She will do as she's told!" Once his flash of temper had subsided, he added, "My mother has great influence with Rome. Perhaps she will take pity on the countess and have them legitimize the marriage. After all, there are extenuating circumstances."

He rose and began to pace. "I want this over with by dinnertime. My stomach is growling." Another thought occurred to him. "We'll need someone to waive the banns. Those Anglican chaplains we brought from Jersey—there wouldn't be a bishop among them?"

Culpeper shook his head. "Nay, sire, but one of our bishops arrived only yesterday with dispatches from your father. He could waive the banns and perform the ceremony. Shall I fetch him?"

"Yes."

Culpeper hesitated. "A minor problem with that . . ."

"What now?" the prince demanded.

"The bishop is elderly," Culpeper said, "and I'm afraid he's rather deaf."

"I don't see how that should make any difference," Wales reasoned. "He can conduct the ceremony, can't he?"

"Oh, aye." Culpeper remained dubious. "But we'll have to shout."

"Then we shall shout," the prince declared irritably. "Now go fetch him." As Culpeper hurried away, Charles looked at the clock. "Quarter past six. We'll have the ceremony here at seven."

"Very good." Ormonde suppressed a smile. "Anything else, your highness?"

"My mother will have to be notified. Send word to her at the Louvre, but be sure it isn't delivered until too late for her to interfere." He waved a finger at Ormonde. "And send someone straightaway to fetch Creighton's things . . . and the countess's baggage and servants. Our newlyweds will be leaving immediately after the ceremony." The prince tapped his bowed upper lip. "They'll need an armed escort, of course. That can be my wedding gift. See to it."

It was all Ormonde could do to keep from laughing. Gift, indeed! Garrett and the countess wouldn't know what hit them—married and bundled off under armed guard in a matter of hours! Ormonde lived for moments like this.

The Prince of Wales rubbed his hands together. "Post a few extra guards outside the waiting room and the exits. Tell them to let no one in or out except you, Culpeper, and the bishop." The prince beamed, looking for a moment like the seventeen-year-old he was. "I love surprises."

Ormonde bowed and backed away.

"On your way out," the prince added, "send Creighton and the countess in."

Ormonde realized he'd be lucky if Creighton didn't challenge him to a duel for what he'd done. He opened the door to find Creighton and the countess glaring at each other from opposite ends of a wooden bench halfway down the empty hall.

After whispering the prince's instructions to the guards, he turned, lifted his eyes toward heaven, said a silent prayer for forgiveness, then announced, "His highness would like to see you both."

# ❧ CHAPTER 7 ❧

*G*arrett listened in stunned disbelief to the prince's pronouncement.

Beside him, the countess choked out a strangled, "What?" For a moment, she looked as if she were going to scream, but she didn't.

Prince Charles laid the marriage contract on the desk between them. "As you can see, the contract is in order. And binding."

Garrett snatched it up, praying that something—anything—would be amiss so he could halt this lunacy. When he read it over, he realized the prince hadn't exaggerated. The contract's wording was ironclad, and the king's handwriting appeared to be genuine, as did his seal. The document lacked only the signatures of the prospective bride and groom—a mere formality. King Charles had authorized this marriage, making it a royal imperative. But why? *When?*

Countess Ravenwold croaked, "Surely your highness is joking. This . . . *marriage by curtain ring* . . . you can't be serious."

Visibly annoyed, the Prince of Wales looked up at her and said, "We are not in the habit of joking about such matters, madam." His heavy-lidded eyes narrowed. "But for your benefit, I shall repeat myself: For the good of the crown as well as your own, we have decided that you shall marry Viscount Creighton straightaway and set out for England tonight." He shot her a look of challenge. "You said you wished to go home. Well, I have granted your wish." He turned to Garrett. "As of this moment, Creighton, you are relieved of your responsibilities in my retinue. I have ordered you transferred back to England on special assignment.''

Garrett felt as if the walls were closing in on him. Every muscle in his body tensed, but he forced himself to maintain a casual pose. He kept his tone light. ''And what assignment would that be, your highness?''

The Prince of Wales leaned back in his chair. ''I want you personally to oversee the shipping of that small package we're expecting from London. Once the package is safely at sea, you shall take three month's leave.'' Charles smiled benignly. ''That should give you time to attend to the business of merging the countess's holdings with your own. Once that's taken care of, you will report to command headquarters in the West Country.''

In spite of his best efforts to the contrary, Garrett's smile faded. Obviously, the prince had worked out all the details, so his crack-pated plan was no idle notion.

Wales's smile broadened. ''You needn't look so grim, sir. You're not being demoted. On the contrary, at Lord Culpeper's suggestion, I have sent word to my father requesting that you be made nineteenth earl of Ravenwold. Contingent upon your marrying the countess, of course.''

Countess Ravenwold gasped. ''What!'' She looked Garrett up and down with scorn. ''I've heard what kind of man you are, sir—nothing but a wanton and a scoundrel!'' She pivoted back to address the prince. ''Ravenwolds have been liege lords to the Crown for centuries—since William the Conqueror— serving with distinction, as have my Compton ancestors! This man is not worthy of such a noble heritage. He's an upstart, a knave! He does no credit to the title he *has,* much less the name of Ravenwold!''

As if the last earl of Ravenwold had been some paragon of virtue! ''Enough!'' Garrett snapped. His neck flushing with rage, he growled, ''If you were a man, madam, those words would be your last. As it is, I will caution you not to insult me further.''

Garrett didn't care if they made him a grand duke; he had no intention of marrying this cold-blooded, conceited parody of a woman. He appealed to the prince, ''Surely I do not deserve to be yoked for life to *that!*'' He turned a contemptuous glance on the countess, only to feel her open palm strike his cheek with surprising force. Garrett grabbed her wrist and forced it behind her waist. ''I have never raised a hand to a woman before, but you tempt me to make an exception." He glanced back to the prince, a sardonic smile twisting his lips. "Would your highness condemn me to marry such an ill-tempered wench?"

"I'd rather marry a leper," the countess spat out, struggling against his grasp. When she realized she could not free herself, her blue eyes widened with fear. "Let me go, you brute!"

"Why? So you can strike me again?" Garrett grinned, still feeling the imprint of her palm across his cheek with every heartbeat. "I think not."

"Varlet!" She tried without success to stomp his toes. "You shall not abuse me, sir! I will not allow it!" Her voice was ragged with panic.

"Stop struggling." Fool woman. Did she really think he would harm her? Garrett loosened his hold a fraction. Still, he couldn't resist teasing her a bit. He grinned evilly. "Tsk, tsk. Such behavior. Hardly worthy of the noble name of Ravenwold."

"Why, you, you . . ." Furious beyond words, she sputtered incoherently, then shrieked, "Aaargh!"

Garrett kept her at arm's length, commenting casually to the prince, "Did your highness know she was subject to fits? I do think that should be taken into consideration."

"Fits?" Countess Ravenwold cried in outrage. "I've never had a fit in my life! It's just the prospect of marrying *you* that's sent me beyond the bounds of reason!"

Prince Charles intervened. "Much as I hate to interrupt, I fear we must get back to the matter at hand." No longer the amused observer, he sobered, every inch the future sovereign. "Understand this, both of you: As far as the Crown is concerned, this marriage is a direct order from my father. Refusal to cooperate will be considered an act of treason."

Treason!

The word shattered Garrett's veneer of nonchalance like a bolt of lightning. He let go of the countess and turned to regard the prince in shock. Surely, Wales was bluffing! But one glance confirmed that the threat was not an idle one.

Wales went on briskly, "I needn't remind you, Creighton, of the importance of your new assignment." He glanced pointedly at the countess. "Absolute discretion is required."

Garrett nodded. "I understand, your highness." Obviously,

Wales didn't want the countess's wagging tongue to endanger the duke of York's escape.

"I knew you would." The prince lifted an eyebrow. "Should anyone question why you have returned to England, simply explain that you are on leave of absence to celebrate your marriage and settle your business affairs."

Garrett's chest felt so tight he could hardly breathe. "As always, I am at your highness's service, but I beg to ask how this marriage . . . that is, *why* your highness—"

Wales interrupted, wagging his hand in dismissal. "I know this seems sudden, but I am certain both of you will see the wisdom in our decision upon reflection." He frowned. "The matter is not open to discussion." The prince pushed the contract closer to Garrett. "This is a legal document expressing the direct will of your sovereign. On behalf of his majesty, I am ordering you both to sign it."

The countess snatched up the document and rapidly read over it.

Superficially, Garrett managed to maintain his self-control, but underneath he was as frantic as a bear caught in a piked pit. He concentrated on breathing slowly and regularly. Mustn't let them see how rattled he was.

Surely, there had to be some way out of this!

Wales busied himself with his ornate lace cuffs, granting them a moment to get used to the idea. The room's silence was broken only by the ticking of the clock and the countess's rapid breathing as she read and reread the contract.

Treason!

Despite the prince's outward charm, Garrett knew all too well that young Wales was far more ruthless than his father. He recalled an incident in the streets of Oxford shortly after he had been assigned to Wales's household. The twelve-year-old prince had stopped a contingent of guards escorting a rebel officer to be questioned by the king. Clearly disappointed that he lacked the authority to order the man executed, the crown prince had told the guards, "You ought to hang the traitor, and quickly, before my father has a chance to pardon him!"

Now that the rebels held King Charles prisoner at Hampton Court and the prince's three eldest siblings at St. James Palace, Wales was even less tolerant of disloyalty—real or imagined. Garrett realized with a sinking feeling that unless he and the countess went along with this marriage, the prince would summarily prosecute them both for treason.

They would be convicted, too. The countess had been caught in the act of spying.

Refusal to sign would probably cost Garrett his head.

The prince was already jealous of him, though without cause. That was doubtless why Wales was doing this, ordering him to marry this insufferable, sanctimonious man-hater and packing him off to England. Sheer jealousy was behind it, and completely unfounded!

The duchesse de Chataillon had flirted with Garrett, not the other way around. Garrett wasn't idiot enough to go after the prince's mistress. Hell, he wouldn't want the Frenchwoman if she sat naked on his face! She was a viper. And speaking of vipers . . . He turned to the countess, who stood pale and shaken beside him. If she hadn't gone snooping around, this never would have happened.

Then a ray of hope broke through Garrett's desperate reasoning: Ormonde! He and Garrett had known and respected each other for years. The prince valued Ormonde's advice. Maybe the marquis could help Garrett wiggle out of this.

The prince glanced up at Countess Ravenwold and said, "Creighton, get the countess a chair. She has my leave to sit. She's not looking at all well."

Garrett swung a heavy wooden chair from beside the desk and shoved it under her. When the edge of the wooden seat nudged her calves, the countess folded into the chair as stiffly as a porcelain doll. Once she was sitting, she managed to find her voice. "Your highness, no one is more loyal to the throne than I, but this haste . . . there have been no banns, and I am in mourning. My sister is dead not yet a week. Surely it is not unreasonable to delay—"

"Madam," Charles snapped, "I have already explained that there are other considerations governing the timing of this union. The bishop will waive the banns and perform the ceremony."

"Your highness," Garrett felt compelled to ask again, "this contract comes as a complete surprise to me. Pray tell, how did your highness—"

Charles answered before the question was fully out. "In light of his majesty's pressing preoccupations and my affection for you, the king assigned me the responsibility of settling your marriage. He left the name of the bride blank, to be filled in according to my best judgment. I received the document before we left Bristol, but had no reason to use it until today."

Bristol! So it wasn't just jealousy over the duchesse de Chataillon, but Lady Wyndham, as well. And in both cases, Garrett was blameless!

But regardless of the reason why, Wales had boxed him into a corner.

Would it really be so terrible, marrying the countess and becoming nineteenth earl of Ravenwold? Garrett had always intended to settle down and marry one day . . .

But not now, and not *her!*

His mind flashed with the vivid memory of the countess three years ago, dancing with drunken abandon on her husband's grave. By thunder, if the woman were forced into this union, she would probably put poison in Garrett's soup, then dance on *his* grave! He rubbed his clean-shaven jaw. If only he had more time . . . but he didn't. The prince wanted the marriage to take place immediately, and Wales was infamous for his stubbornness. Garrett had to respond, and quickly.

Marry the countess or face charges for treason. What a choice! Either alternative could be lethal.

Garrett decided to play his final negotiating card. "Has the marquis of Ormonde expressed an opinion on this marriage, your highness?"

"Actually, he came up with the notion in the first place," the prince replied smugly. "Ormonde's a slick one. He wanted me to think it was *my* idea, but I knew better."

"I'll be damned." Garrett had thought Ormonde was his friend! His last hope of escape bled away as surely as a wounded man's final drop of blood.

The countess let the marriage contract drop to the desk, her eyes brimming. "Your highness, I beg you, do not force this upon me."

Charles said coldly, "Madam, I have said this matter is not open to discussion."

The moving hand had writ. Garrett realized neither he nor the countess had a choice. He turned a defiant grin on her. "Well, Countess darling, it appears we are to be married."

Then he leaned forward, inked the quill, and signed a lifetime lease on hell.

# ❧ CHAPTER 8 ❧

*E*lizabeth watched with sinking heart while the viscount signed the marriage contract. As long as both of them opposed the union, she'd held out some hope, but now . . . Her voice reflected the bitterness that rose within her. "So the brave colonel surrenders without a fight."

To her consternation, Creighton only grinned wider, completing his signature with a flourish. He bowed to the prince. "I am your highness's obedient servant." Then he offered the quill to her. "I trust milady is, as well."

Trapped!

Elizabeth stared stupidly at the quill. She considered running away, but they would doubtless only hunt her down and bring her back. Dear Heaven, what was she going to do?

If only she hadn't agreed to deliver Anne's letter. If only she hadn't stayed behind today to see the prince . . .

*"If only's" are for weaklings!* Her father's harsh voice echoed from the past. *Face what is and do your duty without whining. Privilege and obligation go hand-in-hand. Never forget it.*

She glared at Creighton. Curse the man for rolling over so easily! Obviously, he was as reluctant as she, yet he'd barely protested before signing. Now she had no choice; she could not hold out alone, and they all knew it. With shaking hand, she took the quill and dipped it into the inkwell. But just before she signed, a horrifying thought occurred to her: What would Creighton do when he found out she was barren?

She lifted the pen from the paper. "Before I sign, there's something I must discuss with his highness." She shot a hostile glance at Creighton. "In private."

The Prince of Wales let out an irritated sigh. "Very well." He turned to Creighton. "Leave us."

"As always, I am yours to command." Creighton bowed briefly to the prince, then with insulting exaggeration to her.

After he had left, Elizabeth faced the prince. Despite his youth, he had the imposing presence of a seasoned statesman, but she refused to be intimidated.

*Please, dear God, let my barrenness be of some use to me at last. Please, let it prevent this marriage.*

She flushed with shame at having to mention such an intimate matter. "Your highness, this marriage is not only unfair to me, but also to Viscount Creighton. You see, I am barren."

Her confession had no effect on the prince's impatient expression. He arched an eyebrow and said brusquely, "You have my sympathies, madam, but I assure you, in this case it does not signify."

"Does not signify?" Elizabeth asked, incredulous. "Of course it signifies! Viscount Creighton will want heirs."

"Then he can legitimize one of his bastards. I'm told he has several."

"Bastards?" Elizabeth recoiled. "Surely you don't expect me to—"

Her protest brought the prince to the end of his notoriously short patience. "Not another word, Countess." He rose and leaned over the desk, his long, bony finger pointing to the unsigned space on the bottom of the marriage contract. "I expect you, madam, to sign this contract, marry Creighton, and leave for England tonight. If you refuse, I'll have you thrown into the oubliette. A few hours with the rats ought to change your mind."

He meant it! The cold, determined smile on his face told Elizabeth that he might even enjoy having her thrown into the dungeon for a while.

Abandoning her manners, she sank back into her chair and faced the appalling realization that she had no choice. Sooner or later, she would have to marry Creighton. Prince Charles wanted it to be sooner, and he would be ruthless in obtaining her cooperation.

The prince straightened to every inch of his formidable height. "After the ceremony, you shall accompany Creighton to London and stay out of his way while he completes his assignment there." He shot her a quelling glance. "As for

what goes on behind closed doors, that's between you and
Creighton and of no concern to me.'' He sat behind his desk.
''Now I'm going to grant you permission to speak one word,
and one only. If it's yes, you will sign. If it's no, I will summon the guards and have you taken to the dungeon. The choice
is yours.''

Knowing she was beaten but unwilling to admit defeat, Elizabeth glared at him for fully a minute before she said through
gritted teeth, ''Yes, then!''

Prince Charles exploded. ''That's *two* words! I said *one!*''
He jumped to his feet, prompting a shaken Elizabeth to rise
as well. ''One word! One! Why can't you women manage
that?'' He paced back and forth behind his desk, his arms
waving. ''I swear, I've half a mind to put you in the dungeon
anyway! God help Creighton, married to such a froward, contrary creature. He's likely never to forgive me, or Ormonde,
for this.''

Elizabeth hastily retrieved the quill, inked it, and scratched
her name beneath Creighton's. She shoved the document at
the prince. ''There!''

Suddenly deflated, she felt as if she'd just signed her own
death warrant.

Instantly, the prince's demeanor smoothed. ''Very good. I
knew you'd come around.''' He rolled up the document and
shut it away in the desk drawer. ''Now run fetch Creighton.
We must see to the wedding.''

By the time Ormonde returned with Culpeper and a portly,
white-haired clergyman in Anglican vestments, Elizabeth and
Garrett had been banished to opposite sides of the room.

Ormonde strode over to Creighton and pumped his hand.
''Congratulations, old boy! I always wondered when they
would take you out of circulation.'' Creighton did not appear
amused.

Still seated at his desk, the prince acknowledged the bishop.
''Thank you for coming, your grace.''

The jowled clergyman peered intensely at the prince. ''Beg
pardon, your highness?''

''I said, thank you for coming, your grace!'' the prince
shouted.

The bishop nodded. ''Think nothing of it. My pleasure.''

Prince Charles retrieved the marriage contract and handed

it to the churchman. Everyone in the room winced as he bellowed, "I'd like to have the ceremony immediately. Will you waive the banns?"

The bishop gave the document only a cursory glance before returning it to the prince. "Everything seems to be in order. The banns are hereby waived."

The chiming of the hour prompted the prince to ask loudly, "Will you waive the Mass?"

"In light of the hour, I hereby waive the Nuptial Mass. The marriage shall be binding without it."

Elizabeth had watched and listened in horror. No Mass? And this . . . *heretic* to preside? It had never occurred to her that Prince Charles would not summon a proper Roman priest! Forgetting the prince's order to remain silent in her corner, she swept past Ormonde and the others. "Sire, I am a Catholic! Surely your highness does not intend to allow this—" She stopped herself before she said heretic. "—this . . . *Anglican* bishop to preside over the ceremony. I would be excommunicated!"

Charles's mouth flattened. "Calm yourself, madam. We have no Roman priest in my household. Owing to the pressing considerations of time and the fact that Creighton is an Anglican, we have decided the ceremony shall be Anglican. But never fear. I assure you, you will not be excommunicated. The queen will see to that."

"The queen?" Elizabeth didn't know what to believe. True, Henrietta Maria had great influence with Rome, but everyone knew she and her eldest son were at sword's points. Why would her majesty intervene, particularly on behalf of someone as inconsequential as Elizabeth?

The prince motioned the groom closer. "Come, Creighton. Let's get this over with so we can all eat dinner."

Creighton sidled up to the desk, an arrogant smile on his chiseled lips. He seemed to be enjoying this travesty.

By heaven, but she would love to wipe that smile from his face!

She turned wounded eyes to the prince. "But I can't be married in black. To do so would guarantee bad fortune. And I haven't even had a stitch for luck." It was an ill omen, indeed, to start the ceremony completely dressed—and in black, at that—without a bridesmaid to add a last-minute stitch for luck. "There's not even a wedding cake," she added.

Not that she thought preserving a piece would ensure her husband's fidelity. The ritual hadn't worked with Ravenwold and was even less likely to have an effect on a profligate like Creighton.

Creighton chortled at her superstitious ramblings, but all the others exchanged embarrassed glances.

"We have the necessary documents, a bride, a groom, a bishop, and witnesses. That's all we need," the prince said emphatically. He rose. "So let us begin."

"Here?" Elizabeth's voice was edged with panic. "Surely there's a chapel!" France was still Catholic, so St. Germain's chapel was certain to have been properly sanctified. She turned to the heretic bishop. "I beg you, sir, in the name of our merciful Savior, please let me be married in God's house."

"Eh?"

She repeated her plea at the top of her lungs.

The bishop looked askance at the prince. "Her request is not unreasonable. I seem to recall passing a chapel on my way in."

Charles exhaled deeply. "Oh, all right, we'll adjourn to the chapel. But only on one condition." He pointed to Elizabeth. "You must give me your solemn vow that you will go through with the ceremony without further delays."

Elizabeth nodded. At least she would say her vows in a proper house of God.

"Say it."

"Very well." She crossed herself, scowling at the prince. "I vow before God on penalty of my immortal soul that I shall cooperate without further delay."

When they reached the chapel, Elizabeth was relieved to see a gilded crucifix over the altar and an exquisite statue of the Blessed Mother in a niche. She said a silent prayer of thanks, then asked the Virgin's intervention on her behalf and prayed desperately for escape. Unfortunately, lightning failed to strike any of the men in the room.

The Anglican bishop scowled his disapproval at the chapel's statuary and intricate stained glass windows, but he said nothing as he took up his place in front of the altar.

Prince Charles shouted to him, "We can dispense with the lengthy prayers, your grace. I'd like the abbreviated version."

Ruffled by the prince's frankness, the plump bishop flipped through the pages of his heretic missal until he found the sacrament of marriage. He faced the small group. "The bride will please stand to my right. The groom, to my left."

Creighton took his place, but Elizabeth's feet wouldn't move. They seemed to be glued to the floor. Her mind spun with a singsong melody she and Charlotte had recited as children:

> *Married in white, you have chosen all right,*
> *Married in green, ashamed to be seen,*
> *Married in gray, you will go far away,*
> *Married in red, you will wish yourself dead,*
> *Married in blue, love ever true,*
> *Married in yellow, you're ashamed of your fellow,*
> *Married in pink, of you he will think,*
> *Married in black, you'll wish yourself back.*

The two little girls had shared naive dreams of rescue by handsome, loving husbands, but reality had proved that marriage merely substituted a crueler husband for their cruel father.

Elizabeth looked down helplessly at her heavy widow's weeds. *Married in black, you'll wish yourself back.* A hysterical little giggle escaped her. She hardly needed a nursery rhyme to convince her she would regret marrying Creighton.

She felt a hand close gently on her upper arm. "This way, my lady." The marquis of Ormonde urged her forward until she was standing beside Creighton.

Feeling as if she were living a nightmare, she faced the heretic churchman and heard him say, "In the name of the Father, Son, and Holy Ghost." The men made the sign of the cross while the bishop intoned, "Dearly beloved, we are gathered together here in the sight of God, and in the face of this congregation, to join together this man and this woman in holy matrimony; which is an honorable estate, instituted of God in the time of man's innocency, signifying unto us the mysterious union that is betwixt Christ and his Church; which holy estate Christ beautified with his presence, and the first miracle he wrought at Cana—"

The crown prince stopped the bishop in midsentence by tugging on his sleeve. When the churchman halted, perplexed, Prince Charles made a "hurry-up" motion with his hand.

The bishop flushed, but skipped to the meat of the ceremony. "I require and charge you both, as ye will answer at that dreadful day of judgment when the secrets of all hearts shall be disclosed, that if either of you know any impediment, why ye may not be *lawfully* joined together in matrimony, ye do now confess it. For be ye well assured, that so many as are coupled together otherwise than God's Word doth allow are not joined together by God; neither is their matrimony lawful."

In the brief pause that followed, Elizabeth wished with all her might that there was some legal impediment. Surely, God Almighty could not approve such a union! But no one spoke in the bishop's brief pause.

He turned to Creighton. "Thy name, sir?"

"Edward Garrett, Viscount Creighton."

"Edward Garrett, wilt thou have this woman to be thy wedded wife, to live together after God's ordinance in the holy estate of matrimony? Wilt thou love her, comfort her, honor, and keep her in sickness and in health; and forsaking all other, keep thee only unto her—" Elizabeth let out a derisive snort, but the bishop either didn't hear or decided to ignore it. He didn't miss a beat. "—so long as ye both shall live?"

Creighton turned his insolent grin on her and declared loudly, "I will!"

The bishop addressed Elizabeth. "Thy name, please?"

Sheer frustration tightened her throat, but she managed to say, "Virginia Elizabeth Catherine."

"Pardon?" The clergyman cupped his ear with his free hand. "Sorry, my dear, but I didn't get that."

"Virginia Elizabeth Catherine, Countess Ravenwold!" she shouted angrily.

"Ah." He found his place in the missal and continued. "Virginia Elizabeth Catherine, wilt thou have this man to thy wedded husband, to live together after God's ordinance in the holy estate of matrimony? Wilt thou obey him and serve him, love, honor, and keep him, in sickness and in health; and forsaking all other, keep thee only into him, so long as ye both shall live?"

Obey and serve, indeed! Everything inside Elizabeth screamed "No!" but she had vowed before God to go along with this farce. Yet how could she say the words that would put her at the mercy of this scoundrel?

The silence stretched as taut as a bowstring until she felt

Creighton pinch her arm. "Ouch! Stop that!" She swatted his hand away. Seeing the bishop's shocked expression, she amended, "I mean, I will." When he didn't understand, she shouted, "I will!" A pox on the prince for doing this to her, and Creighton, too!

Visibly relieved, the bishop asked, "Who giveth this woman to be married to this man?"

There was another awkward pause before Prince Charles stepped forward. "I do." He took Elizabeth's cold, limp right hand and placed it into Creighton's large, warm one.

The churchman addressed the groom. "Repeat after me: I, Edward Garrett—"

Creighton's insolent expression lost its conviction. "I, Edward Garrett."

"—take thee, Virginia Elizabeth Catherine, to my wedded wife."

"Take thee, Virginia Elizabeth Catherine, to my wedded wife."

"—to have and to hold from this day forward."

"To have and to hold from this day forward."

"—for better, for worse, for richer, for poorer."

"For better, for worse, for richer, for poorer."

"—in sickness and in health, to love and to cherish."

Creighton recited stiffly, "In sickness and in health, to love and to cherish."

"—till death do us part, according to God's holy ordinance; and thereto I plight thee my troth."

"Till death do us part, according to God's holy ordinance, and thereto I plight thee my troth."

What a mockery! Elizabeth thought. At least Creighton had had the decency to look uncomfortable as he'd uttered such horrendous lies.

The bishop turned to Elizabeth. "Repeat after me: I, Virginia Elizabeth Catherine."

A sudden surge of anger flooded her with energy. She straightened to every inch of her height, lifted her chin, and firmly declared, "I, Virginia Elizabeth Catherine."

"—take thee, Edward Garrett, to my lawful wedded husband."

"Take thee, Edward Garrett, to my lawful wedded husband!"

"—to have and to hold from this day forward."

"To have and to hold from this day forward!" Somehow, it made her feel better to shout the words.

"—for better, for worse, for richer, for poorer."

"For better, for worse, for richer, for poorer!"

"—in sickness and in health."

"In sickness and in health!"

"—to love, cherish, and obey, till death do us part—"

She glared defiantly at Creighton and said in a less strident tone. "To love and to cherish, till death do us part."

Her omission prompted Creighton to lift an amused eyebrow, but the bishop frowned, obviously uncertain whether he had heard her say "obey." Elizabeth shot him a quelling look that dared him to challenge her.

The bishop pulled a kerchief from his vestments and mopped his brow before deciding not to make an issue of the matter. He continued, "Is there a ring?"

Elizabeth saw Creighton slip his left hand into his pocket to conceal the golden seal he wore. He shook his head. "I have no ring for the lady."

The knave wouldn't even grant her that small sacrifice!

As before, the prince came to the rescue. "Here." He tugged a magnificent gold-mounted sapphire from his smallest finger and dropped it into the crevice of the bishop's missal. Prince Charles grinned at Creighton. "Consider it a gift."

"Your highness is most generous," Creighton replied archly.

The bishop handed him the ring. "Place this on the fourth finger of her left hand and, holding it there, repeat after me."

Creighton slid the ring onto her finger. "Ah. A perfect fit." His huge hand dwarfed hers. She noticed several faint scars on his long, spatulate fingers, and one digit had obviously been broken and healed improperly.

The bishop prompted, "With this ring, I thee wed, and with my body I thee worship."

A mischievous spark brightened Creighton's eye as he repeated, "With this ring, I thee wed, and with my body I thee worship."

Indeed! Elizabeth's mouth flattened into a thin line.

"—and with all my worldly goods I thee endow."

"And with all my worldly goods I thee endow."

"—in the name of the Father, and of the Son, and of the Holy Ghost. Amen."

"In the name of the Father, and of the Son, and of the Holy Ghost. Amen."

Elizabeth snatched her hand from Creighton's grasp.

The bishop continued, "Let us pray. O Eternal God, Creator and Preserver of all mankind, Giver of all spiritual grace, the Author of everlasting life: Send thy blessing upon these thy servants, this man and this woman, whom we bless in thy name; that is, as Isaac and Rebecca lived faithfully together, so these persons may surely perform and keep the vow and covenant betwixt them made, whereof this ring given and received is a token and pledge, and may ever remain in perfect love and peace together—"

"Hah," Creighton muttered under his breath.

"—and live according to thy laws; through Christ Jesus our Lord. Amen." The bishop looked up from his missal and boomed, "Those whom God hath joined together let no man put asunder." When he inhaled to launch into the remainder of the service, Prince Charles cut him short by shaking his hand.

"Thank you, your grace. Excellent service."

"But, sire," the bewildered bishop protested, "I haven't finished. There are several more prayers, plus the blessings and excerpts from the Scriptures."

"They're married, aren't they?" the prince asked.

"Oh, aye, they're married," the bishop confirmed, "but there are more blessings—children and such—and the charge to the husband and wife—"

Culpeper addressed the bishop loudly. "I hear there's quite a wedding feast waiting." He took the clergyman's arm and urged him toward the door. "His highness has ordered the finest wines and delicacies in honor of the occasion. We wouldn't want the food to get cold, would we?"

Easily distracted by the mention of a feast, the bishop turned back to the newlyweds only briefly, making the sign of the cross and rapidly reciting, "In the name of the Father, and of the Son, and of the Holy Ghost, I now pronounce you man and wife." He added a hasty, "Don't forget to partake of Holy Communion at the first opportunity. God bless you both." As Culpeper hustled him out of the chapel, he called back to Garrett, "Oh, I almost forgot . . . you may now kiss the bride."

Not if Elizabeth could help it! She glared up at the tall warrior who was now her husband, daring him to try. Wife though she may be, she had no intention of allowing such an intimacy in the presence of Ormonde and the prince.

"Kiss the bride?" Creighton took one look at her murderous expression and laughed aloud. "I think not." Sobering, he turned and addressed Ormonde. "And as for you, sir, I hardly know what to say. I thought you were my friend."

Elizabeth hadn't wanted Creighton to kiss her, but that was no reason for him to insult her, then ignore her.

Ormonde extended his hand to the viscount. "I *am* your friend, sir, in spite of how this may appear."

A sour smile twisted Creighton's lips. He shook the marquis's hand. "With friends like you . . ." He didn't complete the maxim, but instead gave Ormonde's narrow back a playful clout. "You owe me for this one, sir."

"Aye, I owe you." Ormonde chuckled. "But not as much as you might think, milord. You had to marry sometime, and you certainly could have done worse." He led Garrett toward the door. "Wait a year or two. If you still want to call me out about this then, I'll let you choose the weapons." Elizabeth was left standing alone at the altar.

She had endured enough of this rudeness. "Are both of you in the *habit* of speaking as if the ladies present were deaf or simple?"

Looking anything but sorry, Ormonde bowed in her direction. "A thousand pardons, milady." Creighton offered no apology whatsoever.

The prince approached the two men. "Come along, Ormonde. The wedding feast is waiting." When Creighton started to follow, Prince Charles halted him with, "Unfortunately, I'm afraid you two lovebirds will not be able to celebrate with us. The coach is ready and waiting to take you to your ship."

"Now?" Creighton did not conceal his surprise. "I had hoped for at least one night's"—he shot Elizabeth a brief look before finishing—"*rest* before we left."

The prince laughed. "I'm afraid the consummation of your marriage will have to wait. Unless you can manage it in a speeding coach. Farewell." Greatly amused by the idea of Creighton struggling with his unwilling bride in a jolting coach, the prince and Ormonde laughed all the way into the corridor.

Elizabeth's chest heaved with anger. Such coarseness! These

men spoke as if she were a common doxy. Why, she had half a mind to—

"Come, Bess." Creighton's voice filled the tiny chapel. "No time for temperament. We must be off."

"Bess?" Elizabeth turned incredulous eyes on the man who was now her husband. "My name is *Elizabeth,* sir, and I shall answer to no other."

"Elizabeth is far too stiff. I shall call you Bess." He came uncomfortably close, that insolent smile she hated on his lips. "Like it or not, you are my wife—in the eyes of God and of the law." When Elizabeth looked away in disdain, his strong fingers grasped her chin and turned her back to face him. "Oh, I know you did not vow to obey me, but obey me you shall. The law demands it, as does the Church."

"The Church?" she spat out. "Do you actually think the words of that, that *heretic* are of any consequence to me? Nay, sir. In the eyes of the True Faith, you have no claim on me. And no rights to my person or my name!"

Creighton's powerful hands closed snugly on her shoulders, his voice velvet smooth. "Ah, but you're wrong, Bess. I have every right. And not only are you going to obey me, but you're going to like it. Mark my words."

"I'd sooner mark your insolent *face.*" This time when she pulled back to strike him, he was ready.

He deflected the blow, then scooped her into his arms as easily as he would a child. "Now let's see what we can accomplish in the prince's speeding coach."

# ❧ CHAPTER 9 ❧

"*P*ut me down!" Elizabeth struggled to escape as Creighton carried her through the halls of the palace, but he only held her tighter against his broad, muscular chest. She snapped, "I'm perfectly capable of walking on my own two feet."

"I know you are, Bess." Creighton flashed his mocking smile. "The trouble is, if I put you down, there's no telling where you'd go, and I haven't time to chase you."

How had he known? She *had* decided to make a run for it, escape to the Louvre and beg sanctuary from the queen.

She looked up at the man carrying her. Creighton was so much bigger and stronger than her first husband, he could easily strike her dead with a single blow. Dark memories of pain and helplessness sent a shudder through her. Perhaps she should try to reason with this giant of a man. "Please put me down. Everyone is laughing at us."

"That's better, Bess. I like it when you say please." He cocked a tawny eyebrow, but did not slacken his iron embrace. "Let them laugh. We do look silly—you especially, so pale, swathed in black, scowling like that." He peered at her forehead. "Your brow is all wrinkled up like boiled tripe."

"Tripe?" Elizabeth's prudence evaporated. She shot back, "Charming. Is this how you woo all your women? If so, they're even bigger fools than I heard."

Creighton's response was completely unexpected. Without breaking his stride or changing his insolent expression, he tossed her briefly aloft, then caught her securely before she had time to react.

Elizabeth was still waiting for her stomach to catch up with the rest of her when his lips skimmed across her cheek to whisper warmly in her ear, "Watch your tongue, Bess, or the next time, I'll let you land on your bony little rump."

Despite her inner warnings for caution, she had no intention of being bullied. "Don't threaten me, you brute. And stop calling me Bess." Conditioned to violence, she raised her hand to slap him, but before she could make contact with his insolent face, Creighton caught her wrist.

"You know, Bess, I'm beginning to think you're a very violent woman, and I heartily disapprove of domestic violence."

Elizabeth snatched her wrist free of his grip and rubbed the red marks that marred her skin. "I warn you, sir, if you continue to handle me so roughly, I shall be *forced* to strike you."

His smile became menacing. "And *I* shall warn *you* only once more: Do not try to strike me again. If you do, I'll take you to the nearest public square, turn your proper black skirts over your head, and spank your bare ass for all to see. You'll have no one to blame but yourself."

Elizabeth let out a horrified, "You wouldn't!"

"Try to hit me again, and you'll find out." His huge palm slid suggestively across her rump. "I can hardly wait."

He would, the knave! Elizabeth's face prickled with hostility, but inexplicably, her rear end tingled with an unexpected heat where his hand had been.

As they passed from the palace into the dusky courtyard, Creighton looked ahead and said, "Ah. I see everything is ready for our departure, just as his highness promised." Two unmarked black coaches stood waiting in the twilight, surrounded by more than twenty armed musketeers on sturdy warhorses.

Gwynneth scrambled down from the first coach and closed the distance between them. "Milady, are you hurt?" She glared at the huge golden man who carried Elizabeth. "Has she been injured?"

Garrett cocked an appraising brow at the maid. "Calm down, good mother." The round little woman was as fluffed up and agitated as a partridge defending her chicks. "No harm has come to your mistress, and none shall, as long as she is in my care."

"Hmph. And where have I heard *that* before, I wonder?" The maid looked him up and down with open suspicion, then took her mistress's hand. "Are you all right, milady?"

Garrett watched the interchange between the two women with interest. For the first time since he'd caught her snooping in the prince's waiting room, the countess's face revealed her vulnerability. He almost felt sorry for her as she patted her maid's arm and said, "I'm perfectly fine, Gwynneth." Then her vinegar returned. "If this oaf would put me down, I could show you."

"Oaf?" Garrett parodied a wounded response. "Not a very nice thing to call your husband, Bess." Ignoring the maid's gasp, Garrett kept going. He knew better than to put the countess down; she'd take off as fast as her long legs would carry her. Instead, he approached the first coach and called to the soldiers on the far side, "Block the far door, and see that my wife does not leave the coach." Then he tipped Elizabeth neatly into the compartment. Two small lanterns illuminated the padded damask seats inside, with pillows piled into the corners. "Move over, Bess. Make room." He had to bend almost double and twist his shoulders to fit through the small opening, but he managed to get in behind her and close the door.

Eyes wide, the countess scrambled to the window and reached an imploring hand toward her maid. "Gwynneth! Don't leave me."

Garrett leaned out of his window and said firmly, "The countess and I are married now, Gwynneth, so there's no need for a chaperon. I'm sure you can understand why I want you to ride in the second carriage with the other servants."

Gwynneth looked from her mistress to her new master and back again, obviously torn between her devotion to the countess and Garrett's authority. Then one of the musketeers urged his mount toward her. "You heard his lordship," the guard rumbled. "Move along, now."

Gwynneth's face wilted with pity. "I'm sorry, milady." Then she joined the others in the second coach.

The caravan started forward, sending Elizabeth deeper into the cushions piled in the corner of the seat. She looked across the compartment to find Creighton watching her with open assessment.

"Now, for a little privacy." He tugged free the cords that bound the side curtains. The heavy damask panels unfurled, blocking out the cool night air and shielding them from the soldiers who rode alongside.

"Why did you close the curtains? I prefer them open."
Elizabeth clutched one of the pillows to her stomach. Surely
he hadn't meant what he'd implied about consummating their
marriage in the coach.

Creighton made no move to raise the side curtains. "It's
safer if no one sees us. At least until we're well away from
Paris."

Elizabeth slid as far as possible from her husband's looming
presence, but there was no escaping his long legs in the
cramped compartment. His muscular thighs flanked her black
skirts, and his boots disappeared under her seat. He shrugged
off his scarlet cassack and laid it on the seat beside him.

No sooner had she wedged herself against the cushions opposite him than the coach hit a deep rut, tossing them both
aloft, then slamming Elizabeth back into her seat and hurling
Creighton toward her. Elizabeth closed her eyes and braced
herself for the impact of his body atop hers, but it never came.
She opened one eye to find his powerful arms bracketing her,
his face only inches from her own.

"Sorry. I didn't hurt you, did I?" His concern seemed genuine.

"No." She shook her head, suddenly conscious of the masculine energy radiating from his presence. By glory, but he
was big. She wished he would go back where he came from,
but at the same time she couldn't help noticing the fineness of
his tawny hair and the smell of smoke and spice emanating
from his uniform.

Creighton pulled back slightly, his hands shifting to grip the
edge of the seat on either side of her. As the two of them
swayed so close to each other in the dusky compartment, Elizabeth realized he was staring at her widow's cap.

"Is that thing attached? You know, pins or some such."

"No pins," she answered tersely. "Why?"

"Because you don't need it anymore. Not tonight, anyway." His right hand released the edge of the seat just long
enough to pull off her widow's cap and veil. He was so quick,
and the coach was rocking so violently she couldn't spare a
hand to stop him. Creighton's chiseled features lost some of
their humor. "Now why do you flinch like that? I'm not going
to bite you."

Elizabeth didn't answer. She felt her long braid unfurl, and
curly wisps tumble free at her temples.

"Ah. That's much better." An odd sparkle softened his blue eyes. He tossed the cap aside. "You look pale as a bucket of whey in that hat." He followed the insult with a compliment. "Your hair is beautiful, Bess, one of your best features. You really shouldn't cover it up."

There was that hateful name again, and just when she was beginning to feel the tiniest glimmer of warmth toward him. The coach stabilized for a moment, so Elizabeth risked a hand to smooth self-consciously over her drawn-back hair. "I cover my hair, sir, because I am in mourning. Not only for my husband, but for my beloved sister."

"Your *first* husband," Creighton corrected.

He studied her, his brows lowered. "It must be terrible to lose a sister. You and Lady Charlotte were close, weren't you? She spoke often of you, and always with glowing praise."

"You knew each other?" she asked, surprised. Charlotte had never mentioned Creighton in her letters. But then again, the British expatriates in Paris were a close-knit group. Of course they had been acquainted. "I wondered why you came to her funeral."

Creighton leaned back into his seat, his head resting against the vertical upholstery. "Lady Markham and I were friends. She was the gentlest of souls," he said. "One of the few people I've ever met who accepted everyone as she found them, without judgment or criticism. I shall miss her."

To Elizabeth's surprise, she felt unexpected tears slide hotly down her cheeks.

"Blast," Creighton murmured, "I didn't mean to upset you. Here." He fished a neatly ironed kerchief from his jacket and handed it to her. "Would you rather I not discuss your sister?"

"No." Elizabeth accepted his kerchief, her tears stopping as quickly as they had started. "I'm glad you knew her, and I do want to talk about her. It's just . . . This is the first time anyone has spoken of her since the funeral. I wasn't prepared." Suddenly, she felt as drained as an empty wineskin. "I don't know why I'm so emotional. Perhaps because I'm tired. And hungry." So much had happened this day, more than she could face. She turned a vacant stare to the tiny lantern.

"It has been a long day." Without warning, Creighton leaned down and smoothed her skirt against the side of her calf.

Elizabeth stiffened. What was he doing? Her eyes widened. But instead of lifting her skirts, he reached past them and pulled out a basket laden with food. He rooted through the contents until he found a bottle of wine and two silver goblets. "You must be famished. I should have realized." He filled one of the goblets half-full of golden liquid. "Here. Drink this down while I get supper." He unwrapped several meat pies and savory tidbits, then neatly sliced some cheese and bread, piling everything on a heavy damask napkin before transferring it to her lap.

"Thank you." She didn't mean for it to sound sullen, but it did.

Elizabeth bowed her head, blessed the food, crossed herself, then took a bite of one of the pasties. It was stone-cold, but delicious. By the time she had finished it, Creighton was enjoying his own repast. She observed drily, "I hadn't thought of you as the domestic type, but you did quite well with the contents of that basket."

"Domestic?" He smiled and shook his head. "Hardly. But my manservant was killed in the first battle of the rebellion." He exhaled heavily. "We'd been together since I was a boy, and I did not have the heart to replace him. So I've rummaged up many a meal since then."

"Hmm." Weary and hungry as she was, the wine went straight to her head. She ate the rest of her food before finishing the goblet, then eased into the pillows, full and drowsy.

Creighton reached over and removed the empty chalice from her hand. "I think both of us could use some sleep. We'll sort everything out tomorrow."

Elizabeth didn't remember answering him. She didn't remember anything until she simmered up from the depths of an exhausted, dreamless sleep.

She was curled on her side, surrounded by something warm and resilient, and there was a comforting rhythm beneath her ear. Must be the trace horses. Or the escort. Their hoofbeats were so regular, they sounded like a single heartbeat. Without opening her eyes, Elizabeth yawned and nestled into the warmth. It tightened briefly, as if in reassurance, then relaxed.

"Mmm." Her cheek nuzzled deeper, releasing the scent of suede and something else, something pleasant and vaguely familiar.

Only a few more minutes. If she could just stay snug and

secure for a few more minutes, then she would get up.

Elizabeth didn't know how much longer she dozed before a great whoosh of air sounded from the warm firmness beneath her ear. Her eyes opened to see the viscount's long torso stretched out before her in the dim light of dawn.

She gasped, every muscle in her body tensing.

Scanning the coach's dim interior, she saw that sometime during the night the two seats had been converted to a sleeping platform, and now Creighton was angled across the compartment, his long legs bent in the cramped space while she was cuddled like a kitten in his embrace, her cheek on his chest and her leg curled over his muscular thigh!

A hot flush of shame and confusion surged through her. This would never do. She rolled free of·Creighton, jarring him awake.

He yawned and stretched as best he could in the restricted space before opening his eyes. "Ummm. Bumpy night. Sleep well, Bess?"

"As well as can be expected." Elizabeth didn't notice he'd called her Bess until it was too late to correct him. "May we stop now? I need to . . ." She felt herself coloring. "I need to stop."

Creighton's long leg swung up and kicked open the trapdoor behind the driver. "Driver! Is it safe to make a relief stop?"

Gwynneth's face loomed into the opening. "If milady needs to stop, then stop we shall."

Creighton frowned up her. "How did *you* get there?"

"I came over the first time they watered the horses. And I'm not leaving, not until I make certain my mistress is all right."

Elizabeth raised up on her knees, touched by Gwynneth's protective fervor. "God bless you, Gwynneth. I'm fine."

Creighton winked at the maid, his frown shifting to a sardonic smile. "See? All your worries for nothing." He sobered. "Now be a good girl, Gwynneth, and ask the escort if it's *safe* to stop."

"Oh, very well." Gwynneth returned in moments. "The escort says yes, if it's quick."

Garrett nodded. "Tell the driver to stop as soon as he finds a suitable location." He sat up and rubbed the muscles in his arms and shoulders.

Realizing what a fright she must look, Elizabeth poked

around amid the cushions until he asked, "Lose something?"

"My cap and veil. I saw them land over here last night, but now I can't find them." She smoothed self-consciously at the long, loose tendrils that curled around her face. Cap or no cap, she must have Gwynneth dress her hair as soon as they stopped.

"Mmm."

Was that guilt she saw flash across Creighton's features?

He asked mildly, "Don't you have another cap?"

"No." She lifted her chin defensively, refusing to be humbled by her poverty. "The one I had was perfectly good. Why should I need another?"

"Why, indeed?" Money had never been a concern to Garrett, but obviously it mattered a great deal to his new wife. A flash of memory reminded him of the drafty disrepair of Ravenwold, prompting him to look more closely at the countess. She wore no jewelry, not even the customary cameo or pearls permitted for mourning, and the beads that held her crucifix were carved of wood instead of precious stone. The fine fabric of her collar had been subtly mended, and her hem was frayed and soiled. A sobering realization began to dawn on him.

He studied her wan face. Her eyes were dull, her skin dry, and her hair lacked the luster he'd seen in the firelight three years ago.

Why hadn't he seen it before?

Now that he recognized the cause of her paleness, he could kick himself for teasing her about it. The woman hadn't eaten properly—probably for a long time.

Garrett heard hoofbeats grow louder next to the coach, then the sound of a voice through the window curtain. "There's a small wood ahead, sir, and a stream. I've sent half the men forward to secure the area. We'll stop there."

He lifted the curtain briefly, recognizing the soldier as Lieutenant Brumby. "Look sharp after the countess, Brumby. See that no one creeps up on us. I'd hate to die with my britches down."

Brumby grinned and saluted. "Aye, sir."

The coach slowed, then rolled to a stop. Garrett opened the door to a deserted stretch of road flanked by woods.

The lieutenant dismounted. "Sir."

"At ease." Garrett squeezed out of the narrow coach door, then reached inside and offered the countess a hand. "Hurry up, Bess. It's dangerous to linger.''

Ignoring his outstretched hand, she climbed down unassisted. Once she was on her feet, the countess looked up and down the lonely stretch of road before declaring acidly, ''Where's a good highwayman when you need one?''

Garrett chuckled. ''Bess, Bess, Bess. You act as if you've been abducted.''

''Haven't I?'' she shot back.

The maid, Gwynneth, wasted no time getting to her mistress's side.

''You are dismissed, sir,'' the countess said to Brumby. ''My maid will help me.''

''I humbly beg your pardon, Countess.'' Brumby bowed. ''But I must accompany milady. The colonel's orders.''

The countess bristled. ''Am I a prisoner, then, that I must be guarded while I attend to the most private functions of nature?''

Garrett found the countess's posturing amusing, but this was no place for it. He addressed her firmly. ''Lieutenant Brumby is sworn to protect you with his life, Bess. Now run along. Delay exposes all of us to needless danger.'' He started for the far side of the road, then stopped. ''Unless you'd rather *I* stand guard, instead, while you—''

''No!'' The countess took her maid's arm and hurried toward the woods, Brumby following behind.

Gwynneth patted her mistress's elbow. ''Never fear. I'll make sure no one spies on milady.'' She shot a withering glance at Brumby. ''No one.''

Garrett took care of his own needs in only minutes, then oversaw the removal of the sleeping platform. Everything was ready for departure when he heard the women come back. But instead of rejoining him in the coach, the countess and her maid walked past to the second coach and did not return.

He stuck his head out of the window and asked one of the guards, ''What are they doing? I told the countess to hurry.''

The soldier peered past the second coach. ''Looks like her ladyship has your lordship's servants unloading the baggage.'' He leaned forward in his saddle. ''I think her ladyship said something about finding her dresses.'' He shook his head in sympathy for Garrett. ''Women. They'd change their clothes twice a week if you let them.''

"Clothes?" Garrett burst out of the coach. Had she lost her mind? He'd told her it was dangerous to stop, even for a short time. "The last thing we need is to find ourselves between a pack of French Royalists and rebels." He closed the distance between the two coaches with long strides.

Sure enough, behind the second coach, half the luggage and provisions were stacked haphazardly in the road and his servants were removing more at the countess's urging. Gwynneth stood behind her, combing her mistress's hair into a neat chignon while the countess supervised the unloading.

Garrett's servants took one look at him and froze.

The countess turned. "We won't be much longer. I've ordered my things moved to the first coach, where I can find them."

"Put those back," Garrett said to the nearest cowering servant. "And do it quickly." Fighting to control his temper, he grasped the countess's upper arm and pulled her toward the first coach. "Forgive me if I seem more concerned with the safety of this party than your *things,* madam, but I must insist you board the coach immediately." He nodded to the men hastily gathering the scattered trunks and boxes. "We cannot spare time to lash those properly. Just toss them inside the coach. If they won't all fit, leave them."

"Wait!" The countess balked, pulling against him. "I may not have much, sir, but what I have is mine, and I will not allow you to discard my possessions." She pointed to the undisturbed boxes still stacked on the coach platform. "There, Gwynneth. There's my brown box, under that green one. Have them bring it to the first coach." She gestured to one of the servants. "That's it. See? It's brown, about this big." She indicated its size with her hands.

Garrett shook his head. The countess was as stubborn as little Becky, and twice as proud. The harder one pushed such creatures, the more they dug in. He would have to try another tactic. "Take all the time you want then, Bess, but understand—if we are set upon, the consequences shall be on your soul, not on mine." He was pleased to see her haughty expression falter before he turned and headed back for the first coach.

Elizabeth watched him go in consternation. She hadn't meant to endanger everyone; she'd only wanted to save her best dress from the wear and tear of the road. Now she felt foolish for exposing so many to risk over such a trivial thing.

One of the viscount's servants hastened over with a small wooden coffer. "Is this it, milady?" He flipped up the lid, revealing a treasure trove of laces, pearls, embroidered collars, and silver buckles. "It fell off the wagon just now and came open, but nothing spilled out."

Elizabeth stood transfixed. The items were exquisite, as fine as any she had ever seen. She reached out and touched the glowing pearls. One, two, three four, five, six . . . seven strands, of various sizes. And colored gloves as soft as butter. She thumbed the stack, counting seven pairs, some small, some larger. There were seven cutwork collars, too, neatly folded, and seven small bolts of French lace.

What was Creighton doing with a king's ransom in feminine finery? And why seven?

Gwynneth peered over into the box. "Hmph. Didn't see his lordship offerin' any of that to you, milady, did we?"

Elizabeth felt a scalding blush heat her face. Of course these treasures weren't for her. They were for Creighton's other women, the mothers of his bastards. His illicit lovers, all seven of them!

Well, they were welcome to him.

Elizabeth slammed the lid of the coffer. "Put this away. It's not the chest I was looking for. We can find mine the next time we stop." She turned and marched back to the first coach, Gwynneth in tow.

While Gwynneth climbed up beside the driver, Elizabeth allowed one of the coachmen to help her into the compartment. Creighton was waiting inside, the remaining contents of the food basket spread across the upholstery beside him. Elizabeth sat down opposite him just as the coach started moving.

She pushed aside the damask curtain and leaned out of the window, relieved to see that no luggage had been left in the road behind the second coach. Then she settled back into her seat.

Creighton offered her a napkin laden with food. "Here. Eat this."

Elizabeth was grateful for the food, but she didn't like his manner. "You order me to eat? I am not one of your soldiers, sir."

Creighton rolled his eyes. "Pray forgive me, darling Bess."

His generous mouth curved into a mocking half smile. "Please eat, precious wife."

The man's empty endearments stung far more than his sarcasm. Elizabeth would never be able to trust a word he said. Nothing seemed to mean anything to him—except perhaps the safety of his soldiers.

She bowed her head, murmured a blessing, crossed herself, then began to eat.

Several silent miles passed before Creighton spoke. He placed a plum tart on her lap. "Might as well eat this up, Bess, before it goes bad."

Elizabeth dabbed at her mouth with the napkin. "No, thank you. I'm quite full."

Creighton insisted. "Surely there's room for just this one. I'd eat it myself, but I've already had six."

"No, you haven't." Why would he lie about such a thing? "You've eaten only two. I saw you."

"Caught." A mischievous twinkle sparked his blue eyes. "I wanted you to have it, that's all." He grew serious. "You need to eat more, Bess. You're far too thin. Have you been ill?"

So that was it. "I have not been ill." She shifted self-consciously. "And I shall eat or not eat as I please."

Creighton shook his head. "As you wish." He pulled aside the curtain to reveal a glimpse of spring sunshine, then let it drop. "Last night, I said we would sort things out later. I imagine this is as good a time as any."

"Very well." Elizabeth braced herself. Creighton baffled her completely, and she had no idea what he was about to say.

"Our marriage is no love match, but whose is?" He leaned forward, his forearms resting on his thighs. "What I'm trying to say is, I know you are just as unhappy about this as . . . I mean, neither of us wanted this marriage, but it happened. It's a fact. We have to face it, figure out some way to live with it." He examined the back of his hand, his brows drawn together, then ventured a look into her eyes. "There's no reason we can't work out a livable arrangement. You can have your life, I can have mine."

Elizabeth knew what he was driving at. "You can have your friends . . ."

Creighton's face eased. "Exactly."

She finished defiantly, "And I can have *mine*." She said

the words as a meaningless challenge, expecting him to react in typical male fashion and insist that she remain faithful while he indulged his every romantic whim. Just like Ravenwold. But to her surprise—and inexplicable disappointment—he did not protest.

"Exactly." He smiled, his brow smoothing with relief. "As long as you're discreet. I am not an unreasonable man." He hesitated. "But I do draw the line when it comes to children."

Children. Dear Heaven, there was that to deal with. What should she say? Dared she lie, or would that just make matters worse in the end, when he finally discovered the truth? And he would discover the truth. She heard herself repeat the word. "Children?"

"Yes." Creighton's blue eyes darkened. "If there are children, I want them to be mine. I will not foster another man's seed."

She could have told him he needn't worry. Instead, she concentrated on concealing the fear that bloomed within her.

He smiled archly. "My mother says she cannot die in peace unless I produce an heir to the Creighton line."

It was worse than she had feared. Elizabeth shifted the subject to safer ground. "Your mother is alive?" Somehow, she couldn't picture Creighton with a mother. Or a family.

"Oh, aye. Very much so." He nodded. "You'll like her. Everybody does. She lives at Chestwick with my sisters."

A mother and sisters. Did they know about his bastards, she wondered.

Elizabeth's thoughts were interrupted by the sound of dogs barking. The coach slowed.

Creighton lifted the curtain and asked the guard, "What's happened?"

"Cart wreck, sir. Looks like two farmers ran into each other. The road's blocked completely. Pigs and cabbages all over the place."

"Have the men check it out. Make certain it's not an ambush. If it's safe, we'll get out and stretch our legs."

Minutes later, Lieutenant Brumby returned with reassuring news. "No sign of an ambush, sir, but the way's blocked, good and proper. We could remove the wall on the side of the road and bypass the debris, but that's liable to take longer than clearing up the wreckage."

"Assign four of the men to help clear the debris, but keep

the rest on guard.'' When Creighton interacted with his men, his casual manner disappeared. It was almost as if he were two people—one minute the careless, carefree wastrel, the next a sharp-edged, disciplined commander. He turned to Elizabeth. ''Come on, Bess. Let's take a walk.''

''My name is Elizabeth,'' she said without conviction, mellowed by the prospect of escaping the coach. She allowed Creighton to help her down onto the country lane lined by stone fences and poplar trees. Beyond the trees, sheep and cattle grazed in tidy fields that stretched as far as the eye could see.

Elizabeth walked ahead of the coach and saw that two carts had apparently tried to pass each other and hooked wheels, tearing both vehicles asunder and spilling produce and livestock into the confined passage. Now the farmers were shouting at each other in French while four of the guards heaved wagon fragments, baskets, and cabbages over the stone walls.

Creighton's voice sounded behind her. *''Vous! Messieurs! Fermez les bouches et assistez vous mes hommes! Toute a prête!''*

The two farmers stopped arguing abruptly and glared at him.

Elizabeth turned to him in surprise. ''You rattled that off so fast I couldn't understand a word. What did you say?''

Creighton glared back at the farmers. ''I told them to shut up and help my men.'' He motioned to the reluctant Frenchmen. *''Maintenant!''*

Grudgingly, they bent to help the soldiers.

Just then a dozen small pigs stampeded from the wreckage. All but one, a runt far smaller than the others, scampered past. That single squealing, frenzied streak of pink made a beeline for the shelter of Elizabeth's skirts.

Elizabeth looked down in dismay as the creature disappeared beneath her and began rooting frantically at her shoes. ''Shoo!'' She lifted her black gown slightly and stepped back. ''Stop that! Go away.'' But the little pig would not be discouraged. The harder Elizabeth tried to get away, the louder it squealed and the more determined it seemed to climb her ankles. She looked up to find Creighton grinning at her in amusement. Elizabeth asked, ''Are you just going to stand there, or are you going to help me?''

He bowed. ''I am at milady's service.'' He knelt on one

knee in the soft earthen roadway. "Lift your skirts higher, Bess, or I'll never catch it."

Embarrassed, she turned her back to the curious farmers and guards and did as he asked.

At the sight of her calves, Creighton shot her a look of approval. "Now be very still. Don't move your feet. Let the little thing calm down, so I can catch it."

She felt ridiculous standing there with her skirts hiked all the way to her knees in front. The little shoat circled her ankles several times, then finally settled between her feet.

Quick as lightning, Creighton snatched it into his hands. The creature set up an earsplitting ruckus, wiggling frantically. Creighton shouted over its shrieks, "Look, Bess. It's a girl pig." He winked. "I think she likes you. Here." He extended the squalling animal toward her. "Want to hold her?"

"Don't be absurd." Elizabeth backed away. "That's a pig, not a pet. One eats them, one doesn't hold them."

Creighton's generous mouth took on a determined slant. "A pet! Now why didn't I think of that? I'll be right back." He turned and headed for the pig farmer, who by now was trying to round up the rest of the piglets.

Elizabeth watched in amazement as Creighton counted out several coins into the farmer's hand, then motioned for one of the guards to transfer a bag of feed from the ruined wagon to their coach. On his way back, Creighton scooped up a handful of spilled feed. When he rejoined her, the piglet was tucked securely into his elbow, munching grain from his palm instead of squealing.

Creighton smiled indulgently at the little thing. "Can you believe it, she's three months old. Poor little runt. She's a curiosity, really, small as she is. What do you think we should call her?"

"Call her? Are you mad?" Elizabeth had never heard of such nonsense.

Creighton scratched behind the shoat's pink ear. Coarse blond hairs covered the pig's pink body and furred its forehead. Its tiny legs and hooves looked too small to sustain its weight. "I know. We'll call her Mr. Cromwell."

"*Mr.* Cromwell?" She observed drily, "That makes no sense. You said yourself, it's a girl pig."

"Well, in the first place, pet names don't have to make sense. And in the second place, Old Oliver is quite a swine, but as far as I know, his poor wife has done nothing to merit the misfortune of being married to such a scoundrel. So it wouldn't be fair to call her *Mrs.* Cromwell." He regarded the little animal. "I think Mr. Cromwell is perfect. What do you think, Bess?"

The man was ridiculous, but he had obviously made up his mind. A pig for a pet, indeed. In spite of herself, Elizabeth let out a dry chuckle. "I think you dishonor the pig."

"Ha!" Creighton grinned. "You almost smiled, Bess."

Having consumed all the grain, the pig began to struggle. Creighton brushed her snout free of crumbs. "Look at that. Her little nose is most expressive. Makes all sorts of shapes. And it isn't wet. It's smooth and shiny." He held her out toward Elizabeth. "Want to hold her?"

"No." Elizabeth recoiled just in time to avoid the stream of urine that poured from Mr. Cromwell. "And if that's what she's going to do, I suggest you not hold her, either."

"Point well-taken." Garrett extended the dripping creature to the limit of his reach. "Gwynneth," he shouted toward the second coach, where Gwynneth and the other servants were once again rooting through the baggage. "Come at once. I have a job for you."

The maid hastened to stand beside her mistress. She shot a sideways glance at the piglet, but made no mention of it. Instead, she spoke to the countess. "We've just found milady's small trunk. I'll have it brought up straightaway." She turned to Creighton. "The rest of the things should be properly lashed before the wreckage is cleared, milord."

"Very good, Gwynneth. Now I have another responsibility for you." Creighton thrust the piglet toward her. "This is our new pet, Mr. Cromwell. The farmer will give you a basket to keep her in. See that she's properly fed and watered." Gwynneth gingerly accepted the little pig, who set up an immediate protest, rending the air between them. Creighton untied the silk sash from his uniform. "Use this as a tether. I imagine pigs are like puppies. You can feed her when we make relief stops, then walk her."

"A pig, sir?" Gwynneth held the thing at arm's length. "I am no swineherd, your lordship. I'm a lady's maid, and my mother before me. What do I know of pigs?"

Elizabeth agreed. "You can hardly expect her to attend to such a thing. It's beneath her. Give it to one of the footmen."

"What? Our dear Mr. Cromwell, in the care of a mere footman? Shame on you, Bess." Creighton hooked a finger under Elizabeth's chin. "I want Gwynneth to tend her." He turned to the maid, his blue eyes half-lidded but resolute. "I don't know anything about piglets, but it can't be too complicated. Pigs are beasts, like any other. They eat, they drink, they sleep, and they mess. I think you can manage this one."

He turned to Elizabeth. "Come, Bess. They're almost through clearing up. If all goes well, we'll make it to the inn in time to sleep in a real bed tonight."

Elizabeth's stomach knotted. An inn, and a real bed?

That meant that Creighton could . . . that he would expect to . . . He had made it clear that she was his wife, and he intended to exercise his husbandly rights. Once they were alone, he would take her body, and there would be nothing she could do about it. Then she would be well and truly trapped in this heretical union, her soul condemned.

# Chapter 10

"*Les soldats, nos soldats Français, à haut.*" The innkeeper picked up a bottle and mimed a drunkard, then pointed to the ceiling and the rooms above it. "*J'ai une chambre de reste. Une.*" He held up a single finger to confirm the fact that all but one of his rooms were filled with French soldiers sleeping off their revels. The man's wife stood silent and suspicious behind him, her forearms tightly interlaced as she scowled at Garrett's British uniform and carbine.

Garrett didn't blame her for being less than hospitable. Mixing twenty road-weary British musketeers with an inn full of cranky French soldiers might cook up quite a pot of trouble. But there wasn't another inn for miles, and the horses and guards were exhausted. With reasonable precautions, Garrett felt they could all get some rest without incident.

He leveled a piercing look at the innkeeper. The fellow barely topped five feet, but remained stubbornly unimpressed by Garrett's size or his military demeanor. Like most Frenchmen, the proprietor ruled in his own establishment as autocratically as any king, and no amount of persuasion or intimidation could budge him. Garrett decided to try bribery. Surely for a sufficient fee the innkeeper would surrender his own room to house the officers. Garrett extracted a gold sovereign from his jacket pocket and held it up. "*Monsieur, peut-être, votre chambre?* For my officers?"

The innkeeper's eyes widened, but his wife made a noise that sounded like someone strangling a ram. The little man winced and shook his head in emphatic denial. "*Non. Une chambre.*" He shrugged, wiping his hands on his greasy apron. "*Vous voulez, monseigneur?*" Take it or leave it.

*"Oui."* Garrett sat heavily on a crude wooden bench at one of the tavern tables. He aimed a disgruntled frown at their host and ordered, *"Calvados."*

The innkeeper took his time filling the order. On his way to the kegs, he stopped to wipe several nonexistent spills from the worn tavern tables.

Garrett would be glad to get back home where people were grateful to earn an honest coin. He'd grown weary of sullen Frenchmen who acted as if they were doing him a boon to take his money. "Come have a drink with me, Brumby."

"Don't mind if I do, sir." The lieutenant swung his musket from his shoulder and propped it ready against the table, then sat down.

*"Fais ça deux calvados!"* Garrett called to the innkeeper before turning back to Brumby. "Looks like you men will have to bed down in the hayloft with the servants."

Brumby didn't seem to mind. "Better a hayloft than the open road."

Garrett had hoped to give the guards and servants a better rest. The coast was still two days' hard ride away. "Try to stay out of the Frenchmen's way. We haven't time for trouble."

"Aye, sir." Brumby stretched his legs under the table. "We've grown accustomed to avoiding the Frenchies. Had plenty of practice since we came to this godforsaken country."

The innkeeper returned and set down two crude goblets, each containing a generous measure of apple brandy. Garrett took a sip of the searing liquid. Faintly sweet, it burned like molten silver all the way down. "Ah. This stuff will scald the hair off your chest from the inside out."

Brumby took a swig, then gasped, his eyes watering. "Aye. That it does."

Garrett sipped on his drink for several minutes before he addressed the proprietor again. *"Monsieur,* there will be twenty-six for dinner." He held up two fingers, then six. *"Vingt-six personnes manger ce soir.* Understand?"

The innkeeper nodded.

"Give everyone two mugs of ale—*deux bières chacun*— with their dinners, but no more. *Pas de plus. Ma marie et moi, nous mangions en chambre.* Is that clear?"

*"Je comprends."* The little man hustled his wife toward the kitchen, berating her in rapid French.

In the relative quiet that followed, Garrett and Brumby finished their drinks without comment under the envious eyes of the two musketeers. When the last drop was drained, Garrett stood up, prompting Brumby to rise, and said, "Well, Lieutenant, it's time to beard the lioness in her den." He couldn't wait to see the look on the countess's proper, pinched face when he told her they would have to share a room.

On the way out, he instructed Brumby, "See that the guards and servants get settled in the barn, and set up a rotation to stand watch. Post a couple of sentries outside my room, too, just to be on the safe side, but keep the shifts short. I know your men are worn-out." They stepped into the hard-packed yard of the inn. "Keep a sharp eye out for trouble. I don't want any surprises. The last thing we need is an international incident."

"Very good, sir." Brumby saluted, then strode purposefully toward the second coach, calling, "To the barn, men. Servants, too."

At Garrett's approach, the attendant flipped down the step and opened the door of the first coach. Bess was waiting inside, straight as a pike, her hands in her lap. Garrett leaned into the compartment and offered her a wry smile. "Well, Bess, there's good news and there's bad news. Which do you want first?"

"First, I'd like to get out of this confounded coach." She peered down at him imperiously. "Move over, please." Garrett obliged, helping her as she climbed down stiffly and stood to her feet beside him. She straightened her worn, soiled skirts, then confronted him with, "Now, what's the bad news?"

It hardly surprised him that she would elect to hear that first. He inhaled deeply, then said, "There's only one unoccupied room at the inn. The rest are full of French soldiers sleeping off a drunk. I'm afraid you and I will have to share."

Her blue eyes narrowed, but to Garrett's surprise she showed no other reaction. He'd expected a flurry of protest. Instead, she asked, "And what's the good news?"

Garrett grinned. "There's only one room. I'm afraid we'll have to share."

Bess looked him up and down coolly. Oblivious to the milling servants and guards within earshot, she declared, "I may be forced to share a room with you, sir, but make no mistake, I will not share my bed."

"Ah-hah." His smile deepened. "*Your* bed, is it?" So *that* was how she wanted to play it. Well, he would see about that. Garrett put his arm around her waist and guided her toward the inn. "Perhaps we should discuss that over dinner, Bess. In private."

The sun had barely set when they finished a simple but hearty meal of chicken stew, rye bread, apple pie, and stringent wine. As usual, the countess ate sparingly, despite Garrett's urging to take more.

Wine in hand, he crossed the small bedchamber, carefully ducking the low beams that protruded from the ceiling. When he reached the heavy wooden chair at the hearth, he sat down and faced the flames. "We'll be leaving before dawn, so I imagine we ought to get to bed right away. Shall I send for Gwynneth, or can you prepare yourself unassisted?"

There was a moment's silence before the countess responded, "I need Gwynneth. To help get me out of this dress."

"Ah, yes. All those buttons, ties, and hooks." Garrett rose, opened the door, and instructed one of the guards to fetch the maid. Then he shut the door and reclaimed his seat. "Takes women forever just to get into bed," he observed conversationally, staring into the flames. "Do all females go through such a fuss?"

"Based on what I've heard of you, sir, I should think you'd know."

"*Touché.*" He turned to see Bess still sitting very straight at the small dining table. Only the slope of her shoulders betrayed her fatigue. In the candlelight she looked like a young girl up past her bedtime, worn-out and vulnerable. The gentle illumination erased the harshness from her face and softened her thinness.

Poor weary, struggling creature. So old, to be so young. And so hard. Garrett felt an unexpected surge of sympathy.

His wife. He still couldn't believe it, but it was true, and he was determined to make the best of it.

Had she always been this way? He remembered what Culpeper had said about her father—strict, religious, rigid. Perhaps her harsh tongue came from a harsher life. Garrett wondered what she would have been like if she'd had the advantages he'd enjoyed. He thought of Creighton Manor's warmth and laughter.

He couldn't imagine Bess laughing. Ever.

He'd like to make her laugh. Even better, he'd like to hear her sing again, as wild and free as she'd sung that night three years ago. Not for the same reason, of course.

Perhaps he could find some way to release the exotic creature he'd glimpsed that night. He was willing to wager she still existed, buried deep inside and wanting to come out. The prospect appealed to him. It might take time, but Garrett was a patient man. He had nothing to lose and everything to gain by trying.

He rose and crossed to stand behind her. "Since you deem me such an expert at putting ladies to bed, why don't you let me help you get started?" He pulled a pin from her hair, and then another.

As always, she went rigid at his touch. Verbally, she opposed him at every turn, but whenever he got near her, she became inert. Garrett couldn't figure the woman out. All it took to drain the fight from her was a single touch.

He pulled three more pins from her hair, and her chignon unfurled down her back. She did not say a word. Garrett spread his fingers through the fine waves. Though her hair lacked luster, it was incredibly soft. He looked into the open trunk beside her and saw a wide-toothed wooden comb, an implement more befitting her maid than the countess herself.

Garrett resolved then and there that as soon as they reached London, he would buy her ivory combs and the finest silk dresses and sapphires that matched her eyes. Maybe then she would realize her life of hardship was over. He could do that much for her, at least.

He picked up the wooden implement and began to comb her hair. Soon he was pulling long, sensuous strokes through its length. "How does that feel?"

Bess uttered a clipped, "Gwynneth combs my hair every night. I would rather she do it."

He paused. There was fear in her voice—not just apprehension, but fear. He looked down to see that her hands were bloodless as they gripped the arms of the chair.

Garrett laid the comb aside and sat opposite her. "We need to talk, Bess." He offered a reassuring smile. "Maybe it would be easier if you called me Garrett."

She looked at him askance.

"A simple name, Garrett. Is it too much to ask you to say it?"

"Garrett." She spit the name out as if it were a chunk of moldy bread.

"Thank you. Now that we're on a first-name basis, I have a question for you." He peered into her guarded blue eyes. "Why do you fear me?"

She looked away, her voice determined, as if by declaration she could make her words true. "I do not fear you."

"Really? Then why do you freeze whenever I get near you, and flinch every time I touch you?"

"I do not fear you," she said stubbornly. Her gaze leveled with his. "I just don't like you."

Garrett shook his head, smiling. "Don't change the subject. What are you afraid of?"

She rose, her forearms wrapped about her ribs. "I know what you plan for tonight. You've made that perfectly clear." She crossed to the hearth, putting as much distance as possible between them in the small chamber. "You may be able to force yourself upon me, but you cannot make me like it. And you can't make me like you." The countess looked into the flames, her expression bleak. "I am no innocent. Six years with Ravenwold taught me what passes between a man and a woman, and it is all to the man's benefit." She leveled a look of challenge at him. "I know there are guards outside—your men. No one will help me if I cry out. You are stronger than I am, bigger than I am. I cannot prevent you from doing what you wish with me. So if you intend to use my body, all I ask is that you do not hurt me. And that you get it over with as quickly as possible." She stared back into the flames. "Ravenwold usually required only a few minutes. Unless he was particularly drunk; then it seemed to take forever."

Garrett cocked his head at the defiant woman standing across the room. "Was he the only man in your life?"

"Of course he was the only man in my life."

"No sweethearts? No other lovers?"

She looked at him with utter contempt. "Hard as this may be for you to understand, there are decent women in this world, women who come chaste to marriage and keep the vows they make before God. I have been with only one man—my husband."

"Ah." Garrett pursed his lips. That explained a lot. He wondered if Ravenwold's selfish rutting had snuffed out all her warmer instincts. Or did a few remain, frozen solid in that shell of self-righteousness? "Poor Bess," he mused with genuine sympathy. "You don't even know what it means to be given pleasure by a lover, do you?"

"Pleasure?" A bitter chuckle escaped her. "I know little of pleasure, sir. Duty; that I understand. And honor. Work and sacrifice. Those are the principles which order my life." She lifted her chin and recited as if by rote, "Pleasure is a frivolous, transient thing. It serves no eternal purpose."

"Ah, but it does, Bess." Garrett's work was definitely cut out for him. It might take a long time to thaw Bess out. He leaned back in his chair, deciding to be absolutely honest with her. "Rest easy. I have never forced myself on a woman, and I don't intend to start with you." He added archly, "Why should I, when there are those who welcome—even pursue— my favors? I shall not suffer for lack of your affections, Bess."

Her eyes widened in shock at his frankness. "You are impossible."

"Perhaps. But I'm also very, very tired and twice again as sore from that blasted coach." He bent down and pulled off his high boots and stockings, then rose and unbuckled his scabbard. "Just one thing, though." He nodded toward the bed. "I intend to sleep in that bed. If you wish to join me, you may do so; I promise I won't take advantage of you. But I will not give up a decent night's sleep just to humor your misguided sensibilities." He untied his gorget, then doffed his buff coat before shucking off his chamois shirt in a single motion.

Bess stood mute at the sight of his upper torso.

Garrett deliberately rubbed the golden fur scattered across his chest. Let her look. Years of saber training had hardened his body into a chiseled relief of well-defined muscle. Bess had probably never seen a fit man in his prime, for Ravenwold had been a dark, grossly hairy fellow with a bulging belly. Garrett shot her a warning grin. "The breeches come off next, Bess. If you don't want to see what's underneath, I suggest you turn around."

She spun around just as Gwynneth bustled in from the hallway with her mistress's small trunk. The maid took one look at Garrett, shrieked, and dropped the trunk to cover her eyes

with her hands. "Milord! Forgive me, I didn't know you were
. . . indisposed."

Garrett's romantic escapades had long ago inured him to
being naked in front of servants, so he was amused rather than
embarrassed to see Gwynneth peek between her fingers. Her
gaze shifted lower, the slit between her fingers widening
slightly with an accompanying intake of breath.

Bess might be a prude, but her maid was not. Garrett tried
to make his reprimand sound convincing. "Perhaps in future
you will wait outside our bedchamber until someone bids you
enter, Gwynneth."

"Aye, milord." He could see that Gwynneth was trying
very hard not to smile. "Shall I fetch milord's nightshirt?"

"Nightshirt? Never use one when I have a decent bed." He
strolled to the bed. "Why take off your clothes, only to put
on other ones to sleep in?" He aimed his next remark at Bess's
back. "Doesn't make sense. Not when a man has a blanket to
keep him warm . . . or better yet, a woman." He climbed into
bed and pulled the covers up to his waist. "There, now. You
can look, ladies. I'm all covered up."

Garrett wallowed comfortably into the featherbed. It was
stale and lumpy, but felt like heaven after two nights in the
coach. He rolled onto his side facing the fire and punched the
pillow beneath his head. "Put out the candles, would you?
And try not to make too much noise. I'm very tired."

Elizabeth pulled her fur-lined robe tight around her and leaned
toward the fire. Why did she feel so cold? The shuttered room
was cozy from the crackling blaze, but she was chilled to the
bone.

And why did she feel so ashamed, the way she'd felt as a
little girl awaiting her father's harsh discipline? She should be
glad. Her prayers had been answered: Creighton had promised
not to force himself on her. But she wasn't glad. She felt sick
and trapped and forsaken.

Wishing that Gwynneth would hurry back, she chanced a
quick look at the man curled on his side in the bed. When she
saw that his eyes were closed and his breathing deep and even,
she let her gaze linger on the broad brow and straight, aquiline
nose accented now by the flickering firelight. Such a prominent
brow. It would be overpowering if not balanced by the strength
of his jaw. He was handsome, really, but she would have pre-

ferred a man of good moral constitution instead of just good looks.

Not that he didn't have a few redeeming qualities. He seemed to be a competent commander, decisive and self-assured. And when he chose to act like a gentleman, his manners were impeccable. The trouble was, he was no gentleman. Not really.

She turned back to the fire. A gentleman would have given her the bed.

But even as she formed the thought, Elizabeth realized she shouldn't complain that he had taken the bed. Creighton had elected to travel in the coach with her out of courtesy, when he could have passed the journey far more comfortably riding with the escort.

"Bess?"

She jumped at the unexpected sound of his voice. So he'd only pretended to be asleep. She should have known better than to take anything concerning Creighton at face value. "What?"

"You don't have to sleep in the chair, you know. The bed's big enough for both of us, and I've given my word not to take advantage of you."

Elizabeth remembered the way she had wakened the morning after their wedding, wrapped around him, and a hot flush of embarrassment swept over her. Now he was naked under those covers, and she had no intention of sleeping beside him. "No. Thank you. Gwynneth is fetching the cushions and lap robes from the coaches to make me a pallet by the fire. I shall be quite comfortable."

"Suit yourself." She could almost hear his shrug of indifference.

The bed creaked under his weight. "There is one thing you could do for me, though. It would make me very happy."

Alerted by a subtle undertone of mischief in his voice, she asked, "And what would that be?"

"Sing me a lullaby. I'd love to hear you sing." The request sounded smug and mocking.

"What?" Elizabeth shot to her feet and turned to face him. The varlet! He hadn't forgotten what she'd done three years ago, and obviously he wasn't going to let her forget, either. Curse the blackguard! Her low voice shook with anger, "I will never sing for you, sir. Never. And you cannot make me."

She saw a brief flicker of surprise cross his face before he cocked that maddening half smile. "Never say never, Bess." Creighton yawned loudly, then turned his back on her and settled into the pillows. "You needn't have a fit. It was just a thought." Then he promptly went to sleep.

Three days later on the outskirts of London, Elizabeth was waiting in a hackney coach for the viscount to return when Anne Murray burst into the compartment and pulled the door shut behind her.

"Milady! Married, and to Viscount Creighton, of all people. However did it happen? I can't wait to hear, down to the last detail." Rosy with excitement, Anne took Elizabeth's gloved hands into her own. "My sweet Lady Elizabeth and that rascal Creighton. What exciting news. Everyone in England will be talking about it by sunset." Oblivious to the look of pained surprise on Elizabeth's face, she chattered on, "I could hardly get a thing out of your husband. He and Bampfield are so wrapped up in plans. I don't think he'd have told me you two were married if I hadn't asked after you, whether he'd seen you in Paris, and how your sister—" Anne stopped abruptly, her smile fading. "Oh, dear. Stupid me, going on like this, when milady has just lost her dear sister." She planted an impulsive kiss on the back of each of Elizabeth's gloved hands. "I'm so sorry. Please forgive me."

"There's nothing to forgive." As always, Anne's affection, however clumsy, had a bracing effect on Elizabeth. She offered her friend a sad smile. "Now that Charlotte is gone, your friendship means more than anything to me."

Tears welled in Anne's eyes. "And yours to me, milady." She shifted to a less emotional subject. "Isn't it exciting, what Bampfield has planned? I can hardly believe you and the viscount will be working with us. What an adventure."

Elizabeth frowned. "An adventure? Anne, what has Bampfield gotten you into this time?"

"You mean you don't know?" Anne's pretty face reflected her surprise.

"I know nothing of any adventure. The viscount . . . that is, my husband mentioned something about shipping a small package across the channel, but that hardly qualifies as an adventure."

Her eyes sparkling with excitement, Anne leaned forward

and whispered so softly that Elizabeth could barely hear, "The package is a prince, and you can help."

In a darkened corner of the noisy tavern, Garrett nursed a pint of ale while Joseph Bampfield spelled out the details of the duke of York's escape.

Bampfield leaned close, murmuring, "This time, there will be no slipups. I have been permitted regular visits to his highness. I personally delivered the letter outlining the plan. As soon as his highness memorized it, he destroyed the letter."

"You're certain of that?" Bampfield had told Garrett of two previous attempts to free the prince—both of which had been discovered when coded documents were intercepted, with predictably disastrous results for the conspirators.

"Absolutely certain." Bampfield's smile was grim. "I saw it with my own eye." His reference to the patch he wore was hardly humorous.

"So there's no written evidence this time."

"Not a jot."

Garrett was less than reassured. Given his choice, he would never have trusted Bampfield with such a critical mission. Something about the man just didn't add up; he was too slippery, too sure of himself and his plan. Garrett suspected that Bampfield's only true loyalties were to himself. In contrast, George Howard—the prince's master of horse and their contact inside St. James Palace—had long ago proven his devotion to the Crown. "What about Howard?"

"The gate from the palace garden to St. James Park is unguarded. Howard's job was to steal the key, have copies made, then give one to his highness. He's done that."

"So everything is ready?"

"Aye. For several weeks, now, his highness's governor, Northumberland, has allowed the boy to play hide-and-seek with his brother and sister after dinner. Sometimes it takes hours to find his highness. By the time Northumberland realizes the prince is gone, we should be well away."

As Bampfield related the rest of his plan, Garrett listened with alternating admiration and concern. The plot was well thought out, at least. It just might work. Then Bampfield, with typical flair, revealed the nature of the disguise he had devised for the prince. Garrett could hardly believe his ears. "A *dress?*" he whispered. "And he's agreed to it?"

"The lad is game." Bampfield's grin was genuine this time. "I shall be traveling with my sister, Miss Andrews."

Fourteen-year-old Prince James in a lady's curls and petticoats! Garrett shook his head, amazed. "Good glory. I can't wait to see *that*."

"There is one problem, though."

"What?"

"I managed to get measurements so Anne could have the clothing made, but the tailor went on and on about the 'young lady's' thick waist and narrow hips. Anne got very nervous. She doesn't want to go back there, for fear the tailor will be able to identify her. He made such a fuss."

Garrett shrugged. "I could fetch them."

Bampfield shook his head. "No. You're a man. That would be irregular, attract even more attention. It should be a woman."

He considered sending Gwynneth. "When should the clothes be collected?"

"As soon as possible. If all goes well, the package will be shipped tomorrow."

Garrett nodded. "Tell me the tailor's name and address. I'll see to it."

Garrett wasn't surprised when he found Anne Murray still visiting with his wife in the hired coach. He climbed in and squeezed next to the countess. "I trust you two have caught up on your visiting."

"Oh, we've hardly begun," Anne declared. She shot Garrett a sparkling smile. "Guess what? The countess has agreed to fetch the clothes for us. I've told her everything."

"You what?" Garrett stared at Anne in disbelief. Had she lost her mind, dragging Bess into this?

Anne nodded. "I dare not trust my maid to help dress Miss Andrews. The countess will be invaluable." She grinned. "Then afterward, the two of you can go along and act as decoys. Isn't it exciting?" Anne looked Elizabeth up and down. "Milady is almost exactly the same height as Miss Andrews, and you are only a few inches taller than Joseph. Should there be trouble, no one will know which couple is which. We can have a coach waiting at the coast. Once Joseph is safely away, you two can head overland, creating a false trail."

Garrett frowned. She'd certainly adapted the plot to involve Bess in a hurry. And what she said made sense. Her quickness of mind made him wonder if Bampfield had taken credit for plans that were, in fact, Anne Murray's.

Perhaps Bess might prove useful, after all. Expert though he was at *un*dressing women, Garrett doubted that he—or Bampfield, for that matter—could offer Anne Murray much assistance in transforming Prince James into Miss Andrews. With Bess's help, Anne could probably dress the boy much faster.

Garrett considered Anne's other suggestion. If they ran into trouble on the way to Gravesend, he and Bess could provide a critical diversion. But Prince Charles had been quite clear about not trusting the countess. "I'll have to think about this. I'm not sure I want Bess involved."

Bess bristled. "I'm already involved." She looked at Anne. "I'd be delighted to help you, Anne. My husband will just have to get used to the idea."

Garrett eyed the two women. Bess was right, of course. Now that she knew, she was in it up to her neck. He just hoped this latest wrinkle wouldn't cost him his own neck. He leaned back and crossed his legs. "May we offer you a lift somewhere on our way to the tailor's, Miss Murray?"

"No, thank you." Anne pulled up the hood of her cloak. "Joseph and I have plans." She opened the coach door and climbed out, then turned back and winked at Bess. "He's hired one of the rooms above the tavern for the afternoon, and I've promised to give him a bath."

To Garrett's amazement, Bess grinned and let out a musical chuckle. "Anne. You are the most shameless woman in the world."

"I try," Anne said cheekily as she closed the door.

Unaware that Garrett was watching her, Bess watched, smiling, as her friend disappeared into the tavern.

Garrett couldn't believe the transformation in his wife. She was lovely when she smiled. It took years off her, and her whole face came to life. "You ought to smile more often, Bess. You're really quite beautiful when you do."

Her features lost their animation. "I have reason to smile at Anne. She loves me."

"So that's what it takes." Accustomed to smoothing ruffled

feminine feathers with flattery, he bowed slightly and said, "Then I will look forward to the day when you smile for me."

Bess's skeptical frown showed her contempt for his empty words. "It will be a long wait."

# CHAPTER 11

Cloaked in black, Garrett peered from the dark interior of Bampfield's coach into the Spring Garden at St. James and wondered if something had gone awry. Why in blazes had Bampfield insisted on taking a footman instead of Garrett to fetch Prince James? What use would a footman be if there was trouble?

And then there was the matter of Mr. Tripp. Garrett stared across the compartment at the stranger Bampfield had brought along. Bampfield had explained that Mr. Tripp would remain with the coach to lay down a false trail in London after they had left it, but the last-minute inclusion of an unknown conspirator did not sit well with Garrett.

He directed his attention back to the darkening landscape. Bampfield should have returned by now, with or without the "small package" he had gone to fetch.

Garrett scanned the twilit paths and plantings. It was still light enough to recognize a familiar figure, but only a few people strolled the gardens on this cool April evening, and none of them was Bampfield. With every rustle of wind and shifting shadow in the dusky landscape, Garrett's nerves stretched tighter than a hangman's rope. Then he saw three cloaked figures approach from the Royal Garden. He watched with bated breath as the trio came closer, their pace deliberately slow so as not to attract attention. They were less than five yards away before he recognized Bampfield's square jaw and eye patch beneath the broad brim of his hat. Garrett exhaled in relief.

The cloaked footman strode ahead to open the door of the coach for the gangly adolescent who preceded Bampfield into the compartment. The moment Bampfield was inside, the footman closed the door and climbed up with the driver.

As the coach trundled into motion, Prince James immediately snatched off the gray periwig Bampfield had brought him and said, "Creighton! I thought you were in Paris with my brother."

"Your highness." Garrett nodded politely. "The Prince of Wales was gravely concerned for his brother's safety, so he sent me to assist in your highness's escape." In the years since Garrett had last seen him, Prince James had grown to the threshold of manhood, but his eyes were those of an old man. This war had taken more than the boy's parents from him—it had robbed him of his youth.

Prince James turned to Tripp with a look of suspicion. "And who is this?"

Bampfield answered for his friend. "Your highness, allow me to present my associate Mr. Tripp."

Tripp puffed up with self-importance and bowed from the waist. "Yer highness."

The horses picked up speed and exited the gardens, prompting Prince James to let out a peal of triumphant laughter. In an instant, he was a boy again, his cheeks flushed and his eyes sparkling. He swatted Bampfield's shoulder with the wig. "We've done it, Bampfield. We've really done it! At last, I'm free!"

"Please, your highness. Not so loud." Bampfield placed a finger to his lips, his own voice lowered to a discreet level over the clamor of the coach. "Save your celebrations for the Hague. Until then, there is grave danger."

The fourteen-year-old prince did not easily surrender his enthusiasm. "The plan worked perfectly." He turned to Garrett. "First, I told Northumberland I was going to play hide-and-seek with Henry and Elizabeth. He didn't suspect a thing when we went into the garden. I only wish I could see the look on his face when he finds out I've escaped." Prince James leaned back and crossed his legs. "When no one was looking, I locked up Elizabeth's little dog so it wouldn't follow me. After that, the rest was easy. I used the key Sir George gave me to open the garden gate, then I locked it from the other side and smashed the key to bits with the rocks Bampfield left there."

Bampfield frowned. "What did you do with the pieces?"

"I tossed them into the ivy, as you told me to."

"Good," Bampfield answered tersely, discouraging further conversation by watching nervously out the window.

The coach trundled noisily up the cobblestones of Charing Cross, then turned onto the Strand. Within minutes, they slowed to a halt in front of Salisbury House. Bampfield helped the prince back into his periwig and hat, then got out, saying loudly for the coachman's benefit. "Come, gentlemen. We're late already. They're waiting for us at Salisbury House." Tripp remained with the coach, as agreed.

Garrett followed Prince James into the darkened street. He waited until the coach was well away before he steered his two cloaked companions into the dark, narrow lane that led alongside Salisbury House to the river. "Say nothing," he whispered.

His ears straining for the tiniest sound that would betray an ambush, Garrett led the prince down the dark, glistening cobblestones to the riverbank. There on a narrow jetty waited the boatman and his craft. Garrett's hammering pulse eased at the welcome sight. He helped Bampfield and the prince aboard, then murmured discreetly to the boatman, "London Bridge," and climbed aboard himself.

With practiced skill, the boatman pushed his craft into the shallows until the hull floated free, then heaved himself aboard and began rowing downstream. A stiff sea breeze blew against them, slowing their progress but carrying away some of the sluggish current's stink. Slowly but surely, they glided past the elegant dwellings on the Strand. Some of the houses were dark, their occupants already retired for the night. Others blazed with light, the sound of music and revelry coming from their open windows. Then the stately homes were replaced with smaller ones crammed together along the Thames.

Garrett listened intently as they floated past banks now crowded with warehouses, taverns, and shops. He was grateful for the noise of the taverns that covered the steady splash of the oars in the murky water. Not much farther, now. He could see the familiar roofs and spires of London Bridge ahead. He leaned forward and instructed quietly, "Put us out at the north end of the bridge."

The boatman steered left and brought them into the shadow of the bridge at its northern base. When they bumped along the river wall, Garrett grabbed one of the boat's moorings and leapt up onto the ledge that served as a quay.

He reached down and grasped the prince's extended forearm. In one powerful motion, he pulled the boy to the pavement beside him, leaving Bampfield to scramble ashore on his own. As the boat pulled away, Garrett motioned the prince to silence, then searched the shadows, listening for any indication that they might not be alone. Besides the rush of the river, the only noises he heard were the receding splash of the oars and the distant clatter of traffic from the bridge above them.

Garrett straightened the prince's wig, then headed up the steep stairway to the street. Though their destination was only a few blocks away, he was grateful for the milling crowds that frequented Oystergate and the fish markets, even at this hour. The three of them easily blended into the late evening foot traffic. Bampfield led them down several crowded city blocks, then turned into a darkened mews. At the end of the mews, he mounted the stairs of a neat brick structure whose painted sign identified it as the office and dwelling of one Dr. Low, Surgeon.

Anne and Bess must have been watching for them. No sooner had Bampfield raised his hand to knock than the door sprang open and Bess whispered, "There you are. We thought something had gone wrong. It's so late . . ." She shepherded them into the hallway, then locked and bolted the door behind them. That done, she dropped into a deep curtsy. "Your royal highness."

The prince motioned her to her feet. "Quickly. Quickly. Dress me."

Ignoring the royal presence, Anne rushed into Bampfield's arms. "It's after ten. You said if you weren't here by ten—"

Bampfield gave her an impatient hug. "Nothing went wrong; it just took longer getting back to the coach than I had planned." Frowning at her breach of etiquette, he pulled free of Anne's embrace and cocked his head toward the prince.

Stricken, Anne curtsied again. "Forgive me, your royal highness. I was so worried, I completely forgot my manners."

"Think nothing of it. This is no time for formalities." Prince James pulled off the gray periwig as if he were doffing a hat. His thick, dark curls tumbled helter-skelter to his shoulders. "How can I ever thank you for taking such dangerous chances on my behalf, Miss Murray?"

Anne responded with uncharacteristic shyness, "Helping

your highness is reward enough.''

Garrett stepped to Bess's side and took her arm. ''Your highness, allow me to present my wife, Countess Ravenwold.''

''But the countess and I have met on a number of occasions,'' Prince James said, his sidelong glance betraying his impatience to get on with the business at hand.

Bess firmly extracted her elbow from Garrett's grasp. ''I am flattered that your highness remembers. It's been quite some time.''

''I never forget a kindness, madam,'' the prince stated briskly. He turned to Anne. ''Is my disguise ready?''

She nodded, a mischievous smile lighting her face. ''Aye, and a bit of refreshment, as well. If your highness will accompany the countess and me upstairs, Miss Andrews is waiting.''

''Lead on.'' As Anne preceded him up the stairs, the prince focused a very adult look of approval on her curvaceous backside and commented, ''I only hope Miss Andrews can climb stairs as gracefully as Miss Murray.''

Anne chuckled seductively, exaggerating the swish of her hips. ''Mark me well then, sire.''

To Garrett's surprise, Bess let out a chuckle of her own, every bit as seductive as Anne's. She followed the prince up the stairs. ''You'll have to forgive Miss Murray, your highness. She's entirely too candid for her own good.''

After the three of them disappeared onto the landing, Bampfield unclasped his cloak and tossed his hat onto a nearby bench. ''Why don't we wait by the fire?'' He led the way into the parlor, making straight for a decanter of spirits. He poured a stiff measure into a goblet. ''Cognac?''

Garrett wondered if Dr. Low had intended to share his whiskey as well as his house. He declined with a diplomatic, ''Thank you, but I'd better not. I need all my wits about me tonight.''

Bampfield drained the contents of his glass in a single gulp. ''I find that strong spirits improve my wits.''

''Several of my friends used to say the same thing,'' Garrett observed drily. ''Most of them are dead now.''

Bampfield's eyes narrowed briefly, then his expression cleared. Either he hadn't understood Garrett's warning, or he chose to ignore it. He poured himself another liberal dollop of cognac.

Garrett looked around the cluttered parlor. ''Why here?

Wouldn't Miss Murray's house have been safer? Both of her parents served in the king's household. Surely Anne's father would have been willing to—''

Bampfield didn't wait for him to finish. "Anne's father knows nothing about this." He frowned, his voice turning bitter. "The man's an impossible snob, disapproves of me entirely. He forbade Anne to have anything to do with me." He stared into the dark liquid in his glass. "Claims it's because I have no money, but I think he just wants to keep Anne an old maid so she can look after him, now that her mother is dead."

"That's unfortunate." Garrett had met Anne's father. Thomas Murray seemed a decent enough fellow, a bit pedantic but devoted to his family. Little wonder he disapproved of the likes of Bampfield. Garrett wouldn't want any daughter of his mixed up with such a mountebank, either.

Bampfield shrugged defensively. "Anyway, this house is better situated, closer to the river, and Dr. Low owes me a favor. He didn't ask any questions when I paid him for the use of the place and told him to make himself scarce for one night."

Garrett shook his head, a wry smile on his lips. Bampfield had earlier bragged that King Charles financed this escape with twenty thousand pounds from the royal treasury. Twenty thousand pounds! The scoundrel could have *bought* a dozen coaches, a hundred rowboats, and several houses like this one for that amount. Bampfield had no doubt lined his own pockets with most of the money.

Garrett changed the subject. "The barge . . . does the captain know who we are?"

Bampfield shook his head. "I saw no reason to tell him. Safer that way."

"You're sure he'll be there?"

"Oh, aye." The spy grinned. "I paid him just enough to whet his appetite for the tidy sum he'll collect when he delivers us safely to the ship. He's waiting for us now, his greedy little heart going pitter-pat at the prospect of such a fat fee."

"And the ship?"

"A Dutch packet, a pink. She put in at Hope's anchorage three days ago."

"So everything else is ready. Now all we can do is wait for Miss Andrews." Garrett sank into a comfortable chair beside the fire and warmed his hands. Bampfield settled nearby and sipped his cognac in silence as they waited for the prince to reappear.

Upstairs, Elizabeth tugged on the prince's bodice while Anne struggled with his coiffeur. The bodice laces dug into Elizabeth's fingers, almost cutting off the circulation. If the prince could make himself no smaller, she feared the yellow and black striped silk of his gown would rip from the strain. He shifted uncomfortably, prompting her to scold, "Please suck in, your highness."

Prince James let out yet another exasperated sigh. "By my faith, I do not understand how you ladies endure such torment day after day. It's enough to drive a person mad."

"Your highness would do well to remember that the next time he sees a fashionably dressed lady," Elizabeth retorted. She stopped pulling long enough to blow a loose tendril out of her own eyes. She hadn't laced a bodice since she and Charlotte were girls with nothing to bind up. Gwynneth would have had the prince nipped, tucked, and tied in no time, but Gwynneth was on her way back to Cornwall with the rest of the servants. Inhaling as deeply as her own tight stays would allow, Elizabeth renewed her efforts to truss the prince into his gown. "Unless your highness can suck in a little more, it will be daylight before I finish. Exhale, sir."

"I did," the prince grumbled pettishly. "I'm already seeing stars."

Anne tucked yet another tiny braid into the neat bun at the back of the prince's head. "Not much fun, is it?"

Prince James pouted as prettily as any maiden. "Torture, madam, that's what this is." He tugged vainly at the padded garment that encased his ribs. "If I ever have anything to say about it, I'll outlaw contraptions like this infernal bodice."

"I daresay the women of England would be most grateful," Anne declared.

To the dismay of all three parties involved, thirty more minutes passed before the last lace was tied and the last face-framing tendril was curled with a smoking iron. As a final touch, Anne added a demure hint of rouge to the prince's cheeks and lips. His scarlet underskirt accentuated the effect.

Elizabeth and Anne stood back and assessed the startling results of their efforts. Elizabeth said, "Your highness makes a most attractive young lady."

Covering her mouth, Anne suppressed a chortle. "Pray forgive me, your highness, but the change is most unsettling. I doubt if even your majesty's own mother would recognize you.''

''My mother,'' he snapped, ''wouldn't recognize me if I *weren't* dressed up like a girl.'' Obviously, he resented his mother's flight to the safety of her native land.

He took a few awkward steps and almost lost his footing, thanks to the satin slippers they had buckled onto his enormous feet. ''How in blazes does one walk in these things? They feel as if they're shod with ice. And these stockings are too tight. They pull the hairs on my legs every time I move.'' The prince unceremoniously hiked up his skirts and plucked at the silk that encased his surprisingly shapely legs.

Elizabeth slammed her lids shut. ''Your highness! You mustn't lift your skirts, not in front of anyone, or they'll suspect you're not really a woman.''

''Worse yet,'' Anne interjected, '' 'they'll think you're the wrong kind of woman, and you'll find yourself fighting for your virtue.''

To cover his embarrassment, the prince blustered, ''Well, I knew it was safe to, to . . . adjust myself here. Of course I shan't do it in front of anyone else.''

''Of course,'' Elizabeth said mildly, fighting down the urge to laugh. Anne's facial contortions threatened to rob her of her own composure. She couldn't wait to see the look on Creighton's and Bampfield's faces when they beheld Miss Andrews.

Prince James tried again to shift the bodice's iron grip on his rib cage, prompting Elizabeth to chide, ''No pulling at your bodice, either.'' She crossed to the bed and picked up one of three identical dark, hooded cloaks. She draped it carefully over the prince's shoulders. ''Don't forget to raise your hood before we leave, your highness, and keep it pulled forward once we're outside. It's imperative that no one sees your highness's face before we reach the ship.'' She handed the second garment to Anne. ''You, too, Anne.'' Elizabeth pulled the third cloak around her own shoulders. Once their faces were concealed, the three hooded figures would be indistinguishable to anyone who might see them, except for the slight differences in their heights. ''Come. They're waiting.''

Downstairs, Garrett and Bampfield rose from their seats at the sound of Anne's summons from the landing. ''Mr. Andrews, your sister is ready to travel. And quite a fetching lady she is.''

Garrett could hardly wait to see the prince in a dress. "This should be ripe," he murmured, trailing Bampfield into the hall-way.

When the two men looked up to the landing, both of them gasped aloud. Garrett was shocked at just how convincing—not to mention pretty—a young lady Prince James made. Poor Bampfield would be hard-pressed to protect his "sister" from unwelcome attentions. He blurted out, "By thunder, your high-ness makes a most attractive young lady."

"That's just what your wife said. Without the 'by thunder,' of course," Prince James responded. He started down the stairs, picking his way gingerly in the silk slippers. When he reached the bottom, he tried to sigh in relief, but his bodice wouldn't let him. "By all that's holy, I hope I don't have to do a lot of walking. These shoes are dangerously slippery."

Garrett offered the prince a steadying arm. "Rub the soles on the paving stones outside. That will rough them up a bit, give you better footing."

Elizabeth paused. "How did you know about that?"

"The same way I learned everything else about women," Creighton said with a wink.

"Really," she fumed, stung by the open reference to his philandering. "You have no shame, sir."

"Absolutely none, madam." He smiled that insolent smile of his. "You ought to try it, Countess. The results are quite healthy, I assure you."

"Hmph." Elizabeth crossed the hall to pick up a bulky vel-vet bag by its silken drawstrings.

"What in blazes," Creighton demanded, "is that?"

"My medicines," she replied. "I must have them with me."

His blue eyes narrowed. "Are you ill?"

"No, but these herbs and powders are very rare, and very expensive."

"Leave them," he ordered bluntly. "I told you not to bring any baggage, anything that might distinguish you from the prince."

Elizabeth flipped back her cloak and pushed the drawstrings up over her shoulder, tucking the bundle discreetly between her elbow and ribs. When she closed the cloak, there was no sign of the bundle. "There," she said, raising her hood to conceal her face. "Now no one can tell me from his highness."

Before Garrett could protest, Bampfield opened the front door. "Fine. Let's go, then." He motioned to Anne and Elizabeth. "Come along, ladies; we'll go first." He nodded to Garrett. "Creighton, you follow with the prince."

Garrett hesitated only a moment. They had precious little time, as it was. He could scarce afford to spend any of it arguing with a woman as stubborn as Bess. Instead, he offered his arm to the prince. "Shall we go, then, Miss Andrews?"

Prince James bobbed an awkward curtsy. "Indeed, sir." They followed Bampfield and the other two hooded figures into the night.

They reached the four-oared barge at Billingsgate's Lyon Quay without incident, though the bargeman seemed suspicious. Once they were underway, Bampfield bundled the prince into the barge's cabin and joined Garrett on the bow. They watched the shore in tense silence for several miles before the bargeman approached Bampfield.

"Irregular, I would say, that 'young woman' of yours."

Garrett stilled, ready to strike.

"If you mean my sister sir," Bampfield replied, "I must insist that you not embarrass her with such comments, though I myself am well aware of her . . . distinctive stature."

The bargeman was not convinced. "I'm an honest man. Worked all me life to ply this barge. I'm not about to risk it for some scheme, some aristocratic escapade that'll end me up in prison if we're boarded and searched."

"I assure you, good sir," Bampfield said smoothly, "this is no scheme. My sister may be a bit clumsy and thick-waisted, but she is, nevertheless, merely my sister."

"We'll see," the bargeman grumbled. He did retreat, though, leaving the two men alone.

Garrett turned into the wind. "That was close."

"I can handle him," Bampfield said defensively. He stalked back to the cabin and went in.

Several minutes later, Garrett saw the bargeman lurking about the cabin door. He peered through a crack, his face illuminated by a pale shard of light from the cabin's single candle, then recoiled in outrage. " 'Ere, now! Wot's this?" he demanded.

"Blast." As the bargeman jerked open the door, Garrett swiftly closed the distance between them. He arrived to find a surprised prince with one leg propped on the tabletop in a most unladylike fashion, while a flustered Bampfield snatched his hands away from his "sister's" garter. Apparently the prince, annoyed by his unfamiliar undergarments, had asked for help with his stockings.

The bargeman pointed an accusing finger at them. "I never seen no lady hoist 'er leg that way," he growled. "Nor any brother muckin' around up his sister's skirts, neither, I can tell you!"

Bampfield sprang to his feet and preceded the prince out of the cabin, taking up a protective stance in front of his "sister" on deck. "I warned you, sir, not to cast aspersions on my sister."

The bargeman turned his stubby finger to Bampfield. "I smells a rat, I does."

Garrett knew he should have been worried, but he wasn't. Tilbury wasn't far, now, and the current was with them. If necessary, they could reach their destination without the barge-man or his crew. But he'd rather not resort to violence. He put his left arm around the bargeman's shoulders, noting the unrelenting feel of hard muscle beneath his own. "A most observant fellow you are." The bargeman was shorter by nearly a foot, but solid as a piling. Garrett's right hand slipped inconspicuously to his dagger. "And what would be your name, good sir?"

The bargeman shifted under his towering presence, but he did not cower. "John Owen, if it's any of your business."

"Well, John, you're right. We haven't been completely forthcoming, so I'm going to tell you the truth." Even in the silvered darkness, Garrett could see Bampfield's eye widen in shock.

"In the name of heaven, be quiet, man!"

Garrett prayed that candor would be successful. Otherwise, he would be forced to kill the bargeman, and he hated to kill a fellow simply for being observant. "You're right, John." His hand still on his dagger, he nodded toward the prince. "That is no lady." Then he nodded to Bampfield. "And that man is not Mr. Andrews, nor is he brother to anyone here." As he spoke, he heard Anne and Bess hurry up behind him, drawn by the disturbance.

When she realized what Garrett was about to do, Bess gasped and said to Bampfield, "Do something! He's going to tell—"

Fortunately, Garrett hadn't turned his back on Bampfield, so he was ready when the spy lunged for him. Bampfield barely managed to stop short of impaling himself on Garrett's dagger, now unsheathed and pointed toward his attacker. His left arm tightening around the bargeman's shoulders, Garrett cautioned his colleague, "As you were, sir. Rest easy. Let's see what John Owen, here, has to say once he hears the truth. For all we know, he might be loyal to—" He stopped abruptly and addressed the bargeman. "If you please, which side do you favor in this current conflict, sir?" He wagged his dagger from one side to the other. "The Crown or Parliament?"

Beads of sweat formed on the man's forehead. "Wot's it to you?"

"Everything." Garrett's voice was velvet smooth. "Absolutely everything."

The stocky man trembled briefly as he eyed the dagger within easy striking distance of his throat. "Well, I'm loyal to the Crown, sir. Always have been. And if you mean to cut me guzzel for it, then do it and be done. I won't betray my king."

Garrett chuckled, his grip on the dagger easing. "Well said!" He heard Bess and Anne let out a deep sigh of relief behind him and turned to see the two women clinging to each other on the darkened deck.

Garrett gave the bargeman's back a good-natured clout, then motioned to the prince. "Your highness, allow me to present one of his majesty's loyal subjects." He turned back to the bargeman. "John Owen, this 'lady' is the duke of York, and we are taking him to a ship which will convey him to his sister, Queen Mary of the Dutch Republic. Once his highness is under his sister's protection, the Stuart succession will be assured."

The bargeman looked from the prince to the rich clothing of his other passengers, then back to the prince. "It *is* him, innit?" His jaw tightened stubbornly as the gravity of the circumstances dawned on him. "I wish ye Godspeed, yer highness, but I dast not take ye to the ship. I'll land at Tilbury, but you'll have to find some other way from there." His eyes darted nervously to the shoreline. "I've got a family. Wot

would become of 'em, if the Roundheads found out it was me
wot—''

"In for a penny, in for a pound," Garrett interrupted
smoothly, putting his arm around the man's shoulders again.
"You're in this up to your neck already, John Owen, whether
you like it or not. Think about it. We're all far more likely to
be caught if we land at Tilbury. But if you take us all the way
to the ship, who will know? We certainly won't tell."

The bargeman hesitated.

Garrett pressed a clutch of golden coins into the man's hand.
"If you're worried about your own safety, I'm sure his highness would be happy to invite you along." Bampfield and the
prince glared at him, but Garrett kept on talking. Eventually,
John Owen grudgingly agreed to take them to the ship in
exchange for safe passage across the Channel.

"Cut the lights," Garrett advised, "and steer for Hope's
anchorage. Our ship's a Dutch pink." As the bargeman
stormed back to his crew, Garrett added so quietly that only
the passengers could hear, "And hope there's not a pack of
Roundheads aboard lying in wait."

He moved to the bow, his eyes drawn to the northern banks
of the wide estuary. The lights of Tilbury glimmered faintly
in the distance. To his right on the opposite shore blinked the
even fainter lights of Gravesend. He said a silent prayer for
safe passage, then sought out Bampfield.

He found the spy sullen and the prince confused. Bampfield
wasted no time in confronting him. "What were you thinking
of, telling the bargeman who we were? What if he talks?"

Garrett smiled. "He won't."

"And how, pray tell, do you know that?"

"He's going with you. And he declared his loyalty to the
king, even with my dagger under his chin." Garrett laid a
companionable hand on Bampfield's shoulder and gave it a
shake. "Sometimes we have to trust people. It's as simple as
that."

Bess's familiar scent preceded the warmth of her cloaked
figure beside him on the deck. "Trust?" she interrupted, her
voice taut. "I find such talk of trust ironic, coming from you."
Anne was right behind her.

Garrett turned his most engaging smile on his wife. "But I
wasn't talking to you, was I?" Annoyed by her interference,
he added, "I had the situation under control."

"And what if the bargeman had turned out to be a Round-head?" Bampfield challenged.

Garrett shrugged. "I'd have slit his throat, then and there."

Bampfield nodded in satisfaction, but Bess glared at Garrett in outrage. "You would have, wouldn't you? Cut that poor man's throat?"

"Ah, women." He cast a sidelong glance at Bampfield. "They just don't understand, do they?"

"This one does." Bampfield pulled Anne Murray hard against him and kissed her soundly. "God help me if she ever takes the notion to cut *my* throat."

Anne's laughter carried on the stiff sea breeze. "Rest easy, my love. Your throat is safe . . . for the moment, anyway."

On impulse, Garrett pulled the countess hard against him. As always, she went deadly still, yet his body warmed to the feel of hers. He tipped her hooded face up toward his. Even in the darkness, he could see the fire in her eyes. Anger brought an appealing animation to her features. "What about you, Bess?" he purred. "Is my throat safe?"

"Give me your dagger and find out."

He called her bluff, offering the jeweled handle of his dag-ger. "Here, precious girl. My throat is yours." A sudden tug of desire prompted him to propose, "As is the rest of me. Use me as you will."

"Do not tempt me, sir." Bess's voice betrayed an interest-ing note of confusion. "I just might use that dagger."

"Watch out, milord." Bampfield chuckled. "I think she's serious."

"So do I, Bampfield." Garrett sheathed his dagger with a grin. "So do I." Just to annoy her, he kissed his wife, hard and swift, then left her sputtering and walked away.

# ❧ CHAPTER 12 ❧

*E*lizabeth felt her stomach tighten as the unlighted barge neared the waiting Dutch packet. A stiff channel breeze had kicked up two-foot seas, slowing their progress. Still, with every stroke of the bargemen's oars, the ship's dark silhouette loomed a little larger, and the lantern bobbing from its stern shone a little brighter. Elizabeth held the edge of her hood against the wind and scanned the packet for some sign of life . . . or ambush.

Anne huddled close beside her. "Joseph will use a prearranged greeting when we reach the ship. If the ship responds with a simple yes, that means they've been boarded by Roundheads."

"And if they have been boarded?" Elizabeth asked, her heart thumping faster.

"We'll row away as fast as we can."

"They'll catch us, though, won't they?"

"Probably," Anne said matter-of-factly. "But there won't be any Roundheads, and the ship will respond with the proper passwords: 'Greetings from the Hague. Come aboard.' "

"I wish I could be as certain as you are." Elizabeth's gaze shifted from the packet to the barge. Creighton stood poised at the bow with a loaded pistol in one hand and his sword ready in the other. Bampfield and the prince were aft, next to the tiller. In the silvered darkness, she could just make out the dull gleam of gunmetal in Bampfield's hand. She wondered briefly if the others were as frightened as she.

The bow of the barge thudded against the packet's hull, releasing the smell of tar and paint. The ship creaked and groaned beside them on the choppy seas. At a nod from

Creighton, Bampfield cupped hands to mouth and called, "Ahoy the ship."

A pale face appeared over the rail. "Ahoy the barge. Who goes there?"

Bampfield shouted the prearranged greeting, "Mr. Andrews and his sister. Are we expected?"

Elizabeth held her breath, the fingers of both hands crossed for luck as she waited for his response. A simple yes, and all of them aboard the barge, save the prince, would probably end up losing their heads.

To her vast relief, the sailor replied, "Greetings from the Hague. Come aboard." Several other sailors appeared at the rail, and with a clatter of wood and the whir of rope threading through a winch, a bosun's chair was lowered over the side.

The reluctant bargeman was hoisted aboard first, then the empty chair was lowered again. Bampfield caught and steadied it, but before his royal charge climbed in, Prince James turned to Elizabeth and Anne. Staying in character for the benefit of the sailors who were watching, he touched a cheek to either side of Anne Murray's hooded face like a proper young lady bidding farewell to a friend. "Thank you, Miss Murray. May God keep you safe until I return. God save the king."

Anne nodded, her voice thick with emotion. "God save the king."

"And you, madam." Prince James turned to Elizabeth. "I shall remember you every time I see a well-laced bodice." He touched a cheek to either side of her hood. "Farewell and God speed you safely to your home." He cast a wistful glance at the dim shoreline. "I fear it will be a long time before I see mine again."

Then, to Elizabeth's surprise and amusement, he pivoted and executed a passable curtsy in front of Creighton. As he rose, the prince said, "This makes twice you have helped to rescue me, sir. First at Edgefield, and now this. I shall not forget it."

"Think nothing of it." Creighton bowed with a flourish, deftly sheathing his sword and tucking his pistol back into his belt. "I am your highness's obedient servant."

Prince James climbed into the bosun's chair and was hauled aboard the packet. When the empty chair came back for Bampfield, Anne rushed into his arms. He gave her a dismissive peck on the cheek, then pulled free of her embrace. "Please, Anne. I must be off."

"Go ahead and leave me, you scoundrel," she said without rancor. "But you won't be able to forget me. No other woman will ever be as good for you as I have been." She kissed him soundly, then turned and strode aft, never looking back as her lover was hoisted away.

Elizabeth went to comfort her friend. She put her arm around Anne's waist. "Are you all right?"

"I'm fine. Really." Anne's voice was surprisingly calm. "Even in the beginning, I had no illusions about Bampfield. He never was the kind of man to settle down."

"Is *any* man?" Elizabeth observed drily. "They're all faithless, aren't they?"

"Not all of them." Ignoring the darkness and the fact that their features were concealed by their deep hoods, Anne turned to face her. "I think the right woman could settle Creighton. You could be that woman, my lady, if only you'd listen to your heart."

"Don't be ridiculous," Elizabeth countered. "According to the stories Gwynneth passes on to me, my husband has dipped his . . . *finger* into every honey pot at Court."

"I do not doubt she heard such stories," Anne said, "but like most servants' gossip, such tales are only partly true. My sources are more reliable, and I have it on good authority that although many ladies have tried to attract Viscount Creighton's attentions, only a select few have succeeded. Those who fail make up stories." She grew thoughtful. "There's no mystery as to why the viscount knows so much about women. He has six younger sisters and a widowed mother who idolize him."

"Six sisters?" Dear heaven, what a daunting flock of in-laws!

"Aye, six." Anne chuckled. "Think of it: all that feminine adoration, with no strings attached. Little wonder he's felt no need to settle down. But you could tame him, milady."

"Only a fool would care for a man like Creighton," Elizabeth protested.

"Who said anything about caring for him? I merely suggested that milady might tame him. And amuse herself in the process."

"Amuse myself?" Elizabeth shook her head. "Anne, sometimes I think you and I live in different worlds, entirely."

"Perhaps we do. But a little amusement would do milady good." Anne patted her arm, then released it. "Think about it."

Elizabeth sighed. She wouldn't have to think about it long.

The two women returned to the bow of the barge. With a loud clank of metal against metal, the great chain that held the ship's anchor began to retreat into her bow.

"To yer oars, boys, and step lively," the bargeman's mate shouted. "All aft, then make fer Tilbury." By the time the barge was a safe distance from the ship, the packet's anchor hung dripping from her bow and her rigging was alive with sailors preparing to get underway.

Pushed along by the breeze, the barge made rapid progress toward shore, but Elizabeth's gaze remained fixed on the packet. Despite the midnight clouds, there was enough light to see the sails unfurl, flutter, then billow full and smooth. Tacking into the head wind, the ship moved swiftly north, then south, then back again until it was just a speck on the horizon.

Creighton's voice sounded behind her. "We did it, Bess." His warm hands closed gently on her cloaked shoulders.

Instead of taking reassurance from his touch, Elizabeth felt confined, pinned. How easily he handled her, as if she were his personal property. Well, she wasn't. She wanted to slap his hands away, but her self-protective instincts stopped her. She looked over her shoulder to find him scanning the wide estuary.

"No sign of pursuit." He took in a deep, satisfied breath. "He's free. For the time being, anyway." His grip tightened briefly.

"Free," Elizabeth murmured, wondering if she would ever know what that felt like.

Well-past midnight, Garrett climbed onto the wooden quay at Tilbury and helped Bess and Anne out of the barge. Once they were all safely ashore, he waved the barge away, then turned back to the two women. "Keep your hoods pulled forward, so no one can see your faces. And try not to say anything. I don't want anyone to be able to identify your voices." Both of them nodded as he pulled the wide brim of his hat lower to conceal his own features.

He guided Bess and Anne into the shadows beside a stack of barrels. "Wait here. I want to make sure there are no soldiers about.'' Moving smoothly from shadow to shadow, he approached the brightly lit tavern of the quayside inn. He passed half a dozen horses tied in front of the inn. To his relief, not one of them was saddled or equipped like a military mount. Beyond them, two black coaches stood ready, just as Bampfield had promised, their drivers bundled, sleeping, at their posts. The horses shifted and whinnied softly as he passed, but neither driver moved or made a sound. Garrett made a quick inspection. Both teams looked fit and healthy, and the empty coaches and harnesses appeared to be in good condition. He hoped he wouldn't have to put them to the test.

He moved quietly along the side of the inn to the barnyard in back. Faint slivers of lantern light escaped the barn's wooden shutters. He crept up to one of the windows and peered through a crack. Inside the dim interior stood another coach, plus several more horses, but again, none of them looked like the lean, muscular mount of a cavalryman. Satisfied, Garrett returned to the women.

"No sign of an ambush,'' he whispered. "Anne, I'll take you first. Bess, wait here. Stay hidden if there's trouble.'' The two women embraced, then Garrett escorted Anne to the farthest coach.

He prodded the driver awake and gave the password. "I am Mr. Andrews and this is my sister. Are you waiting for us?''

"Aye, sir. I mean, greetings, Miss Andrews,'' the driver responded, rubbing the sleep from his eyes. "Where to?''

"North. The lady will tell you where.'' According to plan, Anne would go to Chelmsford before returning to London. "But wait until the other coach leaves to depart.'' His eyes straining at the shadows, Garrett opened the compartment and helped Anne inside.

"Thank you for all you've done, sir,'' she said. "I pray you have a safe journey home.''

"And you.'' Anxious to be away, he closed the door and turned to leave, but Anne leaned out the window and called after him softly, "Be good to your dear wife. She needs someone to look after her.''

Garrett couldn't imagine Bess needing anyone. He turned. "I'll do my best to see that no harm comes to her.''

In the feeble light that escaped the tavern's smoky window, he saw Anne frown. "I didn't ask you to keep her safe; I know you'll do that. I asked you to be *good* to her.''

What in blazes did she mean by that? he wondered. "I've been nothing but good to her."

Anne peered at him oddly. "She has never known happiness." Without further explanation, she retreated into the coach's dark interior.

Women! They invariably brought up the most baffling things at the worst possible times. Garrett headed back to collect his wife.

She followed him to the unoccupied coach without comment. Their driver now sat erect, reins in hand. Garrett looked up at him. "I am Mr. Andrews and this is my sister. Are you waiting for us?"

"Greetings, Miss Andrews." The driver touched his whip to the brim of his hat. "Where to?"

Garrett opened the door and urged Bess toward the empty compartment. "London, at all speed."

"London?" Bess balked, turning to him in shock. "Have you lost your mind?"

Garrett had neither the time nor the inclination to explain himself. Instead, he heaved her into the coach like a sack of meal, tossed his hat in after her, then angled his broad shoulders to squeeze inside. Ignoring the outraged noises Bess made as she righted herself, he slammed the door and thumped on the roof of the compartment. "On your way, man."

"They know the prince is gone by now," Bess whispered angrily over the clank and jangle of the coach. "London is the last place we should go! They'll search every—"

"Shhh," he quieted her with a gloved finger placed firmly to her lips. "I am not an idiot, Bess, despite the fact that I married you. You must learn to trust me." Bess knocked his hand away and glared at him.

To give the lesson time to sink in, he waited until they were safely away from Tilbury to explain. "I never intended to go to London, but one never knows who might have been listening." He glanced briefly toward the Thames, flowing wide and silent alongside the road. "A few miles down the road, there's a ferry run by a staunch Loyalist. I'll tell the driver to turn when we get there, but not before. Once we're safely across, we'll head southwest for Salisbury. With luck, we'll catch up with Gwynneth and the baggage wagons in only a few days."

"You might have told me," she huffed.

"I might, but I didn't," he said affably, "for your own protection."

She gazed out into the night, her expression oblique. "I'll be glad to have Gwynneth back."

"Gwynneth?" Garrett chuckled. "And all this time, I thought you were so cross because you missed our dear little Mr. Cromwell."

"That pig?" His wife bristled. "Good riddance to it! The thing's always rooting at my shoes or biting my hem." Her eyes narrowed. "Why doesn't it try to eat *your* shoes?"

Garrett smiled, glad she couldn't read his mind. The pig rooted at her shoes because he'd rubbed honey on them while she was sleeping; it nibbled at her hem because of the fine-ground meal Garrett had poured between the stitches. He took great delight in how the little pig's noisy, messy attentions flustered his wife. Bess needed flustering. "Face it, Bess," he said. "That little pig loves you."

"I do not squander my affections on pigs, sir."

"Or on husbands," he retorted playfully. Despite her protests, he was certain she had begun to like Mr. Cromwell; she just couldn't admit it.

It was a start. If she could learn to care for a pig, maybe there was some hope that she could learn to trust her husband. Garrett knew one thing: Only when Bess no longer feared him could he be safe with her. Until then, he wouldn't trust her as far as he could heave a horse.

He leaned forward and adjusted the hood of her cape. "Remember to stay covered. We don't want anyone seeing your face."

"I might say the same to you." Bess briskly raised the hood of his cloak to conceal his hair. "No one who sees that tawny hair would ever mistake you for Bampfield." Her gloved hand tucked a stray curl behind his ear. The gesture was so intimate it left them both awkward, at a loss for words.

Then the trapdoor of the coach flew open, jarring them apart. The driver leaned into the opening and shouted, "There's horses approachin', sir."

Garrett's hand went to the hilt of his pistol. "How many? How far?"

"More than a dozen, ridin' toward us pall-mall. Maybe a mile away."

"Take cover, anywhere you can! Then help me unharness

the lead horses. It's our only chance.''

Bess grabbed his arm. ''Maybe they're not soldiers. How do you know?''

''Who else would be headed this way, at this hour, full-gallop from London?''

''Oh.'' Fear tingled through Elizabeth as she sank back into the seat, the taste of brass in her mouth. If they were captured, would she be strong enough to remain silent under torture? Creighton was out of uniform. He would be accused of spying, and her with him. Her thumb rubbed nervous circles against the side of her forefinger as she remembered the executions her father had forced her to witness. Vivid, gruesome images caused the back of her neck to tingle.

The coach swerved violently, then began to slow.

''The driver must have found a place to stop.'' Creighton gripped Elizabeth's upper arms. ''Can you ride bareback?''

''Father forbade it.'' What was she thinking? This was no time to lie. She blurted out, ''I used to, when no one was watching, but it's been years.''

''You'll do fine.'' He let go of her to pull a bundle from under the seat and thrust it into her arms. The strong smell of goat cheese told her the bundle contained provisions. ''You look after the food.'' He slid to the door. The moment the coach slowed enough, he opened it, jumped clear, then took off running alongside.

With shaking hands, Elizabeth removed her cloak and pulled the cords of her velvet bag over her head, as well as her shoulder, then put the cloak back on. Content that her precious medicines could not fall off, she shifted them into a more comfortable spot behind her arm, then grabbed up the bundle of provisions and waited for the coach to stop. When it did, she climbed out and ran forward.

Creighton and the driver were unhitching the lead horses as fast as they could. Elizabeth laid down the food and began to unbuckle anything she could reach on the first horse. The process seemed endless, and all the while, she imagined the sound of approaching hoofbeats, louder and louder.

At last, the two lead horses were free. Creighton pulled out his dagger and shortened the heavy reins to a manageable length. He motioned to her. ''Hurry, Bess. Get on.''

Elizabeth started forward, then changed direction. ''The food! I almost forgot.''

Creighton caught her at the waist. "I'll carry the food." He swung her onto the huge horse as if she weighed nothing. The gelding skittered sideways at the unfamiliar burden, but settled when she stroked his neck. Elizabeth tugged self-consciously at her skirts in a vain effort to cover her exposed calves. "I'm afraid we haven't time for modesty." Creighton handed her the reins. "The horse's name is Soot. If you have trouble staying on him, grab his mane, but don't let loose of the reins."

While the driver backed the rest of the team away from the discarded harnesses, Creighton threaded his forearm under the knot, scooped up the bundle of food, then pulled himself smoothly astride the other horse. He instructed the driver, "Head back to Tilbury as fast as you can. If we're lucky, they'll chase you instead of us." Then he turned to Elizabeth. "Follow me." After guiding his horse to an almost invisible track that led northwest toward a marsh, he waited until the coach clattered away, then slapped the reins against the horse's neck and dug his heels into its flanks. The horse took off.

Elizabeth did the same, careening after him. For her, it took every ounce of concentration to keep from falling off, but Creighton rode as if he and the horse were one. He led the way with a confidence that belied the darkness and the unfamiliar terrain.

Struggling to hold on, Elizabeth prayed she could keep up. It soon became evident, though, that she couldn't. The distance between them lengthened. She looked ahead and saw Creighton's mount execute a graceful jump. She tried to prepare herself for the jump, but when she reached the narrow creek, her mount balked, hurling her against the steep bank on the far side.

Elizabeth's back struck the muddy bank with such force she couldn't breathe. Dazed, she slid down, feet-first, into the cold waters of the shallow creek while her horse stumbled away. She had barely regained her senses when Creighton's hands closed under her arms. He hauled her up against him.

"Are you hurt?" The anger and exasperation in his voice made it more an accusation than a question.

"No," Elizabeth choked out. "Just wet!" She jerked free of him, her skirts dragging heavily in the brackish-smelling water. "My medicine!" She groped frantically at the cords that crossed her chest. "Where is it?"

"It's still there; makes you look like a hunchback." Creighton reached behind her and shifted the velvet bag through her cloak. "Somewhat squashed, but intact." He brushed the worst of the mud from her back. "Your horse headed straight for mine. Do you think you can ride?"

"Yes." Elizabeth lifted her wet skirts to climb out of the creek, but Creighton stopped her.

"Hold!" He stilled, listening.

Straining to hear, she picked out the faint sound of hoofbeats on the steady breeze.

"They're coming," he said. "Stay here. I'll be right back." He scrambled up the bank and gathered the horses' reins and the bundle of food, then led the animals back down into the creek. "We can't outride them, not with these horses. Our best chance is to try to lose them. But they'll be able to spot us above the banks if we mount." He handed her Soot's reins. "So we'll have to walk the horses in the stream. No tracks." He led the way down the center of the creek. There was nothing for Elizabeth to do but follow.

After what seemed like miles of trudging through the mucky bottom of the stream, her feet ached with cold and the muscles of her thighs and calves quivered with fatigue, but she kept on going. The stream widened and deepened as the land around them leveled to a broad expanse of marsh grass swaying in the wind. When the water lapped at her waist, Elizabeth worried that her medicines might get wet, so she stopped to shift the velvet bag to the top of her head. She secured it by looping the ties over the bag, then hooking them under her chin.

The next time he turned to check on her, Creighton chuckled. "That's some hat you're wearing, Bess."

Cold, frightened, and cross, she retorted, "The day might come when you'll be glad I kept them dry." She pointed to the bundle of food hanging from his elbow. "If that's the only food we have, I suggest you pay better attention. It's about to be baptized."

"Oops." Creighton lifted the food. "You're right." He shoved his pistol and powder bag beneath the knot, then hoisted the bundle to his shoulder.

With every step now, the stream deepened slightly. Elizabeth gasped as the cold water rose above her midriff. When the murky current reached her armpits, she said through chattering teeth, "If you take us any deeper, I'm liable to sink.

My skirts are dragging me down, and I can barely pull my feet from the muck.''

Creighton transferred his reins to the hand holding the bundle of food, then doubled back. He scooped her against him, his powerful arm pulling her feet clear of the sucking mud. "There's a small island just ahead, covered with brush. We can rest there and dry out."

Sure enough, the bottom began to rise. When the stream was only knee-deep, Creighton put her down and listened intently, but the wind bore no sound of pursuit. He bent down and scooped up a handful of water. He sampled it, then scooped up another handful. "Better drink while you can. It doesn't taste very good, but it's not tainted."

Elizabeth nodded. The water was faintly brackish, but drinkable. After she had finished, Creighton allowed his horse to drink and Elizabeth did the same.

"Come on." He led the way into the dense underbrush that covered the marsh island. It took a while to work their way to the small clearing at its center, but as soon as they were safely hidden, Elizabeth sat down and tried to wring the worst of the moisture from her skirts. Creighton dropped the bundle of food beside her. "We dare not risk a fire, but eating should help warm us up. Fix us some food. I'll be right back." He disappeared into the underbrush.

Frowning at his high-handed attitude, Elizabeth grudgingly pulled the pistol and powder from beneath the knot, then untied the bundle. Inside were bread, cheese, dried beef, cold biscuits, and a half-filled bottle of unmarked spirits.

Almost as good as a fire, she thought, uncorking the bottle and sniffing its contents. She recoiled at the familiar stink of malt whiskey—Ravenwold's favorite—but she was freezing, and the whiskey would warm her blood. Holding her nose, she took a deep gulp. The moment she swallowed, her eyes watered and her shoulders twisted spasmodically. Elizabeth inhaled raggedly, then a spell of coughing overtook her.

Creighton came crunching through the underbrush, his arms filled with marsh grass. "What's the matter? Anyone could hear that coughing half a mile away."

"Nothing's the matter," Elizabeth said in a strangled voice. Glaring at him, she took another, smaller, swig from the bottle. It tasted just as bad as the first sip, but this time the effect was far less jarring. Warmth spread down her throat and radiated through her chest.

"Oh." He looked pointedly at the bottle, but did not comment further. Dropping all but a handful of marsh grass, he began rubbing down the horses. Elizabeth took several more swallows of whiskey before he stopped what he was doing and extracted the bottle from her grasp. "Leave some for me."

At least she was warm, now, but she couldn't feel her lips. Better eat something. She broke a piece of cheese from the wedge and popped it into her mouth, then tore off a chunk of bread and ate it.

When Creighton finished rubbing the horses, he removed their bits and gave them some tender shoots as fodder. Then he gathered the soiled marsh grass and shaped it into a pallet beside Elizabeth, topping it with a fresh layer of grass. He sat down on the makeshift bed. "By thunder, I'm almost too tired to eat."

"Phew." He stank of horse sweat. Elizabeth waved her hand in front of her nose. "You smell like a stableboy."

"Really?" He leaned forward and sniffed her breath. "Well, you smell like a drunkard."

He reached for the bread, and Elizabeth swatted his hand. "Oh, no, you don't. Go wash your hands."

"You get bossy when you drink, don't you, Bess?" He rose. "All right. I'll wash, if you'll promise not to drink any more tonight."

She straightened, swaying slightly. "I'm not promisin' anything. Not to you, sir." She could just make out the white flash of his grin.

Creighton shook his head, then pushed through the underbrush. She heard soft splashing, then the soft crunch of his footsteps. When he returned, he was naked to the waist, his soggy clothes draped across his arm and his bare shoulders glistening darkly. "Is that better?"

Elizabeth couldn't help staring at his well-muscled body. He was taut and lean, where Ravenwold had been slack and hairy. She wondered what it would feel like to smooth her hand across the hard surface of Creighton's chest and thread her fingers though the scattered curls that tapered like a golden arrow to his waist. Embarrassed, she looked away. "I didn't say you had to take a bath, for heaven's sake. You'll get a chill."

"I didn't take a bath," he responded good-naturedly. "I just decided that this is as good a time as any to wring my clothes out." One by one, he twisted the moisture from his shirt, coat, and cloak, then put them back on again.

Elizabeth yawned hugely. She was getting very sleepy. She raised her knees and pulled her soggy cloak tighter. "How did you know about this place?"

He cocked that annoying smile of his. "This isn't the first time I've been chased into these marshes, and I doubt it will be the last." He broke off a piece of cheese and ate it. Then he uncorked the whiskey and took a swig.

Elizabeth shivered. The liquor's warming effect was beginning to wear off, but she still couldn't feel her lips. And there was an odd numbness between her legs. "What now?"

"We wait."

"For what?"

"For them to find us." Creighton looked to the horses. A faint vapor rose from their coats into the chill air. "Or until sunset tomorrow. Whichever comes first."

"Oh." She curled into a shivering ball on the thin cushion of dead leaves beneath her.

"You can't sleep like that, Bess. You'll freeze." Creighton patted the thick pallet of marsh grass. "I made this for both of us." He extended his hand. "If we want to get through this night, we'll have to do it together."

Too weary and cold to argue, she crawled beside her husband.

"I'll keep you warm. And safe." Creighton opened his cloak and drew her close, enveloping them both. He cradled her head against his shoulder. "Why don't you sing us to sleep. Just one little lullaby?"

Elizabeth stiffened. "I told you. I will not sing for you. You cannot make me."

"Pity." His arms pulled her snug against him. "But I won't give up asking." His body radiated an almost unnatural heat.

Exhausted, she closed her eyes, feeling his warmth melt the tension from her own body, but she did not go to sleep right away. Intermittent gusts of wind whistled through the marsh grass, and waves crunched against the shore of the tiny island. Overhead, the branches danced erratically with every burst of wind. Every new sound convinced her that she heard the soldiers coming.

Soon it will be next week, she told herself, and I will be safe in my own bed at Ravenwold. Then I'll laugh at myself for being so afraid. To her dulled amazement, she felt herself nodding off.

She dreamed of horses splashing in the water. Then she smelled them, right under her nose, just before Creighton's hand closed over her mouth. "Don't make a sound," he whispered hotly into her ear.

Elizabeth nodded, her eyes flying open to gray morning light. The noise of splashing horses was real, and it was close. Creighton removed his hand from her mouth. She sat up, releasing an explosion of pain in her head and a twist of nausea in her gut.

Creighton pulled free of her and moved stealthily across the tiny clearing to stand between the horses. He soothed the beasts with gentle strokes to their noses.

Elizabeth peered through the heavy overgrowth that sheltered them. She could see patches of cloudy gray sky, but she couldn't tell what time it was. Based on the stiffness of her limbs, she had been asleep for several hours. She stared in fear at Creighton.

Dear God, don't let the horses make noise, she prayed silently.

To the right, probably only a dozen yards away, she could hear the splashing of the Roundheads' mounts in the shallow water and the swish of their sabers as they whacked at the tall marsh grass. Then gradually, the sounds grew fainter.

"They're moving away," Creighton mouthed.

She hardly dared breathe until the sounds disappeared entirely. Then she began to shake with a sudden chill.

Creighton left the horses and pulled her close inside his cloak, but she still shook violently. He began to rock her back and forth, whispering, "There, there, Bess. Everything's going to be all right. All right."

How could he promise that? She knew better; life had taught her often enough.

He smoothed her hair from her forehead. "It will be all right, Bess. I promise. One day we'll look back on this and laugh."

She didn't believe him, but his words were soothing, and it felt good to be held. In spite of herself, she began to relax into his embrace.

Over and over, he murmured softly into her hair, "It's going to be all right."

How she wished that were true.

Garrett kept watch as Bess slept fitfully through the day. By noon, the wind died and the sun came out, warming the air until it felt more like June than April. Garrett waited until the last glimmer of twilight had disappeared before he roused her. "Wake up, Bess. Time to move on." When he shook her, she scowled and turned her back to him, muttering unintelligibly.

He couldn't help smiling. Sleeping so hard, in the middle of a fen! Garrett had to admit, the girl was game. She had kept a level head in the midst of circumstances that would have unraveled most of the other women he knew. And she hadn't complained, though she must have been miserable.

He shook her again. "Time to go."

She yawned, stretching languidly.

Muddy and disheveled though she might be, the sight of her body arching against her damp cloak sent an unexpected surge of desire through him. This is no time for such notions, Garrett chided himself. He stood and pulled her to her feet beside him.

Unsteady, she gripped the front of his jacket as she gained her footing. Bess looked around. "It's black as the inside of a coffin. How will we find our way out of here?" she asked, her voice tight.

"I could find my way back to the road blindfolded." Garrett couldn't blame her for being afraid. Even if the Roundheads had given up searching the marsh, they wouldn't stop looking for them, and Loyalist territory was a long way away.

He reached inside his shirt and pulled out the leather pouch he carried in case of emergencies. Garrett pressed the purse into Bess's hand and closed her fingers around it. "There's enough gold here to bribe your way out of almost anything, with plenty left over for clothes and fresh horses. If we should be separated, use the money to get back to Ravenwold Castle as quickly as you can. I'll meet you there."

Bess's dark silhouette stilled. "Have you kept enough gold for yourself?"

Garrett grinned. "Don't worry. I can manage on my wits alone. Now put that in a safe place." Accustomed to the darkness, he could see her stuff the purse between her breasts. He watched with an odd sense of satisfaction that the purse, still warm from his own body, was now nestled between Bess's breasts. Breasts he had yet to explore.

He steered his errant thoughts back to the matter at hand. "I've already eaten, but you should grab a bite before we go."

"First things first. I'll be right back." Instead of getting food, Bess made for the bushes. After she had relieved herself, she returned and ate some bread and cheese while Garrett got the horses ready. When she started to put her bag of medicines on her head, he laid a staying hand on her arm. "That won't be necessary. I think we can safely ride. The devil couldn't see his own shadow on a night like this."

Bess slipped the loops over her shoulder, then closed her cape.

Taking both sets of reins in one hand, Garrett grasped Bess's fingers with the other. "Just hold onto me." As soon as they were clear of the underbrush, he helped her mount, then pulled himself up on his own horse. He leaned toward her. "Give me your reins."

She handed them over without comment, then rode stiff and silent behind him.

When they neared the road, Garrett led her into a scrub wood on the verge. "Wait here until I make sure there are no Roundheads lurking about." She stilled. If there was one thing Bess knew how to do, it was be still.

Once Garrett was satisfied they were alone, he returned and led her up onto the road. He handed her the mare's reins. "The ferry's not far, and the ferryman is loyal to the Crown. We can cross safely there. Once we're on the other side, we'll set out through open country toward Kingsford. If we can make it before dawn, I know of a cave where we can hide."

They reached the ferry without incident, made the crossing, then set out over open country. After hours and hours of relentless travel, the dark, cloudy sky had lightened to a pale shade of silver when Garrett saw the particular forest he had been looking for. He directed his mount into the thick stand of oak trees and Bess followed, her usually rigid posture now bent with fatigue.

The woodland floor was covered with dried leaves, making it impossible to travel quietly, but soon he spied a familiar outcropping of rock beside a ravine. Garrett dismounted. "There's a cave in that ravine where we can hide."

"This cave," Bess asked, her face wary. "How did you know about it?"

"A schoolmate of mine lives nearby. One summer when I was visiting him, we were hunting in these woods when a storm blew up. He showed it to me."

"A schoolmate? Why don't we go to him for shelter? After all, you were friends."

"We were. Once." Garrett shook his head. "Unfortunately, we came down on opposite sides of this rebellion. He just might turn us in."

"Oh." Elizabeth peered toward the ravine. "You're sure this is the right place?"

"Pretty sure." Garrett checked the landmarks. "Frankly, I can't believe I remembered how to find it after all these years."

"You haven't found it yet," she observed drily. She watched intently as he picked up a fallen branch and retraced their trail to the top of the next gentle rise. He stopped, then began to back toward her, dragging the branch from side to side to obliterate the evidence of their passage. "Where did you learn that?" she asked.

"One of the men in my regiment spent some time in the New World and learned this from the savages." He winked at her. "A little savagery comes in handy every now and then." To his surprise, she colored and looked away.

When he came alongside Bess, she extended her arms. "Help me down, please. My legs have gone completely numb."

Garrett marveled at the way she said it. Not a complaint, just a simple statement of fact. He reached up and helped her off. She tried to stand, but her knees buckled.

He scooped her into his arms. "Put your arms around my neck. That ravine is pretty steep." He led the horses along the rim until the grade softened somewhat, then headed down the embankment. Halfway to the bottom, he swept aside a cascade of wild vines to reveal an opening larger than a door in the hillside. "Ha! There it is."

Bess shrank back. "How do you know this cave isn't occupied already? Looks like just the sort of place serpents and spiders would love."

Garrett smiled, surprised that a woman who had waded through a swamp without flinching now showed fear at the prospect of facing a few spiders. "Don't worry," he teased. "There's room enough for all of us inside. Horses, people, spiders, *and* snakes. Maybe even a bear or two."

She clung to him tightly as he brushed past the vines, reins in hand. At first the horses resisted entering the confined space, but a few tugs convinced them to follow. By now enough daylight filtered through the tunnel to illuminate the dim cavern beyond.

Once Garrett had pulled the horses into the subterranean room, he let go of the reins and lowered Bess onto a large rock. "Give me a minute, and I'll make us a fire."

"What about the smoke? Won't it choke us?" As always, she questioned his decision. Practical questions they were, but questions nonetheless.

"No." He pointed to a deep fissure in the cavern's blackened ceiling. "The smoke all disappears into that crack. It must open to the outside somewhere, sort of like a chimney." Garrett rummaged along a narrow ledge until he felt what he was looking for. "Aha. Just where we left them." He produced several flints. The cave opening provided plenty of dried vines for tinder. Soon, he was fanning a bright flame in the blackened fire pit at the center of the cave. "There. How's that?" When she didn't answer, he turned to find that she was no longer sitting on the rock. "Bess?"

No response.

Heading for the cave entrance, he met her just inside the opening, her arms laden with twigs and branches.

"Here." She dumped what she had gathered into his arms, then limped over to the fire and extended her hands. "Mmmm. Feels good."

"You're limping."

She looked at him as if he had just announced that people needed to breathe. "I can hardly move." She eased herself down painfully to sit beside the fire. "I told you it had been years since I'd ridden bareback. The fact is, I hardly ride at all anymore."

"Oh." Garrett deposited the fuel a safe distance from the fire, then walked over and took a good look at his wife. His own clothes were almost dry, but hers still looked soaked. "If you'll keep the fire going, I'll scout around and gather some more wood."

"Very well." Elizabeth watched him go with some trepi-

dation. She hadn't seen any spiders so far, but she didn't like
being left alone in this place. She fed another twig into the
flame. In the flickering light, she made out a low, smooth ledge
that had been chiseled into the rock. Above it on the stone
wall were several handprints surrounded by reddish pigment.

Forgetting about spiders and snakes, she climbed onto the
ledge and held her hand against one of the imprints. They were
almost the same size.

A loud rustling from the cave opening caused her to pivot.
To her relief, she saw Creighton's large frame silhouetted in
the tunnel. He dragged a bundle of long branches into the
cavern. Selecting three of the smaller ones, he propped them
together, tentlike, beside the fire. "Give me your cloak, and
I'll spread it over these branches to dry."

She climbed down from the ledge and unfastened her cloak.
After handing it over, she huddled close to the fire. Her mud-
died clothes were still soaked, and even though the cloak had
been wet, it had helped keep in what little warmth her body
could manufacture. Now without it, she shivered anew. While
Creighton arranged the cape on the branches, she chafed her
upper arms.

Garrett heard his wife shivering and turned. "Still chilled?"
When he took her hand, it was cold as a corpse's. "You're
freezing," he chided. He circled behind her and sat, enfolding
both of them in the damp fabric and drawing her back against
him. When she resisted, he said, "It won't do you any good
to go all stiff like that, Bess. I'm not going to let you go, not
until your cloak is dry, anyway."

Stubborn woman. She couldn't stand being close to him
unless she was drunk. What was she afraid of? He'd sworn
not to take advantage of her.

Then Garrett remembered the way she had wrapped herself
around him like a vine that first night in the coach, and he
realized why she had kept herself aloof: She didn't trust herself.

Of course. It made perfect sense.

She wanted to be held, but some internal compulsion
wouldn't let her.

He crossed his arms in front of her, but still she remained
rigid in his embrace. *You don't know it yet, but you're going
to be held as often as I get the chance, and you're going to
learn to like it. It might take a while, but I swear, you're going*

*to learn to like it.* Until Bess felt safe with him, he wouldn't be safe with her, and Garrett had no intention in following Ravenwold to an early grave.

Elizabeth soaked in the heat radiating from Creighton's torso and realized to her consternation that she was glad his arms were around her. His heat was as welcome as a hot brick on a cold night. Somehow, she wasn't so afraid when he held her close. She'd grown accustomed to the scent of him, and to his warmth.

She remembered Anne's advice. *Who said anything about caring for him?*

Perhaps she could enjoy Creighton's warmth, after all. It didn't mean she cared. She felt the tension bleeding out of her and leaned back against him. Then she felt the telltale bulge against the small of her back.

She gasped and tried to pull away, but Creighton's arms only tightened, his large hands closing over her forearms. His voice hardened. "Oh, no, you don't. I'm going to warm you up, Bess, and that's that." When she continued to struggle, he snapped, "Stop wiggling! I'm just as tired and sore as you are, and I have no patience for such nonsense. Be still, or I'll—"

Elizabeth froze. "Or you'll what?" Finally, he was showing his true colors. "Go ahead. You'll what?"

"I hate it when you do that," he grumbled irritably. His grip eased, but his muscular arms still cradled her to him. "Every time I show the slightest temper, you get all still and wary, like a rabbit cornered by a pack of hounds."

Elizabeth said nothing, but did not try to escape again. She would take his warmth, and she would allow him to protect her from danger—for the time being, anyway—but who would protect her from Creighton?

She knew the answer. Six years with Ravenwold had taught her all too well.

No one would protect her from her husband. No one could.

# CHAPTER 13

Elizabeth woke the next night curled on her side, her body spooned against Creighton's. She blinked in the oppressive darkness. At first, the cave seemed black as a tomb. Then her eyes made out tiny specks of orange ember shrouded in ashes from the spent fire. She felt as stiff as a corpse, herself, but she did not move. Creighton's arms and cloak enfolded her, creating a cocoon of heat on the cold stone floor. She could feel his breath, warm and even against the crown of her head.

Across the cavern, the horses shimmied, then shifted on their feet, their hulking shadows releasing the strong odor of dung into an atmosphere already thickened by the smoldering ashes.

Glad that Creighton couldn't see her face, Elizabeth closed her eyes and soaked up a few more moments of warmth. She relaxed against his torso, taking comfort not only from his heat, but also from the security of being bound together, enfolded by his arms. Then she recognized the same familiar bulge pressing against the small of her back that she had felt the night before.

Even in sleep, Creighton's body betrayed his lust.

Trying not to wake him, she eased free of his embrace, telling herself he would have responded that way to anything in a skirt. He did not want her. He wanted a woman—any woman.

Miserable and stiff, she groped for a stick to stir the embers, then began feeding twigs into the glowing heart of the fire. A bright tongue of flame kindled, then another. She stared into the growing light, wishing that her own heart could be brought back to life as easily. But it couldn't. Charlotte's death had reduced her to ashes, and being forced into bondage under Creighton had snuffed out whatever embers remained.

Creighton rolled onto his back and stretched. "Ummm. Can't say much for the mattress." In the dim light of the fire, she saw him flex the arm that had cushioned her head. Clenching and opening his fist, he massaged the muscles. Then he stood up and arched his back. Golden stubble glinted on his jaw, and his tawny hair stood out like a mane around his face. Even in disarray, he looked annoyingly handsome.

Aware that she probably looked like a hag, herself, Elizabeth attempted to tuck away the stray tendrils that had pulled loose from her bun.

Creighton yawned hugely. "How much food do we have left?"

She untied the muslin bundle and surveyed its meager contents. "A few bites of cheese and three dry biscuits." The whiskey bottle wasn't there. She looked around and spotted it sitting within easy reach of where Creighton had been lying. Leaning over, she picked it up and held it to the light. "I see you drank up most of the whiskey."

"That I did." Creighton rubbed his backside with a grimace. "Had to do something. Even soldiers aren't accustomed to sleeping on bare stone."

"Hmph." Suddenly struck by an urgent call of nature, Elizabeth rose stiffly to her feet. "Pray excuse me, but I must have a few moments alone outside." When Creighton opened his mouth to protest, she cut him off with, "Don't worry. I'll be careful. But I need my privacy. I will gladly grant you yours when I've finished." She limped out into the night and relieved herself, then returned to find Creighton checking his pistol. "The woods are yours, sir."

Creighton tucked his pistol into his belt. He cocked a wry half smile at her. "I didn't know the woods were yours to grant, milady, but I shall endeavor to return with all speed." He was back almost immediately.

Elizabeth frowned, irritated that even in the basest of functions, men had it so much easier than women. She doled out the remaining food, then took hers to the low ledge and sat to eat while Creighton perched on the large stone nearby. Without any water, the dried food wasn't easy to get down, but Elizabeth's stomach roiled at the mere thought of washing down the dry fare with whiskey. Creighton, however, suffered

no such reservations. In a few brief swigs, he finished off the
bottle without so much as a shudder. When they had finished
eating, he stood. "Time to go. Gather up your things, Bess.
I'll get your cloak." He retrieved the garment from its makeshift drying rack. A few whacks knocked away most of the
dried mud that still clung to the thick woolen fabric. "A little
the worse for wear, but dry."

Elizabeth rose and picked up her velvet bag of simples.
Creighton draped her cloak over her shoulders, his hands lin-
gering. She waited until he released her, then stepped back.
"Thank you."

As she had the day before, she shrugged one side free of
the cloak so she could pull the bag's deep loops over her head
and shoulder. While she pushed the bundle to a more comfortable position behind her arm, Creighton settled her cloak
back into place and fastened it beneath her chin.

He chuckled. "That's a good disguise. As I said yesterday,
you look like a hunchback."

Elizabeth frowned, stung by his observation. "Well, we
can't have anyone thinking that the handsome Viscount
Creighton has married a hunchback, can we?" Fumbling beneath her cloak, she tugged the velvet bag to the front.

"Ah. That's even better." Creighton's tawny brows lifted,
his blue eyes focused on her bulging middle. "Now you look
like you're expecting my child." He grinned. "Any minute."

Stricken, she snapped, "I'd rather be taken for a hunchback." But she did not shift the bundle. This was as close as
she would ever come to being an expectant mother.

She changed the subject. "What about the horses? Don't
they need water?"

"There's a stream nearby." Creighton's long, elegant fingers dusted the tiny crumbs of dried biscuit from the stubble
around his mouth. "We'll go there first, then head for open
country." He gathered the horses' reins. "Remember what
you're to do if we're separated?"

"You told me three times on the ferry." Elizabeth pulled
Soot's reins from his grasp. "I'm not a child. I remember."

"Of course." He motioned her ahead of him, then followed
toward the mouth of the cave. "But if we're separated, and
you cannot find Gwynneth and the others at Salisbury . . ."

Obviously, he wasn't going to leave her in peace until she
repeated his instructions yet again. She stopped, turning to

recite, "I shall go to the Anglican cathedral at Salisbury and find Father Sneed, then buy provisions and return with all haste to Ravenwold Castle."

"Right."

Elizabeth led Soot out into the darkened forest. Fortunately, this night was neither as cold nor as windy as the previous one. Her clothes were still a little damp, but with a dry cloak to protect her, she hardly noticed the lingering moisture in her muddy dress and stockings.

True to his word, Creighton led them straight to a nearby stream. After the horses had had their ins and outs, Creighton helped her mount, then pulled himself atop his own horse. "Follow me." He led them into the open countryside.

How long has it been since he'd walked these woods as a child? she wondered. The man must have total recall. Not to mention an amazing sense of direction. Elizabeth had no idea which way they were going.

Despite her aching muscles, she followed with a little more confidence than she had the night before. She was getting the knack of riding bareback, but still would have traded her eye teeth for a good saddle.

Keeping a steady pace, Creighton led her through fields, into woods as black as pitch, and down long-abandoned roads paved with huge stones edged in weeds. She only hoped the man was as certain as he seemed about where he was going.

They stopped twice to water and rest the horses, but with nothing to eat, Elizabeth's stomach soon felt as hollow as a catacomb. After the second rest stop, Creighton heard her belly growling when he helped her back onto her gelding. "When it's light, I'll go for food. It's a risk, but one we'll have to take." He swung into his own saddle, his usual audacity conspicuously absent. "But if we run into trouble, you must do as I say. If I tell you to run, run. Don't ask questions, just do it. If I tell you to be quiet and stay put, be quiet and stay put. Otherwise, you could end up getting us both killed. Understand?"

Elizabeth straightened on her horse. "Yes." This, indeed, was the sort of man she understood—the autocrat who demanded absolute, unquestioned obedience. Her father and Ravenwold had provided her with more than enough experience with such men. She didn't like it any better coming from Creighton than she had from them.

By the time the eastern sky had lightened to a pale gray, confirming that they had in fact been moving southwest, Creighton reined in his horse at the edge of a thicket overlooking a sleepy little town. He peered down at the village, frowning.

Elizabeth rode up alongside him. "What town is that?"

"I'm not sure. I've never traveled in this area."

"You? Unsure? That's a new twist."

Refusing to be baited, he inhaled deeply, his golden brows drawn together in concentration. "Could be Alton. Then again, could be Farnham, or even Guildford." He pointed to a half-timbered structure with a sign hanging out front. "But I know an inn when I see one." He scanned the eastern horizon. "It might look suspicious if I went down there at this hour. Better wait until the sun's well up." He urged his horse toward a nearby copse of young oaks. "Come on. We can rest the horses for a few hours. Then I'll go into town alone and get some food."

"Alone?" Elizabeth followed. "You would leave me here, defenseless?"

"Somehow, Bess, I can't imagine you as ever being defenseless." Creighton reined his horse to a halt and slid off. "If that town harbors a Roundhead garrison, you'll be far safer waiting for me here. And I'll be safer not having to look after you."

"Oh, really?" Tired and cranky, she slid to the ground and tethered Soot near a patch of sweet grass. Then she sat down beside a tree and leaned her sore, weary bones against a notch in the roots.

Creighton tied his mount beside hers, then took up a post beside a wild lilac bush where he could watch the town come to life. The sun was well up before he stood and brushed the dirt from his breeches. "Look sharp, Bess. I'm going into town." Hat in hand, he untied his horse and led it toward the road.

Elizabeth hurried after him, appalled that he would desert her. "Wait. You can't just leave me here. What if someone sees me? I look like a beggar."

His mocking smile returned. "A very pregnant beggar. If you keep your cloak closed, I doubt anyone will bother you."

*Pregnant?* Elizabeth bridled. A man of good breeding would never use such a term, especially in reference to his own wife. "No decent woman travels the highways alone. What about footpads? And highwaymen. Not to mention the Roundheads. Good glory, man. Do you know what the Round-heads would do to a woman alone? I've heard they—"

"Give it a rest, woman!" He stopped abruptly, forcing her to pull up short to keep from running into him. "Sometimes one must choose from the lesser of two evils. I don't like leaving you alone, but I must." He tipped her face toward his. "If anything goes wrong, don't wait for me. The Winchester road intersects this one a few miles back. Take it, but be care-ful along the way. If there's traffic on the road, head west over open country as fast as you can." He pointed away from the rising sun. "That way."

Elizabeth jerked her chin free of his touch. "I do know the difference between east and west, sir."

His blue eyes weary, he smiled. "Things can get a little mixed up when you're being chased. Believe me, I know." He ran his fingers through the thick, golden waves at his tem-ples. "The Winchester highway will take you into loyalist ter-ritory within a day's ride. Don't stop until you reach the city. You can buy a coach there, and hire a team and driver to take you to Salisbury."

His face troubled, he leaned closer as if to breathe the scent of her. "If you need to find Father Sneed in Salisbury, don't forget to mention my name. He knows me from my school days. He'll help you."

"You told me. *Four* times." She felt her anger fade. Was he really worried about her? Odd, how it pulled at her insides to think of his riding into danger. She had grown used to having him near her. The scent of his skin, the feel of his arms around her ·at night. Until that moment, Elizabeth hadn't re-alized how much strength she drew from his physical presence.

Creighton looked down toward the village. "I wish I could be sure where we are." Then, like a man coming out of a trance, he turned to her and said, "If that village turns out to be a nest for Roundheads, we'll both have to run for our lives." Without warning, he drew her roughly against him and kissed her, hard, his mouth hungry and demanding on hers.

Elizabeth hesitated at first, then felt herself spiraling into a dizzying whorl of sensation. The strong, familiar pressure of his arms around her. The distinctive scent of his skin in her nostrils. The taste of his lips on hers. The surprising fineness of his hair as she threaded her fingers through it.

She was hot, but her feet went cold. Her heart pumped wildly, and her body tingled with a spreading tide that sent sparkles to her very fingertips. For the first time in her life, she knew what it was to enjoy being kissed by a man. And then, as unexpectedly as it had begun, the kiss was over. Creighton eased her to her feet and pulled away.

He untied his horse, then looked back at her, his face serious. "Promise me something, Bess."

Struggling to regain her composure, she breathed a dazed, "What?"

Creighton mounted up, his eyes merry with mischief. "If they do kill me, try to grieve just a little." While she stood groping for a retort, he reined his horse toward the village and trotted away.

Why had he said that? Was the request an oblique reference to that night three years ago at Castle Ravenwold?

She wasn't sure. Nor did she know whether she would grieve if Creighton were killed. Watching him ride away, she considered the prospect, and her heart twisted within her.

No. His death would bring no joy.

But it would free her.

Crossing herself, she said three "Our Fathers" in penance for the thought. Then she hurried back to the lilac bushes at the crest of the hill. Finding a spot where she could see without being seen, she settled to watch Creighton enter the village.

He took his time, slowing to a walk at the edge of town and maintaining a leisurely pace until he reached the inn. She saw him dismount and stroll into the inn. She stared at the building, her thumb rubbing anxious circles against the side of her forefinger.

Several long minutes passed before a small boy emerged from behind the structure. He raced across the green and entered what looked like a guild hall.

Probably nothing to be worried about, Elizabeth told herself. Then she saw a half-dozen dark-clad men emerge from the guild hall and hasten toward the inn. Her chest contracted in fear. Roundheads! Two of the black-clad man went around back, while the rest entered from the front.

Creighton had walked into a Roundhead stronghold.

She heard the distant sound of dogs barking, then saw several villagers scramble out of the inn, waving their arms in agitation. From across the green, several more villagers left their shops and homes, drawn to the spectacle at the inn.

Elizabeth gripped her fist in front of her mouth and groaned.

Below her, one of the black-clad men came flying sideways through the tavern's window and landed in a heap in front of Creighton's horse. Creighton lunged after him, rolling to his feet as deftly as an acrobat.

The soldier started to rise, but Creighton dispatched him with a well-placed kick to the jaw before vaulting onto his horse and taking the north road full-gallop out of town.

Elizabeth watched in horror as two of the black-clad soldiers stumbled out of the inn shouting the alarm. Within minutes, more than a dozen mounted men thundered from behind the guild hall and headed after Creighton.

She had to leave.

West. The Winchester road, a few miles back.

Her heart pounding, she led Soot to a ragged stump and heaved herself atop him. She reined him back the way they had come, then smacked his croup with all her might and dug her heels into his flanks. "Go, Soot! Go!"

Trace horses are bred for strength and endurance, not speed. Even at a gallop, Soot was no match for cavalry. Elizabeth prayed the Roundheads wouldn't come after her.

Her husband had led them away, risked his own life to protect her, but she couldn't let herself think of that now. She had to concentrate. Stay on the horse. Find the road to Winchester.

It seemed like forever before she reached the crossroads Creighton had mentioned, but when she got to the intersection, she reined Soot to a halt and looked for some sign that this was the right place. Then she saw a crude wooden arrow nailed to a tree on the westward track, its faded lettering confirming the way. Cape flying, she tore down the rutted road as fast as her mount could carry her.

Elizabeth wasn't sure how long she galloped Soot before his gait began to falter. Intent on escape, she hadn't noticed the increasing strain the steepening countryside put on the animal. Now she noted with shame that Soot's coat was lathered and his bridle foamed from exertion. She slowed him to a brisk walk, searching vainly for some woods or even a clump of trees where they could hide and rest.

Neatly walled fields and pastures covered the rolling hills

as far as she could see, sure evidence of civilization. She'd met no one on the road so far, but she couldn't count on her luck holding much longer, and there were no trees anywhere, not even a clump of weeds or bushes big enough to hide Soot.

How far away was Royalist territory? she wondered. Judging from the shadows, it was almost noon. Safety was still a half-day's ride away.

Soot snorted, his breathing labored. "Poor beast." Elizabeth patted his neck and slowed him to an amble. "If I asked it, you'd run till your great heart burst, wouldn't you?" She wouldn't ask it, even if the soldiers were on her heels. A dead horse would do her little good. "Just keep going for a little while longer, so we can find some water. For both of us."

She came upon a stream soon enough, but there were no woods nearby. Thirsty and exhausted herself, she decided to risk a stop. She slid to the ground and led Soot across the flat, grassy bank to the stream. The water was clear, so cold it hurt her hands as she scooped up mouthful after mouthful. After wiping the grime of travel from her face, she let Soot drink his fill.

Her stomach growled loud enough to be heard over the horse's noisy slurping.

Elizabeth clutched her empty stomach, then chided herself. It wasn't the first time she had gone hungry. And it certainly wasn't the first time she had been stiff, sore, and exhausted.

Her thighs felt as if every muscle in them had been shredded to pieces. The thought of getting back astride her horse sent a shiver of dread through her. Maybe if she could rest for only a moment . . . The sun shone warm on her shoulders, and the air was sweet with the perfume of spring. Still holding the reins, she lay down on the soft green grass beside the stream to ease her aching bones.

Overhead, puffy white clouds moved swiftly across the deep blue sky. Spring had always been her favorite time of year. She loved the pale new growth and the darling little lambs. But most of all, she loved the beautiful tulips and daffodils and hyacinths that forced their way out of the cold earth, their presence an affirmation of life.

One of her most cherished memories was the day her mother had taken five-year-old Elizabeth outside to see the fragrant clump of hyacinths blooming where the two of them had planted a handful of ugly bulbs the autumn before. "See?"

her mother had said. "Those homely bulbs had beautiful flowers locked inside. All they needed was to be planted in the right place, at the right time, and look what happened."

That had been Elizabeth's first miracle.

Now, lying on the carpet of sweet grass, she prayed for another. *Blessed Virgin, please intercede for my husband. Don't let the soldiers take him. I didn't mean it when I had those thoughts about his being killed. I don't want him dead. I just don't want to be married to him, that's all.* Finishing with the triune amen, she crossed herself, then rolled wearily to her feet. "Come on, Soot. We'll walk a while. Then I'll have to get back on you, and believe me, I'm not looking forward to *that* any more than you are." She led him to the road, her muscles quivering painfully with every step.

She patted Soot's jaw. "Get me to Winchester before midnight, and you'll never have to pull a coach again. That's a promise."

Late in the afternoon two days later, Elizabeth's newly purchased coach rolled through the arched gate into the close at Salisbury Cathedral. Her driver had made numerous inquiries in town about the baggage wagons, but no one had seen or heard anything. Already worried about Creighton, Elizabeth added Gwynneth and the other servants to her concerns. She had no recourse now but to seek out Father Sneed.

She peered out of the coach window toward the Anglican cathedral. Generations of faithful Roman Catholics had sacrificed dearly to erect the magnificent structure, but the Church of England had taken it, and now it stood in Elizabeth's sight as a monument to heresy and division.

She had never seen such a structure. The enormous cathedral towered over the surrounding buildings. Its size and huge, filigreed spires made even Notre Dame seem small by comparison.

Father Sneed must be a man of great importance to merit such a post.

Elizabeth looked down at the tattered, muddy hem that peeked from her new velvet cape and wished she'd taken time to have a new dress made. But that would have meant delaying in Winchester for another day.

As it was, she hadn't reached Winchester until after dark. Alone and unprotected in that strange city, she had wandered for hours, hiding in the shadows when necessary, before finding a decent inn. The proprietor had tried to turn her away at first, sneering at her disheveled state, but a gold sovereign changed his mind. Then he'd ushered her to their best room, where Elizabeth wolfed down a bowl of stew before falling fully dressed across the bed and sleeping until ten the next morning.

It had taken the rest of the following day to find a coach, hire a driver and footman, and rent a team. She'd bought the cloak on impulse after seeing it in the window of a tailor's shop across from the livery stables. But the tailor had had no dresses ready-made.

Now, she self-consciously overlapped the lush fabric of her cloak to conceal her ruined skirts, glad that at least she had taken time to bathe and comb her hair before leaving the inn.

Whatever would Father Sneed think of her?

Would he even believe she was who she said she was? She had no proof, and underneath the fine cloak she looked more like a vagabond than a countess.

The coach rolled to a stop at the entrance of the great cathedral. While she waited for the attendant to open the door, Elizabeth summoned up what was left of her dignity. She exited to the sound of Soot's snorted greeting from behind the coach where he was tied. She made a brief detour to stroke the animal's nose as the coachman hurried up the stairs and opened a small entrance beside the huge, arched doors.

Elizabeth strode up the stairs and into the dim interior of the cathedral. She was halfway down the center aisle when the sexton intercepted her.

"Good afternoon, my lady."

Elizabeth nodded. "Good afternoon. I am looking for Father Sneed."

"Ah. Father Sneed." The sexton's hands curled together at his waist. "And is he expecting milady?"

"No." Careful to keep her cloak closed over her muddy dress, she glared imperiously at him. "Is he here, or isn't he?"

"Oh, he's here, all right." The sexton rolled his eyes as if Father Sneed's mere presence were a source of irritation. "And whom might I say is calling?"

"I am Countess Ravenwold." She paused, unwilling to speak what she must. She forced the words out. "Wife of Viscount Creighton. My . . . husband asked me to find Father

Sneed when I reached Salisbury. It is imperative that I speak with him immediately. Now go and fetch him.''

The sexton eyed her opulent cape. ''Of course, your ladyship. Right away.'' He hurried toward the altar, then cut across the transverse nave to exit through a door at the rear.

While she waited, Elizabeth noted the empty niches and broken stones where Protestant zeal had stripped the interior of its statuary. She was standing there, looking up at the few stained glass windows that had survived the last century, when a voice startled her from close behind.

''So Viscount Creighton has married at last. I've prayed for that.''

She spun around to find her gaze level with dark eyes that glittered bright as buttons in a kind face framed by snow-white hair. ''Father Sneed?''

''At your service.'' He bowed, sending his square clergyman's cap slightly askew on the crown of his head.

''You frightened me.'' Elizabeth placed her hand over her pounding heart. ''I didn't hear you come in.''

''That's because of these.'' Father Sneed hiked up his black cassock to reveal soft leather slippers. He wiggled his toes, his voice dropping. ''The bishop makes us all wear them. He claims it's because he doesn't want anyone disturbed by footsteps. Personally, I think it's so *he* can wear them, and sneak up on us. He's always doing that. But I digress.'' He cocked his head. ''Let me look at you, my child.''

Elizabeth pushed back her hood a bit so he could better see her face.

''You face me squarely. I like that. No false modesty. I hate false modesty.'' He studied her features, nodding in approval. ''A strong chin and resolute mouth. Indicates determination.'' A broad smile caused his cheeks to round like plums. ''You'll need a will of iron, married to Creighton. Takes a firm hand to settle such a man.'' His dark eyes crinkled with affection. ''But, by heaven, you can't help loving the rascal, can you?''

''I've managed, so far,'' Elizabeth said flatly, not taken in by this heretic priest's endearing appearance. She recognized the keen intelligence reflected beneath his shaggy white brows.

''Ummm.'' He pursed his lips, his eyes narrowing. ''The sexton said you had urgent business with me. Might I inquire what brings milady to seek me out?''

Elizabeth glanced nervously at the many niches and shadowed alcoves where someone might be listening. "Perhaps it would be better if we spoke outside."

"Excellent idea." He took her arm and guided her down the aisle, whispering loudly, "That way, the bishop can't sneak up on us."

Once they were out on the broad lawn of the cathedral, he sobered. After motioning her to a walkway that sloped gently toward a small pond, he clasped his hands behind him and walked alongside her. "I sense a great weight upon your shoulders, my child." He glanced briefly askance at her, then down, his steps slow and steady. "What trouble has Viscount Creighton gotten you into?"

Elizabeth hesitated, wondering how much she could safely reveal. She decided to stick to the truth, as much as was prudent. "Creighton and I were married in France. We were returning to my home in Cornwall when some last-minute business delayed us in London. We sent the servants and baggage on ahead, with plans to meet them here, but along the way, we ran into . . . difficulties."

The minister nodded. "These are dangerous times. Until this rebellion settles, an honest man isn't safe in his own front yard, much less on the highways." He looked up in expectation. "What happened?"

"We ended up in the wrong place at the wrong time." Elizabeth's shoulders sagged. "I seem to have quite a knack for that." She forced herself erect. "That's how I came to be married to Creighton—I just happened to be on hand when Prince Charles was looking for a reason to send the viscount packing."

"Mmmm." The priest's mouth flattened. "Still jealous, eh?"

"How did you know?"

"I know Creighton, and I know the prince." He shrugged, the sunlight shining through his snowy mane like a halo. "I had hoped his highness would outgrow such pettiness. After all, it's not always Creighton's fault. But then again . . ." Confronted with Elizabeth's scowl, he steered the conversation away from Creighton's effect on women. "You said you encountered trouble. Is Viscount Creighton all right?"

"I don't know." The remorse in her voice was real. Creighton had risked capture to lead the soldiers away from her. Even now, he might be imprisoned, perhaps tortured. Or dead. "We were separated, and I was forced to go on alone, under the most adverse circumstances."

Father Sneed's features grew grave. "I shall petition Heaven for his safe return."

Elizabeth went on, "As soon as I arrived here, I looked for a place to stay, but the only room available turned out to be in a bad part of town. I don't think it's safe to stay there alone, even with my coachmen guarding the door." She motioned to the center of the city. "My driver has made numerous inquiries in town, but no one has seen or heard anything of Creighton, or the servants and baggage."

A thoughtful expression on his face, the minister repeated, "Creighton."

Despite his benign appearance, she didn't like the way his dark eyes studied her, as if he were analyzing her every word.

Elizabeth wished she could leave. She hated asking anything of anyone, and she particularly hated imposing on a long-ago friendship between Creighton and one of his teachers. Yet she had little choice. Chin up, she faced the priest squarely. "When he saw that there might be trouble, Creighton . . . my husband told me to seek you out if I could not find the servants. He said you could help me locate safe lodgings and provisions for my journey. I have funds"—she looked away, embarrassed by having to discuss such matters with a total stranger—"but no one else to turn to. As I said, I am completely alone."

"Not an ideal circumstance for any lady, especially during this cursed rebellion." Father Sneed regarded her in sympathy. "Never fear. My wife and I live most humbly, but we would be honored if your ladyship would accept our hospitality."

"Thank you, sir," Elizabeth whispered. "I would be most grateful." She hadn't realized just how weary she was until offered the prospect of a safe night's rest.

Then she remembered her dress. "There is one other problem, though." Turning her back to the cathedral, she opened her cloak to reveal the sorry state of her gown. "I'm afraid my journey has taken its toll on my dress, and I have no other."

"Oh, my. I see what you mean." After she shut her cloak, Father Sneed offered her his arm, brightening. "My wife can coax a counterpane from a millsack. She'll be able to come up with something. Never fear. Come along, then. It's not far."

Elizabeth took his arm and walked alongside him toward the coach. "I don't know how to thank you properly for taking me in."

"Nonsense. I'd do the same, even if you weren't Creighton's wife." He cast a look of cheerful appraisal in her direction. "But since you are, please accept my best wishes. You two must make quite a handsome couple."

She steered the conversation away from herself. "You were his teacher?"

"Aye. At Eton." A faraway look came into Father Sneed's eyes. "I'm quite fond of the boy, you know. Liked him from the start, with his angel face and devilish ways. But beneath all that fire and wit, the lad has a heart as big as the world."

Big enough for all the *women* in the world, you mean, Elizabeth thought.

The priest winked. "One could overlook his pranks." He sighed, his smile fading. "Then during his final year, we got word that his father had died." A shadow of remembered grief passed over his features. "I was chosen to tell him." He shook his head. "I've never had a son of my own, but it seemed natural for me to comfort the boy. We became quite close and remained so, even after he had to leave school." His good humor returned. "He writes me often, even after all these years. An exceptional man, your husband. As good as they come."

*As good as they come?* Elizabeth tried to conceal her amazement. Could the man Father Sneed had spoken of in such glowing terms possibly inhabit the same soul and skin as the sly, autocratic manipulator she had married? Creighton was shameless, a self-confessed fornicator! Did all Protestant priests set their expectations so low, or just this one?

The priest pointed across the vast lawn. "Our house is just at the edge of the close. Let's go see what Goodwife Sneed can do about your dress."

# ❧ CHAPTER 14 ❧

*The* next morning Elizabeth had just finished breakfast in bed when a knock sounded at her door. "It's Mistress Sneed, Countess. May I come in? I have milady's dress."

Self-conscious about entertaining her hostess while wearing one of Mistress Sneed's own plain but serviceable nightgowns, Elizabeth pulled the goose down coverlet a little higher on her chest. The movement released a whiff of starched linen into the pleasant, lingering aromas of hot cross buns and mulled cider from her breakfast tray. "Come in. Please."

Mistress Sneed entered with Elizabeth's black dress draped carefully over her arm. After closing the door behind her, she turned, her broad, plain face open with expectation. "Oh, good. I see you're finished eating." She eyed the empty tray. "But perhaps you're still hungry. Shall I have the maid bring more?"

"Oh, no. Thank you." Elizabeth shot a guilty glance at the empty plate. She'd made quite a glutton of herself. Only crumbs remained of the three large buns she'd been served, and she had drunk every sweet, spicy drop of hot apple juice in the ceramic pot. "I'm quite full."

She knew she should have gotten up sooner, but couldn't bring herself to leave the warm, enfolding security of the feather-bed. Bright shards of sunlight peeked from the edges of the heavy brown damask drapes that covered the windows. "What time is it? I was so comfortable, I slept like the dead."

"It's nine o'clock." Mistress Sneed smiled indulgently. "Milady needed her rest, and little wonder, after all milady has been through." She carefully laid Elizabeth's dress across the arms of the Tudor chair by the hearth, then pushed open the window curtains, flooding the room with brilliant spring sunshine. "Ah. Isn't it a lovely day, Countess?"

"Please, call me Lady Elizabeth."

"Very well, Lady Elizabeth." Mistress Sneed's face reflected her pleasure at being granted intimate status with a woman of Elizabeth's rank. "My name is Charity."

"Charity." Elizabeth nodded. "A lovely name. It suits you."

The older woman retrieved the ruined black dress from the chair and held it to the light for inspection. "I'm afraid this is the best I could do," she ventured shyly. "If it doesn't suit, milady could have another made. But even with several seamstresses, that would take at least a day."

Elizabeth stared at the gown in amazement. "Why, if I didn't know better, I would swear you *had* made a new one." The tiny seams that mended the hem all but disappeared in the skirt's folds, and the rich black fabric looked like new. "I thought it was beyond hope, but now no one would ever guess it had been muddy or torn. You've worked a miracle."

"Only God can work miracles, Countess," Mistress Sneed chided gently. She glanced down at her handiwork with satisfaction. "Your dress didn't need a miracle. It just wanted a cold scrubbing, a few repairs, and a careful pressing." She fingered the heavy black fabric. "It's all in the cloth, really. Good, sturdy material like this can survive a few rips and launderings."

Seeing Mistress Sneed in the bright sunlight, Elizabeth realized there were dark circles under her eyes. And she was wearing the same gray dress she'd had on the night before. "You must have worked all night."

Mistress Sneed waved her hand in dismissal. "I'll have plenty of time to catch up on my sleep once you're safely on your way." She laid the dress across the foot of the bed.

Elizabeth still could hardly believe it was the same dress. "You washed it?" She leaned forward and felt the padded bodice. Bone-dry. Her fingers came away smelling faintly of woodsmoke. "The fabric is so heavy. However did you get it dry in so short a time?"

"One of the reverend's contraptions." Mistress Sneed beamed with pride. "A drying box. Hooks up to the fire with four bellows and all sorts of enormous metal tubes. He made such a racket setting it up, I was certain he'd wake you, but he was delighted to have an excuse to use his invention. Once everything was working, all I had to do was keep the fire going while he turned the crank to work the bellows. Your dress dried in only a few hours."

*Only a few hours.* "How ingenious." All that work, after a night of mending and scrubbing. Elizabeth was humbled, indeed, by the Sneeds' hospitality.

Mistress Sneed's silver brows lifted in apprehension. "Unfortunately, milady's blouse was beyond repair." She hesitated before venturing, "One of my daughters was tall, like milady. I saved all her clothes. Her blouses are rather plain, I fear—not as fine as milady's—but perhaps—"

Elizabeth cut short her humble disclaimers with, "I would be honored to wear one of your daughter's blouses. How generous of you to offer it." What had happened to the daughter, she wondered. So many died young. Like Charlotte.

The thought of Charlotte stirred a dull throb of unresolved grief, like the ache of an old wound that had healed on the surface but festered deep within. She looked up at Mistress Sneed. "I shall dress as soon as the blouse is ready."

"Very good." Mistress Sneed picked up the breakfast tray. "My maid is ironing the blouse even now. She'll bring it up and help milady dress." She scanned the room. "Is there anything else I can do?"

"I can't think of a thing." Elizabeth smiled as warmly as she could manage, hoping that her expression didn't look as forced as it felt. She had never smiled easily. "You've already done so much already, taking me into your family, feeding me, staying up all night to repair my dress. Dear Charity, how can I ever thank you?"

"You already have," Mistress Sneed said. *"Lady Elizabeth."*

The borrowed blouse had no lace on its starched collar and cuffs, but Elizabeth was content that the sleeves were long enough and the shoulders did not bind. When she descended the stairs to go shopping with Reverend Sneed—her confidence restored along with her appearance—the priest nodded his approval. He helped her into the velvet cloak, then together they set out to purchase supplies for her journey.

Thanks to his connections in Salisbury, Elizabeth found the

provisions she needed in a matter of hours. She completed her shopping, returned to the Sneeds' for a hearty lunch, and was ready to leave by two o'clock. But when she came downstairs with her bag of medicines, plans took an unexpected turn.

Reverend Sneed was waiting in the entrance hall, hat in hand and tapestry valise at his feet. Mistress Sneed fussed with the fastening of his cloak. "Now don't forget to give Cousin Mary my letter. And the elderberry wine." She turned, meeting Elizabeth's frown of consternation with a serene smile. "All ready, Lady Elizabeth?"

"Yes, but—"

His face calm but resolute, Reverend Sneed put his arm around his wife's shoulders and announced, "Mistress Sneed and I have decided you shouldn't go home alone. I am going with you."

"But it's so dangerous. And your work..." Elizabeth looked into the priest's dark eyes. "Surely you cannot leave on such short notice."

"The bishop has already given his permission. Saw him first thing this morning." In an effort to reassure her, he added, "My absence will cause no great hardship. The cathedral has three other priests, all better men than me."

"Nonsense, Reverend," Mistress Sneed said affectionately, dusting a speck of lint from his cloak. "There are others, indeed, but none better."

The minister gave his wife a look of infinite tenderness. "I'm afraid the rest of the world, my dear, does not share your exalted opinion of my abilities."

"Well, I do," Elizabeth interjected, "and I am deeply grateful for your offer to accompany me, but I cannot allow you to take such a risk." She already had Creighton's fate on her conscience, and possibly Anne's and Gwynneth's. She could not bear for this kind, generous man to risk similar disaster on her account. "There are things I haven't told you." Her right thumb rubbed compulsive circles against the side of her forefinger. "The rebels might be looking for me. They're constantly sending raiding parties into Somerset from Lyme Regis, and into Devon from Plymouth. If the Roundheads should capture me and find out who I am, anyone with me would be tortured."

Both the minister and his wife studied her with curiosity, but she saw no fear in their faces. Reverend Sneed asked,

"Have you committed some crime, then?"

Elizabeth shook her head. "No crime in the eyes of God, but a grave one in the eyes of the rebels."

"Ah." His lips curled inward, then he smiled. "Well, as far as I'm concerned, God is all that matters. Think no more about it."

"But I *must* think about it, and so must you." How could she convince him? "If I should fall into rebel hands, and you with me, I fear that even your priestly office will not protect you."

Reverend Sneed and his wife said as one, "God will protect." Their identical response prompted a chuckle from both of them.

How could they laugh, Elizabeth wondered. Didn't they believe her?

Mistress Sneed covered her husband's hand with her own. "Each of us has prayed about this, Lady Elizabeth, and come to the same conclusion. My husband must accompany you." Seeing the worry in Elizabeth's face, she cocked her head in sympathy. "He goes of his own free will, at God's direction. No matter what happens, God is sovereign. He is in control. We can only obey."

Elizabeth wished she could share Mistress Sneed's unshakable faith, but she couldn't. She had lived with fear so long, she wondered if she had any trust left, even for God.

"We're off, then." Reverend Sneed donned his square clergyman's hat, then picked up his worn tapestry bag.

Mistress Sneed handed him a covered basket redolent of pastries. "Here. Just a few buns and muffins to eat along the way. And some cheese."

"Thank you, my dear." He turned to Elizabeth. "Come along, Countess. We're wasting good traveling light. If we leave right away, we can make Shaftsbury by nightfall. I have a cousin there who will put us up."

"The reverend has cousins everywhere," Mistress Sneed observed wryly. She opened the door to the cool, breezy afternoon. "Godspeed, both of you."

Elizabeth sighed. She realized that even if she argued with the Sneeds till the cows came home, they wouldn't abandon the notion that God wanted the reverend to accompany her. Still, she felt compelled to try one more time. "Father, you know your presence is most welcome, but I must implore you to remain here. Think of the possible consequences, I beg you. I could not bear it if you were to suffer because of me.''

He smiled, shaking his head. ''The matter is settled, Lady Elizabeth. And as always, the consequences will be accounted to God, not to you.''

Resigned, she walked reluctantly toward the doorway. When she reached the threshold, she pressed a cheek to each of Mistress Sneed's. ''Thank you for everything. I promise to do my best to see that Reverend Sneed does not come to harm.''

''Do not trouble yourself. God will be watching over you both. I know it.'' Mistress Sneed shepherded them outside, then waved, calling after them, ''Oh, and Lady Elizabeth, when you stop at Cousin Mary's in Exeter, please remind the reverend to give her my letter. And the elderberry wine.'' She watched them board the coach, then went inside and closed the door. Elizabeth saw no sign of her at the windows as they drove away.

Everything went well for the next four days. Traveling at a reasonable pace from dawn to dusk, they reached Exeter without incident, and the reverend proved to be a wise and entertaining companion.

Mistress Sneed hadn't exaggerated. The reverend's kinsmen were scattered conveniently throughout Somerset and Devon, and all of them were graciously hospitable, regardless of their means. Elizabeth had a room to herself every night, even if it meant that her hosts slept on a pallet by the kitchen hearth.

On the fifth day, Cousin Mary sent them off from Exeter with a reply to Mistress Sneed's letter and a pot of honey in thanks for the elderberry wine. By midmorning, the coach was moving at a bumpy but steady pace along the northern edge of Dartmoor, and Elizabeth had begun to relax at last.

Almost home. Only two more days, and she could stand on the parapet of Castle Ravenwold and look out over the vast Atlantic, the salt wind cold and clean against her face. The ruins of Tintagel would still be there, barely visible as the coastline stretched southwest toward Land's End. Bleak as they were, the towering sea cliffs and wind-scrubbed hills possessed a harsh grandeur that made the works of man seem transient and inconsequential. The land, like Ravenwold Castle, was ancient and worn, but still magnificent. And it was home, where she would be safe.

She only prayed that she would find Gwynneth waiting there, safe as well. And Creighton, of course, though she dreaded thinking what would come next between them.

Elizabeth's thoughts were interrupted by a brutal lurch as the coach speeded up on the bumpy road.

The reverend frowned. "Why do you suppose he's going so fast? I told him not to toss us about unnecessarily." He stood up, pushed open the trapdoor, and stuck his head through it, struggling to keep his balance in the careening coach.

Elizabeth couldn't make out what he was shouting for the rumble of the coach, but she experienced a sickening sense of *déjà vu*. She grasped the windowsill and pulled herself over to look outside. Endless and spare, the rolling terrain of Dartmoor stretched southward to the horizon uninterrupted by fence, forest, or homestead. This was the land of the Gubbings, outcasts so wild and lawless that for more than a hundred years, mothers from Land's End to Taunton had threatened their wandering children with, "The Gubbings will get you!"

*Please, dear God, don't let it be the Gubbings!* Elizabeth had heard horrible tales of the fate suffered by women who fell into their hands. The brutes held nothing sacred.

Reverend Sneed lowered himself back into the compartment and closed the trapdoor, his face grave.

"Is it the Gubbings?" she asked.

He shook his head. "Rebels, or highwaymen dressed as rebels. Either way, we're in deep trouble. It was hard to see clearly with the coach bolting about, but I counted more than twenty of them, and they seem to be well-armed."

Rebels! Her worst fears, realized. Elizabeth's mind raced. Mounted rebels could easily overtake the coach, unless their horses were exhausted. "How fast were they going?"

"Full gallop, and gaining steadily."

She had to do something. She would *not* allow Reverend Sneed to come to harm because of her. Elizabeth stood up abruptly, forcing the trapdoor open. Directly in front of her, the driver was whipping the horses mercilessly while the coachmen watched the troops approach. Neither acknowledged her presence.

Elizabeth shouted, "Driver! When we reach the crest of the next hill, start slowing the coach! I must jump out at the bottom of the grade! Do you hear me? Driver!" He glanced back briefly, prompting her to repeat, "Slow the coach as soon as we clear the next hill! I have to jump out!''

The rebels wouldn't be able to see them. Once she was out of the coach, surely she would be able to find a place to hide. Behind a bush, in a gully, anywhere. The coach could go on without her, and Reverend Sneed would, at worst, be taken to exchange for rebel prisoners. As long as she was not with him, he would be safer.

The driver glanced back at her, his features contorted by effort and fear. ''Slow down? But, milady, they'll catch us even sooner if we—''

Elizabeth cut him off, shouting at the top of her lungs, ''Do as I ordered! If the rebels find out who I am, we'll *all* be tortured!'' When she saw understanding dawn in the driver's eyes, she went on, ''As soon as I've jumped clear, you can speed up again. By the time they overtake you, I'll be deep in the moors. Tell them you were engaged by the reverend, to take him to . . .'' Elizabeth ducked back into the compartment. ''Reverend, do you know anyone near Bude?''

Surprised, he nodded briskly. ''Yes. Willem Broderick, second cousin once removed. He has a—''

Elizabeth didn't wait to hear the rest. She popped back up and cried, ''If the rebels catch up to you, tell them you're taking the reverend to Bude. Bude! If you value your life, do not mention me!''

The driver nodded grimly. ''Bude, it is. And I never saw ye.''

The coachman protested, ''But milady can't jump out here! What about the Gubbings?''

''I'll have to take my chances. It's the only way!'' Elizabeth looked back to see that the soldiers were getting dangerously close—less than a mile behind them, and gaining. Fortunately, the road crested just ahead, then dropped out of sight. She called to the driver, ''Start braking when we clear that ridge. I'll jump out as soon as you've slowed the coach enough. Then whip the horses away.''

She dropped back into the compartment and hastily gathered her medicine bag, securing it once again over her shoulder. ''Reverend, I must leave the coach. For all our sakes.''

Instead of arguing with her as she would have expected, he handed over a neatly tied kerchief full of food. ''Take this, then. It's from the basket. When everything is resolved, I will come back and search for you.''

"No." The coach was slowing now, its iron-shod wheels screeching against the wooden brakes like a soul in hell. Elizabeth made sure her cloak was firmly fastened and her medicine snugly seated. Gripping the food in her left hand, she slid toward the door. "As soon as you can, go to Castle Ravenwold or send them word. My people there know the moors. Organize a search party and send them back for me. Then return to your precious wife."

"Not before we find you. I couldn't—"

"Please do as I ask," Elizabeth interrupted, her voice thick with emotion. "I promised Charity I'd keep you safe."

She heard the driver shouting "whoa" over and over again above the screaming brakes and shuddering harnesses. Elizabeth gripped the door-catch. "Thank you, Reverend. May God protect you."

"And you, my child." He was making the sign of the cross when she leapt out of the coach.

"You don't know where she is?" Garrett stared at his old schoolmaster in disbelief.

Gwynneth had summoned him with shouts of joy when the coach was spotted, but now she stood behind him in the bailey and burst into tears. "Oh, woe! My precious mistress! First that beast Ravenwold, and now this!"

Garrett pivoted. "Ravenwold? What are you talking about?"

"He was a monster, that one," Gwynneth wailed. "Beat my poor lady half to death, he did, and more than once, I can tell you. Broke her ribs. Smashed her face. Blacked her eyes. She's endured enough sufferin' for one lifetime! Why would the Lord let her be lost?"

"Ravenwold beat her?" Appalled, Garrett began to understand far more than he wanted to. "But why?"

"Because she was barren. As if she'd done it to spite him." Gwynneth spat on the ground, her anguished tears turning bitter. "May his soul rot in hell for it."

Shaken, Garrett realized why his strength and stature had caused Bess to fear him. And why she had been afraid of coupling ... and its aftermath. Suddenly everything made sense. No wonder Bess had danced on Ravenwold's grave! "Dear Heaven," he breathed. "If only I had known."

He stepped back and absently put a comforting arm around

the wailing maid. "Hush, Gwynneth. Calm yourself." There
would be time, later, to sort out this shocking revelation. For
now, he had to find out where his wife was. "How can I hear
what's happened to Bess with you carrying on that way?"
Gwynneth's sobs abated. Seeing Reverend Sneed's troubled
expression, Garrett felt an odd tightness thread through his
insides. It took something dire, indeed, to rob the reverend of
his composure. "Reverend Sneed is our guest," he said in a
soothing tone. "I'm sure your mistress wouldn't want us to
forget our manners." He pointed Gwynneth toward the kitchens and gave her a gentle nudge. "Please have some blankets
and mulled wine brought into the great hall immediately."

Gwynneth curtsied, her eyes still glazed with tears. "Yes,
milord. Right away." She headed for the servant's entrance,
her progress interrupted by several apprehensive backward
glances.

"Come," he said to the minister. "We can talk by the fire."
The old man appeared to be exhausted in spirit as well as body.
"You look like you could use a drink." He waited until Reverend Sneed was bundled in a comfortable chair at the hearth
and given a mug of hot mulled wine before he asked, "How
bad is it?"

"I wish I knew." Reverend Sneed's piercing eyes angled
up at Garrett. "It happened along the northern edge of Dartmoor. We were chased by a pack of Roundheads, probably a
raiding party." He cupped the mug tightly in both hands.
"Lady Elizabeth feared they would torture us all if they discovered who she was, so she waited until the rebels couldn't
see us and jumped from the coach."

"Jumped from the coach? Has the woman lost her mind?"
Garrett raked his fingers through the fine hair at his temples.
"Where in perdition would she get an idea like . . ." He
halted, recalling how he had jumped from the coach near Tilbury. "Mmph. So she jumped from the coach. How fast was
it going? Was she hurt?"

Sneed shook his head. "Not fast. She'd ordered the driver
to slow down as soon as we crested a hill. Very clever, her
ladyship." Sneed's knuckles whitened. "I saw her roll onto
the verge, then scramble away toward the moor. I don't think
she was hurt." His kind face crumpled with regret. "I only
glanced away for a moment, to see if the soldiers were coming,
but when I looked back, she was gone."

"So the soldiers didn't see her?"

"No. They kept after us, just as the countess said they would. We managed to get several miles down the road before they overtook us. They did us no harm. Just ransacked the coach and threatened to take us prisoner.".

"But you're here." Garrett paced the hearth, impatient to know everything. "How did you get them to release you?"

"I didn't. A large force of Royal cavaliers appeared from the east and frightened them away. Deus ex machina, quite literally." He looked sheepish. "I should say, Divine Providence." Reverend Sneed took a deep draught of the mulled wine. "The cavaliers were escorting a shipment of arms from Taunton to Lostwithiel. When I told them what had happened, their commander assigned as many men as he could spare to go back and help me search for Lady Elizabeth. Ten of us looked for hours, on foot and horseback, but there was no sign of her."

"Damn." Garrett placed his palms against the massive stone mantel and gazed unseeing into the fire. "Dartmoor, of all places." If the rebels hadn't found Bess, the Gubbings probably would. He didn't know which would be worse for her—to be "interrogated" by the rebels or used and abused by the Gubbings. A subtle shiver passed through him at the thought.

He'd once seen a gentleborn lady who had been ransomed from the Gubbings' clutches. The poor creature had returned a madwoman, never uttering another sound except to shriek and cower at any loud noise. Everyone at Court had whispered behind their hands about it; Garrett had wondered at the time if it wouldn't have been kinder to let the outlaws kill her.

"Is it true?" Reverend Sneed asked. "Would the rebels have tortured us all if they'd discovered Lady Elizabeth's identity?"

"Probably." If only Bess hadn't jumped from the coach . . . But then again, she couldn't have counted on rescue.

"Torture." The minister said the word as if he'd never heard it before. "But why? Can you tell me?"

"Only if I do so under pastoral privilege."

"Then I shall hear you as your pastor."

Garrett pulled up a chair from the far side of the hearth and sat down, his forearms braced atop his thighs. He dropped his voice to a murmur. "I came back to England to help Prince

James escape. I had no intention of involving my wife, but she got mixed up in things anyway. We managed to get the prince out of the country and were on our way back to Cornwall when we were separated. By now, I'm certain Cromwell has discovered our involvement in the escape. He'd relish the chance to rack me, my wife, or anyone who's helped either of us." His hands twisted against each other. "Poor Bess. I never should have left her. None of this would have happened if we'd been together. We could have—"

"I'm sure you had good reason to leave her," Reverend Sneed interrupted. "Who's to say what might have happened if you hadn't? *Both* of you might have been captured by the rebels. As it is, we can hope that Lady Elizabeth is hiding on the moor. A little cold, perhaps, but she has food and a warm cloak." He leaned forward. "Thanks be to God, you can organize a search party to look for her. She told me her people know the moors. They will help you." He gave Garrett's shoulder a consoling shake, then sat back. "If the rebels have her, I know you will do whatever you can to free her. But if the outlaws have taken her, you must pay the ransom and restore her. She's your wife. You owe her that much."

"Yes." Garrett inhaled deeply. "Well, in the strictest sense, she's not my wife."

"What do you mean, boy? You were married, weren't you?"

"Oh, aye. We were married right enough, by an Anglican bishop, with Prince Charles as witness." He looked up at the man who had been like a father to him since his own father's death. Seeing the patience in that kind face, Garrett dropped his defenses and spoke the truth. "But the union was never consummated."

"Why?" Reverend Sneed's question was characteristically direct, but gentle.

"She is a papist and did not want the marriage, yet neither of us had a choice. Prince Charles insisted, threatening her with imprisonment and worse if she did not go along." He looked down at the golden signet ring that bore the unicorn and three stars of the Creighton coat of arms. "I didn't even give her a wedding ring." His eyes leveled with Sneed's glittering dark stare. "Prince Charles provided one of his, instead."

"I asked you one question, yet you answered another." As

always, Sneed went straight for the heart of the matter. "You told me how and why you married, but not why this union has yet to be consummated."

"She fears me, though I have never given her cause." He looked up. "God knows, she had good reason, though those reasons had nothing to do with me. You heard what her late husband did to her." Garrett faltered. "I tried to be patient, to give her time. But whenever I touched her, she reacted like a trapped animal. Now I know why."

"She should have told you."

"I'm sure she was afraid to." Garrett shook his head. "We were strangers. How could she know I was any better?" If only he had known . . .

"Now that you have the truth, you can put things to rights." Reverend Sneed leaned back. "Frankly, I'm surprised you allowed her to refuse you for so long. A lesser man would have taken what was his by rights, regardless. I commend your patience."

"To tell the truth, I had no idea it would take so long to thaw her out." Garrett spread his fingers. "Vain, wasn't I?"

Reverend Sneed said nothing.

"Patience had little to do with it, actually," Garrett confessed. "At first, we had no opportunity to be alone. His highness packed us off for England under armed guard before the ink was dry on the marriage contract. We had little privacy. Then, when we finally reached my town house in London, Bess locked herself in her room every night." He shrugged. "I was working around the clock to help arrange the prince's escape, so I decided not to press the issue." He leaned back in his chair, suddenly weary. "And then, there's always the matter of her faith."

"Ah, yes. She told me she was Roman. Seems devout." Reverend Sneed cocked his head, looking for all the world like some snowy-plumed exotic bird. "She won't consider converting?"

"No more than I would."

"I thought you disdained religion . . . papist *or* Protestant."

"I've little use for religion, sir, but faith . . . ? Faith is another matter." Garrett looked at him frankly, glad for the trust that enabled him to speak his mind in safety. "Do not mistake me: I have no love for the corruptions of Rome. But the travesties England has condoned in the name of reform . . ." He shuddered at the memory of that cold day in January, six years ago at Tyburn. "Bartholomew Roe was a friend of mine, as good a man as ever I have known. I watched him die—hanged, disemboweled, and hacked to pieces, and for what? Because he was a *papist* priest who ministered to the poor, Catholic and Protestant alike!" Garrett's features hardened. "You will forgive me if I want no part of such reform."

Father Sneed considered him closely. "Does it matter to you, that Lady Elizabeth is papist?"

"It matters little to me from a spiritual standpoint, but very much from a practical one." The conversation was getting uncomfortably intense. Garrett stood up and stepped closer to the fire. The drafts of Ravenwold Castle haunted him like ghosts, driving him to the hearth in every cold, threadbare room. No wonder Bess was so cold-blooded.

Gwynneth's voice echoed in the cavernous hall. "Master?"

Glad for the interruption, Garrett turned. "Aye. Come."

The maid approached, a worried look on her tearstained face. "There's a blind man at the door—a beggar, one I've never seen before."

"What does he want?"

"He says he has word of my lady."

Reverend Sneed sat forward, alert.

"Bring him to me," Garrett instructed.

Gwynneth nodded, then hurried away. In a few moments, she returned guiding a ragged, filthy, crippled old man whose useless eyes were hazed white, giving him a spectral appearance. At Gwynneth's urging, the beggar hobbled to within a few feet of the hearth.

"Leave us," Garrett ordered. He studied the smelly, toothless man. "Speak."

His head waving like a hound scenting the wind, the beggar rasped out, "I bring word of the lady. The Gubbings have her." He paused, fumbling in his shirt. "Here. They gave me proof." He pulled out Bess's precious velvet bag, empty. "This is hers, aye?"

A jolt of rage and anguish shot through Garrett.

The beggar held the empty bag at arm's length. "I was sent to tell milord that for a hundred pounds, they will free her. For two hundred, they will kill her."

"Dear God." Reverend Sneed closed his eyes and crossed himself.

With superhuman strength, Garrett gripped the rags at the beggar's chest and jerked the man from his feet. Nose to nose with the disgusting creature, he growled, "If they have harmed her, I swear I'll see every one of them hunted down and hanged, and you with them."

"Mercy, my lord!" The beggar wagged his head in agitation, his legs flailing. The velvet bag fell to the floor. "They took my son, made me come here! If I did not deliver this message, they said they'd kill him. Mercy."

Pulse thundering in his ears, Garrett lowered the man to his feet. "What are the terms of the ransom?"

The old man backed away a few steps, bumping into Garrett's chair. His hands fluttered over the obstruction, then he stepped clear. "Give the money to me. They're watching me. Said they'd return my son if I brought them the ransom without being followed."

Garrett thanked Heaven and all the stars for the small fortune he had withdrawn from his bank in London and sent along with the baggage wagons. He turned toward the kitchens and ordered, "Gwynneth! Fetch the bailiff!" The unexpected shout caused both Reverend Sneed and the beggar to flinch. He turned back to the messenger, his tone now deadly calm. "All right. Once you deliver the money, then what?"

"If milord wants his lady back, then he's to go to the old snag at the middle of Dartmoor, three day's hence. He'll find the lady there."

Gwynneth appeared with Will Goodshire, the bailiff. "Here's Will, sir."

Garrett knew both of them had been listening from the shadows. He nodded to the maid. "Take this beggar to the kitchens and see that he's fed. And give him some decent clothes. But not one word to any of the servants about the Gubbings, or the ransom. Your lady's blood will be on your hands if this becomes a matter of gossip."

Gwynneth went white. "Milord knows I would never cause harm to my lady." She grasped the beggar's arm and pulled him none too gently toward the kitchen. "I will tell the others only that he is a beggar, fed by milord's charity, nothing more."

Garrett picked up the velvet bag and approached the bailiff. Just this morning, nervous and restless about Bess's absence, he'd asked Will to bring the ledgers. Reading through them, he'd been alternately appalled by Bess's poverty and impressed by the bailiff's faithful administration. In Bess's absence, Will Goodshire's able management of her meager funds and needy tenants had more than proved his loyalty. Garrett knew he could trust the man to handle the ransom properly. He handed over the empty bag, instructing quietly, "Take a hundred pounds from the strongbox that came with the baggage wagons and put it in this bag. When the beggar reaches the outer gate, slip him the bag. Watch to see that he's safely on his way, but tell no one about the ransom. Countess Ravenwold's life may depend on your discretion."

Will nodded gravely. "Aye, my lord." He hastened away to the keep's treasury.

Garrett strode back to the hearth. He paced its length over and over again, then stopped, leaning against the mantel with his eyes closed. "Dear God. If they use her, rape her . . ." How could any woman recover from that, much less Bess, after what she'd suffered at Ravenwold's hands? She'd never be able to trust anyone again.

Reverend Sneed's voice sounded over the crackle of the flames. "We must pray for her safety and her deliverance. But regardless of the outcome, we must praise God, to release the power of His Spirit in the midst of this terrible darkness."

Garrett pushed back, staring at his old mentor. "Praise God? I hardly think this situation worthy of praise, sir."

Reverend Sneed met his look of accusation with maddening resignation. "The ways of God are not the ways of a man. We may not understand why He has allowed this, but God is sovereign. We must trust Him."

"Trust Him, if you wish." Garrett drew his pistol. "I'll put my trust in this."

# ❧ CHAPTER 15 ❧

*That* night, wind and rain spawned moaning drafts that licked through Garrett's chamber like invisible spirits, pulling the candle flames in an erratic dance, but he did not retreat to the warmth of his bed. He had spent the afternoon preparing an assortment of firearms for Will to hide away in the coach; now he stayed up late cleaning his own pistols and carbine. It made him feel better to look down the hollow shaft of each bore and imagine his wife's captors on the other end. When the steel shone to a dull luster and the wooden stocks gleamed, he reassembled each weapon, measured in the powder, wrapped his bullets in scraps of greased rag, then shoved the shot down each barrel.

That chore done, he got out his whetstone and sat by the fire, pushing short, angry strokes down the side of his saber until the edge was sharp enough to split a hair. Only when all was ready did he crawl into bed. There he lay in the darkness, listening to the wind and rain and trying not to think of what was happening to Bess. Yet hard as he tried, he could not shut out the images of coarse hands ripping away her clothes to expose her flesh, and filthy mouths plundering her body.

He slept only fitfully.

The dark bedchamber had lightened almost imperceptibly when he gave up trying to rest. The rain had stopped, at least. Not wanting to hear the sound of another voice, he rose and dressed alone. Methodically, he donned his uniform: First came his breeches, then his boots, chamois shirt, neckerchief, gorget, and buff suede coat. Next, Garrett wrapped his scarlet sash around him, buckled his scabbard just below it, and fastened his carbine belt across his chest. Only then did he thrust his saber into its sheath, shove his pistols behind his sash, and slide the loaded carbine into its sling. If he was walking into a death trap, he had every intention of taking down a few of the Gubbings with him.

Garrett pulled his scarlet cassack across his shoulders, glad for its warmth. Ravenwold Castle was cold enough to make the fires of hell seem welcome. Scooping up his hat and gauntlets, he headed for the treacherous open stairway that clung to one wall of the great hall. The castle was silent except for a distant, reassuring stir from the kitchen. On his way down to eat, he was surprised to see light coming from the chapel doorway. He altered his path in that direction, just as he had that fateful night three years ago, but this time he did not peer into the chapel from behind the door. Now master of this house, he walked in to find Reverend Sneed on his knees before the papist crucifix. Every candle in the place was lit, burned down to almost nothing. Garrett could feel the stone floor's chill through his boots and stockings. It must be cold, indeed, beneath the old man's knees. "Reverend?"

The minister crossed himself, then looked over his shoulder. "Ah. Creighton." He glanced up at the pale gray light that filtered through leaded windows decorated with medieval images of the saints. "Dawn already?" Reverend Sneed extended a hand toward Garrett. "I cannot rise without assistance. Time passes quickly in earnest prayer, but my old bones punish me afterward."

Garrett helped the old man to his feet. "How long have you been here?"

"I never went to bed. I was praying for Countess Ravenwold. And for you." Reverend Sneed leaned heavily on Garrett's arm and stretched the stiffness from his legs. "Come. I'll keep you company while you break your fast. I know you're anxious to be on your way." He hobbled alongside Garrett toward the kitchen. "You do well to make an early start. It might take every bit of three days to reach that snag."

When they entered the kitchen, they found the servants up and busy with the myriad chores that started every day in a great house.

Garrett scandalized the help by insisting that he and Reverend Sneed be served their breakfast at a worktable near the kitchen's enormous fireplace. His presence made the cooks so nervous they could hardly work for looking at him, but Garrett didn't care. The kitchen was the only island of life and warmth in this cold, drafty castle.

He and the minister had just finished a rasher of bacon and bowls of porridge rich with cream when one of the grooms approached them. The boy bowed to Garrett. "I've saddled the strongest warhorse, milord, as ye asked." He looked up, his young face apprehensive. "But the stallion bain't rid proper lately. The onliest groom who could ride 'im was tooken two weeks ago fer the king's army. I fear the beast is fair wild."

"You needn't worry, boy." The horse hadn't been born that Garrett couldn't ride. "Is the small coach ready, and the team?"

"Aye, sir, and Will set to drive it." The boy hesitated, obviously perplexed that Garrett would choose the bailiff to drive the coach when there were others of lower station far more qualified.

Garrett stood. "Fetch my horse, then." He turned to Reverend Sneed, extending his hand for a vigorous farewell shake. "Thank you for everything." Donning his leather gauntlets, he told his old friend, "The coach you came in is yours to keep. Please accept it with my gratitude. I've paid the driver and coachmen to take you back to Salisbury as soon as you're ready." He picked up his hat. "I hope you will return home right away."

Reverend Sneed nodded. "I shall, but only because the countess asked it. I'd rather go with you." He leveled a piercing gaze at Garrett. "Lady Elizabeth is an exceptional woman, Creighton—intelligent, resourceful, brave, self-sacrificing . . . Regardless of the irregularities of your marriage, you are fortunate to have married her."

"Fortunate?" Garrett smiled at the irony of such a statement. Glad that no servants were close enough to overhear, he confided, "Perhaps after I've *had* her as my wife, as you so aptly put it, I'll agree with you. Until then, I shall reserve judgment."

The minister shook his head in disapproval. "I would chide you for such talk, but I know it would be a waste of breath."

"I am as I have always been, sir. The same yesterday, today, and tomorrow." Garrett donned his hat. "And now, my friend, I am off to rescue my brave, intelligent, resourceful wife."

The minister made the sign of the cross. "May God go with you."

Exiting the kitchen, Garrett noticed that all the servants seemed to have disappeared. He wondered where they'd gone, but when he strode into the bailey, he found out.

They were waiting for him, cloaked and silent, behind the groom who held Ravenwold's huge chestnut war stallion. Some of the servants carried pitchforks, some staves, some only their meager provisions, but every member of the castle's staff stood ready to travel. And with them were at least seventy others, obviously Bess's tenants, all of them marked by famine—old men whose feet were bound in rags; women standing flushed and defiant, their ragged shawls knotted across their bosoms; young boys awkward with the first signs of manhood.

No one said a word. They all just looked at him, silently declaring their loyalty to Bess by the set of their postures and the resolution in their sunken eyes. Garrett could see from their faces that their mistress's welfare was a matter of personal concern to every one.

Garrett doubted his own tenants would come to his aid so readily; he'd been away from Chestwick too long. A sudden pang of homesickness disquieted him.

A haggard woman stepped forward, trailing a flock of thin, dirty children, her hand on the shoulder of a lad who couldn't be more than ten. She halted in front of Garrett and curtsied. "G'mornin' yer lordship. I'm the Widow Edmunson. We heered our lady was lost, and we all come to help." She pushed the boy forward. "This is Tannie, me eldest. He's a strong lad and can run very fast." She pulled her thin shawl tighter against the dawn mist. "I'd go meself, but I been sick. Be dead and burried, but for 'er ladyship. An angel, 'er ladyship is, God's own angel, cleanin' and cookin' and lookin' after me all those months so these younguns bain't motherless."

Bess, cleaning and cooking for peasants?

Mistress Edmunson swiped at the shock of dirty hair on her son's forehead. "Now you mind his lordship, Tannie, and don't make him ask ye twice. It's fer our lady, God love 'er, so do yer best." She urged the lad toward Garrett. "Off with ye."

Garrett's glibness deserted him. Now he understood with wrenching clarity why Bess rarely smiled. For years, she'd been struggling to keep these people from starvation while her husband squandered his birthright. Seeing Bess through the eyes of her tenants, he gained a new perspective on his wife— a woman who went without so others could eat; highborn, yet humble enough to do menial work helping the least of those who looked to her for protection.

A surge of unexpected emotion made it difficult to speak. Garrett cleared his throat, then said, "As master of Ravenwold, I am deeply touched by your loyalty to the countess." How much should he tell them? "Your lady will be most gratified to hear how readily you came to her aid, but happily, there is no longer any need. I know where she is and have made arrangements to bring her back."

A murmur of speculation rumbled through the crowd.

"I shall not rest until she is safe," he vowed.

While the tenants discussed this latest revelation, Garrett turned to Gwynneth. "Find out from Will where he keeps the strongbox and fetch it, then go tell Cook to prepare food for everyone here. While they're eating, take ten pence from the strongbox for every man, woman, and child present. Hand the money out as they leave, and tell them that their privation is at an end."

"Very generous, your lordship," Gwynneth murmured, frowning, "but if we feed all these folk, however will we manage afterward? There's precious little left in the storehouse, certainly not enough to last till harvest, and—"

"Gwynneth, I have plenty of money, even with the war. No one need go hungry here again, not as long as I possess the means to prevent it." He scanned the ragtag collection of servants and tenants. "Now run along and do as I asked. Will and I must be on our way."

As Gwynneth hurried toward the coach to carry out Garrett's orders, Tannie sidled up shyly and bowed. "I know yer lordship said there bain't no need fer 'elp, but I'd like to go along, just the same. I could rub down the 'orses and gather wood, and maybe even carry a message, if there's call." He shot an anxious glance at his mother. "Please, master. Ma'll have a fit if yer lordship don't let me come."

Impressed by Tannie's initiative, Garrett nodded. "Very well." The lad might come in handy. "Climb up onto the coach beside Will." Then he raised his hands to quiet the crowd. "Good people of Ravenwold!" The buzz of conver-

sation subsided. "I've given instructions for food to be prepared. Her ladyship and I would be honored if all of you would
accept our hospitality, along with a small token of our gratitude." He looked up at the gray clouds overhead, then back
to the tenants. "Please, go inside and warm yourselves by the
fire." While the murmuring tenants filed into the castle, Garrett
mounted the enormous golden stallion and turned it toward the
gate. Motioning for the coach to follow, he spurred his horse
for Dartmoor.

The trip back to the moor proved difficult. Last night's rain
had turned the road into a quagmire. The coach got stuck more
than a dozen times, making it necessary for Garrett to dismount every few miles and help Will and Tannie free the
wheels. By the time they reached the northwestern boundary
of the great moor, two days had passed and all three weary
travelers were covered in mud.

Garrett reined his horse to a halt at the edge of the moor
and peered through the moisture-fogged air. When the coach
pulled alongside, he pointed out a distant rise barely visible
above the mists. "What's that?"

Will stood for a better look. "High Willhays. On a clear
day, yer lordship could see most of the moor from there, but
I doubt a body could see more than mist in this weather." He
looked up at the low clouds blowing in from the north Atlantic.
"Might rain again, though. That should clear the air, but
there's little use settin' out until it does." He cocked his head
toward the bleak, shrouded landscape. "I've hunted these
moors since I was a boy, but I wouldn't risk goin' in with this
fog and no sun to reckon by. Too easy to get lost. A body
could wander around fer days, gettin' nowhere."

The stallion snorted and skittered sideways, sensing Garrett's tension. Then a drop of rain hit Garrett's shoulder, and
another. Soon, a steady drizzle was rinsing the air of fog. Garrett adjusted the broad brim of his hat to channel the runoff
away from his back. "Wait here. And keep those pistols I gave
you cocked and ready. God willing, I'll be back with Countess
Ravenwold by this time on the morrow." He spurred his horse
into the moor.

After three hours of careful travel, he reached the crest of
High Willhays. The rain had stopped, and spread out before
him was the vast, rolling expanse of the moor, its drab brown

surface brightened by patches of fresh spring growth. Garrett looked southeast toward the heart of the moor.

Then he saw it, a lone projection atop a hummock on the horizon.

The snag. It had to be.

He urged his mount down the far side of the hill, his progress slowed by the unfamiliar terrain. Mist had began to collect in the low-lying areas, sometimes obscuring his view of the snag, but by dusk, Garrett reached the bleached, hollow tree trunk.

Bess wasn't there.

He hadn't really expected her to be—not yet, anyway—but he felt a sharp pang of disappointment when he didn't find her.

Cold and weary, he tied the stallion to a broken branch of the snag, then ate a hasty meal of dried chine and cold biscuits from his saddlebag, washed down with beer. Soon, the light began to fade. He shivered from more than the damp. The Gubbings were watching him. He could feel it, but the quiet of the moor was broken only by the wind.

Wrapping his cloak tight against the night chill, Garrett settled next to a thicket and waited. Above him, the cloud cover began to break up, revealing an irregular, shifting pattern of starry sky. He tried to stay alert, yet dozed off several times, only to wake to the unnatural silence that follows a disturbance in the wild. Each time, he crept through the darkness to the tree, but there was no sign of Bess or the Gubbings.

The last time he nodded off was just before sunrise. He wakened in the silvery predawn light to the muted sound of something moving on the moor. A fog had risen, so thick he could only see a few feet in front of him. He stood up and cautiously approached the snag.

Bess was there, bound to the tree, her head slack, a tangled fall of blond hair concealing her face. The red velvet bag hung heavily from her neck.

His heart pounding, Garrett approached her prepared for the worst. Gently, he lifted her chin and smoothed back the snarl of golden curls. What he saw caused a sharp intake of breath.

Her once-shapely lips were split and swollen, her fine ivory skin bruised. The front of her blouse had been torn away, revealing more dark bruises above her bodice. But she was alive. A strong pulse beat in her throat, and her breathing was

slow and regular. "Thank God." Garret put his arms around
her and leaned close, inhaling the faint, distinctive sweetness
that lingered despite the filth of her ordeal. His shoulders
sagged with a release of tension so profound he could scarcely
stand. Then he straightened. They weren't out of danger yet.

First, he had to get that cursed bag off her neck. He carefully
lifted off the silken cords. The weight of the bag surprised
him, and when he removed it, he heard the unmistakable clink
of coins. He opened it to find most, if not all, of the ransom.

A coarse female voice called from the fog, "For our children!"

Another voice, this one male, bellowed, "Take 'er, and
good riddance!" followed by the muffled thunder of retreating
hoofbeats.

Instantly alert, Garrett shielded Bess with his body, but after
the hoofbeats died away, he heard nothing more. They were
alone.

He stuffed the bag of gold into his sash. Why had the Gubbings returned the ransom? They were infamous for their
greed, never letting so much as a farthing slip between their
fingers.

He drew his dagger, anxious to be away from this eerie
place. Bracing his wife's unconscious form with his own body,
he cut the ropes that held her upright. She fell against him,
dead weight, and he scooped her into his arms.

Garrett put his stubbled cheek on hers and whispered
hoarsely, "It's all right, precious girl. You're safe now." Her
skin felt cold and inert against his own warm flesh. He tried
not to think what they might have done to her.

A dark speck leapt from her hair to his cloak, and another.
Garrett felt something moving on his neck. Fleas! She was
probably crawling with them—and God knew what else—after
several days with the Gubbings. He would deal with that later.
For now, he had to get her home to safety. Garrett carried her
to his horse and laid her as gently as he could across the saddle
before mounting and gathering her against him.

How long would she remain this way, he wondered, and
what remembered horrors would she wake to?

Morning sun had burned away almost all of the fog by the
time the stallion bore him and his still-unconscious wife past
High Willhays. Moving rapidly now thanks to the brilliant sun-

light, Garrett neared the road in a fraction of the time it had taken him to pick his way across the moor the evening before.

He saw smoke ahead and prayed it was Will's campfire. Cresting the last rise, he was gratified to find Will and Tannie huddled next to the coach, a small peat fire smoldering nearby. Garrett urged his mount down the hill. At the sight of him, the two servants jumped up and ran forward.

Will's expression was bleak when he saw his mistress's condition. "You've found her, then." His eyes searched Garrett's. "Is she dead?"

"She's alive, but unconscious." Garrett halted his horse beside the fire. "I don't know what's wrong. She hasn't stirred since I found her. Take her gently." He lowered her into their ready hands, then dismounted. "Here. Give her to me." Unwilling to surrender her even for a short while, he gathered her back into his arms. "Bring us some blankets. She's cold as stone."

It wasn't easy, but with much shifting and squeezing, he managed to get himself and Bess into the coach. Cradling her against him, he sank into the seat. A dozen flea bites deviled him, but he did not abandon his hold on Bess to scratch them. Fleas were the least of his worries.

Will appeared with two thick woolen blankets. While the bailiff tucked them around his unconscious mistress, Garrett asked, "Anything happen while I was gone?"

"Aye, milord." Will perched on the opposite seat. "Bad news, I'm afraid. A company of Cavaliers saw us and stopped. They almost took Tannie for the army, but I was able to talk 'em out of it. Told 'em milord would be fair angry if they took your servant, you bein' a colonel and all, so they let Tannie go."

"What were they doing out here?"

"Huntin' rebels. Seems there's a raidin' party from Plymouth on the loose somewhere between here and Bude. The soldiers said we shouldn't go home that way."

"There is no other way," Garrett said wearily. How in perdition was he supposed to get Bess back to Ravenwold?

Then it occurred to him that he might not want to. The castle was cold as a grave digger's shovel and had no proper doctor, not to mention the pall of gloom that seemed to hover over the place. Why go back to Ravenwold at all? Exeter was closer. With the ransom money, Garrett could easily engage a doctor, rent decent lodgings, and have clothing made. Then, as soon as Bess was able to travel, he would take her home to Chestwick.

He should have taken her there in the first place, but he hadn't wanted his family to see how his wife scorned and despised him. He was beyond such vanity, now. If the Gubbings had used her, Bess would need help to heal—the kind of help no man could give, but his mother and sisters could.

Garrett gazed down at the battered creature in his arms. The dark bruises on her fair skin contrasted starkly with her golden lashes and tumbled curls, giving her the look of a broken angel. Was this the way she'd looked after Ravenwold had beaten her? "Wake up, Bess," he urged, his voice thick with remorse. "Open your eyes. It's Garrett." He shook her gently, praying for some spark of life to prove her spirit still survived. But there was no sign. She lay unresisting in his arms.

"Oh, Bess," he breathed, "I'm so sorry. But it's over, now. You're safe." He rocked her close against him, feeling a deep, possessive tug for the first time since they had married. She was his, for better or for worse.

He couldn't consider asking for an annulment, not after the disgrace and abuse she had suffered because he had left her unprotected. No matter what the Gubbings had done to her, he would acknowledge her as his wife and stand by her. Chestwick would be her home, now, too.

He leaned out of the window and called to Will, "Lady Elizabeth needs a doctor. I've decided to take her to Exeter. Do you know the way?"

"Aye, sir. It's just a few hours down the road."

"Good. Get us there as quickly as you can."

The coach had been making slow but steady progress for three hours when Bess stirred for the first time. She moaned softly in Garrett's arms, her tongue sliding over her swollen lips.

"Are you thirsty, precious girl?" Garrett pulled out his flask of brandy, but realized it would sting the open cuts on her mouth. Reconsidering, he said to Tannie, "Hand me that cup of cider, lad." He'd tried, earlier, to get her to drink, but the liquid had run from the corner of her mouth. This time when he tipped the cup, she swallowed.

Bess grimaced, her blond brows drawing together. Briefly,

her golden lashes fluttered open, then closed again, tears coursing silently from beneath them.

"Are you in pain?" Garrett asked, haunted by the torment he had glimpsed in that moment of consciousness.

"The babies," she whispered. Her body began to shake, and a sob escaped her.

Garrett held her closer. "Shhh. It's all over, Bess. You're safe. No one will harm you."

"Dear God, the babies. Fever. So many. So helpless." She writhed in his arms, then tried to push free. Her eyes flew open, looking up at him without comprehension, her pupils so dilated only a thin ring of blue surrounded their black depths. Garrett felt as if he were looking into her soul as she stared at him in despair, tears flowing freely. "I tried. Really I tried," she muttered. Her voice sounded unnaturally thick, the words slurred. "But there was nothing I could do. Nothing." She buried her face in his chest and started to sob again, clutching at his cloak.

Anguish twisted sharp as a razor inside him. "Bess, it's all right. It's over now, and you're alive." He stroked the blankets covering her back. Poor creature. None of this should ever have happened. If only he hadn't left her . . . "Shhh. Go back to sleep. You're safe now. I'm taking you home, Bess. Home." Rocking her gently, he was gratified to feel her body relax.

Whatever had happened to her, she would heal at Chestwick.

# ❊ CHAPTER 16 ❊

$\mathcal{I}$t was dark when Elizabeth woke up screaming. For a brief moment of confusion, she didn't know where she was, only that something immense and horrible had happened. So dark, and there was so much noise. Everything was moving.

Why couldn't she think straight? Someone must have drugged her. She had hurt like this before; her head was splitting, and she ached all over. Thirsty. So thirsty. Ravenwold . . . had he beaten her again? No. He was dead.

Strong arms tightened around her, rocking her back and forth in the clattering, jolting darkness. ''Shhh. It's all right, precious girl. You're safe now. We're going home.'' The male voice was soothing and familiar, but the confinement of his arms awakened sharp fragments of memory—rough hands pulling her down; a stinking mouth with rotted teeth covering her own until she bit the probing, foul tongue and tasted blood; then brutal open-palmed blows to her face, delivered with such force she thought her neck would snap. The Gubbings had held her down, then tied her. Remembering how the ropes had burned her wrists, Elizabeth struggled now to free herself, but the harder she fought to escape the arms that held her, the tighter they became.

Then she remembered, saw it all spread out before her like a vast, vivid painting. She stopped struggling. The images were so real she could almost smell the stench of the Gubbings' camp and the smoke that hung over their dank hovels carved into the moor. Coarse, dirty women had peered at her from the doorways, their hard faces filled with suspicion, hate, and envy.

Elizabeth had tried to keep walking, her head held high, but the mud was so deep her feet sank to the ankles with every step. Impatient, one of her captors heaved her roughly over his shoulder and carried her like a sack of grain into the leader's hut, where he dumped her onto the dirt floor.

She'd struggled to her feet, choking from the cloud of peat smoke that competed with the stench of urine and dung in the sod hut. The leader—a fat, freckled man in soiled clothes— looked at her with an unnatural light in his eyes. His woman had actually growled when the outlaw's meaty fist tore away Elizabeth's blouse and roughly handled her breasts.

If it hadn't been for her medicines, he would have taken her then and there. Now in the darkness, Elizabeth heard her own voice murmur, "The medicines."

The soothing voice asked, "What about the medicines, Bess?"

Bess? Nobody called her Bess. Nobody but—"Where am I?" she asked with surprising clarity.

"Safe in the arms of your husband, Bess. It's all over. They won't hurt you anymore."

"Creighton," she said flatly, going still. So she was yet a prisoner, after all. The viscount must have escaped the Round-heads and ransomed her.

"Ah, Bess." He sighed. "After all we've been through, don't you think you could call me Garrett?"

Elizabeth did not answer. Why had Creighton bothered to save her? He hadn't wanted this marriage any more than she had. Wouldn't it have been simpler for him to let the Gubbings kill her? She'd heard them plan to, regardless of the ransom.

But that had been before she learned about the fever, before she had won her own life by trying to save the outlaws' chil-dren. Now, thinking back over those terrible days and nights, a wrenching sob rose from the depths of her soul.

She curled against Creighton's warmth, her fingers gripping his suede jacket. "Dear God, the babies, and the children . . . they died in my arms. I tried so hard to save them. I used my medicines, taught their women everything I knew, but nothing worked." Their keening echoed through her memory. "Gypsy Fever. The babies never had a chance. In the end, only eight out of thirty survived." Her own immunity had protected her, but the children—ragged, filthy, and malnourished—had been defenseless against the deadly disease. "So helpless. So trust-ing. Their eyes, looking up at me. And then they were dead."

One by one, those deaths had stabbed away at her, shredding her carefully constructed defenses, tearing open a lifetime of suppressed pain and loss. Now Elizabeth held onto Creighton in the darkness as if he were her only anchor in the vast, consuming vortex of anguish.

She wept for the helpless infants who had died in her arms. For her sister, Charlotte. For her mother. For the child she had never been. For the child she would never have. She cried until there were no more tears.

Garrett found a doctor in Essex, who assured him Bess's injuries were superficial. Though she had been heavily drugged by the Gubbings, she could travel safely. Unfortunately, the physician explained there was not a room to be had in all of Essex. Inns, barns, and civilian homes alike were filled to over-flowing not only with garrisoned Royalist troops, but also with country folk seeking protection from rebel raids. Garrett quickly discovered that in war, sometimes even gold and rank were not enough to buy a bed. They were forced to set out for Bristol.

He finally found lodgings just outside the sea port, and none too soon. After Bess's wrenching breakdown, he feared for her sanity. She hadn't spoken a word since, just stared dully into space or curled in the corner, away from him, in troubled sleep. Now, at least she was clean and in a decent bed.

He stretched his arms over his head and arched against the bedside chair, yawning. When he turned back to Bess, she was looking straight at him, her features calm and a welcome spark of animation in her blue eyes. Garrett lifted an eyebrow. "Well, it's about time you woke up. How do you feel?"

To his surprise, she answered. "Thirsty. And sore." Bess sniffed. "Phew. Smells like rotten eggs." She blinked, then looked around the room, frowning. "Where are we?"

"Bristol." He said nothing about the sulphur powder he'd put in her hair. First things first. He rose and poured a generous measure of red wine into a goblet. "Here. Try some of this." Lifting her pillow, he tipped the goblet to her lips.

She took a sip, then made a face and turned away. "Ugh. Wine?"

"You're welcome, I'm sure." Garrett lowered her pillow abruptly before setting the wine aside.

"Isn't there any broth," she grumbled, "or sweet cider? Anything but wine."

"Broth? I'll have some sent up right away, your highness," he said, hiding his relief with sarcasm. She must be getting better. Crankiness was a definite improvement over the wounded, incoherent torment she had shown for the past two days.

Bess frowned. "Bristol?"

"Still a little slow on the uptake, aren't you, my girl?" He sat beside her. "Yes, Bristol. I've decided to take you home."

"But Bristol's more than thirty miles in the opposite direction from Ravenwold. Why—"

"Ravenwold?" He shook his head. "Not that drafty, depressing place. *My* home. Chestwick, in Shropshire."

"Shropshire!" She bolted upright, then winced, bracketing her temples with her hands. "Oooh! My head." Bess squinted balefully at him. "Shropshire's halfway to Scotland! Need I remind you, sir, there's a civil war going on. Why in Heaven's name would you set out across six counties when Ravenwold Castle was only a day's ride—"

Pleased though he was by her show of spirit, Garrett quickly had his fill. He cut her off with, "I have my reasons, Bess, and they're good ones." *And I'll be flayed before I explain myself to you.* He'd almost forgotten how irritating she could be. He leaned back, lacing his fingers behind his head. "Chestwick is your home, now, too. After all, we *are* married." If looks could kill, he would not have drawn another breath, but he ignored her obvious displeasure. "Anyway, it's time you met my family."

"Your family?" Elizabeth couldn't imagine what sort of family would spawn a man like Creighton. Odd, though, that she hadn't considered meeting her in-laws before now. What would they think of her, and she of them?

Creighton cocked that annoying half smile of his. "Admit it: You're curious. I can see it in your face."

"It still doesn't make sense, traveling all that way," she protested weakly. She looked around. "Where's Gwynneth?"

"She'll join us there. I sent Tannie and Will back to Ravenwold yesterday with instructions for Gwynneth to come to Chestwick straightaway. She'll bring our belongings. And Mr. Cromwell, of course. Wouldn't dream of leaving your pet behind."

"That pig?" Her injuries throbbed with a fresh flush of hostility at the thought of the annoying creature—and Creighton's obvious delight at her irritation.

"Think of it," he said. "By the time Mr. Cromwell reaches Chestwick, she'll be the most traveled pig in all of England."

"You are impossible, sir." Elizabeth pulled the quilt up higher on her chest. For the first time, she noticed the unfamiliar lace cuffs of her nightshirt. "Where did this gown come from?"

"I bought it while you were sleeping."

"And how, pray tell, did I come to be wearing it?"

"I put it on you. After I took off your clothes and bathed you. *And* dusted you with sul—"

"Bathed me?" Elizabeth interrupted. She slid lower in the featherbed. "You couldn't have. I would remember it."

Creighton sobered. "When I found you, you'd been drugged, with a dangerously high dose, according to the doctor in Essex. He said it was a miracle you didn't stop breathing. You've been in and out for days." He shifted the topic back to her bath. "I couldn't wait for you to wake up to bathe you, Bess. You were covered with fleas, and so was I. Both of us needed a good wash."

"Fleas?" Her jaw dropped. "I've never had fleas in my life."

"Well, you had them when I found you, and half the little varmints took up residence on me." He gave his scalp a scratch at the mere mention of them. "I got rid of most of them."

Elizabeth snatched open the neckline of her gown and looked down to make sure none of the creatures was crawling around inside. When she saw the angry purple marks on her breasts, she let go of the gown. Her hand flew to her swollen lip, then she pushed up one sleeve to see more bruises and the angry red welts circling her wrist. She didn't need a mirror to know her face was marred and swollen, as well. "I can't meet anyone looking like this." She turned to him, her eyes awash with tears. "Your family . . . I can't let them see me like this."

He regarded her with grave compassion. "Don't be silly. You have nothing to be ashamed of, Bess. My mother and my sisters are most solicitous. They'll do their best to help you recover from your ordeal." For once, he seemed sincere. "The past is past. You're alive. That's all that matters. And you have a chance to start life all over again in a new place. We're going home, Bess."

Despite clear skies and a fair wind that dried the roads, it still took a week to reach Shropshire by way of the Severn road. By the time they passed the county boundary marker, Elizabeth had decided the Gubbings must have killed her after all, and this was hell, trapped eternally in a coach with Garrett Creighton and an indestructible supply of fleas. Her bruises had begun to heal, but now she was covered with itching red bites, and so was Creighton. He tried to joke about it, but she could tell he was annoyed by the infernal pests.

Scratching his arm, he pointed out the window. "Look, Bess. There's the pond where I used to swim as a bare-assed boy. And that orchard, there. I was always getting into trouble for climbing the apple trees."

Elizabeth scanned the pleasant, rolling countryside. So this was where Creighton had grown up. It must have been a carefree childhood, from the sound of his voice and the look of fond recollection in his eye. "How long has it been since you were home last?"

"Five years." He stared out of the window, his expression sober. "Far too long."

Garrett had told her about his family, but she was skeptical of the glowing picture he painted. If the Creightons were such a happy clan, why had he stayed away so long? Still, what Anne had said made sense. His secure childhood might well have left the doted heir with little need to risk his affections elsewhere. Elizabeth could only guess at that, having no idea what it would be like to be part of a happy family.

Creighton pointed ahead toward a pair of magnificent sandstone pillars bridged by ornate ironwork. "There it is."

Elizabeth was fascinated by the emblem over the gates—a rampant unicorn on a shield bearing three stars. Fitting, that a man like Creighton would have such a whimsical crest.

The gatesman opened up immediately at the sight of his long-absent master.

Once inside the gates of Chestwick, Elizabeth tried to conceal her awe at the vast, manicured grounds. She had never seen a more beautiful setting. Placid streams wandered through the pastoral landscape. Swans glided on serene ponds that reflected the blooming laurels and water iris at their banks. Then the graveled drive rounded a curve, and she almost gasped aloud. Aligned in perfect, majestic symmetry, an allée of an-

cient oaks led up to a gracious three-story brown brick manor
house.

Her hand smoothed self-consciously at her hair. She'd
known Creighton was rich, but this . . . such perfection could
only be maintained by immense wealth. And she had worried
about the expensive gowns and accoutrements he had bought
her in London! Elizabeth wished now she hadn't insisted on
plain black wool for the dress she'd had made in Bristol. She
should have chosen the moire silk, regardless of the cost. She
cringed inwardly, realizing how ridiculous her efforts to save
a few pounds must have seemed to her husband. Smoothing
the sturdy black fabric, she was suddenly aware of how plain
she looked.

"Don't worry," he said. "You look fine."

"I wasn't worried," Elizabeth snapped. She found it dis-
concerting how easily he invaded the privacy of her thoughts.

Six footmen in immaculate livery were waiting at the edge
of the brick courtyard when the coach came to a stop.

"Welcome to your new home, Bess." Creighton climbed
out and spoke to one of the footmen, who hurried back to the
house. With an ease born of privilege, he waited while two of
the footmen helped Elizabeth exit the coach.

She stepped onto the courtyard and saw that its intricate
brickwork depicted a vast serpentine dragon that twisted and
looped in an enormous wreath around the stars and rampant
unicorn of the Creighton crest. Forgetting herself, she exclaimed, "Why, it's a maze. How clever."

"Aye, and not an easy one. I was six before I made it from
the dragon's tail to the unicorn." He offered her his arm.
"Shall we?"

Elizabeth frowned. "The maze? Now?"

Creighton chuckled. "No, silly." He cocked his head at the
house. "Are you ready to meet my family?"

Elizabeth didn't get a chance to answer. A tide of chattering
girls poured out of the front door, trailed at a dignified pace
by a plump, attractive middle-aged woman with gray hair.
Elizabeth counted six girls dressed in vibrant spring colors.
They ran across the maze and descended on Creighton, their
bright skirts swirling in the breeze.

"Garrett! Why didn't you tell us you were coming?" the
tallest, a brunette, asked, hugging him.

He hugged her back. "I didn't know myself."

"Knave, sneaking up on us like this," chided the redhead in an emerald green dress. "I thought Mummy was going to faint when the footman said it was you." She stood on tiptoe and kissed his cheek.

The two youngest, identical twins of about ten, looked most like him. They had his wavy golden hair, fair skin, and bright blue eyes. Both girls wiggled past the redhead to circle his waist with their arms and gaze up adoringly while two of their less vocal companions lagged back, watching.

Creighton stooped down to scoop the twins up, one in each arm, then moaned with effort when he straightened. "Aargh. Either you two have grown up, or I've gotten too old for this."

Elizabeth was amazed he had the strength to lift both girls at once. They had to weigh at least six-stone apiece!

One of the twins smiled shyly, revealing a charming dimple. She cupped Creighton's cheek tenderly in her palm. "Of course we're grown. We're eleven." The other nodded earnestly, her dimple the mirror image of her sister's.

"Well, have mercy on an old man and get down, before I strain something." He eased them back to the ground.

Elizabeth shifted on her feet, uncertain whether to be relieved or annoyed that no one had acknowledged her presence. Watching these lovely young women flutter around Creighton was like looking at a whirlwind of brilliant spring blossoms.

Before the other two sisters had a chance to say anything, the gray-haired matron glided past Creighton to stop in front of Elizabeth. She smiled warmly, her dark eyes merry, then pivoted to swat at a passing girl with her folded fan. "Girls! Girls! Have you forgotten your manners entirely? Can't you see we have a guest?" She turned an expression of gentle acceptance back to Elizabeth. Without looking away, she said to Creighton, "Garrett, you churl, introduce your young lady."

"Of course." Far from chastened, Creighton bowed, taking Elizabeth's arm. "Mother, allow me to present my wife, the Countess Ravenwold. I call her Bess." In the stunned silence that followed, he cocked a half smile and said, "Bess, this is my mother, now *dowager* viscountess of Chestwick." He gave his mother an insolent wink to emphasize "dowager."

Fourteen female eyebrows headed skyward and stayed there for several heartbeats. Then everyone started talking at once. The girls surrounded Elizabeth, their questions running together into an unintelligible jumble.

Creighton threw up his hands. "Sorry, Bess. They're wild women, all of them."

"Girls! Quiet! You sound like a flock of magpies!" Ignoring the fact that her admonition had no effect, the viscountess took Elizabeth's hands and leaned forward to kiss each cheek. "Welcome, my dear. Please call me Catherine. Or would you prefer Mother?"

Elizabeth didn't now what to say. "I . . . Lady Catherine will be fine." She tried to smile, but the corners of her mouth quivered so, she abandoned the effort. "My name is Elizabeth."

"Well, Elizabeth, welcome to the family." She gave Elizabeth's hands an affectionate squeeze, then released them. "Girls! If you don't behave yourselves, I shall have to send you to your rooms without being introduced to Elizabeth!"

Instantly, there was quiet. "That's better." As her six daughters lined up, Lady Catherine nodded to her son. "Introduce your sisters, Garrett."

Creighton stepped behind the tallest, the brunette who had greeted him first. "Bess, this is my sister Mary. She's seventeen, and she used to burn worms when she was a little girl."

Mary spun on him, outraged. "Garrett! I can't believe you told her that!"

"It's true." He grinned. "She said she liked the way they crackled—" The rest was muffled by Mary's hand over his mouth.

"Just wait, Lady Elizabeth," Mary countered, "I can tell you a few stories about Garrett that—"

Creighton pulled away, cutting her threat short with, "All right. All right. Truce."

Elizabeth listened in amazement. Judging from Lady Catherine's lack of reaction, this type of raucous behavior was commonplace at Chestwick. She couldn't help contrasting it to the somber tension of her own childhood.

Creighton moved to stand behind the redhead. "This is Edith. She's fifteen—"

"Sixteen," Edith corrected in a wounded tone.

"Oh, that's right." He nodded to Elizabeth. "She turned sixteen the twenty-eighth of April. She loves to ride but hates to read."

He moved to the next girl, a somber-looking creature with

wide hazel eyes and hair the color of honey. "And this is Becky. She's fourteen."

"My name is Rebecca," she said with just a hint of sullenness, then curtsied.

"Rebecca," Elizabeth repeated.

Creighton placed his hands on the shoulders of the slender brunette with enormous brown eyes and a heart-shaped face. "This is Amy. She's twelve." He leaned closer to ask in a stage whisper, "Do you still hate boys?"

Blushing, she looked back at him and murmured, "Depends on the boy."

Creighton recoiled, the surprise in his voice convincing. "By thunder, you *are* growing up."

He stepped between the twins and bent to their level, his eyes alight with a special fondness. "And these are the twins." Elizabeth could see they were favorites. Without hesitation, he looked left. "Hope." Then right. "And Honor."

Five years since he had seen them, yet he could tell them apart. They looked indistinguishable to Elizabeth.

"All right, girls," Lady Catherine called. "Inside. You'll all be brown as Gypsies if you stand about outside all afternoon." She put her arm around Elizabeth's waist. "Come, child. You must be exhausted from your journey. Would you prefer to rest first, or eat, or have a nice, hot bath?"

"A bath sounds wonderful," Elizabeth ventured, suddenly conscious of the bruises on her face and neck. And the fleas! She'd never be able to lift her face again if Lady Catherine got fleas from her. She tried to pull away, but Lady Catherine's plump arm only tightened around her.

"Then a bath it shall be." Creighton's mother guided Elizabeth toward the house, but she stopped short just outside the door. "Good gracious. Look what I almost did." She smiled at Elizabeth, her eyes suddenly bright with unshed tears. "Garrett's father carried me over this threshold almost thirty years ago. Now it's your turn." She extended her hand toward her son. "Come. Carry your bride over the threshold."

His face unreadable, Creighton stepped forward and lifted Elizabeth into his arms, arms that had sheltered and protected her, yet possessed the power to crush her. "Welcome home, Bess." He took an exaggerated step inside, to the giggling approval and applause of his sisters.

In all her life, Elizabeth had never dreamed of such a wonderful house. The large chambers were made warm and welcoming by wooden floors and paneled walls polished to a golden gleam. Colorful decorations adorned the exposed beams that traversed the whitewashed ceilings. Dozens of diamond-paned windows admitted the afternoon sunlight, and richly hued oriental rugs brightened every room. And there were fresh flowers everywhere.

"Do you like it?" Creighton asked.

"It's beautiful."

He smiled. "It's yours."

Lady Catherine beamed with pride. "The maids will have the master suite ready for you two in no time."

Creighton tensed. "Mother, that's your room."

Elizabeth wriggled down from his arms. "Please, Lady Catherine," she pleaded, "don't give up your room. I couldn't bear to cause such an imposition."

"Nonsense, dear. It's no imposition." Lady Catherine turned to the girls. "Edith, go tell Bridget and Mavis to meet me upstairs with fresh linens. Mary and Becky, come with me. Amy, please ask Wynton to fire up the boiler and bring the slipper tubs to the master suite." She put her arms around the twins. "You two shall have a very special job. See if you can find the most beautiful flowers in the garden for your new sister's room."

The sisters scattered to their appointed tasks with a surprising lack of discussion.

Lady Catherine watched them go. "They're good girls, really. I only wish they would act like proper ladies." She started up the stairs, then paused. "I'll only be a few minutes. Then the two of you can retire." A knowing smile curled at her mouth. "And don't worry about coming down for dinner. I'll have it sent up." She left them alone in the entry hall.

Elizabeth looked to Creighton in desperation. How could she ask for her own room without exposing the farce of their marriage and humiliating him in front of his family?

He shrugged, smiling that cursed cat-in-the-cream-house smile of his. "Any suggestions, Bess?"

"I don't know." Her right thumb rubbed agitated circles against the first joint of her forefinger. "Your mother has been so kind. I do not wish to offend her. Nor do I wish to embarrass you. But everyone thinks we're . . . that we'll be . . ."

"We *are* married, Bess." A resolute cast darkened his

bright blue eyes. "When are you going to give up and admit it?"

"Admit what? That I was forced to submit to a heretic ritual my faith does not acknowledge?"

"No one put a pistol to your head, madam." Creighton took her firmly by the wrist. "You signed the contract. You participated in the ceremony. In the eyes of the law, we are married. In the eyes of God, we are married. And in the eyes of my family, we are married." He pulled her toward the stairs. "I have been very patient, waiting for you accept the truth, but my patience is at an end. We are married, madam." He deftly swept her back into his arms to carry her up the stairs. "Before this night is over, I shall be your husband, indeed, Bess. Get used to the idea." He leaned closer, his whisper warm in her ear. "Who knows? You might just like it. I've had no complaints from the ladies so far."

# ❄ CHAPTER 17 ❄

*G*arrett held up one of the shirts he had left behind on his last visit. The fabric smelled musty after five years in a trunk, but at least it was big enough, which was more than he could say for the rest of the clothes he'd been rummaging through for the past half hour. He heard the door of his old room open and turned to see his mother enter.

She closed the door behind her and approached, her face composed but grave. "Well, son. Are you going to tell me what happened?"

"What? About getting married?" He directed his attention back to sorting through the musty clothes.

"That, too. But mainly, I want to know what happened to Elizabeth. She's been beaten." There was no judgment in her voice. Unlike Garrett, his mother never jumped to conclusions. She watched and listened, slowly digesting the facts, then invariably decided to see things in the most generous light.

Her dark gaze bored into him. He never had been able to fool her the way he had so many others. Those eyes—eyes that saw through every lie, even the well-intentioned ones. His mother was made of truth, just as much as he was made of mischief. He never could lie to himself without knowing it instantly upon telling her.

So now he told her as much of the truth as he dared. "I had a mission in London, a very dangerous one. I can't go into the details, but Bess and I were forced to flee through rebel territory. Before we reached Royalist country, I left her to get food and ran into a nest of Roundheads. It was all I could do to lose them." He turned and gripped the side of the trunk, unable to face his mother when he said, "We could have managed without food for another day, but she's so thin. I worried . . ." His voice grew hard with recrimination. "I should never have left her alone in the first place. On her way from Salisbury to Cornwall, she was captured by the Gubbings. They . . . abused her." He looked up to see his own torment reflected in his mother's face. "I cannot bear to think what else they might have done to her."

"Oh, son." Lady Catherine circled him in a comforting embrace, just as she used to when he was a lad, and pulled his head down to her shoulder. "How my heart goes out to both of you." She gave him a brief, hard hug, then pulled away. "You got her back, though. That's the important thing."

"Yes. And for some reason I still don't understand, they returned the ransom." Garrett paced to a chair by the hearth and sat down, staring into the cold, empty fireplace. "When I found her, she was so . . . wounded—more in spirit than body—that I didn't ask many questions. It's only been in the last few days that she's come to her senses."

Watching him stare into the fireplace, his mother said in an odd tone, "Your father used to do that."

Garrett looked around the high-backed chair. "What?"

"Stare into the fireplace, whether there was a fire or not, whenever he had to speak of something painful."

He leaned back into the chair. "Not as painful for me as it must be for her."

Lady Catherine approached and stood beside him, her hand on his shoulder. "She hasn't told you what happened?"

He shook his head. "No. And how can I expect her to? It would be like making her live it all over." Suddenly weary, he leaned forward, his forearms braced on his thighs. "Dear God, Mother, the Gubbings." He looked up. "It tears me apart to imagine them striking her, tying her, *using* her like animals in rut. Filthy, disgusting—"

"Don't." His mother crouched in front of him. "Nothing can be served by such dark imaginings." She tipped up his chin, her brown eyes resolute. "What's done is done. Neither you, nor I, nor Elizabeth can change that. But you can help set things to rights. Elizabeth is your wife. Only you can restore her dignity. She needs you, Garrett."

"Needs me?" Garrett stood and paced to the windows, gazing out over the serene landscape. "I wish it were that simple."

She followed him to within an arm's length. "Why isn't it?"

He turned to see his mother's reaction. "Well, for one thing, the marriage was forced upon her, as it was upon me. And for another, she's a papist."

"Ah." An expression of thoughtful concern settled onto Lady Catherine's face, but she hardly reacted with the shock Garrett had expected from such a fervent Protestant. "That does complicate matters."

"There are other, more basic, complications, but I do not care to discuss them."

A deep sigh escaped her. "Oh, dear. Problems in the bedroom." She studied him shrewdly. "Has the marriage been consummated?"

Garrett pivoted. "Mother, what in blue blazes possesses you to ask such a question?"

"Women notice things, dear." She faced him frankly, enumerating, "You're prickly as hedgehogs with each other. She never called you by your first name. And I saw the panic in her eyes when I said I was making up a single room for the two of you."

Garrett regarded his mother with renewed respect. "You don't miss a thing, do you? You'd make an excellent spy."

"One observes." A small, secretive smile softened her mouth. "I suppose it might seem odd for me to discuss such matters with you, son, but perhaps it will help if I tell you a few things about your father and me." She folded her hands primly at her waist. "Haven't you ever wondered why so much time elapsed between your birth and your sisters'?"

"No. I never really thought about it."

As calmly as if she were telling him what to expect for dinner, she announced, "I'd never even seen your father until our wedding day. I was only fourteen, and he was an old man of twenty-five and big, like you. I was frightened to death of him. And after our wedding night, I was terrified."

"Mother!" Garrett peered at her in amazement, her revelations stirring his curiosity but embarrassing him at the same time. "But you and Father seemed so happy, so devoted to each other."

"Not in the beginning. After that first night, I wanted nothing to do with him. Poor man, he meant well, but that first time he was more than a little drunk, and woefully clumsy. I

was so naive that I thought it would always hurt like that, and
frankly, I'm not certain your father knew otherwise. I wouldn't
let him near me after that." A fond look softened her eyes.
"We couldn't talk about it. You know how shy your father
was about discussing private matters."

"I remember." Garrett chuckled. "If it weren't for the stableboys, I never would have figured out what Father was trying
to tell me when I was twelve and we had that father-son chat."

"It took me a year to get him to tell you that much." She
went back to her original thought with, "Our wedding night
wasn't a complete failure; we managed to conceive you. My
condition provided a perfect excuse to avoid my conjugal responsibilities." She chuckled. "Delivering you wasn't easy.
Afterward . . . well, the thought of letting your father back into
my bed frightened me more than ever. Every time the dear
man tried, I carried on like a spoiled child, wailing and pulling
at my hair until he left me alone. We went on that way for
three years."

"Three years?" Garrett was stunned.

"Aye." Lady Catherine shook her head in wonder. "Can
you imagine? A patient man, your father." She gazed down
at the garden. "Then something unexpected happened: Your
father was called away to fight. Though we hadn't shared a
bed in years, we'd rarely been separated for more than a few
days. Without our being aware of it, your father's life and mine
had been knit together by our love for you and the countless
daily intersections of living. Then he left, with no idea of when
he'd return.

"He was away for seven long months." A wistful smile
turned up the corners of her mouth. "The oddest thing happened; the house seemed so empty without him. Only when
he was gone did I realize how much I'd come to depend on
his presence." She patted Garrett's arm. "I had you, of course,
but every time you did something funny or smart or preco-
cious, I'd catch myself wanting to bring you to your father to
show him." Her voice warmed. "Not a day passed when I
didn't think of something I wanted to tell him, only to realize
I would have to write it in a letter. How I missed that man."

Her smile widened. "He'd been away about a month before
I realized I loved him." The glow of that discovery reverber-
ated across time to light her features. "Everything was differ-

ent after that. From the moment he came home, we couldn't get close enough.''

The glow faded, along with her smile. ''In the next seven years I bore three sons, but none of them lived more than a few days. I sometimes wonder if that was a penance for my rejecting your father for so long.'' As if coming out of a trance, she turned to him and brightened. ''But God is merciful. He gave us your sisters. And now He has sent us Elizabeth.'' Her manner became brisk. ''Where is she now?''

''In the master suite. Wynton and the others are preparing her bath.'' Garrett's mouth flattened. ''Under the circumstances, I thought it would be a good time to come look for some clothes.''

''A wise impulse. Give her time, Garrett.''

''I hope you don't expect me to give her three whole years.''

''If that's what it takes.''

Garrett shot a baleful look at his mother. ''I am not my father, madam.''

Her laugh was as young as his sisters'. ''No, you're not, you wicked, randy thing. I've heard the gossip about your romantic escapades.'' She sobered. ''God rest his soul, your father was as faithful as the sunrise, and he was neither impatient nor impulsive, as you are. But you inherited his good heart.'' She reached over and took his hand, the mother-love in her eyes denying her recitation of his faults. Her fingers tightened reassuringly. ''Being a man isn't easy in times like these. Being a good one is even harder, but I know you can do it. You've never had reason to settle down before, Garrett, but you do now.'' She let go of his hand and crossed to open the door, pausing to look back. ''This can end well only if you make it end well.''

She left him with a lot to think about.

The one thing Elizabeth did not envy this opulent household was its complete lack of privacy. The dressing room was crowded with people. Three laundresses were helping the man named Wynton fill an enormous, muslin-draped metal tub while two scullery maids stoked the fire to a crackling blaze. Meanwhile, Lady Catherine's personal servant Luella hovered over Elizabeth, slowly using a wide-toothed comb to unsnarl the wreckage wrought by Elizabeth's clumsy efforts to dress her own hair during the week-long coach ride from Bristol.

A distant knock sounded at the bedchamber door, followed by, "Lady Elizabeth, it's us. May we come in?"

Elizabeth nodded for the maid to admit "us," whoever that was.

The moment Luella opened the door, the twins rushed through the bedchamber and into the dressing room, each of them bearing a crystal vase filled with fragrant lilacs, laurel blossoms, early roses, and lilies. The girls looked identical, down to the lace on their sky blue dresses and the style of their hair. "Where do you want us to put them?" one asked.

Elizabeth blinked, searching their faces for some identifying trait. They were mirror images, indistinguishable except for the fact that one dimpled right, and the other left. Elizabeth had no idea which was which, but the twins' smiles were contagious. "Thank you so much, both of you." She had an inspiration. "Honor, why don't you put your flowers here, on the dressing table? And, Hope, yours will look lovely on the chest beside the bed."

Honor beamed, dimpling left, and placed the vase at the edge of the dressing table.

*Honor, left* Elizabeth engraved into her memory. And Honor had spoken first. She made a note to notice who spoke first in the future. That might be an easier clue than the dimples.

Hope carried her flowers into the bedchamber, then returned. She did not speak, but reached out to stroke Elizabeth's long, golden hair, completely unselfconscious.

Honor smiled, the deep dimple on her left cheek betraying her identity. "You have beautiful hair, Lady Elizabeth. It's fairer than ours. Yours looks like sunshine."

"And yours looks like honey," Elizabeth responded. "So lovely." She discerned that, of the two, Hope was the toucher and Honor the speaker.

Another, more forceful, knock sounded on the bedchamber door.

"I'll see who it is, milady." Luella hurried away, her swift, gliding pace similar to her mistress's. She returned almost immediately. "It's Lady Mary, Countess."

Another sister. Elizabeth wondered if the whole family would be there to witness her bath by the time it was ready. After the past few weeks with Creighton, she was desperate

for some privacy, but she did not want to offend anyone.
"Show her in."

Mary's rigid posture and no-nonsense gait declared for all
to see the importance of her position as eldest of the sisters.
A hapless maid struggled behind her, arms so laden with clothing that Elizabeth couldn't see the poor girl's face.

"Good afternoon, Countess." Lady Mary swept into the
crowded dressing room. "Since you and I are about the same
height, Mummy thought you might wish to borrow a few of
my clothes until your baggage arrives."

"Thank you. There was time to have only one dress made
in Bristol." Elizabeth glanced around the crowded room.
"Perhaps it would be more comfortable if we looked through
your clothes in the bedchamber."

Mary smiled, her mask of maturity dissolving. "Good
idea." Obviously, she couldn't remain aloof for long. She
turned to the beleaguered maid. "Patsy, lay everything out on
the bed."

A muffled "Aye, mistress," caused all three sisters to giggle.

Elizabeth rose and led her visitors into the welcome expanse
of the bedchamber. How long would it take, she wondered,
before she became accustomed to having people around her
all the time? At Ravenwold, she could easily escape the few
remaining servants when she wanted to be alone. She wasn't
certain she would ever adjust to the constant comings and go-
ings at Chestwick. And despite the outward acceptance of Garrett's warm, close-knit family, she felt very much like an
intruder.

Another knock sounded at the door. "Elizabeth, it's Catherine. May I come in?"

"Please." She nodded for Luella to open the door. When
Lady Catherine entered, her silvered brows rose at the sight
of Mary, the twins, and Patsy. Peering past them to the dressing room, she counted aloud, "One, two, three, four, five.
Goodness. So much fuss." She glanced at Elizabeth. "Poor
child. Leave this to me." She glided to the door of the dressing
room, murmured a few quiet instructions, and the bath attendants retreated down the back stair. Then she turned to her
daughters. "Run along, now, girls. How can Elizabeth take a
bath with all of us visiting? Say good-bye."

The twins hugged Elizabeth long and well. "We'll bring

you more flowers tomorrow, Countess.''

Feeling awkward in their embrace, Elizabeth stammered, ''Thank you. I . . . I shall look forward to that.''

Mary bobbed a curtsy. ''Good evening, Countess. I hope the clothes please you. If you don't find anything to your liking, I have more. Just send Luella.'' She urged Patsy and the twins into the hall ahead of her, leaving only Lady Catherine and Luella behind.

Garrett's mother turned to her maid. ''Patsy will take over your duties to me while you attend the countess, Luella.'' When Luella shot a skeptical sidelong glance at Elizabeth, Lady Catherine's tone firmed. ''Countess Ravenwold is now mistress of Chestwick. Do everything in your power to assist her. You may begin by going into the dressing room and making certain everything is ready for the countess's bath. And close the door behind you. I'd like a few moments alone with my daughter-in-law.''

Elizabeth watched the maid leave with some trepidation, certain that the viscountess was going to ask questions she did not want to answer. But Lady Catherine asked no questions. Instead, she stroked the shimmering curtain of hair that hung about Elizabeth's shoulders.

''What beautiful hair you have, and what wonderful cheekbones. Like a queen. Come.'' She crossed to the two chairs that faced the hearth. ''Let's sit by the fire, where it's warm.''

Elizabeth obliged in silence. When she was seated, Lady Catherine took the opposite chair and said, ''I have many happy memories of this room. And now it is yours and Garrett's. Another generation.''

Elizabeth shifted. ''Lady Catherine, I feel very uncomfortable about putting you out of your room.''

''Nonsense. You aren't putting me out. You belong here now.'' The viscountess's gaze moved around the room, focusing briefly here and there, then moving on, the way a child would touch her precious toys to make certain all of them were still there. ''Life is change. It's been more than ten years since my husband died; I've rattled around in here alone too long. This room is better suited to two people.'' She brightened, her smile convincing. ''I'm looking forward to cozier quarters, near my girls in the east wing. So you see, you're not putting me out at all.''

She leaned forward, shifting the conversation. ''My son tells me you are a devout Roman Catholic.''

Elizabeth tensed. "Yes, I am." What dared she say to this Protestant woman? "My faith is very important to me. It has been my only comfort in . . ." She looked down into her lap to avoid those kind dark eyes that seemed to see into her soul. "It has often been my only comfort."

Lady Catherine leaned back in her chair. "My faith has sustained me, as well. I am pleased to find that we have that in common."

"In common?" Elizabeth looked up. "But you are a Protestant."

"Aye, but the Lord has many vineyards, Elizabeth. You were born to serve in one, I, another. Yet we both serve the same master. That is enough for me." She extended her hands toward the fire's warmth. "I hope you won't think me presumptuous, but I have arranged for you to have Latin lessons every morning at dawn." She shot a meaningful glance at Elizabeth. "I trust you are an early riser."

Bewildered, Elizabeth answered, "Aye, Lady Catherine. I rise for my devotionals before sunrise every day, but—"

"Good, then. Your tutor's name is Stephen Wolcox, a fascinating man. He's a farrier by trade, but has a marvelous education and a wide acquaintance in the village. I think you'll find you two have a lot in common." She beamed smugly. "It will be best if you meet for your lessons in the chapel."

Latin lessons, from a farrier? At dawn, in the chapel! It made no sense, but Elizabeth did not want to appear ungracious, so she accepted. "As you wish, Lady Catherine."

"You can start tomorrow." When she saw that Elizabeth was confused, Lady Catherine leaned forward and whispered, "I've heard rumors that he's a Roman priest, but of course I wouldn't want to know, since that's been a capital offense these last seven years." She winked at Elizabeth. "Good farriers are hard to find. I would hate for anything to happen to Stephen."

Elizabeth could hardly believe her ears. Lady Catherine was willingly harboring a Roman priest in her own household! And the Latin lessons . . . ? The truth dawned on her. Wolcox wasn't going to tutor her in Latin; he was going to say the Mass! Garrett's mother had arranged everything so discreetly that no one else in the household would have to know. If anyone overheard the Mass, Elizabeth could simply explain that her teacher was reciting.

For more than a hundred years, England's Protestants and Catholics had been in constant and often bloody conflict. Expecting her faith to cause suspicion and hostility in this Protestant family, she was completely unprepared for the viscountess's generosity of spirit. "I . . . I hardly know what to say. How very kind of you." She found herself fighting back unexpected tears. "Thank you, Lady Catherine." Did Creighton know? she wondered.

"You are more than welcome, child. Now I shall leave you to your bath and some well-earned rest." She rose along with Elizabeth, then started for the door. Halfway across the room, Lady Catherine halted. "Gracious, I almost forgot the most important thing, the reason I came." She lifted the two long strands of magnificent matched pearls she was wearing over her head. "Bend forward a bit, dear. These are yours now, as mistress of Chestwick."

Elizabeth bent her head and felt the pearls slide down to nestle on the hair blanketing her neck. She straightened, at a loss for words.

"There." As casually as Elizabeth's own mother had done when she was little, Lady Catherine stepped behind her and pulled her hair out from under the pearls. "Now, let's see how they look on you." She circled around to regard Elizabeth with satisfaction. "Perfect—you *and* the pearls."

Lady Catherine's dark eyes glazed with nostalgia. "My mother-in-law gave me these pearls when I married Garrett's father. Garrett's great-grandfather was a sailing captain who made his fortune in the Orient so he could come home to marry Garrett's great-grandmother. He brought these pearls back with him." She chuckled. "The old man claimed to have dived to the bottom of the South Seas for every one of these himself, but no one really believed him. Still . . ." Her fingers straightened the strands. "It was a gift of love, and now I pass it on to you, as Garrett's wife."

"Please, Lady Catherine," Elizabeth struggled to explain. "Your gift is most generous, but I cannot accept it. Nor can I take your place as mistress of Chestwick. It wouldn't be right."

"My dear, you have taken nothing from me." Lady Catherine's face reflected a peace Elizabeth could not help but envy. "I *give* you my place as mistress of this house, and gladly. Running Chestwick is hard work. It's a relief to turn it over to such capable hands."

Clearly, Garrett's mother expected Elizabeth to remain here—permanently. Trying to hide the desperation in her voice, Elizabeth equivocated, "But I don't even know how long I . . . we will be staying."

"This is your home, now. No matter where you go, it will always be here for you, as will I."

"But you don't understand." How could Elizabeth explain to this gracious, generous *Protestant* woman that she considered her marriage to Creighton was not binding because it had been performed by a Protestant priest? That she planned to file for an annulment as soon as possible? Elizabeth couldn't. Instead, she stammered, "I . . . I do not deserve such kindness."

Lady Catherine leveled a piercing look at her. "May I speak frankly, my dear?"

"Of course."

"I have no illusions about my son, Elizabeth. Like every man, he has his faults." She interjected wryly, "I've long suspected men are happiest when they're completely out of emotional context, and Garrett may be no exception." Her voice became earnest. "But Garrett has many wonderful qualities. I only hope that you will one day come to appreciate them. Foremost, he possesses a good and noble spirit." The viscountess straightened to every inch of her diminutive height. "As his mother, I ask you to be a good wife to him. A decent marriage can make the best of a man. A bad marriage will destroy the best of men." Her face softened with sympathy for Elizabeth. "I love my son. If you give him a chance, I think you will, too."

Abruptly, she shifted back to sociable detachment. "Now, I've kept you from your bath too long. I must be off." She kissed each of Elizabeth's cheeks. "I'll see that you're not disturbed." A sly smile curved Lady Catherine's lips. "Even by Garrett. We women need our privacy." She left Elizabeth in blessed silence.

Half an hour later, Garrett quietly opened the door to the master's chamber and entered, his bare feet soundless as he crossed to the rug. What he saw by the fire set his pulse pumping. Clad in only a thin shift, Bess leaned back, long and luscious, in a chair by the hearth, her eyes closed and her body draped luxuriantly in complete relaxation. Her hair cascaded to the floor in a cloud of golden curls as Luella stroked a comb through it. He could clearly see the rosy circle that crowned each breast, and the faint, dusky shadow at her loins. In the soft firelight, he could barely make out the faded bruises that had marred her breasts and face so lividly only a week ago.

She was lush, unguarded. Beautiful. This was the exotic creature he had glimpsed that night three years ago. His body responded with a surge of desire so strong that his manhood shifted as if it had a life of its own.

Luella spotted him and froze.

"Why did you stop?" Bess murmured. Still lying back, she opened her eyes and saw the look of distress on Luella's face. She sat up abruptly, her body tensing.

By thunder, Bess was a fine-looking woman when she let her hair down. Garrett sipped the potent liquid in his glass and strolled closer.

His wife stood in rigid defiance, never taking her eyes off him. "My robe, please, Luella."

"Aye, milady." Luella hastened to the bed for the robe.

Garrett waited until she neared her mistress to intercept her. "I'll take that." He pulled the garment from Luella's hands. "Leave us."

Luella hesitated, visibly torn between her duty to her master and her loyalty to the new mistress of Chestwick. But one more look at Garrett's steely expression, and prudence won out. "As you wish, master." She retreated into the dressing room and down the back stair.

Alone, at last.

Garrett tossed the robe into the dressing room and decisively closed the door.

"Pray excuse me, sir," Bess said in a martyred tone, "but I wish to put on my nightgown and retire."

"Go right ahead. I'm not stopping you." He moved so close he could feel the heat of her body, but he did not touch her. Instead, he leaned in and inhaled the scent of lilacs in her hair. "Mmmm. You smell as delicious as you look, Bess."

Elizabeth knew she was not a beautiful woman, yet she could almost believe he thought so, the way his brilliant blue eyes devoured her. Anxious to escape the towering heat of his presence, she crossed to the bed, where Mary's clothes were laid out in neat stacks of gowns, shifts, petticoats, skirts, and bodices. She selected a long-sleeved, bleached muslin nightgown with a high, ruffled collar and held it up to cover what the thin shift revealed. She was determined not to let him intimidate her. "If you insist on invading my privacy, you might at least turn around while I dress."

Creighton cocked that annoying smile of his. "Not unless you call me Garrett."

"Please turn around, *Garrett*."

"Now, that wasn't so difficult, was it?" He turned his broad back to her, the hard, muscular lines of his form outlined by the light from the fire.

Elizabeth hastily pulled the heavy muslin over her chemise and buttoned herself up as tight as a nun. She faced her husband. "I don't wish to be rude, but I'm very tired, and I'd like to go to bed."

"Don't mind me." Garrett pulled a chair alongside the one at the hearth and sat down, facing her.

Exasperated, she laced her arms across her chest. "Please leave."

"Garrett," he prompted.

"Please leave, *Garrett*."

"I do not wish to leave, Bess." A dangerous glitter sparked in his blue eyes. "Not until we've talked."

"Talked?" Elizabeth scowled. She recognized that look, and it had little to do with talking. "About what?"

"About us." He patted the empty seat beside him. "Come. It won't take long, I promise."

She knew why he wanted her within easy reach. She would just as soon sit herself in a scavenger's daughter.

"Just talk, Bess."

"Oh, very well." She stormed over and dropped into the chair. "Talk, then."

Creighton faced her, his expression unreadable. He did not speak for several moments, but when he did, his voice rolled out as soft as summer fog. "I told you I would never force you, and I meant it, but I want to make love to you. Now. Tonight." The backs of his fingers brushed her cheek. "Let me give you pleasure, Elizabeth."

Elizabeth pulled away from his touch. "You know I cannot, and you know why."

"No, I don't." The flames accented the clean, strong lines

of his face, sparking a flicker of amber in his eyes. By firelight, he really did look like a great, golden lion. "Be honest, Elizabeth. Do you really want an annulment?"

She straightened, appalled that he knew what she had been planning. But how? "I never said anything about an annulment."

"You didn't have to." He stretched his long, muscular legs toward the hearth, crossing them at the ankles. His large hands curled over the ends of the chair arms. They were exceptional hands, strong and artistic, with just a dusting of golden curls on the back. "What will happen to your people then, Elizabeth?" he asked. "You know I have the means to ensure their well-being. Would you let them starve rather than accept me as your husband?"

"I . . . I hadn't considered that," she said honestly.

"And what about you?" Garrett sobered. "Is being married to me so onerous that you would give up everything I have to offer, everything my family has to offer, simply so you can be free?" When she did not answer, he shook his head. "Even if you did secure an annulment, the king would not allow you to remain single for long, and you know it. You cannot afford to pay the fines."

Elizabeth rose and warmed her hands near the flames. As much as she hated to admit it, he was right. The king would force another match, and even if her next husband were a Roman Catholic, there was no guarantee he wouldn't be as bad as Ravenwold.

At least Creighton had never harmed her, even when she had angered him. And he had kept his word about forcing himself on her. So far.

Which alternative offered the lesser evil? Should she sacrifice her soul for her people and allow Creighton to plunder her body? Or should she stand fast, denying the marriage, and let her people starve?

Her faith taught that sacrifice was the purest form of love, yet that same faith would damn her for accepting an unbeliever as a husband. She was so confused.

Creighton's voice cut through her indecision. "I'm giving you a choice, Elizabeth. Accept me as your husband in every way, and I will provide for your tenants and do my best to make you happy. Refuse, and I shall send you back to Ravenwold tomorrow, then file for the annulment myself."

She pivoted. "You would release me?"

"I don't know what kind of monster you think I am, but I have no desire to be bound to a woman who does not want me—though I have given you no cause to hate me as you do. Yes, I would free you."

"I do not hate you," she murmured, her mind spinning. If she accepted the marriage, there was always the hope that he would convert, allow the union to be properly solemnized. "Would you agree to convert, have a Roman Catholic priest marry us?"

He inhaled long and deep. "I might consider it, but I make no promises." Garrett looked up at her. "I'm being completely honest with you, Bess. I do not want there to be any lies between us."

"I appreciate that. Really. But what you ask, to abandon my faith . . ."

"No one is asking you to abandon your faith. I'm sure there's a priest hiding somewhere in Shropshire who will serve you the Mass."

Did that mean he knew about Wolcox? Elizabeth wasn't sure, and she certainly didn't trust Creighton enough to ask. Instead, she said, "No priest will serve me Mass, sir. If I am married to an unbeliever, I cannot partake of any of the blessed sacraments."

"I am not an unbeliever," he asserted quietly, his voice steel cloaked in velvet.

"You know what I mean." She sank back into her chair, miserable. "And there are other reasons why we should not be married, reasons you do not know."

"What reasons?" His eyes narrowed. "Because you had no children with Ravenwold?"

Elizabeth lifted her chin. She owed him the truth. "Yes. I am barren." The words stabbed like rusty knives. "Every man wants children. Your mother wants grandchildren. I cannot give them to you."

"How do you know?" he asked.

"You said so, yourself." She fought down the tears that welled in her eyes. "Ravenwold and I had no children, and it was certainly not from lack of trying."

"Bess, Bess, Bess." Creighton actually chuckled. "That's no proof. Has a doctor told you you cannot have children?"

"No. I've seen several, and they could find nothing specific wrong, but—"

He leaned forward. "I hate to speak ill of the dead, but in the many years I knew him, your late husband sowed his seed in every doxy he could get his hands on, from Gravesend to Land's End, and never got a single bastard. My guess is, it was he who was barren, not you."

Elizabeth scowled, humiliated to have her private shame discussed so openly. But if what Creighton said was true, if she could conceive . . . Her frown shifted to an expression of dismay.

"What?" Creighton looked at her with apprehension. Then his face hardened. "Oh. The Gubbings." He stood and gazed into the flames. The room behind them was getting dark, so his figure was a silhouette edged in gold. "You're worried about what would happen if there should be . . . consequences, from what they did to you when you were abducted."

"Consequences?" Baffled, Elizabeth asked, "What do you mean?"

"A child." He turned back, his eyes haunted. "I could find a good home for it among my tenants. Regardless of how it was conceived, the babe would be innocent. No one need know. I will stand by you."

"You will stand by me?" Elizabeth felt an unexpected—and completely inappropriate—chuckle escape her. She tried to keep it down, but she was helpless to control the bizarre laughter that bubbled up and escaped. Soon she was hooting, doubled over, arms wrapped around her aching sides as tears ran from her eyes.

"What's so blasted funny about that?" Creighton asked.

"You . . . ha . . . you thought . . ." Elizabeth couldn't get the words out. It wasn't funny. She knew that, but for some reason, she laughed even harder.

Creighton grasped her upper arms and drew her to her feet. "Are you telling me they did not rape you?"

"Yes. No." At his look of confusion, she struggled, without success, to regain her dignity. She wanted to explain, especially after seeing the genuine relief in his eyes. His offer, though unnecessary, had been kind, even gallant—anything but laughable. Yet she had kept her emotions bottled up for so long, she could not control herself. Her laughter took on an edge of hysteria. "They didn't rape me," she managed to gasp out.

Creighton flung his arms around her and pulled her close. "Thank God. Thank God."

Inexplicably, her laughter turned to tears. Shaking and weeping, she allowed him to hold her.

He murmured softly, "Let it out, precious girl. Let it out." He kissed her forehead, her temples, her cheeks.

Slowly, her tears subsided. He was so warm, so strong, so gentle. She felt protected in his arms. Unafraid. Without realizing how or why, she kissed him on the lips, tasting the salt of her own tears.

Creighton's mouth was tender at first, then hungry. Abruptly, he pulled back. "I'm sorry. I don't want to take advantage of—"

"Don't be sorry." Elizabeth looked up into his azure eyes, her hands sweeping across the broad, muscular planes of his back. "Be my husband, Garrett. May God have mercy on my soul, I want to help my people. I want to be a part of this family." She admitted to herself as much as to him, "I want to know what it feels like to live in a house where there is love."

"You won't regret it, Bess." Garrett swept her into his arms and carried her across the room to the bed. He brushed the borrowed clothing onto the floor, then laid her atop the coverlet. "We'll take it slow and easy. Tell me what you want, what you like, and it's yours."

"I want you," she whispered.

# CHAPTER 18

"Wait." Garrett stepped back, away from the bed. "I'll be right back."

Elizabeth watched him cross the room. When he opened the door to leave, she asked, indignant, "Where are you going?"

"I'm not abandoning you," he responded equably. "I just want to make sure everything is perfect for us." His slow smile was eloquent with promise. "Believe me, I won't be gone one minute longer than necessary."

It seemed like a long time before she heard footsteps approaching in the hallway outside their room. Garrett entered, followed by two footmen bearing silver trays laden with several bottles of wine, an assortment of blown-glass goblets, and several plates piled high with tempting morsels. After the servants had set everything out on a table and stoked up the fire to a roaring blaze, they exited.

Garrett locked the door behind them, then disappeared into the dressing room. She heard the metal key slide into the lock of the servants' entrance, then the sound of the mechanism sealing that door, too. For one brief, chilling moment, she wondered if he were locking the others out or locking her in.

Her fears eased when he returned and handed her the key. "Just so you won't have to worry about someone walking in on us."

He crossed to the table bearing the wine bottles. "What's your favorite spirit, Elizabeth?"

Her tastes were so unsophisticated, she hesitated to tell him. "Sweet sack."

His smile broadened. "Good. I guessed right." He filled a diminutive glass with the amber liquid, then picked up another

bottle and poured a scant three fingers of a darker spirit into
a goblet for himself. Balancing a plate of pastries precariously
on his arm, he carried the drinks over. ''Oop. Quick, get the
plate, before I drop it.''

Elizabeth rescued the food, then took her glass. She watched
out of the corner of her eye as Garrett circled the bed and
reclined beside her. His drink in one hand, he propped himself
on his side and stared, half-lidded, into her eyes. His frank
gaze unsettled her. Elizabeth looked away, her focus shifting
to his bare lower legs. An aura of golden curls covered his
muscular calves, and his feet were long and well-formed. She
might have known that even his feet would be handsome.

When she glanced back at his face, his smug half smile
rattled her so badly that her first gulp of sack was far larger
than she intended, burning her throat and causing her to cough.
She took another, smaller, sip and avoided his gaze by in-
specting the pastries. The salty flavor of the meat pie she chose
proved a perfect complement to the sweet sack.

Garrett swirled the dark liquid in his glass, releasing the
unmistakable, potent scent of applejack into the air. Somehow,
Elizabeth finished her first glass of sack before he had drunk
even a fourth of his.

''Here.'' He took her glass. ''Let me get you another.''

She nodded, still so nervous she felt no effect from the wine.
By the time her second glass was empty, Garrett's applejack
was still more than half-full. His expression sober but his eyes
merry, he asked, ''Another?''

Desperate to take the edge off her tension, she nodded.
''Please.''

Her third drink didn't seem nearly so strong as the first. She
finished it in only a few long, delicious swigs, then yawned
hugely, settling back into the pillows.

''Elizabeth, I only wanted to help you relax a little, not get
you drunk,'' Garrett said. ''Are you all right?''

''Mmmm.'' She yawned again and looked beyond the bed-
posts. The windows were dark now, reflecting the firelit chamber, and the air was hot from the crackling flames. She liked
this room, with its warm wooden floors, intimate scale, and
low ceiling. Snug. Her gaze circled back to Garrett. He had
loosened his robe, exposing a tantalizing vee of muscular
chest.

He plucked at the thick muslin of her nightgown. "Aren't you hot in that thing?"

"S'warm. Yes. Verrrry warm." Her lips were singularly uncooperative, making it difficult to speak clearly. Garrett watched with open amusement as she rose unsteadily to her knees on the bed and struggled to unfasten her prim nightgown. It took some time, but she finally managed to loose enough buttons to shuck the garment off over her head. "Whew. That's better." Oblivious now to the fact that she was wearing only her shift, she flung the nightgown aside. "I was roasting." Elizabeth plunked most ungracefully onto her backside. After another sip of sack, she licked her lips with deliberation. "Mmmph."

"What?" Garrett asked, his eyes never leaving her face.

A ridiculous giggle escaped her. "I think I've had enough. My lips have gone numb." Suddenly drowsy, she dropped back against the pillows and closed her eyes. Elizabeth felt Garrett roll closer, then smelled his clean, masculine scent mingled with the musty odor of his clothes.

The tip of his finger traced a gentle path across her lower lip. "Can you feel this?"

"A little." She kept her eyes closed. Somehow, she felt safer in the dark.

"How about this?" With a rustle of fabric, his warmth grew nearer, hovering above her, then his lips were on hers. At first his kiss was tender, almost innocent, then it deepened, lingering, exploring, igniting an unexpected flicker of desire.

It had never been like this with Ravenwold. His kisses had been harsh, demanding, but Garrett kissed her as if the act were an end unto itself. She found herself actually enjoying it.

She heard his breathing quicken, and her own heart answered by thumping rapidly in her chest. Garrett's palm stroked the side of her cheek, then slid through her hair to cup the back of her head. She relaxed in his hands and savored the glow that radiated from his touch and his lips.

Then he drew away, leaving her empty. "Well?"

She opened her eyes to find him propped next to her, his hair backlit into a golden halo by the firelight and his face in shadow. "Well, what?" she asked breathlessly.

"Could you feel that?"

She nodded.

"And?"

"And I'd like for you to do it again."

Without a word, he drew her to him and kissed her again, this time so thoroughly she barely noticed his hands threading through her hair, exploring its fine texture, pulling it down over her shoulders. When at last she drew away, faint from lack of air, he searched her face hungrily, then descended once more.

Next, it was he who came up gasping. He looked down on her with an odd expression on his shadowed face. Slowly, his fingers untied the ribbons that laced her shift. Elizabeth let him, feeling strangely detached about it, almost as if she were a spectator watching from a corner instead of a participant. But she was not afraid.

His touch as sensitive as that of a blind man learning the shape and feel of an unfamiliar find, Garrett's hand slid up Elizabeth's calf to caress her thigh, raising her chemise with it. "This shift is getting in the way," he said raggedly. "I want to take it off. I want to see what you look like."

Suddenly constricted by the delicate garment, she nodded. What would he say when he saw her? Would he be disappointed? She sat up and started to pull the shift and gown off over her head, but Garrett stayed her hands.

"No. Let me." The raw desire in his voice triggered an odd contraction deep within her. Slowly and deliberately, he lifted the delicate fabric, revealing her body inch by inch. Exposed to the warm air, her skin came alive at the feel of the hem brushing against it, higher and higher. When she was completely naked, he sat back on his haunches, his eyes devouring her. "You're beautiful, Elizabeth. Just as I imagined you would be."

She did not believe him, but she was glad he'd said it. "And what about you?" Elizabeth reclined on the pillows. "Don't I get to see what you look like?"

Her boldness sparked a gleam of lust in his eyes. "Indeed." Untying his sash, he rolled out of bed and dropped his robe from his shoulders, exposing the tight contours of his entire back side. Then slowly, he turned, less than an arm's length away from her, the firelight gilding the hard planes of his body. Elizabeth gazed at his broad shoulders and muscular abdomen, then looked lower to his proud, erect manhood. Her eyes widened. It was enormous.

Without thinking, she reached over and touched it.

Garrett closed his eyes and moaned, a look of exquisite suffering on his face. "Have mercy, Bess. If you do that, I won't last more than five minutes."

Appalled at her own brazenness, she stammered, "I'm sorry. I didn't mean . . . I mean, I didn't think . . ."

He slid into the bed on his stomach and smothered her explanations with a kiss. Then he pulled back, smiling, "You're full of surprises, aren't you?" His lips brushed across her cheek to whisper into her ear, "I liked it when you touched me, Bess. Liked it so much that I almost lost control, and I don't want to rush things. Not this first time."

His mouth moved down her neck, across her chest, and brushed seductively across her nipple. A charge of white-hot sensation bolted through her. Gently, his teeth tightened on the tender flesh and his tongue flicked back and forth across the sensitive, erect tip. Elizabeth gasped aloud.

When he lavished her other breast with the same exquisite attention, tiny noises of delight escaped her. With every sound she made, his own ardor increased, but he remained patient, deliberate. His lips moved lower, the feathery pressure burning across her waist and abdomen. But when his mouth brushed the shallow depression between her belly and her hip, Elizabeth cried out, "Ah! Don't do that."

He looked up at her, his face intense. "You don't like it?"

She felt herself blush. "It tickles." His touch magnified every sensation, even the inappropriate ones.

"Ah. I know what to do about that." His hand slid firmly over the affected area, wiping away the ticklish sensation. But his fingers did not stop there. They threaded lower, probing, separating, until they found the nub of her desire. Elizabeth arched her back and closed her eyes, overcome by the erotic torrent his strokes released.

Touch by touch, Garrett opened a world of sensation she had never dreamed of. In all those years with her first husband, Ravenwold had never given her pleasure. Even in the beginning, he had used her, roughly and quickly, then rolled over and slept. But now, under Garrett's skillful manipulation, she felt her body come alive. Like a poor, half-frozen creature rescued from the cold and given refuge by the fire, she began to warm and come to life. "You were right," she breathed.

Garrett raised up, his eyes glazed with passion. "About what?"

"I have never had a lover. Not until now." She grasped his shoulders and pulled herself to him, kissing his chest. She reveled in the distinctive scent of him, so close against her, the feel of his scattered golden fur brushing her skin, the taste of him on her lips. Elizabeth pressed her cheek hard to his flesh. "I want you inside me. Now." Her nails dug into his corded muscles. "Fill me up, Garrett." She laid back, the hunger patent on her face.

Before her eyes, she saw Garrett's control dissolve. His skin burning, he rolled atop her, then parted her legs and thrust into her, hot and deep, taking her beyond thought, beyond circumstance, beyond everything but the primal compulsion to be joined. This was how it was supposed to be between a man and a woman. Lost to herself now, she met him thrust for thrust.

Garrett grasped her waist and changed position, pulling her hard against him as he rocked back onto his knees. Elizabeth's body arched convulsively. She closed her eyes and pushed against the pillows above her head. His thrusts became sharp and rapid, each one stabbing some unknown, mystical part of her that released wave after wave of pure ecstasy. Responding instinctively, she locked her legs behind him to draw him even deeper.

Garrett's hands played over her breasts, stroking, massaging, intensifying the assault of pleasure. Her passion grew and grew until it bloomed within her, like some huge, exotic flower bursting open in the moonlight.

With that, Garrett arched his back and let out a guttural cry of satisfaction. Then, still joined to her, he bent forward and tenderly kissed her lips.

Elizabeth pulled him down atop her, wanting to feel his heart beating wild as her own, wanting the sweat that glistened on his fair skin to mingle with hers. He tried to brace himself so as not to crush her, but she urged him to let go. "No. I want to feel you on top of me. All of you." He relaxed, his weight somehow reassuring.

She tightened around him, and an answering shift of his manhood sent a fresh stab of pleasure through her. Taking his head into her hands, she kissed his eyelids, then his cheeks, then his lips, then his neck.

A contented growl escaped Garrett as he rolled onto his back, pulling her close beside him. Then he drew her head to his chest and stroked her hair in silence.

Elizabeth closed her eyes and snuggled against him, the rhythm of his heart now strong and slow beneath her ear. She felt as if she could breathe underwater, drifting peacefully beneath a warm, salty sea.

Odd, for him to be so quiet. She wondered for a fleeting moment if she had done something wrong, but the memory of his cry of exultation reassured her. Her fingers threaded absently through the golden fur of his chest, then she gently teased at his nipples by brushing her hand across them. He shivered at her touch. She propped her chin on his chest and looked up at him. "I liked that very much, Garrett. Do you think we could do it again?"

He raised his head. "Now?"

She nodded. "Oh, yes. That is, if you want to."

"I'd like nothing better." Laughing, he rolled over, taking her with him to the other side of the bed and ending up atop her again. He kissed her softly. "Touch me now, Bess. Touch me all you want."


The sun was well up before they were wakened by several brisk knocks and a muffled, "Breakfast, master," from beyond the servants' entrance to the dressing room.

Garrett reached across Elizabeth and retrieved the key, then rose, naked, to unlock both doors. She scarcely had time to find her shift and gown, put them on, and pull up the covers before he slid back into bed beside her and called, "Come in!"

A parade of servants entered, prompting Elizabeth to cross her arms self-consciously in front of her. She felt uncomfortable about being seen in bed with her bare-chested husband beside her, but Garrett didn't seem to mind at all.

None of the servants looked at them directly. The footman seemed intent on arranging the wood he'd brought for the fireplace, and the chambermaid busily fanned the embers. The manservant, Wynton, wordlessly draped Garrett's robe across the foot of the bed, then disappeared through the dressing room.

Trying to hide her embarrassment, Elizabeth said to the maid who was opening the draperies nearby, "Please pick up Lady Mary's things from the floor and see that they're properly pressed." A blush stung her cheeks. "And don't let anyone know how you found them—particularly Lady Mary. I do not wish to offend her.''

"As milady wishes," the girl responded. She gathered the garments and left along with the footman and the chambermaid. The two remaining maids carefully placed breakfast trays on either side of Elizabeth and Garrett on the wide bed, then retreated.

Watching them go, Elizabeth whispered to Garrett, "I'd die if Mary found out I'd left her lovely dresses all over the floor."

"You needn't worry about Mary. She cares little for dresses." Garrett poured a cup of coffee from the ceramic pot on his tray, releasing a savory, robust aroma. "Mary pretends to be a proper lady, but she's really still a tomboy." He handed the coffee to Elizabeth, his voice dropping. "I happen to know she wears breeches under her skirts.''

"She doesn't!" Surely, he was jesting.

"Oh, aye." Garrett cocked a half smile. "Mother has tried for years to break her of riding astride and climbing trees, but Mary does as she pleases. She's as stubborn as the rest of us. The breeches were a compromise . . . for modesty's sake.''

Elizabeth eyed him skeptically as he lifted the napkin covering a basket of aromatic pastries. "Raisin pasties and raspberry jam." He chuckled, shaking his head.

"Don't you like them?''

"I used to. They were my favorites when I was ten." He poured himself a cup of coffee and took a sip. "Now I prefer shortbread and butter, but once my mother gets it into her head that a person likes something, she'll feed it to him until doomsday.''

"I like your mother very much." Elizabeth plucked up one of the pasties. "And the twins. I can see why they're your favorites." She bit into the delicious, chewy morsel.

"I love *all* my sisters," Garrett protested, but his frown of indignation did not reach his eyes. "Who told you the twins were my favorites?''

"No one told me. It was written all over you. You melt whenever you see them.''

"That doesn't signify. They're the babies, that's all." He propped a few pillows behind him and leaned back. "I love all of my family just as much, and so will you, once you get to know them.''

"Your sisters are very pretty." Elizabeth sipped from her

own cup, relishing the exotic, bitter flavor. It had been years since she'd been able to afford a luxury as expensive as coffee. "Tell me about them."

"Well, I've already told you about Little Mother Mary." He cradled his steaming cup in both hands. "Edith is next in line. She's always wanting to change everything around, move the furniture, rearrange the gardens. I don't think she could sit still if her life depended on it."

"I envy her energy. She seems so alive."

"She's a live one, all right. The poor fellow who marries her will never know another moment's peace."

"Then you shall have to find her a husband who wants an industrious wife." She took another sip of coffee and cut her eyes up at him. "That shouldn't be too difficult, should it? Perhaps a Scotsman . . ."

"A Scotsman! Bess, you can't be serious! Mother would—" He stopped, his outrage abruptly fading. "By glory, so you do have a sense of humor. You really had me going, there."

Elizabeth felt a smile tug at her own lips. Maybe around Garrett, in this house, it wouldn't be so hard to smile. "What about Amy?"

"You skipped Becky. She's next," he corrected.

"Ah. Becky, then."

"Becky's a quiet one. I never know quite what to make of her. But one thing is certain: She's the stubbornest of the lot. If you push her, she just digs in her heels and balks." He shook his head. "She gets her way by *not* doing what you want her to." His blue eyes shifted appraisingly to Elizabeth. "Reminds me of someone else I know." When she frowned in suspicion, he introduced a safer topic, "Becky loves cats, perhaps because the creatures are so silent and aloof—rather like she is. Take care with Becky, though. She never forgets a slight."

"I'll remember that," Elizabeth said. "Now, Amy."

Garrett brightened. "Amy's a sweetheart, kind and generous to a fault, but impulsive. She's always thundering around, rushing into things with the best intentions, only to find herself neck-deep in trouble." He chuckled. "Rather like a big, affectionate dog who accidentally flattens the children with its tail." Elizabeth marveled at the affection in his voice. "Amy's very dramatic, a real romantic." He shook his head. "I hope she grows out of that before it's time to find her a husband."

"You disapprove of romance?"

"No." His features sobered. "But a realistic attitude will serve her better, especially in marriage."

Elizabeth wondered if Garrett's pointed observation was a veiled warning directed at her. He needn't bother. She had no illusions about the passion they had shared. Last night had been wonderful, and she was looking forward to more amorous revelations, but she did not expect the excitement to last. Garrett was a man who relished new things, new conquests, new experiences. Once Elizabeth was no longer new, he would find another lover.

As if he had read her thoughts, Garrett frowned, then turned his attention to his breakfast.

She put the rest of her raisin pastie into her mouth, chiding herself. It shouldn't matter, his taking another lover someday, but deep down inside, Elizabeth realized it would. She told herself to be realistic, accept what he had given her: safety, financial security, sisters and a mother, a lovely home. Not to mention last night's physical awakening. That should be enough.

She must be realistic. Garrett had not promised her more than he could give, never pretended to be anything more than he was. It wouldn't be fair to expect him to provide the love she craved. Such notions were for naive girls of twelve, like Amy.

A knock sounded at the door. "Garrett, it's us. Are you awake?"

Elizabeth recognized the twins' voices, but before she could protest that they were hardly in an acceptable state to receive anyone, Garrett boomed, "Come in! Come in!"

The two girls opened the door and ran inside, their arms brimming with fresh-cut lilacs, apple blossoms, lilies, and silver bells. Neither of the twins seemed embarrassed by the circumstances, but Elizabeth blushed and pulled the covers up under her chin. At least Garrett was decently covered from the waist down.

He stretched open his arms and said, "Come here, you two. Give us a hug."

Elizabeth watched the twins scamper over and hug their brother, then circle the bed to hug her. She felt awkward when each of them embraced her and kissed her cheek, but their warmth was contagious, and she was smiling when they stepped back.

Honor scratched her wrist. "Oooh! Something's been biting me."

"And me," Hope chimed in, vigorously rubbing the waist of her dress.

"Come here, bunny rabbit," Garrett said to Honor. When she obliged, he pushed up her sleeve to inspect the area she had been scratching. "Oh, good glory!" He glanced at Elizabeth. "Take a look at that and tell me what you think."

Elizabeth leaned over. The mark on Honor's arm was identical to the bites that had marred her own legs and torso. "Dear Heaven, we've given them fleas."

"Looks like it, but I can't imagine how. We were only together for a few minutes when we arrived, and then we both bathed," Garrett reasoned. He looked Honor full in the face. "Do you have any more itches like this one?"

"Yes," she responded guiltily. "And so does Hope. But not where we can show them."

"Hmm." His eyes narrowed. "Let me guess. You've been playing in the coach, the one I brought Elizabeth home in, haven't you?"

Honor's eyes widened. She spun to her sister. "I told you Mary would tattle!"

"Whoa, now. Nobody told me anything. On my word as a gentleman," Garrett assured her.

Both his little sisters frowned, but it was Honor who asked, "Then how did you know we'd been playing in the coach?"

He put his forehead to hers. "I can read minds." Garrett frowned without rancor. "I think it would be best for you two to stay away from the others until Mother gives both of you a good dusting with sulphur powder."

"Sulphur powder?" Honor exclaimed. "But it smells like rotten eggs. *We'll* smell like rotten eggs!" Hope nodded, her indignant expression identical to her sister's.

"Sorry, my little princesses, but it's the best way to get rid of fleas." He motioned them toward the door. "Run along, now, straight to Mother. Tell her what I said, and don't leave out the part about the sulphur."

When they had gone, he rose from the bed, splendidly naked and unselfconscious. He gave his ribs a vigorous scratch. "Makes me itch just to think about those fleas."

"Fleas." Elizabeth tried to act nonchalant about his walking around in broad daylight with no clothes on. "Oh, Garrett, it's all my fault. First I gave them to you, and now—"

Garrett cut her off. "None of that, now. I can't abide a martyr, Bess." He shrugged. "Fleas are a fact of life. The girls shouldn't have been playing in the coach, anyway. Maybe a few itches will teach them a lesson." He strode into the sunshine pouring through the diamond-paned windows. "I'd forgotten how beautiful May is here." He pushed open one of the casements, admitting a surprisingly warm breeze. "How about a picnic, Bess?"

"A picnic? But don't you think I should be helping your mother? After all, I—"

"Nonsense. There's all the time in the world to take over running this house." He leered at her. "I promise to make it a picnic to remember." When she hesitated, he coaxed, "We're on our honeymoon, you know."

Since it seemed to mean so much to him, she ignored her more practical instincts and agreed. "Very well, but only if your mother doesn't need me."

"Mother," he said, "will be the first one to tell you to go." He bowed. "And now, dear wife, I beg your leave to shave and dress."

He looked so silly, bowing formally without a stitch on, that she actually chuckled. "You have my leave, husband, but might I remind you this isn't a barracks. I suggest you put on your robe, or you'll embarrass us both."

"I refuse to be embarrassed, especially in my own house," he said with mock haughtiness. "But in deference to milady's gentle sensibilities, I shall wear my robe." He put it on, over-lapped it, then tied it closed. "Meet me on the front lawn at one, and wear something comfortable."

He grew serious. "As long as we are here, Bess, I would prefer that you not wear black." When she started to protest, he shook his head. "I mean no disrespect to Charlotte. I ask it simply because it would please me to see you in something besides those widow's weeds."

Elizabeth realized there was little point in arguing. Mary had lent her a dozen colorful gowns, but not one of them had been black. Her own two black dresses were doubtless being laundered. The truth was, after the week she'd spent in her old dress, she'd rather burn it than wear it again, and the gown she'd had made in Bristol was far too plain for this exalted household. "Very well. As long as we are among family, I will forego wearing black."

A satisfied smile eased Garrett's face. "Thank you." He strode out into the main hall, calling back, "See you at one."

# ❧ CHAPTER 19 ❧

"*Exhale*, milady." Luella tugged at the back of Elizabeth's borrowed bodice. "By heaven, this bodice is wee. Good thing it's stoutly made." She managed to hook the waist fairly easily, but midway up the back, she ran into real trouble. Her voice thickened with effort. "I'm not sure I can close it."

"You must," Elizabeth gasped. If only she hadn't promised not to wear black . . . "Lady Mary was closest to my size. This will have to do." She took a few shallow, panting breaths, then exhaled deeply, mashing the bodice front as hard as she could to flatten her ample breasts. "Now. Quickly."

Luella renewed her struggle with the sapphire-colored silk. After much grunting, mashing, and straining on both their parts, she finally succeeded. "There!" She circled Elizabeth to survey the results. "Mmmm." The maid's eyebrows lifted.

Elizabeth looked down and frowned. Her displaced bosom bulged provocatively beneath the almost-transparent white batiste of Mary's blouse. "Tinkers and tacks! I'm indecent."

"Nay, milady. It looks most fashionable." Luella's dubious expression shifted to a knowing smile. "I daresay milord will like the way it fits."

"Well, I don't; I can scarcely breathe." Elizabeth wedged her feet into Mary's matching slippers. "Thank goodness the shoes aren't quite as tight as the dress. I should be grateful for that, I suppose." At the sound of the bedroom door bursting open behind her, Elizabeth turned to see Amy skipping toward her.

Halfway across the room, the twelve-year-old stopped, crestfallen, and exclaimed, "Oh, dear! I forgot to knock." She spun around and hurried back toward the door.

"Amy," Elizabeth called after her, "come back. It's all right." When the girl obliged, she added, "Just this once, though. I know you'll remember to knock in the future."

"I'll try," Amy offered, unabashed. "I just couldn't wait to tell you how happy Garrett has been this morning. He's whistled all over the house getting things ready." She took Elizabeth's hands, her attention shifting to the borrowed dress. "What a perfect shade of blue for you." Amy's gaze bobbed from the dress to Elizabeth's face and back again. "It matches your eyes exactly." She cocked an auburn brow. "Mary never looked half as good in that dress, I can tell you."

"Amy," Elizabeth chided gently, pulling her hands free. "You mustn't say uncomplimentary things about Mary, especially after she was kind enough to share her clothes with me." She still wasn't used to the way Garrett's family kept touching her.

Amy shrugged. "I wasn't being uncomplimentary. Just telling the truth."

The clock in the hall gave one deep, dignified chime, prompting Elizabeth to say, "I'm afraid we'll have to finish our visit later. I'm supposed to meet Garrett outside right now." She turned to Luella. "My hat, please." Mary's hat, to be more accurate.

"Milady will not be wearing the Creighton pearls?" Luella asked.

"Not today," Elizabeth said firmly. Not on a picnic. She'd be foolish to take such a chance with the priceless heirlooms. She motioned to the elaborate broad-brimmed hat of finely woven white straw. "Just bring the hat. His lordship is waiting."

"Aye, milady." Luella smoothed a faint crease from the wide brim, then settled the hat on Elizabeth's head. She pulled back the two wide, white ribbons and tied them at the nape of Elizabeth's neck. "If milady will please tip her chin down, I'll have this bow done in no time."

While she worked, Amy reached up to touch the cunning white silk roses piled against one side of the crown. "Don't you just love the roses? They look so real." She plopped onto a footstool and hugged her knees. "They came from Paris," she said importantly. "Last Christmas. Garrett sent each of us a whole basketful of silk flowers, all kinds and colors. It was like having spring in the middle of winter." She smiled proudly up at Elizabeth. "He's always sending us presents, you know."

"I think that's because he loves you all so much," Elizabeth confided honestly.

Finished with the ribbons, Luella pulled a tall, free-standing mirror into place and adjusted it to reflect her mistress from head to toe. "Is everything satisfactory, milady?"

Elizabeth hardly recognized herself. She looked elegant, indeed. Mary's gown showed off her small waist, and the tight bodice accentuated her bustline. The sapphire color really did match her eyes.

For one fleeting moment, she almost believed that she could hold her own with Garrett's comely sisters. Then she almost laughed aloud at herself for having such a silly, vain notion. She was plain—skinny as a beggar and twice as pale. It was only the dress that was beautiful. "Come, Amy. Walk me outside."

Amy took her hand. "I can't wait to see the expression on Garrett's face when he sees how beautiful you look."

Elizabeth cocked her head in wonder that the dress had worked its magic on Amy.

On the stairs, they met Becky carrying one of her ever-present cats. Remembering Garrett's warning, Elizabeth stopped despite her hurry. "Good afternoon, Rebecca." She reached out to stroke the cat's long white fur. "What a beautiful cat. What's its name?"

Becky pulled the cat closer, her expression oblique. "*Her* name is Pearl."

"I can see she loves her mistress." She looked into Becky's large hazel eyes, eyes that gave away no more than a cat's. "Do you have any other pets?"

Becky nodded solemnly. "Five cats."

"I should like to see them." Obviously, Becky wasn't going to make this any easier.

"We have to go now, Becky," Amy announced. She tugged Elizabeth after her down the stairs.

Elizabeth shot a smile of apology over her shoulder. "Good day, Rebecca."

Lady Catherine intercepted them at the bottom of the stairs. "Why, Elizabeth, you look beautiful!" She said it with such conviction, Elizabeth almost believed her.

"It's the dress. And the bonnet," she responded. "If you

see Mary, please tell her how much I appreciate her generosity."

"I shall." Lady Catherine turned an affectionate smile on Amy. "And you, missy. Have you been making a nuisance of yourself?"

"No, Mummy. Truly, I haven't."

"She's delightful," Elizabeth interjected.

Lady Catherine chuckled. "Well, I happen to know that a little bit of Amy goes a long way." She pulled her daughter close and gave the girl's chin a wiggle. "Come along, my precious butterfly. Time for your harpsichord lesson. I think Garrett and Elizabeth can manage quite well without us." Ushering Amy toward the music room she called back to Elizabeth, "Enjoy your picnic, dear. We'll keep your supper warm."

Outside under a flawless blue sky, Elizabeth blinked in the bright sunlight. A warm breeze billowed her skirts behind her.

Garrett was waiting in the center of the brick courtyard, his back turned as he adjusted the harness of a stallion hitched to an odd little two-seated cart. Strange, that there were no footmen or stableboys to help him.

Elizabeth crossed the winding pattern of the maze. Busy with the harness, Garrett kept his back to her and gave no indication that he heard her coming. Her husband cut a dashing figure, even dressed in a simple white shirt, dark breeches, plain black boots, and unadorned riding gloves. No one would ever mistake him for a stableman.

What would he think of her, she wondered, in her borrowed finery? She stopped just behind him and made her presence known with, "That's an awfully big horse for such a small cart."

Garrett turned, wearing his usual mischievous smile, but with one look at her, his smile faded to a blank stare. "I got the cart in Ireland," he murmured absently. "It's light, but very strong. Fast."

"Oh." Elizabeth tried to hide her disappointment. Garrett was usually so free with compliments. He might have at least pretended to be impressed by her transformation. She wished now she'd worn her comfortable black dress, after all.

Garrett resumed his customary lighthearted manner. "Perfect weather for a picnic, isn't it, Bess?"

"How can we have a picnic?" she challenged, peering into

the cart. "I don't see any food."

"Don't worry. I've taken care of everything." He helped her into the padded wicker seat, then circled to get in beside her. Garrett picked up the reins. "Hold on." He flicked the stallion to a steady trot.

Elizabeth grabbed her bonnet to keep it from blowing off. "Where are we going?"

"It's a surprise." He shot her a winsome grin. "But we must travel a bit to get there. Just sit back and enjoy the ride." He turned his attention to the road.

The cart seemed comfortable enough, but Elizabeth's tight bodice made her wonder just how far "a bit" was. She leaned back and tried to enjoy the unseasonably warm sunshine and the pastoral beauty of the Cambrian plain.

Leaving Chestwick behind, Garrett took them westward at a brisk pace along a well-traveled road. Within half an hour, they had crossed the Welsh border and entered the foothills of the Cambrian Mountains.

Elizabeth made several awkward attempts at conversation, but when her efforts fell flat, she lapsed into uneasy silence as the country became wilder, steeper, and more isolated. The scenery was spectacular, but she couldn't help thinking how vulnerable they were on the long, lonely stretches between towns and homesteads.

Her anxiety increased when she saw a dray wagon crest the rise in front of them on one particularly isolated piece of road. She edged closer to Garrett.

"Don't worry, Bess," he reassured her. "It's one of ours."

Sure enough, when the wagon passed them, the driver bowed in recognition. Elizabeth subsided, relieved.

By the time an hour had elapsed, they were deep in hill country, and Mary's dress felt as if it had shrunk two sizes. The stays gouged into Elizabeth every time the cart hit a bump, but discomfort was the least of her worries. They hadn't passed a house or farm for miles. Unable to remain silent any longer, she asked, "Are you certain it's safe to travel here?" She nervously scanned the mountains all around them.

Garrett didn't take his eyes from the road. "Yes."

Unconvinced, she shifted in her seat. "What about bandits? They could be hiding anywhere."

Garrett pulled hard on the reins, bringing the stallion to a halt. He turned to her with a serious expression. "I can understand why you're worried, Bess, especially after what you've been through, but I would never risk your safety again. Watch this." He let out a shrill, piercing whistle. Within moments, armed, mounted men appeared out of nowhere on the surrounding hilltops.

Elizabeth clutched his arm.

"They're my men, Elizabeth, all of them. I wanted to take you to a favorite spot, so I sent them ahead to stand guard. They'll keep watch until we return, then escort us home." He smiled. "At a discreet distance, of course." When he waved his hand in a circle, the mounted men disappeared from sight.

Elizabeth was impressed. "You are not what you appear to be, are you?"

"I'm not sure I know what you mean by that." Garrett urged the horse forward.

"You only pretend to be carefree and careless. You're really a very clever man." Her eyes narrowed. "Or would calculating be a better description?"

"You've seen through me, Bess."

At the crest of the next ridge, they veered onto an almost invisible track that meandered down into a deep, closed valley. Elizabeth looked below them and saw a sparkling stream beside the moss-covered ruins of a Gothic church. Thick woods grew just behind the ruins, and beyond that, a thundering waterfall spilled down the high cliffs that closed the far end of the valley.

"I love it here," Garrett murmured.

Elizabeth nodded. The valley seemed almost magical— apart, somehow, from time or circumstance. In this isolated, mystical place, she could almost believe they were the only two people in the world.

As they neared the ruins, Garrett pointed to the waterfall. "That's where we're going, but we'll have to leave the cart and walk a bit."

"Walk?" Her tight bodice left little breath for exertion.

"Don't worry. It's not far." He reined the cart to a halt, then pulled off his gloves.

Elizabeth didn't wait for him to help her out. She hopped down to the ground and arched her back. Blast this bodice! Her ribs ached almost as much as they had when Ravenwold had broken them, years ago.

Garret climbed out on her side. He lifted the wide brim of

her bonnet and looked underneath. "Are you all right?"

"Fine," she lied.

"Good." He grinned like a little boy. "I can't wait for you to see this." He led her under an abandoned arch into the ruins, their footsteps muffled by the mossy ground. Garrett halted when they reached the center of the deserted church. "Close your eyes and listen, Bess," he said in wonder.

Already short of breath, Elizabeth was glad for an excuse to stop. She closed her eyes and listened. There was no wind. No birdsong. No hum of insects. Only the distant rushing of the falls. The effect was almost eerie.

Were there ghosts here? She shivered, her lids flying open at the thought.

Garrett's voice broke the hushed spell. "Wonderful silence." He brightened abruptly and tugged her toward the woods. "Come on."

Elizabeth did her best to keep up, but even in the shade of the huge oak trees, she quickly grew breathless and overheated. Fortunately, they hadn't gone far before the forest ended in a laurel thicket.

"We're here," Garrett announced proudly. He pushed back the branches so Elizabeth could pass, then followed her into a sunlit setting as beautiful as any she had ever beheld.

Her mouth dropped open in amazement.

Garrett chuckled. "I thought you'd like it."

A pristine clearing spread out before them. At the far side of a small, sparkling lake, the waterfall tumbled white and brilliant down the cliffs. Between the woods and the lake, a crescent of meadow sloped gently downward to the grassy shoreline, where a lavish picnic had been laid out on an enormous Persian rug. Behind them, dense laurels and pines stretched unbroken to climb the base of the cliffs.

"It's perfect," Elizabeth whispered. "Perfect." She crossed the sunny meadow to the rug. Never, in all her life, had she seen such an opulent spread. Huge cushions of every imaginable color were piled around a flat box draped in damask and set with silver and crystal for two. Baskets of fruit and assorted trunks and boxes of food had been arranged within easy reach. She turned to Garrett. "You've thought of everything."

"I tried to." He dropped to the rug and pulled off one of his boots. "Come on, Bess. Take your shoes off." After tugging off the other boot, he shucked his stockings, then wiggled his toes in the sunlight. "It feels wonderful."

Elizabeth flexed her cramped toes. Mary's slippers *were* small. Trapped in her tight dress, she *could* take her shoes off. "Why not?" She stepped out of the slippers, but did not remove her stockings. Her feet sank into the sun-warmed softness of the rug. "Mmm. You're right. It does feel good." Mindful of Mary's dress, she descended carefully onto a fat pillow next to the "table." The down-filled cushion beneath her felt as soft as it looked.

Garrett rubbed his hands together. "Before we do anything else, let's eat. I'm starving."

"Eat?" She dared not eat; she'd split the seams.

"Yes, eat," Garrett repeated cheerfully. "As in picnic." He rummaged around in the trunks and boxes, setting out wine, a basket of fritters, a large bowl of salad, an enormous cold Florentine, an olive pie, several kinds of cheese, cold roast goose and venison, baked chewits, braised cabbage, pickled turnips, and a platter of quince tarts. "Mmmm. Looks good." Garrett served up a little of everything onto two silver chargers, then laid them on the "table" and sat down opposite her. He bowed his head and rattled off, "For what we are about to receive may the Lord make us truly thankful amen," before digging in with gusto. After several hearty mouthfuls, his spoon paused halfway between plate and mouth. "You're not eating."

Elizabeth poked her spoon into the pile of food on her plate. "Yes, I am."

"No, you're not. You're just pushing it around. You haven't eaten a bite." Puzzled, he asked, "Don't you like it?" He waved his knife. "Gwynneth told me these were your favorite foods."

"The food's wonderful." Elizabeth shifted uncomfortably. A stay was digging into her hip.

"Are you ill?" Garrett's face reflected real concern.

"No. I'm fine, really."

"Then what's the matter, Bess?" When she didn't answer, he threw his hands up and fairly shouted, "For heaven's sake, woman, I can see that something's wrong. Why in blazes won't you *tell* me? Just open your mouth and—"

"My dress is too tight!" Elizabeth blurted out. She glared at his surprised expression. "I can hardly breathe, much less eat!"

Garrett burst out laughing. "Of all the . . ." He shook his head. "Why did you wear that one, then, if it's too tight?"

"Because you asked me not to wear black," she shot back. "I only have two dresses, and both of them are black!" She tried to rein her temper. "Mary was very gracious to share her clothes with me, but she and I are *not* the same size." Barely aware she was doing it, she tugged at the top of her bodice where it dug into her squashed breasts. "My . . . *bones* are much bigger than Mary's."

Garrett followed the motion with an appreciative eye. "You're right, Bess. I'm happy to say your *bones* are much larger than Mary's."

Elizabeth couldn't endure sitting any longer. She struggled to her feet. "Blast! This thing is stifling me."

Garrett got up and came around the table for a close look at the offending garment. "Hmmm." His concerned expression gave way to a beatific smile. "There's a simple solution, you know."

"Really?" Elizabeth regarded him with hostility from the shade of her bonnet. "And what, pray tell, would this simple solution be?"

"I'm surprised you didn't think of it." He circled behind her and grasped her waist, his long fingers curling around her sides. "Take it off." His thumbs pressed together, unfastening the bottom hook of the bodice.

"Garrett! Stop that!" Before she got away, he'd managed to unhook several more. Elizabeth groped the gaping fabric at the back of her waist. "Now look what you've done. How will I get them closed? Luella could hardly manage—"

He cut her off. "Calm yourself, Bess." Garrett held out his large, shapely hands for her inspection. "These are much bigger and stronger than Luella's. I can get you unfastened in no time, and fastened back up just fine."

He probably could. Elizabeth surprised herself by actually considering his suggestion.

"Take the silly thing off," Garrett urged. "Unless you'd rather suffer." He lifted a critical eyebrow. "I hope that's not the case. I told you, Bess, I can't abide people who wallow in their misery."

"I do not wallow, sir, in anything," she huffed. She *was* miserable, though. And she certainly didn't relish the prospect of passing the rest of the afternoon trussed so tightly. Bad

enough, that she had to ride home that way. Elizabeth wavered.
"What if someone were to come upon us?" she asked lamely.

"No one's going to come upon us." Garrett's face was all
innocence. "You have my word on it."

"And how can you be so certain of that?"

"Because I own this place, and the land for miles around.
My men are posted along the borders, with orders to let no
one past."

He owned this place? Elizabeth looked at the natural splen-
dor surrounding them and began to understand just how rich
her husband was. "Your men," she blustered, "how do you
know *they* won't spy on us?"

"They wouldn't dare." He pulled off her hat and drew her
close, a dangerous glitter in his eyes. "If any man should look
at my wife that way," he growled, "I'd put his eyes out and
cut off his tongue." There was no question that he meant it.

Elizabeth went still at the violence resonant in his threat.

Garrett turned her around, his hands circling her waist as
they had before. "Now, don't fight me." Mistaking her lack
of protest for consent, he swiftly unhooked every cursed hook.
Then, smooth as butter, he reached around her and unbuttoned
the straining fabric of Mary's blouse. "There. That's better,
isn't it?"

It felt so good to be free of the bodice's grip, she was almost
grateful. Elizabeth bent forward and sucked in deep, gasping
breaths of air. The bodice slipped down her arms, then slid to
the ground.

When she straightened up and rubbed her aching ribs, Garrett stared frankly at her gaping blouse. Her breasts were
clearly visible beneath her thin shift.

"Why don't you take off the rest?"

Now that she could breathe, she put her foot down. "I think
not," she snapped. She tried ineffectually to close the blouse.

"Suit yourself." Garrett dropped onto the pillows and
stretched out. He yawned hugely, closing his eyes. "Nap
time."

The knave, Elizabeth fumed. How dare he dismiss her that
way, ignoring her as if she were a servant? She flounced down
onto a pillow and shoved Mary's bonnet haphazardly back
onto her head. She glared at him, but Garrett dozed away in
blissful oblivion.

After several minutes, growing hunger supplanted Elizabeth's anger. Now that her dress was undone, she reasoned, there was no reason to starve herself. She leaned over and retrieved her heaping plate. Perhaps just a bite.

Fifteen minutes later, she stifled a belch and put down the empty plate. She glanced over at her husband. Sleeping like a babe—or so it seemed. His breathing was deep and even, his handsome features completely relaxed. Maybe he really was asleep. Full and drowsy herself, Elizabeth pulled up two of the large cushions and curled into their welcome softness, propping her bonnet over her face to protect her from the strong sunlight.

So peaceful, here. Before she knew it, the rushing waterfall sang her to sleep.

She awoke to the feel of Garrett's hand on her cheek. He was sitting beside her, holding her bonnet to shade her face. He peered at her as closely as she had earlier inspected him. "Wake up, sleepyhead," he coaxed.

Elizabeth yawned, then stretched. Even without the bodice, her clothes had grown damp and sticky in the heat. She asked sleepily, "Is it time to go home?"

"Not yet, but it is time to get up." Tossing the hat aside, he rose and pulled her to her feet. "Come. I have another surprise for you."

"Just what I need," she muttered, "another one of your surprises."

"Grumpy when you haven't slept your nap out, aren't you?" he asked affably. Garrett lifted her chin with his finger. "You liked my first surprise, didn't you?"

"I liked it very much," she confessed.

"Well, you'll like this one, too." He stepped into the meadow. "Follow me."

Elizabeth raised a staying finger. "Shoes."

"No shoes."

"But my stockings—"

"Take them off," he ordered cheerfully. As soon as she did, he strode back to take her by the wrist. "Just watch your step." Garrett pulled her toward the laurel thicket near the base of the cliffs.

"Slow down!" Elizabeth picked her way after him, her bare feet tender on the uneven ground. "At least give me time to look where I'm stepping." When they reached the thicket, she followed him through it, only to encounter a dense stand of pines on the other side.

He held back the pungent branches. "It's right on the other side of these pines."

When Elizabeth broke clear of the resinous boughs, she found herself standing in a sun-dappled woodland at the base of the cliffs. Her eye was drawn immediately to a heavy rectangular table of white stone that stood on a carpet of moss beneath the towering trees. No fallen trunks or broken branches marred the leafy forest floor.

Garrett slid his arms around Elizabeth from behind. "What do you think?"

"It's lovely."

"So are you." Garrett bent to kiss her. His lips were sweet and lingering, then insistent.

Elizabeth turned into his arms and kissed him back with an ardor that surprised them both. A surge of heat coursed through her.

Garrett pulled back and looked at her. "My, my. You're quite flushed, Bess. Are you feeling a bit warm in those clothes?" His hands stroked over her shoulders, smoothing them free of her unbuttoned blouse. "You would look like a woods nymph, naked in this place."

Elizabeth closed her eyes and felt his mouth, hot and feathery, on the side of her neck. She hardly noticed when he pulled her blouse away. Dizzy, she murmured a halfhearted protest. "Would you take me here, on the ground like some rutting animal?"

"I must admit, the idea has its merits," he said, expertly untying the ribbons of her shift. "But if you do not wish it, there's always the table."

Elizabeth looked at him askance. "The table?"

"We have complete privacy here," he assured. Slowly, he drew her to the table. "Think of it, the cool, smooth feel of marble underneath against your bare skin . . ."

"Hmmm." Hungry for the pleasure her husband could give her, she slid her palm across the polished slab. "It is cool. I must admit, I'm tempted."

"I told you you'd like it." Garrett skillfully loosed the waist of her skirts and petticoats. The garments fell to her ankles with a whisper of silk. Now she was standing in the warm, dappled shade in nothing but her shift. Damp with perspiration, the thin fabric clung to her body. He pulled the neckline open and peeled it off her.

Part of Elizabeth wanted to protest, but the greater part of her was transfixed by the hunger in his eyes. He wanted her. And she wanted him, even here, exposed, in the woodland.

His hands slid down her ribs. "More lovely than I remembered." He kissed her, long and tenderly, then guided her to the end of the table. There, he buried his face between her breasts, pushing her back against the edge of the slab.

Elizabeth closed her eyes and breathed deeply, inhaling the dusky smell of moss and humus along with Garrett's sharp, masculine scent. She knew he didn't love her, but she told herself it didn't matter. Better this pretense than what she'd had with Ravenwold. She wanted to feel loved, even if she could not be loved.

The pleasure was real, at least.

His lips traced a trail of heat across her breasts. Then his teeth tightened gently on her erect nipple, sending a stab of desire clear through her. "Ah." She threaded her fingers into his hair and savored the hungry pressure of his mouth.

She heard his breathing quicken. Garrett straightened and kissed her with renewed ardor, his tongue plunging, probing, tasting in her mouth.

Elizabeth felt as if she were breathing liquid fire.

Garrett's strong arms closed around her, lifting her hard against his erect manhood, but he did not penetrate her. Instinctively, she wrapped her legs around his hips to tighten the contact between them. She opened her eyes to find his blue gaze probing her own. Afraid that he would see too deeply, she closed her eyes and kissed his ruddied lips with unexpected urgency.

Her legs still wrapped around him, Garrett sat her on the end of the table. Beneath her bare buttocks, the cool, polished slab provided a delicious contrast to the heat that coursed from her lips to her breasts to the deepest, hungriest part of her.

His hands smoothed over her naked torso, followed by his darkened gaze. "Beautiful," he murmured.

Elizabeth let herself believe the lie, even if only for a moment. Here, in this place, so far removed from reality, she could be beautiful.

She stroked the taut muscles stretched across his ribs. "I think *you* are beautiful. I like to look at your body." She felt his manhood jump. "Love me, Garrett," she demanded. "Love me beyond sensibility, till I cannot think, only feel."

"Patience, Bess." Though his tone was even, his voice sounded hoarse. "In due time." One by one, he pulled the pins from her hair, releasing a blond cascade across her shoulders onto the marble table that supported her. His fingers combed a cloud of curls loose down her back. "Like sunshine on a winter morning. And soft. So soft." He nuzzled behind her ear, inhaling the scent of her. Then, his muscular thighs hard against the edge of the slab, he lowered her shoulders to the table, but still, he did not penetrate her.

The table's height was perfect, as if it had been made for this. Perhaps it had.

Garrett's hands explored her body with a deliberation contradicted by his rapid breathing. His touch awakened wave after wave of sensation. She writhed closer, every shift in pressure triggering sharp stabs of pleasure at the seat of her desire. The emptiness inside her grew until she could bear it no longer. She sat up abruptly and gripped his shoulders, rising sharply against him. "Now," she panted harshly. Then she thrust down atop his pulsing manhood.

Garrett's eyes fairly rolled back in his head. Locked to her in flesh, he pushed her shoulders back down onto the table. Slowly he began to thrust, deeper and deeper. Every hot, powerful stab released an explosion of joy inside her.

What secret place was he touching? Did he know what he was doing to her?

She opened her eyes to find him smiling down, an exultation as old as the world in his expression.

He knew exactly what he was doing. "You like that, don't you, Bess?"

A husky yes escaped her. She gripped the edges of the marble table and met him thrust for thrust.

He took her to the brink of release, then slowed, leaving her wild with wanting. Conscious only of a desire to be fully joined, she unwrapped her legs from his hips and stretched them up his torso. Garrett gripped her ankles. She flexed her knees, rising sharply, then shifted downward, feeling his manhood flick at something deep inside her.

Garrett gasped aloud with pleasure. "Do that again, Bess."

She did, robbing him of his self-control completely.

He shoved into her with a rhythm as rapid as his own ragged

breathing. Elizabeth added her own force to each pulse of join-ing until Garrett executed a final, magnificent thrust at the very moment of her own release. He cried out, then stilled, his head back.

Elizabeth pulled herself up and buried her face in the resil-ient curls on his chest, wishing they could stay this way for-ever. To her dismay, he withdrew from her abruptly and staggered backward.

Like a man who had suddenly lost his equilibrium, Garrett steadied himself on the mossy ground. Standing tall and golden in the shade, he looked like a sun-god exploring the shadows, but his blue eyes were dark with confusion.

"What's wrong?" Elizabeth asked.

"Nothing. Nothing's wrong."

Suddenly, she felt vulnerable, exposed. "Something's wrong," she said softly. "I can see it in your eyes." She curled her legs onto the table and covered herself as best she could with her long hair.

"Nothing's wrong." A practiced smile slid over his face. He took her hand. "Come on," he said with forced enthusi-asm. "Let's go swimming."

"Swimming?"

"Yes, swimming. In the lake. Naked."

"You can't be serious," she scoffed.

"I'm as serious as the plague," he said, his expression now bright with mischief.

"Don't jest about such a thing!" Elizabeth chided, making the sign of the cross, then spitting for luck. The mere mention of plague was an invitation to disaster. "It's bad luck."

"I don't believe in luck, Bess," he said with a wicked smile. He lifted her off the table and set her to her feet. "You look for your hairpins. I'll pick up our clothes." While he gathered their things haphazardly under his arm, she initiated a hasty search for her hairpins. When she'd had found most of them, she tucked the pins into one hand and extended the other to-ward Garrett. "My clothes, please."

Instead of handing over her things, Garrett took her hand and pulled her toward the lake. "No clothes. Not until we've been swimming." He grinned back at her. "Trust me, Bess. You'll like it."

Elizabeth wouldn't trust him any more than she would a Gypsy, but she had liked everything else he'd said she would.

Still, she felt obliged to protest a little. She tugged against him as he drew her along. "This is, by far, the most addlepated thing you have ever come up with." When they reached the laurel thicket, she dug her feet into the soft earth and pulled against him in earnest. "Stop! I can't go out into the open this way."

"The trouble with you, Bess," he said, "is you don't know how to have fun." Without even dropping the clothes bundled under his elbow, he scooped her off her feet. "Swimming naked is *fun*." Garrett carried her through the thicket and out into the meadow, making straight for the lake. A few yards from shore, he let their clothes fall to the ground. Elizabeth hastily tossed her hairpins atop the heap of silk and velvet.

Garrett stepped off the grassy bank into the water and waded in, knee-deep. A satisfied sigh escaped him. "Ahhh! It feels wonderful." Wading deeper, he looked askance at her. "You *can* swim, can't you?"

"Of course I can." She let go of his neck. "You may put me down, now."

"Very good, milady." He eased her to her feet.

"Why, it's warm as a pond," she declared when her legs slipped into the temperate water.

"I know." Garrett waded backward until the water reached his chest. "There must be a hot spring somewhere beneath the surface, but I've never found it."

Elizabeth followed, stopping a few feet away from him, the water lapping at her shoulders. She closed her eyes and turned slowly in place, reveling in the feel of the comfortable current on her bare skin. "You're right. It *is* fun to swim naked."

A rude splash brought her up short. "Garrett!" She coughed and wiped the water from her face. "Stop that!"

"What? This?" Smiling that insolent smile, he splashed her again, harder.

"Yes, that!" She twisted away from him in anger. "I don't like to be splashed."

"Oh, I think you need splashing, Bess." He swiped a sheet of water into her outraged face.

"Why, you knave!" She charged after him. "Stand still! Let's see how well *you* like it underwater!"

Wading backward, he taunted, "You'll have to catch me first!" Garrett rolled into a smooth, powerful crawl and struck out toward the falls.

Bent on teaching him a lesson, Elizabeth took off after him. She was a good swimmer, but Garrett easily outdistanced her. She lowered her face into the water and stroked harder, kicking with all her might. When she came up for air near the far side of the lake, he was nowhere in sight.

She slapped the surface in frustration. "Tinkers and tacks!" Where was he? She twisted around, checking the shoreline, then looked again, just to make sure, but he wasn't there. "Garrett!" Even above the noise of the falls, her frightened shout echoed off the cliffs, but he did not answer.

He couldn't have gone the other way. The last time she'd seen him, he'd almost reached the rocky shoreline beside the falls. He must be here somewhere. Elizabeth swam to the edge and called again, "Garrett!"

Still no answer.

"This isn't funny, you know," she grumbled, clambering up the water-slicked rocks. They were treacherously slippery here, next to the falls. She almost fell when she straightened to look for him from the higher vantage point.

What if Garrett had fallen climbing out? He might have hit his head and . . .

Nonsense, she told herself. The man was surefooted as a goat. She cupped her hands around her mouth and shouted, "All right, you win. Now show yourself!"

Less than five yards away, a figure emerged from the curtain of water. Garrett had been hiding behind the falls all along. He stepped forward onto a smooth boulder that parted the cascade. In the sunlit mist, his bare skin glistened with a thousand brilliant droplets and his thick, tawny mane was burnished against his head. He grinned at Elizabeth. "Race you to the other side!" Before she could scold him for frightening her, he executed a shallow dive and splashed away.

Elizabeth knew she could never outswim him—especially with his unfair head start. Instead, she leapt recklessly from rock to rock until she reached a long spit of shale that projected halfway across the little lake. When she reached the end of the spit, she launched herself across the water and swam full-out for shore. By the time Garrett emerged from the water, she had tumbled, dripping and gasping, onto the rug. "Ha! I beat you!" She pulled a sheet of cotton damask from the open trunk and secured it around her. "Even though you cheated, I beat you."

Towering over her, Garrett chuckled between heavy breaths. "So you did, Bess. So you did." He shook his head briskly, peppering everything—including Elizabeth—with a shower of cool droplets. She rolled aside onto the cushions to avoid the worst of it. Lying there in the warmth, she watched Garrett draw a towel from the trunk and begin to rub the water from his hair.

Elizabeth marveled, as she always did, at how unselfconscious he seemed to be about his body. His lean muscles rippled in the amber afternoon light as he scrubbed the moisture from his arms, legs, and torso. She felt an inward contraction of desire just watching him move, followed by an undeniable flicker of disappointment when he pulled on his breeches and buttoned them.

Her husband looked as golden as Apollo, and just as magnificent.

Like a storm cloud in an azure sky, a dark thought intruded: *He is beautiful—so beautiful he can have any woman he wants, and he knows it.*

How long would it be before he bored of playing the adoring husband? Garrett would revert to his old ways eventually. Only a simpleton would think otherwise.

Elizabeth looked away, wishing she could be content with what she had. Garrett had given her so much: a loving mother, sisters, a beautiful home, passion, wealth—even the hope that he'd convert. Why couldn't she be happy with that?

In a rare flash of insight, she wondered if she would ever let herself be happy with anything.

He dropped onto the cushions beside her. "By glory, you look bewitching," he rumbled, "all smooth and shiny, like a water sprite." He bent his forehead against the damp damask that covered her hip. "Mmmm. How I wish we could stay and play the rest of the afternoon. But we can't." Abruptly, he changed from carefree playmate into efficient commander. "It's getting late." He rose and gauged the narrowing distance between the sun and the western horizon. "We were having so much fun, I didn't notice. Time to go home, Bess." Taking her hands, he drew her to her feet. "We'll do well to make it back before dark, as it is. Come along, my love."

Elizabeth went deadly still.

*My love.* The empty words echoed through her.

He said them so easily, but she knew they meant nothing. Nothing.

Suddenly deflated, she pulled her hands from his.

"Why do you look at me like that, Bess?" Garrett asked. "What's wrong?"

"Nothing." Elizabeth said it just the way he had said it to her earlier. "Nothing's wrong."

# ❧ CHAPTER 20 ❧

*T*he next week at Chestwick was perfect. By day, Garrett acted every inch the considerate, devoted husband. By night in the privacy of their room, he made love to Elizabeth as if she were the only woman in the world.

His methods varied with her mood. If she was pensive, he loved her long and slow until her blood ran hot as his own. If he found her withdrawn, he became masterful, his passion controlled but relentless. If she was in a pleasant humor, he became playful and adventurous, coaxing her with hot, teasing touches into experiments she would never have imagined. Yet no matter how their lovemaking began, it always culminated in a panting, sated tangle.

With each night, his hunger for her seemed to grow, and Elizabeth wanted him as much as he seemed to want her. At first, she confessed this weakness to Father Ignatius, but the priest only shook his head and declared Prince Charles and the king culpable. Soon she gave up mentioning her fleshly pleasures altogether, since her halting confessions only seemed to embarrass the cleric, and he never gave her penance.

Elizabeth didn't know whether it was Father Ignatius's lack of condemnation or the comfort of the daily Mass, but something good began to happen inside her. Slowly but surely, the fears and failures of her past released their death grip on her heart, leaving her room to breathe at last. Like a tight bud opening in the sun, she bloomed.

She was changing.

Her opinion of Garrett was changing, too. His family adored him, and she could easily see why. Garrett treated her and his mother and sisters as equals, clearly esteeming their ideas as

well as their company. He was never high-handed or conde-
scending, even with the eleven-year-old twins. Though it went
against all her past experiences with men, Elizabeth realized
that her husband actually liked the women of his family and
valued their opinions.

Did he like her, too?

He said he did. He was always spouting glib endearments.
Yet her strong self-protective instincts warned that such flattery meant nothing. She often caught him looking at her with
an odd, unsettled expression she did not understand. Still, she
was happier at Chestwick than she could ever remember being.

Garrett wasn't the only reason: The warmth and affection
of his family were chipping away at her reserve, too. Rain or
shine, the walls of Chestwick resonated cheerful activity and
laughter. Lady Catherine lavished Elizabeth with the same affection she showed her own daughters. And with the occasional exception of moody Becky, the girls were constantly
competing for Elizabeth's attention and bringing her little
handmade treats. She knew they were only being kind, but
their kindness had its effect.

Now instead of greeting each day in fear of new trials or
abuses as she had at Ravenwold, Elizabeth awoke contented,
her husband by her side. She savored every peaceful moment
here, but she never let herself forget that these peaceful days
would end. They always had, before.


Saturday night at dinner, she noted that Garrett seemed unusually quiet. He scarcely ate anything, nor did the twins. Concerned, Elizabeth watched him and his two youngest sisters
poke unenthusiastically at their food. When everyone else had
finished, the twins pushed their plates away and slumped back
in their chairs.

Elizabeth took a close look at her husband. His eyes were
red, and the creases beside his mouth seemed deeper than
usual. "Are you all right?" she asked softly.

Garrett arched a golden eyebrow. "It's nothing, really. Just
a headache. Had it all day." He pressed his forefingers to his
temples. "A good night's sleep will get rid of it, I'm sure.
Perhaps I'll turn in early. But first . . ." Tapping his knife to
his empty wineglass, he brought the soft murmur of feminine
conversation to a halt. "Now that everyone's finished eating,

I have a little surprise." He stood. "Last one into the study is
a rotten Roundhead!"

His challenge revived even the twins. Their excited voices
overlapping, Garrett's sisters turned to their mother. "May we
go, Mummy?" "Please, Mummy?" "We're finished."

"Girls, remember your manners." Lady Catherine looked
to Elizabeth. "May we be excused, Lady Elizabeth?"

"Of course." Elizabeth stood, feeling awkward, as she always did, that Garrett's mother was obligated to defer to her.

"Very well," Lady Catherine rose. At her cue, the girls
sprang to life. "To the study, it is." As the twins scrambled
past her, Lady Catherine snared one with each hand. "Have
you two been sneaking honey cakes before supper again? You
barely touched your food."

"No, Mummy." Honor hugged her mother impatiently. "I
just wasn't hungry."

"Nor I," Hope added.

"Hmmm. I hope you're not coming down with something."
Lady Catherine pressed the back of her hand to Honor's pale
cheek, then to Hope's. "Not warm." She waved them after
the others. "Run along, then." Elizabeth didn't miss her small
frown of worry.

"Ladies." Garrett escorted Elizabeth and Lady Catherine
from the dining hall. He said to Elizabeth, "I must beg your
pardon for not including you in the surprise, Bess. When I did
my shopping in Paris, I didn't know I was to be married." He
cocked a wry smile. "Will you forgive me? I promise to make
it up to you at the first opportunity."

"Garrett, you bought me far too many presents in London,"
she reminded him. "They'll arrive with Gwynneth any day
now." Elizabeth didn't mind being excluded, yet for some
reason the idea triggered a small, nagging sense of disquiet.

When they walked into the study, she knew why. There on
the desk was a wooden box she recognized immediately. She
had seen it that day on the road: the coffer full of expensive
feminine trinkets she had assumed were purchased for Garrett's paramours. Now she realized why there were seven of
everything.

She sank numbly onto a footstool by the fire.

"Sit down, everyone." Garrett drew up a chair for his
mother. The twins perched side-by-side on the cushioned win-

dow seat, and the rest of the girls hastily claimed the remaining chairs.

Garrett rubbed his hands together. "Now, everyone but Elizabeth close your eyes, and don't open them until I touch you." He grinned at Elizabeth and mouthed, "Watch this." The box lid creaked when he opened it. "No peeking," he chided. "Not even you, Mother." Garrett carefully gathered up all the pearls and arranged the various lengths over his hand. Though each necklace was a perfectly matched set, the subtle hues varied. Two identical shorter strands had a pinkish cast. Of the four intermediate lengths, two were ivory, two purest white. The seventh, and longest, strand glowed almost silver. "Remember, keep your eyes closed until you receive your gift."

He crossed to the twins, who were rocking nervously back and forth, their eyes squeezed shut. Garrett placed one of the short strands over Hope's shining blond head, then draped one just like it over Honor's.

The twins opened their eyes at the exact same moment, their delighted expressions identical. With the precision of an image reflected in a mirror, each reached out to touch her sister's pearls in admiration. "Oh, Garrett, they're beautiful," they said in unison. "Thank you!" They bracketed him with a crushing hug, then hugged each other, their laughter as sweet a sound as Elizabeth had ever heard.

Ashamed that she had so easily believed the worst of Garrett, Elizabeth stared into the fire. Her unworthy suspicions had twisted Garrett's generosity into something dirty. In this matter, at least, the man was innocent, his motives wholesome. Garrett hadn't bought these treasures to secure his lovers' favors; he had carefully selected each gift with his mother and sisters in mind.

How cruelly she had misjudged him. Elizabeth couldn't help wondering how many other things concerning her husband she had misjudged.

"Lady Elizabeth," Honor called from across the room. She pointed to Hope's pearls. "Aren't they wonderful?"

"Almost as lovely as the wearers." Elizabeth did her best to smile, but the result was unconvincing. Chastened, she watched Garrett distribute the rest of the pearls. By the time he settled the last necklace on Lady Catherine, the room resonated with merry chatter as his sisters admired each other.

Elizabeth watched the happy scene like a traveler standing in the cold, observing a warm celebration through a window. The closer Garrett's family seemed, the more out of place she felt. This was his family, his house, not hers. She would do well not to forget it. Still, she allowed herself to bask in the distant warmth, even if it were only for a little while.

While Mary preened demurely in her best adult manner, Edith lovingly stroked her own strand of smooth, perfectly matched pearls, and Amy flitted in noisy exuberance from one sister to the other. Meanwhile in the corner, Becky smiled softly and dangled her pearls for a playful swat from the cat in her lap.

A cat named Pearl, Elizabeth reminded herself.

Garrett's mother assayed her new necklace with appreciation. "They're beautiful, son." She got up and gave him a kiss on each cheek. "How you spoil us."

He urged his mother back to her chair. "Sit down, Mother. I'm not through spoiling you, yet." Accompanied by escalating squeals of delight from Amy and the twins, he distributed the gloves, collars, buckles, and laces.

Only when the last of the gifts had been handed out did Elizabeth notice the twins whispering between themselves. They shot her several worried, furtive glances. After another whispered exchange, they broke into smiles and removed their pearls. Holding hands, Hope and Honor approached her shyly.

As always, Honor spoke. "We want you to have these."

Hope placed her pearls into Elizabeth's hands.

Honor nodded. "We didn't want you to be left out of the presents." She and Hope exchanged satisfied smiles. "We only need one pair, anyway. We always share."

Stunned, Elizabeth stared at the pearls. "I . . . thank you. That is the kindest, most generous gift I have ever received." She smiled up at the girls, her eyes brimming with unexpected tears. "But, you see, I haven't been left out." She glanced at Garrett's mother. "Lady Catherine has already given me the Creighton pearls." Blushing, she lied, "I just forgot to wear them. Silly me."

She gathered the two little girls awkwardly into her arms. "So we all have pearls." She pressed the necklace back into Hope's hand. "But I shall never forget your kindness. Never."

The twins frowned, skeptical. "You're sure?"

"Cross my heart and hope to die." Elizabeth rose. "Wait.

I'll show you.'' She bobbed a brief curtsy. "Pray, excuse me. I shall be right back.'' She fairly sprinted for her room and the drawer where she had locked the precious heirlooms. Never again would she lock them away, for now—thanks to the twins' heartbreakingly generous offer—these pearls would remind her that she was heir, at least in part, to the legacy of love that bound the Creighton family as strongly as blood. She draped the lustrous strands around her neck and vowed to wear them always.

Elizabeth raced back down to the study and sank, breathless, onto the window seat beside the twins. "See?'' she panted, lifting the pearls for their inspection. "Here they are. And I shall never be without them again.''

"Well. Now that that's settled . . .'' Garrett rose. "I think I'll call it a night.''

A footman opened the study door. While the girls crowded around Garrett, thanking him and kissing him, Wynton picked up a silver candelabra and stood by, ready to light his master's way. Garrett, just a trifle unsteady, turned glittering eyes toward Elizabeth. "You needn't come up if you're not ready, Bess.''

Elizabeth frowned. She didn't like the way he looked. "No. I'm tired, too.'' Was he ill? "Wait for me. We'll go together.''

She said her good-nights to the family, then took Garrett's arm. To her alarm, she could feel the heat of his skin through his shirtsleeve. He was burning up! Concerned, she slowed her pace as they mounted the stairs behind Wynton, but Garrett's steps did not falter.

Only when they reached their bedchamber did he sink onto the bench at the foot of the bed and murmur, "Wynton, you're dismissed. I'll undress myself later.''

"Very good, your lordship.'' Wynton bowed, then left them alone.

"Garrett, you're ill.'' Elizabeth reached under the turned-down covers and removed the bed warmer. Then she urged Garrett to his feet and guided him to the side of the bed. "Into bed with you.'' He sank to the mattress and eased his head down onto the pillows without even taking his feet from the floor.

"I don't know why you sent Wynton away,'' Elizabeth grumbled, her brusqueness hiding a growing fear. "Now I'll have to undress you myself.''

Garrett shot her a bleary smile. "Maybe that's why I sent him away."

"Well, the least you can do is help me. Point your toes." She tugged off his boots, then removed his stockings before lifting his ice-cold feet onto the bed. She covered them, then felt his hands. Freezing. Elizabeth chafed them, but to no avail. "Sit up, so I can take off your shirt."

Garrett obliged, raising his arms. "Sometime when I'm feeling better, remind me to discuss bedside manner with you, Bess. Yours leaves something to be desired." As she pulled off his shirt, he muttered through the fabric, "Easy, there. I'm merely ill, madam, not a felon."

Elizabeth's heart sank when she saw the rash on his chest, but she managed to remain outwardly calm. Garrett leaned against her, his face buried in her bosom. "Mmmm."

"No nonsense, now." She pushed him back onto the pillows. Hastily unbuttoning his pants, she was dismayed to see more red, grainy blotches at his waist. "Help me get these breeches off." She tugged his breeches lower. "And no monkey business."

Garret arched his hips so she could strip him naked. Clearly, he was in no mood for romance. He shivered and pulled up the heavy covers. "Cold in here."

"I know you're cold, but you mustn't huddle under the quilt. It will only drive your fever higher." Elizabeth pulled away all but the sheet.

She had seen these symptoms before, most recently in the Gubbings' camp. Fighting a surge of panic, she told herself it was probably only a coincidence. Surely there were other, less lethal, illnesses with similar symptoms. She prayed so.

A hard chill rattled Garrett's teeth. "Get me some blankets, woman! I'm freezing."

"Oh, Garrett." Elizabeth smoothed her palm across his brow. "You mustn't cover up. Not until the fever breaks." She prayed Lady Catherine had a well-stocked apothecary. The Gubbings had stolen what few medicines she hadn't used in her efforts to save their children.

"Damned grippe," he murmured. "S'always worse when you get it in the summer."

If only it *were* the grippe! "Try to sleep." Elizabeth rang for Luella. "I'll fix you some medicine."

She met the maid at the back stair. "The earl has taken a

fever. Please ask Lady Catherine if there's any aspen bark or willow bark in her apothecary. I'll need both." She instructed Luella to bring several other things from the kitchen.

Luella's usually cheerful expression fell. "Right away, milady."

Elizabeth added, "Just to be on the safe side, I think we should keep everyone away until we know what's wrong. I can care for the earl myself."

Luella blanched. "You don't think it's—"

Elizabeth cut her off. "I don't think anything." For Luella's sake, she hid her suspicions. "The earl says it's the grippe." She tried to smile. "You know how quickly the grippe can run through a family. Experience has taught me to separate the sick from the well. Now go ask Lady Catherine for the aspen bark. And some plasters."

"Aye, milady." Luella hastened away, leaving Elizabeth to worry alone. She sank into a chair by the fire and wrapped her arms tight across her ribs.

Gypsy Fever. If Garrett had Gypsy Fever, he could die. So could the others. Wherever the disease struck, it spread like wildfire.

Elizabeth shivered at the thought of losing him.

Her mind churned. Garrett had ridden into the noxious humors of Dartmoor to rescue her, but he hadn't gone near the Gubbings' camp. Only she had been directly exposed to the fever among the outlaws. Now that she was at Chestwick, there was fever, here, too. Had she brought the sickness with her, somehow?

It seemed the only explanation. Dear heaven, had saving her brought pestilence to Garrett and his family?

A brisk knock on the door interrupted her recriminations. "Elizabeth, it's Catherine. May I come in?"

Elizabeth swiped away the tears that had escaped. "One moment." She hurried to the hallway door and cracked it open.

Lady Catherine extended a basket of medicines, herbs, and poultices. "I put in a few extra things: a little poppy syrup and some camphor, in case he starts coughing." She craned her neck for a better look at her ailing son.

"Thank you. Luella is bringing me a kettle of water to make an infusion." Elizabeth deliberately blocked the doorway. "I fear it would not be wise for you to come in. Garrett's fever is very high, and he has a rash."

The older woman's gaze locked with hers. "Where is the rash? Is it smooth, or raised?"

"Scattered in patches on his torso. It has a slight texture."

Lady Catherine's eyes closed in dread. "Gypsy Fever."

"I pray not, but the symptoms are all there." Elizabeth's heart ached so, she could hardly breathe. "If it is, though, I can care for him. I had Gypsy Fever as a child and survived."

"So you are protected. Thank God for that, at least." Lady Catherine gripped Elizabeth's arms. "The twins. They didn't look at all well at dinner. You don't think they might—"

"Do they have a fever?" Elizabeth's stomach knotted. "Where are they?"

Lady Catherine thrust out a staying hand. "You take care of Garrett. I'll check on the twins." She turned and hurried away.

Elizabeth pushed the door closed and leaned against it. Dear God, she prayed, please don't let the twins have it, too. Then she straightened, concentrating on caring for Garrett. At least he was strong, a man fully grown. Gypsy Fever was hardest on the young or infirm. The disease progressed quickly, killing within days or sometimes even hours. If Garrett could hold on until the fever broke, he would recover.

Luella's knock signaled that she had brought the supplies. Elizabeth took them without comment. Trying to ignore the dark fears that crowded the edges of her thoughts, she set to work brewing the aspen-bark tea. While she was waiting for it to cool, she wiped Garrett's limbs down with cool cloths, even as he shivered and grumbled at her for doing so.

"Can't you see that I'm freezing, woman!" he railed. "Quit mopping me with cold water and bring me a blanket!"

Despite his illness, he was still quite capable of overpowering her. Afraid that he might shove her aside and get the blankets himself, Elizabeth was forced to dose him with poppy syrup. At last, he slept.

Deep in the night, another knock sounded from the hallway. When Elizabeth opened the door, she found Lady Catherine waiting outside, still in her dinner gown. "Elizabeth, the twins are ill, their symptoms the same as Garrett's."

Elizabeth leaned her forehead against the doorjamb in despair. "Oh, no."

"With your permission," Lady Catherine continued, "I

would like to have them brought here. That way, you and I can take shifts caring for them."

"Of course." Elizabeth straightened. "By all means, bring them here. But I can care for everyone alone. I wouldn't want you to catch—"

Lady Catherine shook her head. "These are my children, Elizabeth. As much as I appreciate your offer to nurse them, I must stay with them, too."

"Have you had Gypsy Fever?" Elizabeth challenged.

"No," Lady Catherine announced calmly. "And I'm fully aware of the danger." She looked in sympathy at Elizabeth. "It's not that I don't trust you, dear, but I'm their mother. No matter how old they are, children want their mother when they're ill. I know you can understand that."

Elizabeth understood so well she could not speak for the emotion that twisted inside her. She nodded.

"Good. Then there shall be no more arguments." Garrett's mother took Elizabeth's upper arms firmly in hand. "When I return with the girls, I'm staying." Her hands bestowed a reassuring pat as she released Elizabeth. Lady Catherine's eyes narrowed in thought. "Wynton's had Gypsy Fever. He can safely move the girls, then help us look after them." A sad smile pulled at her lips. "We'll put the twins in one bed. I long ago gave up trying to separate them when they're ill. They carry on so . . ." She fell silent when Luella came hurrying down the hall.

"You sent for me, milady?"

"Yes." Garrett's mother turned her attention to the matter at hand. "Find Wynton. Have him direct the footmen to bring a large bed from one of the guest rooms here. Wynton can assemble it in the master suite. Once that's done, he can carry the twins here for me. No one else is to get near my son or the twins except Wynton or Lady Elizabeth or I. Do you understand?"

Luella's eyes widened. "Aye, milady."

"After you give Wynton his instructions, wake the maids. We'll need several cots, the ones we use on outings in the summer, and plenty of fresh bed linens. Quickly and quietly, have everything brought here, into the hallway, but no farther. Remember, the sickroom is forbidden. Only Wynton may come in."

"Milady, the fever . . ." Luella's voice faltered. "It's not the cholera, is it?"

"No, good woman, it's not cholera," Lady Catherine hastened to reassure her. "You may serve me best by keeping such conjecture to yourself, Luella," she chided gently. "Wild talk will only alarm the others. It helps nothing."

Luella's gaze dropped to the floor. "I beg milady's pardon."

"Elizabeth," Garrett's mother asked, "can you think of anything else we'll need?"

"More syrup of poppies and aspen bark. Cups. Spoons. A pot of plain broth. Plenty of water. Some good-sized kettles and basins. Compresses." Elizabeth paused in the rapid-fire recitation, trying to remember what else she'd needed while tending the Gubbings. "Wood for the fire. Some strong spirits. Bread."

Lady Catherine listened with approval. "Very good." She turned to Luella. "Fetch Wynton, then see to the supplies. I'll be with the twins." She headed down the hallway. "We'll have everything you need within the half hour, Elizabeth."

Elizabeth crept back into the bedchamber, closed the door, and sank to her knees. *Blessed Mother, intercede for Garrett and his sisters. Please, don't let it be Gypsy Fever.*

It was Gypsy Fever.

In less than twenty-four hours, Garrett's room became a sick ward for not only the twins, but the two stablemen who had unloaded the coach Garrett and Elizabeth had arrived in. Then the laundress who had washed Elizabeth's clothes fell ill. She was joined within hours by the three maids who had helped Elizabeth bathe.

Everyone who fell ill had come in contact with Elizabeth or the flea-ridden coach.

Elizabeth knew there was some connection, but she was too tired to figure out what that connection might be. As it was, she merely felt responsible.

By sunset on the second day, she saw Wynton pick up the young laundress and carry her toward the dressing room. "Wynton?" she asked in dread, noting that the laundress's arms hung limp and her head was bent back sharply.

Wynton stopped but did not turn around. His shoulders heaved in a deep sigh. "She's gone, milady," he said softly. He straightened. "Don't worry. The minister's downstairs in the chapel. We'll see she's buried proper." He disappeared into the dressing room and shoved the door shut behind him.

The laundress was barely fourteen. Elizabeth hadn't even known her name until yesterday. Lily, like the flower, she had murmured shyly. Now she was dead.

Elizabeth crossed herself. God help her, she was glad it hadn't been Garrett or the twins. But it could be, yet. Spurred by the laundress's death, she doubled her efforts to force cool aspen bark tea down her patients. She changed their compresses twice as often, but felt herself growing wearier with each passing hour.

Even with Wynton's help, she and Lady Catherine could scarcely get medicine and liquids into the patients, much less rest themselves. Catching only a brief nap here and there, the three of them had battled the fever for three full days before she saw the first sign of encouragement.

The sun had just set on the third day when Elizabeth leaned over her husband and pressed her hand to his stubbled cheek. For the first time since he had fallen ill, she felt perspiration on his skin, and he was cooler. Relief flooded through her. "Lady Catherine!"

Garrett's mother was holding Honor in her arms, trying to force some camphor tea past the child's cracked lips while Hope slept fitfully beside them. The cup in Lady Catherine's hand stilled. "What? He's not . . ."

"His fever's broken." Suddenly so weary she could hardly speak, Elizabeth sank to the edge of Garrett's bed. "It's broken, and his breathing is much easier." As if on cue, Garrett let out a loose, rumbling cough. Elizabeth felt tears running down her cheeks, but she was too tired to care who saw them. "I think he's going to be all right."

"Thank God!" Lady Catherine closed her eyes briefly, then glanced down at the child sleeping beside her. "Hope seems better, too, but I'm worried about Honor." She tipped the cup again, but the pungent liquid escaped out the side of Honor's mouth. "She can hardly breathe. Her fever doesn't respond to anything, not even the cold water Wynton brought from the springhouse. I've sponged her with it and poured it down her for hours, but it hasn't done any good." She set the cup amid the clutter of bottles, bowls, herbs, and decoctions that crowded the candle stand. "I've tried slippery elm, aspen bark, willow bark, and camphor. Nothing works. I don't know what else to do.''

Hearing the desperation in Lady Catherine's voice, Elizabeth roused herself. ''You've been holding her for hours.'' She crossed to the twins' bed. ''Let me take her for a while.'' She gathered Honor away from her exhausted mother's arms and into her own. ''Try to get some rest, Lady Catherine. I'll keep watch.''

Garrett's mother pushed a tendril of silver hair out of her eyes. ''Perhaps you're right.'' Wynton had nodded off beside the sleeping servants, and only a few candles lit the dusky room. ''After I check on the others.''

''Garrett has passed the crisis, and the servants are fine,'' Elizabeth insisted. ''Please sit down, Lady Catherine, before you fall down.'' When Garrett's mother just stood there, she added, ''Stephen and the others are holding their own. Perhaps it's their peasant blood, but this hasn't hit them as hard.'' She shifted Honor higher so the little girl could breathe more easily. ''Please get some sleep. You'll be no good to anyone if you wear yourself out. I promise to wake you immediately if you're needed.''

Lady Catherine rubbed her hands over her face. ''Very well.'' She lowered herself stiffly into the high-backed chair beside the bed. ''Perhaps I should take a little nap.'' She was asleep before her head touched the damask upholstery.

Honor woke just as twilight surrendered to darkness. Her blue eyes bright with fever, she looked up at Elizabeth and wheezed, '' 'Lizbeth. I'm glad it's you.''

Elizabeth tried to hide her concern. ''Your mother's close by.'' She shifted Honor so she could see her mother dozing in the chair beside the bed. ''Shall I wake her?''

''No,'' Honor gasped. Her hand groped weakly for Hope's. ''Hope?''

''She's sleeping. And Garrett is out of danger. Now you must get better, too.''

A hard chill wracked the child. ''My heart hurts. And my back.'' Honor squirmed uncomfortably. ''Please put me down. On the pillows.''

''All right.'' Elizabeth plumped the pillows as best she could with one hand, then eased Honor into an almost upright position. Elizabeth settled back beside her, arm stretched across the girl's shoulders. ''Is that better?''

The poor child scarcely had breath to speak. "Much . . . better."

Elizabeth looked down at Hope, still sleeping beside them. The other twin was breathing freely, and the sheen of moisture on her forehead meant her fever had broken. She'd passed the crisis. Elizabeth said a silent prayer of thanks for the Blessed Mother's intervention. Now, if only Honor's fever would break. But Honor's continuing chills did not bode well.

Honor stirred. Her hand fluttered weakly. "Hope . . . hold hands." Elizabeth reached over and placed the sleeping girl's hand into hers. As their fingers linked, Honor smiled. "Now I can rest."

"Sweet dreams, precious girl." Elizabeth stroked her temple. "Sweet dreams." So softly it was almost a shadow of a song, she began to sing a lullaby, her voice high and clear.

Sometime deep in the night, Elizabeth woke to the sound of screaming, and realized Honor was no longer propped against her. She sat bolt upright and opened her eyes to see Hope frantically rocking her twin sister's lifeless body.

Lady Catherine shot to her feet, and everyone else in the room sat up.

Hope's screams ripped through the air with inhuman agony, as shrill and jagged as shattering glass. Her dead sister's eyes were fixed, her limbs slack.

Garrett's mother crawled onto the bed and pulled her daughters—one alive, one dead—hard against her. Her own, wrenching wail joined Hope's.

Elizabeth backed away in mute denial.

"What is it?" Garrett demanded. He struggled out of bed, wrapping the sheet around him as he staggered toward his sisters. "What's happened? Hope?" When he saw what had happened, he sank to his knees beside their bed. "Oh, God, no . . ." As long as she lived, Elizabeth would never forget the agony in his face, any more than she could wipe away the memory of Hope's wild, inhuman shrieks.

Garrett slumped against the coverlet. Alarmed, Elizabeth rushed to support him. She put her arms under his and tried to pull him up. "There's nothing you can do, Garrett," she heard herself say. "You must get back into bed. If you don't, we might lose you, too."

"No!" He turned angry, uncomprehending eyes on her.

Garrett rose with unnatural strength, his fist tightening the fabric at his waist. "You don't understand how it is with twins! Hope and Honor are like one person! They share the same thoughts, the same feelings! They cannot exist alone! One is only half-alive without the other."

Lady Catherine wept softly, her hands caressing the two girls.

Elizabeth didn't know what to do. "Garrett, please," she pleaded. How could she make him understand? "Have pity. Your mother has already lost one child. The last thing she needs is for you to have a relapse. Let me help you back to bed."

Garrett reached out and stroked his dead sister's hair. "Be quiet, Elizabeth," he said wearily.

"Oh, Garrett, I'm so sorry." Hot tears spilled over Elizabeth's cheeks. She tried one more time to pull him away, but he shook loose.

"Leave me alone." He sat on the edge of the bed and stared at Honor's face.

Elizabeth couldn't imagine how things could get any worse, but they did. Wynton finally managed to get Garrett back into bed and administer a strong sleeping draught, but Lady Catherine was unable to pry Honor's body from her fevered sister's hands. Despite Hope's illness, the child showed uncanny strength when anyone—including her mother—tried to take Honor from her.

As dawn approached, Lady Catherine was forced to allow Hope to hold her dead sister's hand while their mother bathed and dressed the body for burial. Worse yet, Hope insisted on being dressed identically. Then, still holding Honor's lifeless hand, she rebuffed her mother's effort to separate them with, "No! You cannot bury her without me! Swear it!"

No one could convince her otherwise. After Elizabeth and Wynton tried, Lady Catherine stood beside Hope and pleaded, "Dearest, Honor isn't here. She's with the angels, now. This body is nothing without her spirit. Her spirit is in Heaven. She doesn't need this body anymore. She's gone. You must let go."

"No! You don't understand!" Hope's face crumbled. "She never told anyone, you see, but she doesn't like the dark. I always have to hold her hand." Her grip tightened on her sister's cold fingers, an edge of hysteria in her voice. "Promise, Mummy! Bury me with her! You can't put her into the dark without me!''

It was more than Lady Catherine could bear. She collapsed, weeping and insensible, into Elizabeth's arms.

''Wynton, come help her ladyship,'' Elizabeth called. She handed her mother-in-law into his care. ''Take her ladyship to her room and see that Luella looks after her.'' She turned back to Hope. ''Oh, child. Sweet child.''

The two little girls were laid out side-by-side on the bed, distinguishable only by the bluish pallor that had begun to tinge Honor's skin. For one jolting moment, Elizabeth wasn't certain either child was still breathing. Then she saw the rapid, shallow respirations beneath Hope's embroidered bodice.

She sat on the mattress beside her. ''Hope, we cannot keep Honor with us, but we don't have to put her in the dark.'' She smoothed the damp curls away from Hope's forehead. ''What if we laid her to rest above the ground, in a special little house with a door of open ironwork to let in the light?'' Elizabeth had seen such a tomb in London. ''Then she wouldn't be in the dark, and you could bring flowers there every day.''

''No.'' Hope's mouth set into a grim line. ''You must bury me with her. It's the only way.'' Her lids squeezed shut. ''Dear God, please take me to be with the angels, too. I want to go with my sister.''

''Oh, Hope, you mustn't say that.'' Elizabeth moved closer. ''Lady Catherine loves you so much, and so does Garrett—as much as they loved Honor. Think how they would suffer if they lost you both.'' Her voice sharpened. ''Look at me, Hope!'' The child opened her eyes. When Elizabeth saw the depth of loss reflected there, she realized Hope was serious about wanting to join her sister.

Elizabeth had to do something. ''Hope, you cannot be selfish. I know you don't want to be separated from Honor, but your mother needs you to stay here, with us. So does Garrett. And Mary. And Edith and Amy and Becky. We all love you too much to lose you.''

A flicker of indecision crossed Hope's face.

Desperate, Elizabeth went on, ''How can we remember Honor without you? Your face is hers. How can we remember her without you?''

''Go away.'' Hope's eyelids drooped. ''Leave us alone.'' With all the strength she had, she was letting go of life.

At a loss for what to do next, Elizabeth covered her face and slumped in despair. Perhaps she should go away. She had brought this pestilence to Chestwick. "Dear God," she blurted out, "I wish now that Garrett had never rescued me from the Gubbings. If only he hadn't brought me here, everything would still be all right. I should have been the one who died, not Honor! If only it could have been me, instead." Unable to remain strong any longer, she broke down. "I'm so sorry. So sorry." Great, gulping sobs shuddered through her.

She didn't realize Hope had let go of the dead to comfort the living until she felt the child's arms circle her. "It's not your fault, Elizabeth. Don't cry."

# ❧ CHAPTER 21 ❧

*E*lizabeth did not recognize the bed in which she woke, but the unfamiliar room was cool and quiet. She pulled the starched sheet up over her shoulders and burrowed deeper into the featherbed.

She was so tired. If only she could go back to sleep. Her lids drifted shut, hiding from the terrible weight that consciousness would bring, but her mind would not allow her to run away. Instead, a sluggish internal whisper prodded her awake. She blinked the sleep from her eyes and focused on her unfamiliar surroundings. The room was well appointed, but devoid of personal effects. Probably one of the guest chambers.

How did she get here?

The last thing she remembered was caring for Hope after they had taken Honor away . . .

Honor.

Elizabeth curled miserably onto her side as her mind flashed through last night's tragedy in a jagged progression of image and emotion: Honor's death; the agony on Garrett's face; Lady Catherine's collapse; the heartbreaking tenderness with which Wynton had carried Honor away when Hope had at last let go of the body; and then, just before dawn, Hope's renewed terror when she had wakened to find her sister gone. The little girl had wept in Elizabeth's embrace until her child's voice was only a hoarse, ragged cadence of suffering. Elizabeth had kept on holding her long after the child subsided into exhausted slumber, taking comfort from her reassuring solidness.

Elizabeth could not bear the torture of remembering, yet there was no escape. Not this time. She had only eluded grief when Charlotte died; she'd channeled her pain into a dark reservoir somewhere deep inside her and covered it over. But in the Gubbings' camp, that flood of grief had filled to overflowing, shattering forever her means to close the hurt away. Now she felt as if she were drowning in this huge new churning tide of sorrow.

She heard the bedchamber door open and gently close, followed by careful footsteps. Elizabeth rolled over to see Garrett's eldest sister, dressed in deep mourning. Though Mary's brown eyes were swollen from weeping, she seemed composed.

"Lady Elizabeth." Mary sat on the edge of the bed. "You've slept the clock around. How do you feel?"

"Garrett . . ." Elizabeth searched the young woman's somber face. "How is he? And Hope?"

"Their health is much improved," Mary answered, "but I fear their hearts are broken, as are our own." She touched her sodden kerchief to the tears that leaked from weary eyes. "Hope is sleeping, and Garrett . . ." Her gaze dropped briefly to her lap. "Poor Garrett. I've never seen him take anything so hard. Suddenly, he looks like an old man. He's barely spoken since . . ." Unable to speak of her sister's death, Mary's voice trailed away.

Elizabeth covered her face with her hands.

"Forgive me, Lady Elizabeth," Mary begged, remorseful. "How could I be so thoughtless? I should have realized that would upset you."

"No. You were right to tell me." Elizabeth took in a shuddering breath, then lowered her hands. "I need to know how he is," she confessed brokenly. "I *must* know."

Mary peered into her eyes and saw something Elizabeth had not admitted, even to herself. "You love him." The revelation prompted a small, sad smile. "I'm glad."

"He's my husband," Elizabeth equivocated. "Of course I'm concerned."

Garrett's sister seemed puzzled by her defensiveness, but she let the matter drop. "I'll have Luella bring you something to break your fast."

"No. Please. I'm not hungry," Elizabeth said flatly.

"Perhaps later, then. You must keep up your strength." Mary stood, her face in stark profile. "The . . . funeral will be tomorrow, in our own chapel. Because of the fever, Mummy said it should be private."

"How fares Lady Catherine?" Elizabeth asked with genuine concern.

"She slept a little after . . ." Still, Mary could not say it. "After. Then, she got up and insisted on returning to the sickroom. Garrett . . ." She paused, a sudden awkwardness overtaking her. "Well, he finally managed to get Mother back to bed. She's sleeping now."

Elizabeth wondered just how much Mary wasn't telling her. "The fever . . . your mother hasn't fallen ill?"

"No, by the mercy of God," Mary assured her. "No one else has fallen ill."

"Thank God." Elizabeth felt a tiny easing of the weight that crushed her soul.

Mary curtsied. "I've worn you out with talking. I'll leave you to your rest." She crossed to the door and opened it, then paused, glancing back at the crystal bell on the candlestand beside the bed. "If you need anything, just ring."

"Thank you, Mary." Elizabeth watched her leave, then rolled onto her side and drew her knees to her chest. How could she ever face Lady Catherine again? Or Garrett? Or manage to get through the funeral?

*Sleep.* The word whispered inside her, promising oblivion. Later, she would do what she must, but for now, she would sleep. Elizabeth closed her eyes and prayed she would not dream.

She awakened to the sound of someone noisily pulling back the window curtains, then clattering the shutters open to admit the light of a gray, overcast day. Elizabeth turned her eyes into the pillows. "Close those draperies," she ordered crossly. "I'm not ready to get up."

The intruder's only response was, "Hmph."

Elizabeth turned her head and peered through slitted eyes at the overweight figure silhouetted against the windows.

"Milady has slept long enough," a brisk, familiar voice chided. "Everyone will think milady has taken ill, and we can't have that."

"Gwynneth!" She pushed herself upright. Never had she been so glad to see her faithful servant. "You're here."

"Aye, milady." Gwynneth swept over and kissed Elizabeth's hands. "What a wretched business this has been." The maid set to fussing over the covers. "Tell Gwynneth what's happened."

Elizabeth did, her halting narrative bathed in silent tears.

When she had finished, Gwynneth's own face was wet. "My poor lady." She abandoned station and threw her arms around Elizabeth, drawing her close. "My poor, precious lady. Gwynneth's here," she crooned, in the same soothing tone Elizabeth had used with Hope. "The worst is over, now. Gwynneth's here. Everything will be all right."

"Oh, Gwynneth." Elizabeth laid her head on Gwynneth's shoulder and held on for dear life. "I fear nothing will ever be all right again."

It was midafternoon before Elizabeth, at Gwynneth's urging, dressed and summoned up the courage to visit her husband. Side by side, the two women set out toward the master's chamber. As they neared the unattended door, Gwynneth coaxed, "Talk to him, milady. Grief shared is grief lessened. You can help each other." She reached for the door handle, but Elizabeth stayed her hand.

"Wait." She dreaded seeing Garrett. What would she say? What could she say?

Sympathy clouded Gwynneth's face. "Perhaps this would be a politic time for me to go see how fares Lady Hope." She curtsied. "Pray excuse me, milady." She left Elizabeth to confront Garrett in private.

Elizabeth knocked softly on the door. When no one answered, she knocked again, louder. "It's Lady Elizabeth. May I come in?"

"One moment, milady." She heard footsteps, then Wynton opened the door and bowed, stepping back. "Milady." The cares of the past few days were etched deep into his face.

Elizabeth looked past him and saw that the room had been restored to its original state, and the bed was empty. She stepped inside. "Where is everyone?"

"They've all been returned to their own beds, milady." Wynton closed the door behind her. "Once their fevers went away, Lord Ravenwold said it would be safe. There have been no new cases for three days."

Lord Ravenwold . . . it sounded so strange to hear Garrett called by that name, a name that did not suit him. Garrett was light to Ravenwold's darkness. "My husband, where is he?"

Garrett's voice came from a tall, upholstered chair by the window. "Here." He rose but kept his back to her. Illness had scarcely diminished his powerful frame. "Leave us, Wynton."

Seeing her husband, Elizabeth wanted to rush into the shelter of his arms, to comfort and be comforted, but she did not. Instead, she crossed the room and sat facing him on the window seat.

For one brief moment, Garrett allowed her to see his grief, but he made no movement toward her. "Bess," he breathed, her name heavy with all he could not say. Then his features solidified into a mask of grim resolution. Keeping his distance, he walked past her to stare out the window toward the chapel yard.

Elizabeth felt the silence spread between then like a vast, bottomless chasm. Suddenly, they were strangers. When she could endure the quiet no longer, she murmured, "Do you think it's wise for you to be up?"

His stance rock-solid, Garrett clenched his hands behind his waist, but he did not look at her. "Arrangements must be made. Mother . . ." The muscles in the back of his neck constricted. "Mother wanted to do everything herself, but she was on the verge of collapse. I sent her to bed." He paused. "Someone has to take care of things. I feel well enough."

"Well?" Elizabeth asked, incredulous. "Garrett, your fever has scarcely left you. I'm surprised you can stand."

He granted her a brief glare of warning. "I'm fine."

What inner power kept him going? she wondered. Elizabeth had no strength left. Mute, she watched him turn away again.

She wanted to tell him what she was really feeling: that she was soul-sick with remorse for bringing the fever to this once-happy place; that she would give anything to live the last few weeks over again. Had she but known the destruction that rode on her coattails, she would never have allowed Garrett to bring her here. Better to have been killed by the Gubbings and left to rot on the moor. She ached to tell him, but she couldn't, any more than he could speak the grief and rage that resonated in his silence.

Elizabeth rose to stand beside him at the window. She followed Garrett's line of vision to the chapel yard, where five stonemasons were constructing, block by block, a small mausoleum in the style of a Greek temple.

Garrett spoke, his voice dry as ashes. "Hope said you promised not to put Honor's body in the ground." His gaze remained fixed on the tomb. "How came you to make such a promise?"

"She wouldn't let us take the body. The harder we tried, the more desperate she became. After your mother collapsed, Hope confessed that Honor was afraid of the dark." Elizabeth's voice broke, but she spoke on. "She said she always had to hold Honor's hand in the dark, to keep her from being afraid." She saw Garrett's shoulders sag, yet she owed him the truth, no matter how it hurt them both. "Hope was frantic at the thought of leaving her sister in darkness forever. She . . . she begged God to take her, too, so she could be with her sister. It was such a selfless prayer, I feared God would grant it." Below, the masons laid a stone into place. It took two men to lift each one. "So I promised not to bury Honor's body in the ground. It seemed the only way."

"They'll have to work all night to finish it in time for the funeral tomorrow," Garrett murmured. He turned veiled eyes to her at last. "For Mother's sake, I suppose we should go to the funeral together." He said it without emotion, a mere formality for the sake of appearances.

Elizabeth quailed at the darkness in his eyes. The light had gone out of him completely. Perhaps the name of Ravenwold suited him after all. "As you wish," she murmured, then left him.

When she entered the chapel the next afternoon on Garrett's arm, the crowd of servants standing at the rear of the chapel parted to make way.

Black. All around her, black, even draping the empty Protestant cross. Only the minister's plain, white surplice and the flower-strewn coffin provided contrast.

Elizabeth kept her eyes on the cross. She dared not look lower, to the polished coffin. Nor could she face the servants' open sorrow, permitted by their station but denied by hers.

The family was seated facing the altar, close enough to reach out and touch the casket. Beyond the empty chair at Lady Catherine's right, Mary, Edith, and Amy held hands, but Becky sat rigid and alone, her chair pulled slightly away from the others.

Cradling a listless Hope in her lap, Lady Catherine nodded to the two empty chairs on her left. "Sit next to me, Elizabeth," she whispered. As Elizabeth sat, Garrett's mother looked up at her son. She patted the vacant seat on her right. "I need you close beside me, son."

Garrett settled between Mary and his mother. His long arms stretched around their shoulders, and Hope slipped her hand into his. Elizabeth would have sworn she had no tears left to shed, but her eyes welled at the sight of that small hand finding refuge in Garrett's large one.

The minister began the service. As his voice droned through the little chapel, Elizabeth noted abstractly the similarity of the English rite to the Latin sacrament she knew so well. She rose, knelt, and sat to words that expressed almost identical principles of faith. And she sought comfort in the same assurances of resurrection and reunion.

Midway through the ceremony when they were all seated, Garrett drew his little sister from her mother's arms, murmuring, "Come to Garrett, precious butterfly. I need a hug." Hope clung to him with her arms and legs, but she did not cry. Elizabeth almost wished she would. Anything would be better than the huge, unspoken suffering in the little girl's glazed blue eyes.

Having seen the reluctance with which Garrett's mother had surrendered her bittersweet burden, Elizabeth circled Lady Catherine's shoulders in support. Lady Catherine shot her a look of gratitude, then turned her attention to the funeral Mass.

When the host and wine were offered, Elizabeth did not hesitate to partake. The unity of this loss was stronger than any human doctrine that would deny her communion with Garrett's family. At this moment, such man-made differences seemed meaningless, as fragile as spider's webs. After she had taken the Blessed Sacrament, Elizabeth closed her eyes and silently prayed her anguish to God.

One by one, the rest of the household approached the altar across the gravestones that paved the little chapel from wall to wall.

Garrett hadn't thought himself capable of feeling anything, but he experienced a tug of gratitude when Bess knelt with the rest of the family for Holy Communion. The gesture would mean a lot to his mother.

He tried to pray while he waited for the minister to finish, but he could not. He couldn't even remember the minister's name. All he could do was stare at the dark, burnished wood that held his little sister's remains.

Dead.

Garrett had buried his father, many of his friends, scores of his comrades, hundreds of his soldiers. He'd walked battle-fields heaped with death on a brutal and overwhelming scale. He should be used to death by now. But this death—this un-timely, rending loss—wounded him so deeply he could scarcely breathe.

Hoping that the coffin lid would stay in place later, he tried not to think of this morning, when Hope had seen her sister's body in the coffin for the first time. She had cried fierce tears, doggedly insisting that the lid not be closed. Both Garrett and his mother had tried to reason with her, but Hope was unre-lenting. Her determination to protect her dead sister from the dark seemed to be the only thing that kept the child going. How could he refuse her? In the end, he had promised her the lid would only be closed, never nailed shut.

The minister droned on, "... O death, where is thy sting? O grave, where is thy victory? The sting of death is sin, and the strength of sin is the law. But thanks be to God, which giveth us the victory through our Lord Jesus Christ. Therefore, my beloved brethren, be ye steadfast, unmovable, always abounding in the work of the Lord, forasmuch as ye know that our labor is not in vain in the Lord."

Garrett did not realize the minister had stopped for several seconds. Then he looked up and saw the cleric signal him with a nod.

It was time. Time to do the hardest thing he had ever done.

Garrett forced himself to his feet. He stepped forward and took hold of the head of the coffin as Wynton, tears running down his cheeks, took the other end.

Please, God, Garrett prayed earnestly, don't let the lid come off.

It didn't, yet Lady Catherine quaked visibly when they lifted the casket from the bier. Garrett hesitated, afraid she would faint, but Elizabeth supported her until his mother could stand alone. When he was certain his mother was all right, he fol-lowed the minister past Amy and Edith, their arms around each other, and Mary, who had drawn an unwilling Rebecca to her side.

Poor Becky. She would brood about this forever. Mary and Edith and Amy would heal in time, but Garrett wasn't certain about Hope and Becky. Or himself.

Someone opened the side door of the apse, admitting bright sunlight and a warm gust of wind. Slowly, the minister led the way out into the small enclosure of sanctified ground, the breeze whipping at his vestments. With measured steps, he walked between the weathered gravestones toward the little tomb alongside Lord Creighton's monument.

Garrett and Wynton followed him into the light. It didn't seem right, that the sun should shine on a child's funeral. When a child died, the skies should weep.

Close in their wake, Lady Catherine guided Hope at the head of the grim procession that trailed behind them.

The tomb looked raw and out of place next to the muted patina of his father's reclining marble effigy. Could it really have been more than ten years since his father died?

Garrett approached the gaping ironwork doors. The narrow mausoleum enclosed a raised bed of stone only slightly wider and longer than the coffin itself. When he reached the opening, he paused to shift his grip to the side, then laid the end of the casket onto the slab. Gently, as if he might disturb the child inside, he slid the casket into its final resting place. His hand lingered only briefly, then he took his place beside his mother and sisters in the strong sunlight.

The minister cleared his throat, then spoke above the wind. "Man that is born of woman hath but a short time to live, and is full of misery. He cometh up, and is cut down like a flower—" The words stopped short when Hope pulled away from her mother and headed for the casket.

"Wait," Garrett ordered quietly, holding his mother back. He knew what Hope was doing. "Let her go." He turned to the minister and shook his head. "Let her go."

Oblivious to all the eyes that watched her, the little girl stepped resolutely across the soft, muddy ground until she reached the tomb. Her child's hands lifted the lid a fraction, just to make sure Garrett had kept his promise. Satisfied, she let the lid fall back into place. Then she laid her head on the casket and smoothed her hands across the polished surface in a gesture of farewell so poignant that Garrett wavered on his feet from the force of anguish that rose within him.

Behind him, a ragged chorus of grief swelled from the servants.

Unable to look away, he watched Hope pick up an iris from

atop the coffin. Then, flower in hand, she reached over and slowly closed first one heavily wrought iron door, then the other. Ignoring the sturdy padlock that lay ready at the base of the tomb, she threaded the stem of the flower through the hasps. Her task completed, she turned and plodded back to her mother's side.

Struggling to retain his composure, Garrett nodded to the minister, and the all-too-familiar, droning words resumed. "... he fleeth as it were a shadow, and never continueth in one stay. In the midst of life we are in death ..."

After that, he heard only fragments. "... it hath pleased Almighty God ... to take unto Himself the soul of our dear sister here departed ... ashes to ashes, dust to dust ... in the sure and certain hope of the resurrection ..."

Garrett remembered little of the brief service. He only knew that it took every ounce of his strength to get through it. And when it was done, he wondered if he would ever smile again.

Elizabeth could not sleep. Though a brisk wind had blown the clouds away, darkness had brought an oppressive silence to Chestwick. Now, after long hours of tossing and turning in the guest chamber, she felt as if the house, itself, were smothering her.

She missed Garrett's solid, reassuring presence beside her, but he had not invited her back to his bed, and out of respect for his grief and recent illness, she had not asked him to.

Quietly, lest she waken Gwynneth, she put on the elegant robe Garrett had bought her in London. Then she gathered her Rosary and crept, barefooted, out into the hallway.

Its shadows deepened by the frail light of a half-moon, Chestwick slept in unnatural stillness. Elizabeth tasted sorrow in every breath as she eased down the stairs and through the moonlit hallways to the chapel. There, she knelt and began the Rosary for Honor's soul.

Halfway through the cycle of prayer, she heard the unmistakable sound of metal against metal from the graveyard. Elizabeth froze. The tomb was unlocked. Surely no blackguard, no matter how base, would dare to desecrate ...

Gripping her Rosary, she scrambled to her feet. The side door of the apse was locked, and she could not reach the high windows of the chapel to look out. She hurried into the hallway and searched out the first window she could find that overlooked the graveyard.

When she saw the figure kneeling in the moonlight at the door to the tomb, Elizabeth's heart broke.

Shoulders heaving, Garrett gripped the heavy padlock he had threaded into the hasps and sealed.

She could hear his muffled sobs even through the glass.

# ❧ CHAPTER 22 ❧

$\mathcal{E}$very morning, Elizabeth went alone through silent, empty halls to meet Father Ignatius in the chapel for Mass, then returned to the guest chamber to spend long, stuffy hours with only Gwynneth for company. Day by muted day, she wondered when the shattered Chestwick family would try to gather itself together again. Not that she expected them to, so soon. She understood all too well why meal after meal passed without a summons to the dining table.

Who could blame the family for not wanting to face the cruel, undeniable testimony of that empty chair?

She could not think of it without remembering the day her mother had died. Only hours after a servant had brought word, Elizabeth's father had coldly insisted his daughters dress for dinner and join him at the table. "Almighty God saw fit to take my newborn son, and your mother," he'd said without emotion. "In this, as in all things, we must accept God's will with dignity, not with tears. Those of our station must set the example." Precise as ever, he'd laid his napkin in his lap and proceeded as if the empty chair at the other end of the table had never been occupied. "You girls would do well to remember that we all die, sooner or later."

*We all die, sooner or later.*

At this moment, Elizabeth wouldn't mind if it were sooner. She had no wish to spend a lifetime this way—as a painful, alien presence in this place, like a thorn imbedded in the body of her husband's family. No one had come to see her since the funeral. It was almost as if Honor's death had made her invisible.

Elizabeth wasn't even useful here. Chestwick had suspended

all but the most basic activities. The servants spoke in whispers, treading softly as they went about their duties, then disappearing. They did not come to Elizabeth for direction. She could only suppose they sought out Garrett or Lady Catherine, as they always had.

There was nothing for her to *do*.

All these years, work had been her refuge and her shield. Work defined her, kept her too busy to think. Ever since her mother's death, she had risen with the sun and labored until dark, managing first her father's household, then Ravenwold's. Now, trapped in idleness, the woof and warp of her suppressed emotions wove a dark, oppressive pattern she could no longer ignore. Anger and regret became her silent companions as she passed day after day in her room, embroidering or reading aloud to Gwynneth.

She had not heard from Garrett since the funeral. Her only contact was an occasional brief glimpse of him as he strode away into the countryside alone or returned with labored steps and bent shoulders. Soon, she found herself listening for the sound of him below her window.

She knew he must be getting stronger, for his lonely sojourns lengthened day by day, but still, he did not send for her or even ask about her. Elizabeth wondered about him, prayed for him, and worried about him, but did not intrude upon his grief.

Then, eight days after they had buried Honor, she woke just before dawn to the distant sound of retreating hoofbeats.

Somehow she knew Garrett had left her even before Lady Catherine knocked softly at her door. Elizabeth had felt it—a strange sense of loss, as if she had wakened missing some essential part of her.

"Elizabeth, it's Catherine. I know it's dreadfully early, but may I come in?"

"One moment." She slid out of bed, smoothing the straggled tendrils that had worked loose in the night, and hastily donned her robe. "I'm coming." She hastened to the door without taking time to locate her slippers.

In the dark hallway, the flickering light of Lady Catherine's candle revealed that she, too, had been roused from her bed. Her long silver hair, still braided for sleep, trailed over the collar of her nightgown and robe. "I'm sorry to wake you, but I've just spoken with Garrett, and I thought it wise to come at once, so I might speak with you in absolute privacy."

"He's gone, isn't he?"

"I'm afraid so," Lady Catherine verified. "May I come in?"

"Of course." Eyes downcast, Elizabeth admitted her mother-in-law. Why did it hurt so much to hear he was gone? She'd known it would come to this, sooner or later.

*Sooner or later* . . . her father's voice whispered like a curse.

Lady Catherine crossed to the cushioned window seat and sat. "Come, child. Sit beside me."

After she had closed the door, Elizabeth settled more than an arm's reach away.

Lady Catherine promptly closed the space between them. "First," she began, "I must beg your forgiveness for not coming to visit you before today." She sighed. "The girls have had such a difficult time, particularly Hope and Becky. All my girls needed me. I tried to give each of them as much individual attention as I could. So many sad, endless hours I spent with them. But strangely, the days just slipped away. Before I knew it, a week had passed." In trying to explain, she seemed to be speaking as much to herself as to Elizabeth. "I did not stop to think that you might need someone to talk to, too. I had hoped Garrett . . ." She paused, regret evident on her kind face. "I hoped you two would comfort each other."

"We tried," Elizabeth confessed, "but we could not. There were no words . . ." Her voice trailed into awkward silence.

"How well I know. I offered Garrett words of comfort, but he could not hear them." Lady Catherine stared across the room into the empty fireplace, her voice distant. "It's so different with men. His father would have known what to say." Garrett's mother crossed her arms tightly over her chest. "Men build such complex fortresses around their emotions. They want us to think they're so strong, but they're not always. Not on the inside. Once something penetrates their defenses, I suspect they shatter far more easily than we. And then they add silence to the weight of their affliction."

Her gaze dropped to her lap. "Before Garrett's sisters were born, I bore three sons, none of whom survived infancy. Perhaps that marked Garrett, somehow. I don't know." She shivered, remembering. "Even as a child, Garrett was absolutely fearless, laughing at danger, but he has never risked his emotions, not beyond this family." She lifted sympathetic eyes to

Elizabeth. "My son loves his sisters and me without reservation, but apart from us, he's done his best to keep from caring too deeply for anyone or anything. For years, we have been the only constant in his life." She faltered. "Now one of us is gone. Do you understand, Elizabeth, why he went away? He could not bear to look at us and see only six, instead of seven."

Six, instead of seven . . .

Counting Elizabeth, there *were* seven, but she realized neither Garrett nor the rest of his family would be able to see *her* for the one that was missing. In trying to justify her son, Lady Catherine had succeeded only in confirming what Elizabeth had suspected all along: There was no place for her in Garrett's house, or in his family.

"Oh, child. He did not leave *you*." Garrett's mother put her arm around Elizabeth's rigid shoulders. "He left the pain."

Either way, he was gone.

Elizabeth felt more alone now, abandoned in the midst of this kind, loving family, than she had ever felt at Ravenwold. But telling Lady Catherine would only injure the woman who had shown her nothing but kindness. So she said nothing.

A gentle knock sounded from the hallway, followed by a soft, "Good morning, Countess. It's Gwynneth, with milady's clothes."

"One moment, Gwynneth." Elizabeth rose, pulling free of Lady Catherine's embrace. "Thank you for coming to see me, Lady Catherine," she said stiffly. "I appreciate your speaking so candidly, but now I must beg your leave to dress for . . ." She almost said Mass. "For my Latin lesson."

"Of course." Lady Catherine's expression remained troubled. She opened the door to a surprised Gwynneth, then turned back briefly to add, "We'll talk again, later." Like the good mother she was, she left to attend to the needs of her real daughters.

Elizabeth had almost reached the chapel when Becky, her eyes red from weeping, stepped out from the shadows to block her path. Becky glanced left, then right, to make certain no one was watching before she hurled an angry whisper at Elizabeth: "It's all your fault, you know. Everything was fine until he brought you here. Now Honor's dead, and Garrett has gone away. I hate you.'' Her face crumbled. ''I hate you!'' She burst into tears and ran away.

For a few, pounding pulse beats, Elizabeth couldn't move. Then she forced one foot in front of the other until she reached the chapel.

As always, she found Father Ignatius on his knees before the altar. But this time when he rose to greet her with an expectant smile on his face, she did not wish him a good morning as she usually did. Instead, she erased his smile with, ''Please go back to your work immediately, Father, without speaking of this to anyone. There will be no Mass today. There will be no more Masses in this house.''

Without waiting for his reaction, she turned and went upstairs to pack.

What was keeping Gwynneth? And what was so important, that she'd left behind? Just when Elizabeth had thought they were at last ready to leave Chestwick, Gwynneth had cried, ''Oh, good glory, I almost forgot!'' and scrambled out of the coach.

Elizabeth was relieved when she finally saw the front door open, but her relief was short-lived. It wasn't Gwynneth who hastened through the door, but Lady Catherine, cloak in hand. Four burly groomsmen, armed to the teeth, followed in her wake. Elizabeth recognized two of the men from the guards who'd escorted her and Garrett home from the picnic.

Lady Catherine marched purposefully toward the coach. ''Thank goodness. I was afraid you'd get away.'' She motioned to the footman. ''Open up, Martin.''

Surely Garrett's mother wasn't planning to go with them! Lady Catherine had done her best to talk Elizabeth out of leaving, but . . .

With a rustle of black silk, Garrett's mother entered the coach and sat opposite Elizabeth. ''Close the door, Martin.'' When she was safe from curious ears, she said, ''I'm sending four of our best men with you. They're excellent shots, and very loyal.'' She pressed a small, supple leather pouch into Elizabeth's hand. ''Here, dear. Tuck this well out of sight.'' Her voice dropped. ''In times like these, a lady should never travel without a little insurance.''

Elizabeth opened the drawstrings and saw the glint of emeralds, diamonds, and rubies deep inside. Jewels! She was holding a fortune in the palm of her hand! She looked up in shock.

"They're real, all right," Lady Catherine affirmed, as if she had read Elizabeth's thoughts. "When it comes to bribery, I've found that jewels make far more compelling currency than gold." Her practical tone told Elizabeth the lady spoke from experience. "Those stones are cut shallow, to maximize their brilliance. Each one is just big enough to be irresistible, but not so large as to tempt someone to slit your throat for the rest."

"But . . . I couldn't . . . I mean, I . . ."

Lady Catherine lifted a hand to silence her, whispering, "Don't worry, child. Garrett's great-grandfather brought home a whole box full from Damascus. We have plenty more." She leaned back. "Try to save those for emergencies. And do take care not to let anyone see where you hide them." She winked, tapping the bodice between her own breasts.

"Of course, you'll still need money." She laid the cloak across Elizabeth's lap. "Once I realized you were determined to leave us, Luella and I spent the rest of the morning sewing gold coins into the lining of this cloak."

She leaned forward and grasped Elizabeth's upper arms, kissing her on both cheeks. "Ah, how I wish I could dissuade you from going." Her eyes brimmed, but she retained her composure. "I shall not say good-bye. Only *au revoir,* for we shall see each other again, very soon. Mark me." She turned to the window. "Open up, Martin!" As briskly as she had arrived, Lady Catherine sailed back into the house.

Elizabeth sat in confused silence for a few moments, then stuffed the little purse between her breasts. This was but another evidence of her husband's wealth. Why did it surprise her so, that she was entitled to share it? Wasn't that the reason she'd consummated the marriage? The stones would come in handy this winter, when food became scarce at Ravenwold.

She waited for several more minutes before hearing the front door open again. Elizabeth peered out the coach window to see Gwynneth hesitate on the threshold as if something were holding her back.

Gwynneth scowled, then turned around, tugging at some unseen object. "Come on, then. No one's going to eat you." She bent down and struggled to lift whatever it was. "Oof! Faith, you weigh two stone, if you weigh an ounce!" When the maid straightened and turned back around, she was carrying a plump, shiny pig half as big as she was. A thick leather strap trailed from the animal's neck.

"Oh, good grief," Elizabeth exclaimed. It was Mr. Cromwell—big as a hunting dog and three times as heavy!

The coach door opened and Gwynneth heaved the animal inside. "Sorry, milady. What with everything that was goin' on when I arrived here, I forgot all about her." Retrieving the strap, she climbed in behind Mr. Cromwell and closed the door. "They'd put her in the swine cote, so I had to get one of the stableboys to bathe her, quick-like." She rubbed a spot of mud from her skirt. "The pig came out better than I did, in that one."

As always, Mr. Cromwell went straight for Elizabeth's ankles. Too large to fit under her skirts, the animal simply flipped everything out of the way with her snout. The next thing Elizabeth knew, her petticoats were on display in her lap, and her black-stockinged calves and ankles were being rudely pommeled by Mr. Cromwell's formidable snout. "Scat!" she cried. The more she tried to push the pig away, the more eagerly Mr. Cromwell rooted against her. "Grab her leash, Gwynneth, and get her off me!"

"Sit, you wicked, heathen beast," Gwynneth commanded, pulling the leash with all her might. She had to apply a great deal of force to overcome Mr. Cromwell's affection for Elizabeth. In protest, the pig set up a rending squeal, but at last Gwynneth managed to wrestle the animal into the seat beside her. "Stay!" Arms wrapped around the pig's neck, she panted, "I think the beast was so glad to see milady, she forgot all I taught her." She puffed away a strand of hair that had fallen into her eyes. "She's tame, really. Sits. Eats out of a bowl." As Gwynneth spoke, she scratched behind the pig's ears, eliciting a grunt of satisfaction. "There, there, you wicked little beastie," she crooned. "That's it. Settle down." She looked up at Elizabeth. "She's hardly any trouble—never messes inside, which is more than I can say for most *dogs* I've known."

"Out," Elizabeth demanded, ignoring the affection she heard in Gwynneth's voice. The last thing they needed was a pig to worry about.

"Oh, please, milady," Gwynneth begged. "Don't make me leave her."

Elizabeth frowned. In all her years of service, Gwynneth

had never asked for any personal favors, and now she was asking this? "Are you so attached to this . . . animal?"

"Nay, milady." Gwynneth straightened defensively. "It's just that, well, she's fattening up nicely." She shrugged. "Who knows? We just might need another pig in the smokehouse at Ravenwold next winter."

Judging from the way Gwynneth was holding the creature, Elizabeth thought it far more likely they'd be saddled with a three-hundred-pound pet. "Very well. You can keep her. But only if she minds her manners. If she attacks my legs again, we'll cook her for supper that very night!"

Gwynneth blanched, confirming Elizabeth's suspicions, and patted the pig's shoulder. "Be good, now. Be good."

Already regretting her decision to take the animal along, Elizabeth leaned toward the window and directed, "Driver! We're off!"

And so, with a pig, a pouch full of jewels, and a cloak lined with gold, she set off for Cornwall, once and for all.

Eight weeks later, she walked into the Great Hall at Ravenwold only to find Mr. Cromwell sleeping contentedly on the threadbare Turkish rug. Again.

"Gwynneth!" Mr. Cromwell didn't even stir. How in blazes had the sow gotten loose *this* time? Elizabeth wondered. By now, the animal must have chewed, rooted, wiggled, or climbed her way out of every pen and pasture on the place!

"What is it, milady?" Gwynneth hurried into the hall, only to stop short at the all-too-familiar sight. "Oh."

"We cannot have a pig lying about in the living quarters," Elizabeth said for the twentieth time. "Great Goshen! I vow, I cannot fathom how she manages to get in." She walked over and gave Mr. Cromwell a none-too-gentle nudge with her slipper. The pig grunted as if she'd just been given an apple instead of a poke. At the sound of Gwynneth's giggle, Elizabeth cocked a critical eyebrow at her maid. "Why, Gwynneth. You've been letting her in, haven't you?"

"Nay, milady!" Never any good at lying, Gwynneth reddened. "She's a sneaky beast, that one. Too clever for her own good. Lurks about until someone opens the door, then creeps in behind them." She grabbed one of Mr. Cromwell's ears and pulled. "Come along, then, you wicked, willful creature. You'd be chops by now, if it weren't for those piglets you're carryin'!'' Ignoring the indignant animal's squeals, she led the sow toward the kitchens. "Why couldn't you stay in the laundry, where I put you? Keep this up, and the countess will soon have enough of *both* of us.''

Elizabeth shook her head. She'd been entirely too lenient with Gwynneth about this problem. Some day soon, she'd have to put her foot down.

Mr. Cromwell had grown so large, she could easily knock over the furniture. Not that the beast ever did. She was surprisingly delicate of foot, to be as fat as she was, and fastidious about her habits. The sow disdained the other swine, and used the pond to wash, not to wallow.

Elizabeth told herself she tolerated the animal for the sake of the brood Mr. Cromwell was carrying, but the truth was, she could not look at the huge, lumbering thing without remembering the sight of Garrett, grinning, with the piglet in his arms.

She had few enough happy memories in her life. Perhaps it was worth the bother, to be reminded of that long-lost smile.

"Countess?'' Will stood at the archway to the kitchen.

"Come in, Will.'' She could tell he was worried. "What is it?''

"A rider just rode in full-gallop from tenant Wilson's, down by the Launceston road.'' He stopped a respectful distance away. "Coaches comin'. Three of 'em. And wagons, more than a dozen. Looks like enough provisions to feed an army.''

At the word *army*, a chill shot through Elizabeth in spite of the August heat. So the Roundheads were coming, at last, to confiscate her holdings. She'd known they would, ever since learning King Charles, though captive, had renewed hostilities by convincing the Scots to fight for him.

Elizabeth wasted no time making for the bailey. "To the keep. Maybe we can see them from the tower.'' As Will followed her out under an overcast sky, she asked, "How far away?''

"Less than an hour,'' was his grim response. "They're movin' fast.''

"Were there any troops?'' She led the way into the narrow spiral staircase.

"Word is, only the armed guards ridin' alongside, but they're not in uniform.''

Elizabeth didn't know whether to be relieved or terrified.

The lack of uniforms wasn't reassuring, for Cromwell's bankrupt puppet Parliament had no money to pay their troops, much less provide them with uniforms.

She reached the parapet almost too breathless to stand.

"Are you all right, milady?" Will asked, steadying her.

"Fine. It's just the heat. Made me a little dizzy, running up all those stairs." Elizabeth leaned against the warm stone merlon and peered eastward to the horizon. The distant invaders snaked toward her, each link of their procession dark and distinct against the green countryside. She squinted, counting three coaches, more than a dozen mounted men, and fifteen heavy laden wagons.

For once, she was glad she lived in a fortress. "Will, I don't suppose the drawbridge still works . . ."

"Nay, milady. We dismantled the mechanism for scrap, years ago."

"What about the portcullis?" Take her home, they might, but she had no intention of making it easy for them. "When's the last time the portcullis was lowered?"

"I can't remember ever doin' it, milady." Will frowned. "But never fear. The lads and me, we'll do our best. We've got plenty of rope, and more than a little chain. Maybe we can manage to get it down before the coaches arrive."

"Try." Elizabeth followed him to the spiral stair. "While you're doing that, I'll gather our provisions to send with the women into the countryside."

Half an hour later, she was working alongside the cook and scullery maid in the larder, frantically emptying the turnip bins into baskets when Will found her.

"Milady!" Black and perspiring from his efforts to repair the portcullis, Will paused, out of breath, in the doorway. The three women froze until he regained enough wind to say, "I don't think it's soldiers. They've sent a messenger ahead. Asked me to give you this." He proffered a folded letter.

Elizabeth clambered out of the turnip bin and snatched the letter with shaking hand. She ripped it open and scanned the feminine script.

"Tinkers and tacks!" She couldn't believe it!

Elizabeth peered in dismay at her filthy hands and the dirt on her dress before turning to Will with an incredulous, "It's my mother-in-law! She's come to live with us."

\*　　\*　　\*

There was barely time to set the staff in motion and change her clothes before the family arrived. Lady Catherine was first out of the coach, followed by a noisy exodus of black-clad daughters and maids. Arms open, Lady Catherine made straight for Elizabeth. "Ah, my dear. Can you forgive us for descending on you with so little notice?"

"An unexpected honor, Lady Catherine," Elizabeth managed, awkward at the smothering affection of Lady Catherine's embrace. No sooner had her mother-in-law released her, than she felt Hope's arms about her waist in a brief, silent hug. She watched the child retreat into the shelter of Mary's arm.

The sisters appeared to be in good health, despite their dusty dishevel from the journey. All five of them curtsied and murmured, "Countess."

Elizabeth nodded. "You are most welcome, all of you." She made a hasty count of the servants swarming around the coaches and wagons. Almost thirty. Ravenwold had plenty of room, but the castle larders were only half-full. Unless most of the heavily loaded wagons were filled with food, they would all go hungry within weeks.

"We're refugees," Lady Catherine declared. Her voice dropped. "Garrett headed straight from Chestwick to the king's delegation in Scotland. He sent back word that there was trouble in South Wales, and the Scots were already marching south through Lancashire. With Cromwell and his hateful Puritans heading north to meet them, we saw ourselves too close to the middle for comfort. So I packed up everything and made for safety, here. I knew you'd take us in."

"Of course," Elizabeth assured her, though both women knew that nowhere in England was safe for Royalist sympathizers now that Cromwell controlled the rebel army, and with the army, the government. "As you can see, though, Ravenwold is far less commodious than Chestwick. I hope you will not be too uncomfortable here."

Lady Catherine cast an appraising eye over the bleak, dilapidated fortress. "Given the choice between luxury and safety in times such as these, I gladly choose safety." As another wagon rumbled through the gate, she smiled and waved, prompting Elizabeth to turn around.

Father Ignatius! She caught herself before his name escaped her lips.

"I hope you don't mind my bringing Stephen along," Lady

Catherine said, all innocence. "I thought you might have need of a good farrier. And some Latin lessons."

"I can think of nothing I'd like better than having Latin lessons again," Elizabeth responded, keeping up the pretense for Lady Catherine's sake. "Stephen will be far safer here, under my protection, than back in Shropshire."

"Such evil, perilous times." Garrett's mother cast a worried glance at her daughters. "If Cromwell manages to crush this new offensive, I do not know what will become of us all."

"We will endure, Lady Catherine." Elizabeth scanned the activity that crowded the bailey. "That is our lot, as women, isn't it? To endure." Now that she had the priest and a family to protect, she resolved to repair the castle's defenses at once.

She took Lady Catherine's arm. "Come. Let's get you settled. Gwynneth is making ready your chambers."

They had taken only a few steps when a subdued Rebecca, cradling her long-haired white cat, intercepted them. "Hello," she murmured.

"Hello," Elizabeth responded, tensing.

"What is it, dear?" her mother asked softly.

"I must speak with Lady Elizabeth," an abject Becky whispered. "It's very important."

"Very well." Lady Catherine turned to the others. "Come along, girls. Let's make ourselves useful." Shepherding them toward the wagons, she called back over her shoulder to Elizabeth, "Once the unpacking is all done, I plan to take to my bed for a week, but not before."

Elizabeth braced herself and focused on the fourteen-year-old before her. "You wished to speak with me, Becky?"

"Yes." Becky's big hazel eyes welled with remorse. "I'm so sorry, Lady Elizabeth, about what I said to you back home. It wasn't fair, and I knew it. I never meant to drive you away." Her fingers threaded compulsively through the cat's fur. "I don't know why I said it. Can you ever forgive me?"

"Oh, Becky, of course I forgive you." Elizabeth sighed. "And I understand why you said it. Everything *was* fine until Garrett brought me to Chestwick." She felt her own eyes sting. "But I never intended any harm to your family. Do you believe that?"

"Yes," Becky said with conviction, then looked away. "Mummy's always telling me that blaming does no good when things happen that none of us can control." Her hand stilled on the cat. "Hope said you were so kind to her, promising the tomb, and all."

"Poor Hope." Elizabeth could ônly imagine how terrible it must have been for the child to leave her sister's tomb behind. "I know it must have been difficult for her to leave Chestwick so soon after the funeral."

"Yes. It was hard for all of us, but we understood why we had to go." Becky turned to regard her youngest sister, who was still clinging to Mary's waist. "But Hope has done better than any of us expected. Since we were all together in the coach, we talked a lot, even Hope. I think the trip has been good for her." Stricken, Becky murmured, "Mummy told us how hard you fought to save Honor, and how kind you were to Hope and Garrett." She paused, suddenly awkward. "Thank you for taking us in, Lady Elizabeth."

"I'm glad you came, Becky," Elizabeth said, and meant it.

The presence of the Creighton family transformed Ravenwold in more ways than one. Overnight, the castle's bare walls and floors were brightened by colorful tapestries and thick Persian rugs. Two wagon loads of sturdy, comfortable furniture now graced the castle's once-sparse chambers. And the larders brimmed with more than enough food to carry the household through the winter. But most important, there was life again inside the walls.

Thanks to the army of servants, Elizabeth was free to spend her mornings helping with the girls' lessons and her afternoons overseeing her tenants. One particularly fine August afternoon, Lady Catherine stopped her and Gwynneth on their way to the stables.

"Are you going out, Elizabeth?"

"Just to take some food to the Edmunsons. Mistress Edmunson is still weak from her illness."

"Might I go along?" Lady Catherine asked, almost apologetic.

"Of course. I'd be delighted for the company. The only reason I didn't invite you sooner was that the weather's been so bad. I never dreamed you'd want to go out with the roads in such a mess."

"I'm used to mud, Elizabeth," Lady Catherine confided. "It's inactivity I'm unaccustomed to."

Elizabeth stopped in her tracks. Without realizing it, she'd

done the same thing to Garrett's mother that had been done to
her at Chestwick. "I could use your help. This year's crops
were very poor, and there is much need among my tenants."

"Thank you, my dear," Lady Catherine responded with
touching gratitude. "Let me just run inside and change into
my boots. I won't be a moment." She hurried away, more
animated than Elizabeth had seen her since their arrival.

"Now, why didn't I think to ask her sooner?" Elizabeth
asked Gwynneth without expecting an answer. "I am hope-
lessly stone-pated when it comes to other people."

"Milady mustn't be so hard on herself. After all, milady's
been alone for so long now, it can't be easy, all of a sudden
havin' such a large family to consider."

"The Creightons are so kind to me, they make it easy,"
Elizabeth said. "I'm just afraid I'm not doing a very good job
of being a sister, or a daughter."

"Milady's doing fine." Gwynneth looked past Elizabeth's
shoulder, and her reassuring smile faded.

"What's the matter?" Elizabeth pivoted to see Hope strid-
ing across the bailey toward the living quarters, an attentive
Mr. Cromwell in tow. Wearing one of Hope's bonnets, the pig
trotted along at the end of an insubstantial hair ribbon. Hope
reached the door just as Lady Catherine exited. The little girl
showed off her new companion and would have taken the pig
inside, but for Lady Catherine's intervention.

"Oh, dear," Gwynneth murmured guiltily. "I told the precious child to use the *back* door. Now her mother won't let
her bring Mr. Cromwell inside."

"The back door?" Elizabeth asked, appalled. "Gwynneth,
why in Heaven's name did you tell her she could bring the
animal in at all? Even peasants don't let their pigs into the
house. What will Lady Catherine think of us?"

"Well, Lady Hope was so taken with Mr. Cromwell, and
the pig with her, I didn't have the heart to keep them apart.
And when the dear little girl found out there were going to be
piglets, she actually smiled."

"She smiled?" Elizabeth turned back to Hope, remembering how she had despaired of ever seeing another smile on
that thin, solemn face. Now she couldn't help but notice the
protective way Hope's arm circled Mr. Cromwell's shoulders.
"Wait here, Gwynneth. I'll be right back."

She crossed the bailey and waited for a pause in Lady Catherine's patient explanations. "Forgive me, Lady Catherine, but I fear there is a misunderstanding." Elizabeth patted Mr. Cromwell's back, now level with her own hips. "You see, Mr. Cromwell was Garrett's wedding gift to me. Thanks to Garrett and Gwynneth, the creature doesn't know she's a pig; she thinks she's a person. She's tame, really, and quite fastidious in her habits. Never messes in the house." Elizabeth winked so only Hope could see her. "If you would not object, I see no reason why Hope shouldn't play with the animal wherever she wishes."

"Please, Mummy," Hope pleaded, seeming like herself for the first time since her sister's death. "We won't bother anybody, I promise. We'll just play dress-up in my room."

"Very well, dear. If Elizabeth says it's all right." Lady Catherine's response was strangely husky. "But take care not to let the creature knock anything over."

"Goody!" Hope grinned and led her porcine playmate inside.

Lady Catherine watched the door close, then covered her face with her hands and bent forward, weeping.

"Lady Catherine!" Elizabeth grasped her shaking shoulders. "I didn't mean to upset you. Please forgive me. I only . . . Hope seemed so happy, I didn't think it would do any harm for her to bring the pig inside."

"Dear, precious Elizabeth." Lady Catherine circled her with a fervent hug. "I'm not upset, I'm grateful. So grateful." She drew back, wiping her tears away, a curious mixture of elation and pain on her face. "God bless you. Do you know what it means to me to hear her talk of play again?" She took both of Elizabeth's hands and kissed them. "First, you saved her life, and now you have given her back her smile. How can I ever repay you, Elizabeth?"

"You already have, Lady Catherine," Elizabeth said quietly. "You came here when you were in trouble."

Understanding dawned on Lady Catherine's face. "Oh." She stroked Elizabeth's cheek with the back of her fingers. "Did you know, precious girl, that God had sent you to us? Counting myself, now we are seven, indeed." Garrett's mother took her arm and headed for the coach. "Come, daughter. There's work to be done."

# ❦ CHAPTER 23 ❦

*G*wynneth opened the shutters to admit the cool tang of the sea breeze into Elizabeth's chamber. "Ah, but it's fine today, milady. Crisp and sunny."

After the heat of August and the rains of September, Elizabeth was glad to see October come in so fair. "This is one year I'm actually looking forward to the cold." She rubbed her thickening waistline, deciding that the beautiful weather was a good omen. Perhaps she should tell Catherine about the baby today.

Gwynneth draped a lightweight cloak over her shoulders. "Well, we can't have milady taking a chill, just the same." She tied the ribbons under Elizabeth's chin. "The food and medicines are all loaded in the coach and waitin'. With milady's permission, I'll go fetch Luella and the viscountess and meet milady at the coach."

"Very good. But, Gwynneth, would you and Luella mind riding with the driver while we make today's rounds? I'd like to speak with Lady Catherine in private."

Gwynneth grinned, her eyes dropping to Elizabeth's protruding tummy. "That'll pose no hardship atall, milady, on such a fine day as this." She curtsied, then left.

Elizabeth leaned on the windowsill and looked down into the bustle of activity that crowded the once-deserted bailey. Things were so different, now. The Creightons had brought Ravenwold to life, brightening its once-dark halls as much with their energetic presence as with their colorful, elegant belongings. The nation might be in turmoil, but within these walls, all was orderly and secure.

The ringing sound of Father Ignatius's hammer drew her

attention to the stables, where Mary, Edith, and their governess mounted for an excursion into the countryside. Beyond them, a dozen servants chattered companionably outside the guardhouse as they rendered tallow and fashioned wooden barrels in the sunlight. Just below Elizabeth's window, Becky and Hope coaxed a lumbering Mr. Cromwell, due to farrow any moment, toward a hay nest the girls had fashioned in a snug, sunny spot at the west curtain wall of the bailey.

Elizabeth watched, fascinated, as Becky lowered her cat onto the sow's back. The two sisters shrieked and giggled when the terrified cat leapt immediately onto Becky's skirt, hanging by her claws. What a blessed sound that laughter was, after the summer's sorrows. Elizabeth felt her throat tighten with gratitude at the way Hope and Becky played. The two grieving survivors had found comfort in each other and begun to heal. Now, faithfully accompanied by Pearl and Mr. Cromwell, the girls were inseparable.

Elizabeth had begun to heal, too, thanks to the determined efforts of Lady Catherine and Garrett's sisters. Each of the Creighton women in her own way had accepted her—not as a replacement for the daughter or sister they had lost, but as a consolation in that loss. Adversity had not broken the fragile bond between them, but instead had tempered the union of heart and will that drew them closer. That union proved stronger than the shadows of Elizabeth's past, more important than the differences in their faiths, and far more reliable than the uncertain future they all faced because of the war.

At last, Elizabeth had found a love she could count on, a love that had nothing to do with the whims of circumstance or the flesh. The only dark cloud that remained over Ravenwold was the lack of word from Garrett.

Elizabeth crossed to her desk and took his last letter from the drawer. It was dated in August, on the eve of the disastrous defeat at Preston. Until then, his correspondence had been frequent and entertaining, full of witty observances about the Scottish Court, amusing stories, and personal messages to each member of the family. Granted, sometimes the cheerful tone seemed forced, but Elizabeth and the others always found comfort in his words, no matter how superficial. But this last letter was different. Had she not known the handwriting so well, she would have sworn someone besides Garrett had writ-

ten it. Now she reread it again, as she had so many times in
the past two months.

> To my family,
> Shortly, we will face Cromwell's army for what may be
> the last time. We are greatly outnumbered. With the king
> yet imprisoned, this offensive may be an exercise in fu-
> tility, but duty compels me to acquit myself honorably
> in defense of my sovereign. I bid you all adieu.
>
>     Garrett, Viscount of Chestwick, Earl of Ravenwold

Such a terse, impersonal message from a man facing death—
so unlike Garrett. Elizabeth folded the paper and placed it back
into the drawer. After the battle, she and Lady Catherine had
sent letter after letter inquiring about Garrett, but the fragmented Royalist command could scarcely keep up with its few
remaining soldiers, much less those who had gone missing.

Wondering again if he were hurt or killed or captured, she
unconsciously rubbed her thumb in worried circles against the
side of her finger and she said yet another silent prayer for his
safety.

"Elizabeth!"

She looked down to see Catherine waving beside the coach.
Good glory! She'd kept everyone waiting with her daydream-
ing. Elizabeth hastened downstairs.

Only when the coach was well on its way did she venture,
"Catherine, I have some very good news to share with you."

Garrett's mother came instantly alert. "You've had word
from Garrett?"

"No." The anxious question blunted the edge of Elizabeth's
excitement. "This is personal." She looked with longing into
Catherine's eyes, almost afraid that by revealing her miraculous blessing, she would set some unknown evil into motion
to take it away. Yet she could not keep her joy a secret any
longer. "I . . . well, I'm going to have a baby. Late this winter."

"Thanks be to God! I knew it! I knew it!" Lady Catherine
enveloped her, kissing her cheeks and beaming. "Even in the
midst of darkness, our Lord gives us light. Oh, child, I'm so
happy for you and Garrett!" She let go of Elizabeth and sat
back. "A grandchild. Just think of it." Eyes sparkling, she

exclaimed, "At last, I'm finally going to be a grandmother! And the girls aunts, all of them! They'll be so excited. I can hardly wait to tell them." Abruptly reining in her enthusiasm, she said sheepishly, "Listen to me, chattering like the silly old woman I am. I'm sure you'll want to tell them yourself, in your own good time."

Elizabeth smiled. "I would be happy for you to tell them. And Luella."

"How long have you known?"

"What with everything that happened at Chestwick, then the difficult journey home, I didn't realize anything was amiss for almost two months." Elizabeth basked in the joy on Lady Catherine's face. "I began to hope in August, just after you arrived, but I didn't want to say anything until I was certain. The birth should be in mid-February, by my calculation."

"Has the child quickened?"

"Yes. At least, I think so." Elizabeth rubbed her abdomen, her smile broadening. "Such a delicate sensation, like the bubbles in sparkling wine."

Lady Catherine's gaze became nostalgic. "Ah, how well I remember." She took Elizabeth's hands. "Garrett will be thrilled. We must double our efforts to find him."

Elizabeth glanced away, afraid that Lady Catherine would see the fear reflected in her eyes. Her child might be fatherless, even now. "I'll send another inquiry tomorrow."

Lady Catherine nodded. "Have you had the morning sickness? I did with three of mine, but not the others." For the next half hour, she asked dozens of questions about Elizabeth's condition and shared many memories of her own—some funny, some informative, but all encouraging.

Elizabeth was enjoying their conversation so much that she didn't notice the coach had stopped until she heard Luella and Gwynneth climb down from their perch beside the driver. She gave Lady Catherine's hands a squeeze. "We can talk more, later. Now the Edmunsons want to thank you personally for sharing Chestwick's bounty."

"Nonsense." As always, Garrett's mother dismissed Elizabeth's efforts to give her credit for rescuing Ravenwold's starving tenants. "They should direct their thanks to God, not to me. It was He who provided the ample harvest and the means to transport it, and His Providence brought us here."

"Just the same," Elizabeth insisted, "Ada and the children

are looking forward to being presented. They're so proud that
their new lord's mother shares their faith.''

"You shame me, Elizabeth," Lady Catherine said as she
followed Elizabeth from the coach. "Ministering to your tenants, Protestant and Catholic alike. I never even knew Chestwick *had* Catholic tenants until God's Providence brought
Stephen to our doorstep. Our poor Catholic folk had done their
best to go unnoticed, despite their need. If ever God sees fit
to allow me to return there, I mean to make amends for ne-
glecting them.'' She took one of the baskets laden with food
from Luella's arms.

"You'll see your home again," Elizabeth said with conviction. She lightened Gwynneth's heavy basket by a sack of
parsnips. "The war will end eventually, and Chestwick will
still be standing. Somehow, I just know it.'' Carrying the turnips like a baby in her arms, she started down the hill toward
the Edmunsons' cottage.

"I hope you're right," Lady Catherine said. She followed,
falling in alongside Luella. "Guess what, Luella. The most
wonderful news . . .''

Word of Garrett reached them less than a week later. The
messenger had first gone to Chestwick, then been directed to
Cornwall by the few faithful servants who had stayed behind
to protect the house. By the time the poor man reached Ravenwold, he was exhausted and half-starved.

Elizabeth noted the unfamiliar hand on the letter as she
accepted it. She questioned the messenger briefly, then thanked
him. "God bless you, sir. Your diligence and courage will be
most handsomely rewarded.'' She turned to Gwynneth, who
was hovering at a discreet distance. "Gwynneth, see that this
man is made comfortable, fed, and given clean clothing, then
tell Will to pay him generously.'' As the maid led him away,
Elizabeth retreated, alone, into the study and closed the door.

She sat at the desk and read the message with a heavy heart.
She had just laid her head down in despair when Lady Catherine burst in.

"Forgive me for intruding, but I heard there was a messenger from . . .'' She looked at Elizabeth's haunted expression
and stopped dead. "Oh, no. He's not—''

"No." Elizabeth rose. "But he was badly hurt at Preston,
left for dead. After the battle, an Anglican minister heard him

moaning and hid him from the Roundheads. Then, when dark fell, the minister fashioned a makeshift sledge and dragged him all the way to Ormskirk, where a Royalist sympathizer took him in." She tried not to make things sound as terrible as they really were. "Garrett's horse must have fallen on him during the fighting. He wasn't shot, but his pelvis was broken clear through on one side and his hip dislocated on the other. The minister did his best to set the bones back into place, but Garrett cannot move his legs without agonizing pain."

His mother paled. "When was the letter written?"

Elizabeth looked for the date. "September eighteenth."

"Weeks ago." Lady Catherine dropped into a chair and covered her face with her hands. "My son. My son."

Elizabeth rapidly calculated what must be done, then knelt before the distraught woman. "Do not despair. He's alive, and once we have him back at Chestwick, we'll make him well."

"Chestwick?" Lady Catherine uncovered her face, brusquely wiping away her tears.

"Yes. The messenger said Chestwick is secure; the fighting never got near there. We can all go back. I'll send Will and Wynton ahead on the warhorses immediately to fetch Garrett. Meanwhile, we'll throw together the bare necessities and take the girls to Chestwick straightaway in the coaches. The remainder of the servants can load up the wagons and follow as soon as they're able. With luck, we'll have everything settled and ready for Garrett by the time Will and Wynton bring him home." She hesitated, hoping sincerely that the answer to her next question would be no. "Should we bring the food with us?"

"No." Lady Catherine's expression firmed. "Before we left, we hid far more than we brought. There's plenty for the winter back at Chestwick."

"Thank God. I could not bear to leave my people hungry." Elizabeth drew her mother-in-law to her feet. "Come. With the girls helping, we can be ready to leave by dawn." She offered Lady Catherine a consoling smile. "We'll even bring Mr. Cromwell, to keep Hope company."

Resolute now, Lady Catherine gave her a swift hug. "You always do exactly as I would, myself. We're cut from the same bolt, Elizabeth. No child of mine could be more like me. I thank God that Garrett married you."

Elizabeth fought down the surge of emotion that threatened

to reduce her to tears. "So do I," she whispered. Then she set about the business of rescuing her husband.

By the grace of God, the coaches safely reached Chestwick in only two weeks. The moment they came to a halt in front of the house, Hope jumped out and made straight for her sister's tomb, but this time she seemed to find reassurance there instead of pain.

The family quickly settled into an uneasy routine, their preparations for Garrett's arrival accomplished with one ear cocked for the sound of hoofbeats on the road. Ten long days passed before they heard the rumble that signaled the arrival of the wagons and the rest of the servants. Once the brief furor of unpacking was accomplished, the entire household waited anxiously for any word or sign of Garrett.

By November ninth, Elizabeth had worried herself into a state about her missing husband. Desperate for anything to take her mind off her growing concern, she upset the staff by insisting that she, personally, would harvest the last of the season's carrots. She directed the gardener to rake away the heavy straw mulch, then dropped to her knees and rooted with her trowel and gloved fingers through the still-warm, loamy soil. The chore proved therapeutic, despite the cold wind that chilled the rare November sunshine. She had harvested half a bushel of sweet, slender carrots before she was interrupted by the sound of Gwynneth's voice from one of the upstairs windows.

"Come quick, milady! It's Will and Wynton, with the master! They're almost home!" Gwynneth closed the window and disappeared to raise the alarm inside.

Elizabeth dropped her trowel and leapt to her feet. Without even bothering to brush the dirt from her hands and clothes, she ran for the front of the house. By the time she reached the courtyard, most of the staff and family were waiting there. She was gratified to see two of the footmen ready with a well-padded litter, and several of the maids standing by with blankets.

She turned to the closest chambermaid. "Bring me some soap and water and a towel, Jane. Quickly." As the maid hurried away, Elizabeth pulled off her apron and sought out Lady Catherine. Mary, Edith, and Amy stood close behind their mother. "Has anyone told Hope and Becky?" Elizabeth asked.

"Yes." Catherine answered, "but I gave them leave not to come. It seems Mr. Cromwell has chosen just this moment to farrow. Without the first sign of warning, the animal lay down during their science lesson and delivered a piglet on the governess's feet. As easily as one might spit out a cherry pit, according to Patsy."

"Most educational," Amy interjected. Strained laughter fluttered among the girls when she added, "Hope and Becky were spellbound, but the governess fainted dead away."

"Perhaps it's just as well that they're not here," Elizabeth said. Too nervous to stand still, she crossed for a better look down the empty driveway, then returned to Catherine's side. "You don't suppose the wagon's broken down?"

Garrett's mother followed her gaze to the leafless allée. "Wynton sent one of the tenant lads ahead with word. The boy said they were taking the road very slowly, owing to Garrett's condition."

*Garrett's condition . . .* the words sent a wisp of dread through Elizabeth.

Several anxious minutes later, the chambermaid interrupted their tense vigil to offer Elizabeth a steaming basin of water, a small disc of scented soap, and a towel. Elizabeth hastily splashed water onto her face, swiped her skin clean with the towel, then scrubbed her hands as best she could without taking her eyes from the horizon.

"I see them!" one of the footmen called from a third-story window.

All eyes focused on the wagon that crawled to the crest of the ridge. Even at this distance, Elizabeth recognized Will's weary, stooped figure at the reins.

Lady Catherine frowned, squinting. "Wynton must be inside with Garrett." She took hold of Elizabeth's arm. "I should be praising God for their safe return, yet I can hardly bear to think what we might find inside that wagon."

Elizabeth felt the same fear; her own heart was thumping wildly in her chest. "He's alive," she asserted. "He must be."

"There are worse things than death, Elizabeth," her mother-in-law said ominously.

Elizabeth could bear the suspense no longer. Oblivious to the others, she gathered her skirts and ran full-out toward the slowly approaching vehicle. She did not feel the jarring impact of her feet on the graveled drive. She paid no heed to the cold wind that pricked her lungs with every heaving breath. All she knew was that Garrett lay in that wagon, and she had to see him. Stride by stride, she closed the distance. When she streaked past Will, he pulled the horses to a halt. Elizabeth swung around the back of the wagon, gasping, and pounded on the wooden doors.

Wynton opened up, his expression grave, and extended his hands. "Come in quickly, milady, before he takes a chill." He hoisted her inside, then pulled the doors shut.

Inside was dim, and foul with the sour stench of agony. As the wagon started up again, Elizabeth struggled to keep her balance on the lumpy mattresses beneath her feet, almost falling atop the bundled figure laid out from one end of the load bed to the other. She shifted her weight and lowered herself carefully beside him. After a leveling breath, she pulled the oily blankets away from his face. She scarcely knew the ravaged features that looked back at her. "Garrett?"

"Not anymore," he murmured thickly.

A cold cloud of dread radiated from Elizabeth's heart, enveloping her completely. Her golden warrior was thin as a scarecrow, his hair now colorless as sooty water, and his cracked lips thinned with pain. "Oh, Garrett, what have they done to you?" She stroked his forehead, relieved to find it cool to the touch. "You're home now," she whispered close in his ear. "Everything will be all right. You'll see." Her lids closed briefly. "We're going to have a child, Garrett. Did you hear me? You're going to be a father."

His eyes fluttered open to look straight through her without comprehension.

Elizabeth frowned.

"We had to give him poppy syrup—more every day," Wynton volunteered. "It was the only way we could move him, milady." He waited until Garrett lapsed back into unconsciousness to lean close to her and murmur, "When Will and I finally reached Ormskirk, we found the master in such pain we dared not move him. Every day, we hoped for some sign of healing. Then, after a week without improvement, we had to move him anyway, because the Puritans were nosing around, putting all of us at risk, especially the good soul who sheltered us. We left under cover of darkness and made straight for Chester. It's been a slow trip back, and more than hard on his lordship.''

Elizabeth gently extracted Garrett's hand from beneath the blankets. "He's home now. We can nurse him back to health."

Wynton looked doubtful. "Will and I took him to a doctor in Chester, milady. The physician was very blunt with his lordship. He said it isn't likely his lordship will ever stand again, much less walk.''

"No." Elizabeth's lungs constricted, robbing her of air.

"Aye," Wynton confirmed sadly. "Afterward, when I dosed the master with poppy syrup, he grabbed the bottle and tried to drink the whole of it down, but him bein' weak as he was, I was able to take it away before he did himself in. Since then, he's asked me to finish him off every time he comes to his senses, which isn't often. I can hardly blame the man; the slightest movement from the shoulders down, and he suffers the tortures of the damned.''

Elizabeth groaned, remembering the winsome jackanapes Garret had once been. "Does any rogue, no matter how black his sins, deserve to suffer so?''

"Cromwell does," Wynton answered grimly.

Elizabeth's protective instincts abruptly overrode her despair, focusing all the pain and frustration of the past year into a white-hot burst of anger. "I shall not give my husband over to the devil," she declared. "Hang the doctor, and all his ancestors! What in blazes do doctors know?" She turned burning eyes to Wynton. "If the Good Lord could raise Lazarus from the dead, he can heal my husband. God will do his part. Now we must do ours.'' She squeezed Garrett's inert hand. "Garrett, you must get well, if not for yourself, then for the child I carry. You will walk again, but only if you fight back. Don't give up. You *will* walk again.''

Wynton's face brightened momentarily at the mention of the child, but upon hearing Elizabeth's impassioned plea, his expression became skeptical, yet sympathetic. "If anyone can put his lordship back together, milady, I believe you could. But it won't be easy.''

"Nothing in my life has been easy." Elizabeth laid her cheek to the soft golden curls on the back of Garrett's hand. "He'll walk again. You'll see.''

\*　　\*　　\*

The next few weeks proved just how hard it could be to restore a man who lived with constant pain.

Baths were the worst. Though his hip was back in place and his broken pelvis showed no sign of swelling or dislocation, Garrett still gritted his teeth and went pale at the slightest movement of his legs. He stopped losing weight, but despite Elizabeth's urging and the cheerful patience of his family, it soon became evident that agony and apathy were the only two emotions he had left. When he was not grim-faced and drawn with pain, he stared listlessly into space, eating little and asking only for the poppy syrup.

He did not know that Elizabeth had slowly been substituting herbs, coloring, and honey for the opium he craved. The weaker the syrup, the more irritable Garrett became, plagued by insomnia, tremors, and bouts of violent muscle spasms. Yet she was determined not to let him dream his life away, no matter how unpleasant the cure. Some day he would thank her, she told herself, but for now, she and the family bore the brunt of his sharpening pain and escalating irritability.

One morning early in December as she approached Garrett's room, the door opened and Hope ran weeping into the hallway. The child was clutching a small piglet that looked for all the world like Mr. Cromwell, made over.

"Hope, what's the matter?" Elizabeth pulled her close and looked over Hope's blond curls to see Garrett staring at them from his bed, his face a mask of anger and shame. "Must everyone be as unhappy as you, Garrett?" she challenged. "Is that what you want?" She slammed the door, then turned her attention to Hope. "Come now, precious butterfly, tell Elizabeth what's happened."

Hope held up the little pig. "See, he looks just like Mr. Cromwell." She handed the piglet to Elizabeth, and it immediately nestled against her. "He's so dear. He'll curl up in your arms like a cat, if you'll just scratch him."

Elizabeth rubbed the little animal's belly and was rewarded with a contented sigh when her fingers passed over the hairy little stump of navel at its center. He did look almost exactly like Mr. Cromwell had that first day back in France.

"Becky and I, we thought it might cheer Garrett to have a pet," Hope explained. "Gwynneth said he used to be so fond of Mr. Cromwell when she was little. So we picked this one from Mr. Cromwell's first litter, because he looks so much like his mother. We named him Hamlet."

"Very clever," Elizabeth observed. Hamlet protested when she tried to stop scratching his navel, so she resumed with vigor. "Goodness, he likes to have his little navel scratched."

Hope peered over and said matter-of-factly, "That's not his navel, Lizbeth."

Then what . . . ?

Horrified, Elizabeth thrust the ecstatic Hamlet back into Hope's arms. "Perhaps you'd better take him." She wanted to wash her hands immediately, but Hope, unaware of the implications, merely cradled the animal and turned huge, limpid blue eyes toward Elizabeth.

"I thought Garrett would be pleased, but when I took Hamlet in to show him . . ." Fresh tears streaked down her cheeks. "Oh, Lizbeth, why is Garrett so cruel all the time? I think he hates us, because he's sick and we're not."

"No, dear one, he doesn't hate us." She started to stroke Hope's hair, but remembering where her hand had just been, she caught herself and kissed the top of the child's head, instead. "Garrett's just cross because I've had to change his medicine. He won't be so ill-tempered forever." Elizabeth wished she were as convinced as she sounded. She pulled back to look at Hope. "As a matter of fact, you should be pleased that he's so grumpy these days. That's a sure sign he's getting well." When Hope's brows drew together, Elizabeth added, "Think about it. Remember how still and sad and thin he was when he first came home? I think he was much worse then, don't you?"

Hope searched her gaze. "Is Garrett going to die, Lizbeth?" she asked softly. "Does he want to be with Honor?"

"No!" Elizabeth tightened her arms around the child. "He is not going to die. We won't let him."

"We couldn't keep Honor from dying," Hope whispered.

Elizabeth faltered. "No, we couldn't." Unable to face the silent confirmation she had seen in Garrett's eyes, she held Hope for a long time in the empty hallway.

"I don't know what to do, Father," she admitted in the chapel before dawn the next morning. "My husband's body is beginning to heal, but the pain and helplessness have done something terrible to his spirit."

The priest sighed. "God's perspective on suffering is so

different from our own. The Scriptures tell us that suffering perfects us, and Christ himself endured the cruelest suffering imaginable.'' He paused, groping for the right words and, as always, finding them. ''When I make a horseshoe, I first melt the metal white-hot, burning away the impurities and drawing off the dross. After I pour the molten metal into a mold, I must hammer the iron into shape, alternately plunging it into the water to harden what is properly formed, then placing it back into the fire to soften what is not. In the hand of the Master, we are not so different from horseshoes. Suffering refines us, burning away the dross, and tribulation shapes us into something useful.''

He went on, ''Considering the life he's led, I would imagine Lord Ravenwold has accumulated much dross. That leaves him with precious little to hold onto, now that he is being shaped by the hammer of God.''

''The hammer of God . . .'' Elizabeth frowned. ''It's destroying Garrett, and the whole family with him.'' She slumped back in the tiny cubicle. ''I've tried everything, but nothing works: not patience, nor kindness, nor bullying, nor babying, nor goading. Every day, he grows more distant and sullen.'' She looked down at her swollen stomach. ''My condition is obvious, yet he refuses to acknowledge it, even when I speak of it openly. What can he be thinking?''

''Perhaps of how like a helpless babe he is, himself, and might remain.''

''That never occurred to me,'' Elizabeth confessed, ashamed that it hadn't.

''It's a hard thing for any man, especially a man as powerful as his lordship, to face spending the rest of his life on his back, completely dependent on others.'' Father Ignatius let out a long breath. ''But it is when we admit our helplessness before God that He can best use us. Though I understand his lordship's bitterness, I would not encourage it. Bitterness poisons everything it touches. Surely he would not want to poison his whole family that way.''

''Not intentionally. I know he loves his family, but lately he seems to be pushing even them away. It frightens me.'' She could not tell the priest about Garrett's attempt to take his own life. ''Would you talk to him? I am no good with words; I can feed him and bathe him and mix him potions, but I do not have the words to heal his soul.''

"Does he know I'm a priest?"

"I'm not certain." Nor was she certain what Garrett would do should he find out. "If he isn't aware already, counseling him could be very dangerous." They both knew that exposure would mean hanging, disemboweling, and butchery, but Elizabeth could not imagine Garrett capable of bringing down such a hideous punishment on anyone, especially a man as decent and selfless as Stephen Wolcox. "No matter how bitter he's become, I do not think he would betray you."

"I would speak with him, regardless," he said calmly. "That is my calling, to bring comfort to the comfortless." He considered for a moment, then asked, "Since prudence forbears my going as a priest, what reason could I give for visiting his lordship? I need some device to bring the earl and the blacksmith eye-to-eye—perhaps something to provide a distraction from his pain. Most men, noble or base, converse far more comfortably with some diversion."

"Rumor has it," Elizabeth observed drily, "that my husband finds his diversions solely in the company of women."

A garbled sound halfway between a gasp and a chortle escaped the priest. He covered it by pretending to cough. "I was thinking more of chess or cards," he said mildly.

"Hmmm. Chess." Elizabeth searched her memory. "Now that you mention it, I recall that Lady Catherine once told me his lordship used to play chess as a lad, but he gave the game up when he'd beaten everyone in the fief."

"Bless me, I quit the game for lack of a worthy opponent, myself," Father Ignatius declared in surprise. He rubbed his big, rough hands together in anticipation. "*Deo gratias!* How perfect is the Lord's economy. It will be my pleasure to provide his lordship with a rousing contest at chess while I challenge his spirit."

"Good." For the first time since Garrett had come home, a ray of hope warmed Elizabeth's steely determination to restore her husband's health. "He gets particularly restless in the afternoons. Would it be convenient for you to come at two? I'll have everything ready and tell him then."

"Two, it is." Father Ignatius smiled. "I pray this will be the beginning of a long and fruitful relationship."

"I hope so," Elizabeth said. "I hope so, indeed."

\*    \*    \*

It took some effort for Elizabeth to refer to Father Ignatius as Stephen, but as his visits with Garrett became routine, she began to see small signs of progress. Curious as she was about their meetings, she made certain the two men were alone and undisturbed for three hours every afternoon except Sunday. To keep herself busy and avoid the temptation to eavesdrop, she resumed the custom she and Catherine had established at Ravenwold: Six days a week, weather permitting, she and Garrett's mother set out to take food, clothing, and medicine to their needy tenants, Catholic and Protestant alike.

She wasn't above asking Father Ignatius about the less-confidential aspects of his sessions with Garrett, however.

Though the priest never mentioned their conversations, he was able to report that his lordship's initial resentment had soon mellowed to a grudging acceptance. And, after much grumbling and feigned indifference on his lordship's part, Father Ignatius was happy to tell her that their chess games had steadily improved, along with Lord Ravenwold's memory and concentration. At first, he said, his lordship remained flat for their matches, tiring after only a few moves, but as time went on, the injured man insisted upon being propped with pillows a little higher each day, until he was able to sit up for more than an hour before the pain forced him to lie back down.

As the cold, gray days passed, Elizabeth saw steady improvement in her husband's color and disposition, as well as the muscle tone in his arms, but still, he could not bear to move his legs.

By mid-December, the servants reported hearing conversation, and sometimes even laughter, when they passed the master's room of an afternoon. Everyone in the family agreed that the visits were doing a great deal of good.

Then the moaning started.

Elizabeth heard it for the first time the week before Christmas. She was on her way to fetch a heavier shawl when the low, groaning sound echoed through the hallway from Garrett's door. Alarmed, she tried the door, but found it locked. Hearing nothing further, she decided it must have been a vagrant spirit. She crossed herself and said a brief prayer for protection, then forgot about it.

Soon, though, dark whispers circulated among the servants about the dreadful noises they heard when the blacksmith shut himself up in the master's room. Why did Stephen lock the doors and stuff the keyholes all of a sudden, they asked. What were the two men hiding, that no one else could see? And what was that unearthly moaning? Gwynneth faithfully relayed the staff's increasingly wild conjectures, adding to Elizabeth's concern for Father Ignatius's safety.

She had her own ideas about what was really happening. She presumed that Father Ignatius had at last gotten through to Garrett, perhaps opening up the anguish of past sins and present disappointments. That would explain the need for privacy, as well as her husband's muffled cries. Yet she dared not share that explanation with anyone, not even Garrett's mother. Since Pride's Purge had eliminated Cromwell's remaining opposition from the Rump Parliament, England now faced the chilling possibility that King Charles would be brought to trial for his life. His majesty would lose his head if Cromwell got his way, and then there would be nothing to prevent the rebels from wreaking untold horrors upon the king's supporters. As Royalists, the Creightons were in enough jeopardy already, without the added crime of harboring a Catholic priest. Elizabeth worried, with good cause, that the servants' suspicions might prompt them to ferret out Father Ignatius's true identity and report him.

When she shared her concerns with the priest, he merely smiled and reassured her there was no cause for alarm. He steadfastly refused to discuss the source of the moans, or why he now locked the doors and covered the keyholes.

For Garrett's sake, she wanted the priest to stay, but for Father Ignatius's own safety, as well as the family's, she knew she should send him away. On New Year's Eve, she asked him to leave.

To her dismay, he politely but firmly refused without offering an explanation.

That night, lying alone in her bed as the clock struck midnight, Elizabeth greeted the year of our Lord sixteen-hundred-forty-nine with a growing belly, a house full of whispering servants, a crippled husband who had yet to acknowledge the fact that she was carrying his child, and a dangerous secret that could bring them all to ruin, perhaps even death.

# CHAPTER 24

## Chestwick—January 12, 1649

"At this rate, I'll end up taking longer than my sisters to dress!" Garrett's complaint lacked the corrosive anger of a month ago. It had taken two hours just to bathe, shave, and put on a proper shirt and one stocking, but he was determined not to face the entire household in his nightshirt.

"I dare not go any faster, my lord," Wynton responded. He carefully rolled the other stocking onto Garrett's bare foot, then eased the soft woolen knit over his heel and up onto his calf. Despite Garrett's best efforts, his muscles tensed with every movement, betraying his pain. Wynton paused. "I'm hurting your lordship, aren't I?"

"It hurts," Garrett admitted, "but not nearly as much as it used to." He focused all his concentration on slowly bending his knee up off the bed, steeling himself to the sharp pain that shot up his thigh and exploded with predictable intensity in his hip. Better to be the master of his own agony than its helpless victim, he reminded himself. That small measure of control had given him back something, at least, of the man the pain had stolen.

"I can see a great improvement, master." As Stephen had instructed him to do, Wynton gently kneaded Garrett's knotted calves. Every pressure sent a sour, twisting throb through the spasmed tissue. "The exercises are working. Soon your lordship's legs will be good as ever."

"You've been saying that for weeks," Garrett grumbled. He pushed himself up into a sitting position for an objective look at his withered limbs, ignoring the resulting pain that bloomed in his lower back. Once his legs had been as powerfully chiseled as turned newel posts, but not anymore. Yet

Garrett had to admit that his wasted muscles had begun to thicken and the stiffness in his joints was subsiding, thanks to Stephen's gentle, relentless tortures. Progress at last, after all those secret hours, day in and day out, of stretching and flexing. Garrett eased himself back down onto the bed. "I'll wear the dark blue woolen breeches."

"Very good, your lordship." Wynton fetched the breeches.

It wasn't so bad when Wynton tugged the pants legs over his own, but beyond that was agony. Garrett could lift his buttocks off the bed for only a few seconds before he had to rest. Such a simple thing, pulling his britches over his hips, but like many simple functions Garrett had once taken for granted, the process now exhausted him. Still, he persevered until he had his pants on for the first time in five months.

When he felt strong enough, he said, "I'll have the gold-embroidered doublet. And my black boots."

"Boots, master?"

Garrett responded to Wynton's concerned frown by flexing his foot. "Yes, boots."

"Aye, master."

When Wynton returned with them, Garrett pushed himself up and eased his legs over the edge of the bed. The process was brutal, but he took perverse pleasure in putting his feet to the floor, a thing he hadn't done since August. "Small victories, Wynton. Now I must content myself with small victories."

Wynton steadied him on the side of the bed. "Enough small victories, sire, and any war can be won." He knelt to put on Garrett's boots.

"I've only fought in one war," Garrett said bitterly. "We lost it." And everything with it. He looked around the familiar room, remembering his happy, sheltered childhood in this house. "I do not know how much longer we shall be allowed to remain here, Wynton," he confessed.

Cromwell, always vindictive, would never let him keep Chestwick, despite the huge fines and bribes the Creightons' London agents had already paid. Garrett had been too close to the king, and to his sons. Cromwell would punish him for that. The desperate, bankrupt puppet Parliament would bleed Chestwick's coffers dry. Even Garrett's vast reserves were not enough to ransom his and Bess's extensive holdings in cash. Now it was only a matter of time before all his lands and titles—and Bess's—went forfeit as the spoils of war, to be sold or doled out to Cromwell's supporters.

Things might be different if he hadn't invested so heavily in the Virginias at the start of the war, but he took some comfort from the fact that Cromwell would have a hard time tracing the partnerships, much less seizing them. The Creightons might have to emigrate, but at least they wouldn't be penniless.

Stripped of his pride, his strength, his home . . . Garrett could scarcely bear to look at Elizabeth's growing belly, knowing that their baby might be baseborn and rootless, the child of a cripple.

Wynton fastened the final button of the elegant doublet that used to fit like a glove, but now scarcely touched Garrett's chest. "There. Done at last." He dragged Garrett's favorite chair over and pushed it side-on against the bed. "Shall I call Will, now, to help lift your lordship into his chair?"

"Hand me my staff." Garrett motioned to the polished shaft Stephen had carved from a resilient sapling. With it, he might be able to stand and pivot himself into the chair. When Wynton brought the stick, Garrett took hold of it three-quarters of the way up and planted it securely beside his feet. With grinding agony, he pulled himself slowly to his feet.

"Merciful heaven, lordship," Wynton protested. "You've gone white as a bleached bone." He grasped Garrett under his arms and lowered him back to the bedside.

"Fetch Will then." Frustrated and clammy with perspiration, Garrett leaned his forehead against the staff. "The two of you can carry me to the window in the chair."

Proud of his master's hard-won progress, Wynton countered, "Now that the earl has recovered himself, it'll take more than two stout men to lift that heavy chair with your lordship in it."

"You're just saying that to make me feel better." To see for himself, Garrett peered across the room at his reflection and felt a surge of hopeful recognition, as if he had glimpsed a long-lost friend on a crowded street. Pale and drawn though he was, he almost looked like his old self. Except for the hair that straggled from his head.

He straightened. "Send a footman after Will and Stephen, then bring my comb and a ribbon to tie back my hair."

By the time everyone began to arrive, he was impeccably groomed and seated in his chair as far from the bed as possible.

His rigid features gave no sign of what it cost him to maintain the illusion of strength.

Seven empty chairs had been set up on either side of him for the family. As the servants entered, most seemed pleased to see him up at last, but when they met his steely stare, they retreated into subdued huddles at the back of the room.

His mother arrived with Hope and Becky, and all three females rushed toward Garrett, exclaiming joyfully. Afraid of what would happen if they so much as touched him, he kept them at a distance with a harsh, "Take your seats, please. I wish to get this matter over with as soon as possible."

Garrett's mother frowned with wounded concern. She urged Becky back toward the door. "Quickly, dear. Run and fetch the others. We mustn't keep your brother waiting."

Within minutes, everyone but Elizabeth was silently crowded into his room.

His wife arrived last—whether by design or coincidence, he wasn't sure—but when she reached the open door, she took one look at Garrett and stilled, her face unreadable. Her hand moved unconsciously to the mound that sheltered their unborn child.

"We're waiting, Elizabeth. Please sit down," he said with a forcefulness he did not feel. When she had taken the empty seat to his left, he addressed the servants sternly, "It has come to my attention that some of you have been engaging in idle gossip concerning my personal affairs." Appropriately, most of them betrayed guilt with downcast eyes. "Understand this," Garrett warned, "as long as God and the king allow, I am master of this house, and I will not tolerate such behavior. I shall summarily dismiss any and all servants who disrupt the peace and security of my home by meddling in matters they cannot understand."

Family and servants alike tensed, clearly convinced that he meant what he said.

He looked pointedly at Stephen, his expression easing. "However, those who obey me with loyalty and discretion will be rewarded. That is why I have summoned you here today, to announce that I am promoting Stephen to serve as my valet. He has graciously accepted that responsibility." He paused, waiting for the news to sink in. Then he defused any resentment that might have arisen. "In recognition of his diligence, I had intended to settle a fairly large sum on Stephen, but he

asked me to distribute the sum equally among the rest of you,
instead." The servants looked at each other in surprise, then
turned to stare at Stephen. "Out of respect for Stephen, I have
decided to grant his request. That should come to five pounds
apiece." An excited murmur erupted among the staff.

Two hundred and fifty pounds that Cromwell won't get his
greedy hands on, Garrett thought with satisfaction. He'd made
arrangements to send significantly more than that back to Ravenwold with Will, when he could spare him. Garrett quieted
the servants with, "What you do with the money is, of course,
your own affair. But considering the present turmoil, I would
advise against spending your largesse. I have received confirmation from my agents in London that our sovereign is presently being tried for his life." A tense buzz of alarm rose from
the gathering. Rumors had been flying for weeks, but this
made it official. "With such a shadow hanging over our nation, we would all do well to make provision for an uncertain
future."

Suddenly Garrett felt so weary he could scarcely move his
lips. It took almost everything he had to order, "Everyone but
Stephen and Wynton is dismissed. Please leave immediately."
While the servants bowed and curtsied, his mother hurried the
girls away, ignoring their murmured questions.

Elizabeth remained seated and whispered something to
Gwynneth, after which the maid nodded and followed the rest
of the family. Only when Wynton and Stephen closed the
doors on the last of the servants did his wife rise and approach
Garrett. Desperate to be back in bed, he wished she would
leave, but her subtle smile perplexed him. He'd never seen her
wear such a soft expression.

To his amazement, his very pregnant wife lowered herself
clumsily before him and took his clammy palms into her own
cool ones. She kissed the backs of his hands, then looked up
at him with guileless gratitude. "Thank you," she said quietly.
"For Stephen." Slowly and deliberately, she continued, "And
for our unborn child. And the mother and sisters you have
given me to love." Her eyes glistened with unshed tears. "But
most of all, thank you for having the courage to win your life
back. I know it would have been easier to turn your face to
the wall and give up. I've missed you, Garrett."

Garrett's heart contracted. How could he make her understand, when he didn't understand anything himself anymore?

His quiet talks with Stephen had turned everything upside-down, forced him to face questions he had never even wanted to ask. "Elizabeth, I am not the man you married, and I never will be again." He tried to pull his hands from hers, but she only gripped them tighter.

Clearly speaking of more than his hands, she declared calmly, "I will not let you go, Garrett."

"You don't understand, Bess," he said wearily. "Parliament is bleeding me dry. Soon, there will be almost nothing left. I won't even be able to protect your people, or my own, from Cromwell's madness. How could I protect them, or you and the family? I can't even walk."

"You'll walk again," she said, still smiling up at him. "And ride, and work, and hold our child upon your knee. I've seen it in my dreams."

"Dreams," he said bitterly. "Dreams are mere illusions, and after this past year, I have no illusions left."

She arched an eyebrow, her softness evaporating. "Goodness, you are feeling sorry for yourself, aren't you." A spark of mischief in her eye, she threw his own words back at him. "You know I can't abide people who wallow in their misery, Garrett." She motioned to Stephen. "Help me to my feet, please. I've kept his lordship up past his bedtime, and I fear he's growing cross."

Stung by her patronizing sarcasm, Garrett retorted, "By all means, madam, leave."

"Oh, I'm not leaving."

"What?" Garrett wasn't the only one who was surprised. Stephen and Wynton shot sidelong glances at each other.

Bess glided toward the dressing room. "Since you seem so much improved, I've decided to move back in with you. Gwynneth is bringing my things, as we speak." She opened the dressing room door and smiled back at him. "I'm tired of sleeping alone, Garrett." She glanced pointedly at the wide mattress. "Huge though I may be, that bed is big enough for both of us." She grinned—actually grinned! "The way I see it, since our respective conditions have rendered us both uncomfortable, we might as well be uncomfortable together." She added gravely, "If you'll promise not to bump into me in the night, I'll promise not to bump into you."

Garrett watched her close the door, scarcely able to believe what he'd just seen and heard. Bess, speaking of such things

in front of Wynton and Stephen, and brazenly coming back
into his bed . . .

For the first time he could remember, he didn't want a
woman in his bed! Not until he was well enough to enjoy it,
anyway. Of course, considering her condition . . .

"For mercy's sake," he blustered at the two men who were
doing their best to act as if nothing had happened, "put me
into bed and undress me, before she gets back!"

Over the next three weeks, Bess systematically dismantled
Garrett's stubborn isolation. When she wasn't underfoot herself, resolute in her quiet optimism, she destroyed his solitude
by constantly sending the tenants to him to have their disputes
settled.

Garrett rose from his chair after resolving yet another of the
inevitable conflicts between one of his Catholic and Protestant
farmers. It still took a moment to steady himself on his feet
with the aid of his staff, but with each passing day his legs
grew stronger, though he still paid dearly for every step. He
had made it halfway to the door when Stephen returned from
showing the tenants out.

"Allow me to compliment your lordship. Solomon himself
could have done no better. I feared those two were about to
murder each other when they arrived, but they seemed respectful, at least, when they left." He did not offer to help Garrett,
but walked along beside him, ready to assist if needed.

"I solved the immediate problem," Garrett said, "but I fear
no one can solve the hatred that has festered between Catholic
and Protestant in this country."

"Over the past few months, the countess and viscountess
have accomplished much on their rounds," Stephen confided.
"Small acts of kindness and tolerance, most of them, but they
add up. And my people are most grateful for the food."

"Your people." Garrett voiced what he had known for
weeks, "Your flock, you mean."

Stephen smiled without hesitation. "How long has milord
known?"

"I'm not sure. I suspected something right away. The Latin
lessons . . . in the chapel, at dawn? That was a little obvious."
A wry smile twisted Garret's lips. "Should I call you Father,
now?"

"Stephen is fine, milord, and far less dangerous for both of us."

"Your secret is safe with me, Stephen, but now that I know your true calling, I have quite a few questions for you."

The blacksmith-servant-priest fairly glowed. "I thought you would, my lord."

Chuckling companionably, the two men strolled slowly down the hall.

By the time an unseasonably fair February arrived, Garrett had made steady progress walking with his stick. At last, he could stand up straight on legs that were almost as muscular as they once had been, but he still moved slowly with a slight limp. Even so, he managed to come downstairs almost every day to attend to his family and responsibilities. His only concession to his injuries was the cot in his study, where he rested after lunch.

One unusually warm, sunny Saturday at the end of the first week in February, the house was empty except for Garrett, Stephen, Gwynneth, and Bess. Since the baby wasn't due for two more weeks, Garrett's mother had arranged a mammoth outing for the entire household. She'd claimed her purpose was to give Bess and Garrett some privacy, but Garrett suspected his wife's outburst this morning had been the real reason.

Poor Bess. When one of the maids had looked askance at her enormous belly, his wife had burst into tears, wailing that unless everyone stopped looking at her as if she were about to explode, she'd go mad. Garrett's mother had calmed her down, then come up with the idea to clear the house. A most perceptive woman, his mother.

Garrett had to admit, he was grateful for the peace and quiet, though he imagined the picnic-goers were chilly, even with the sunshine. "I believe my wife is resting upstairs," he told Stephen. "Quite an upset that, this morning." He looked up from the accounts spread out on the study desk before him. "I wonder if she's all right."

"Shall I inquire, milord?"

"Good idea." Garrett rose and crossed to the cot. "Give her my regards, and take your time coming back. I think I'll stretch out for a while."

"Very good, milord. I'll leave the door open, in case milord needs anything. Just call out."

"Fine." Garrett had barely dozed off when he heard the front door creak open. A gust of wind blew into the study, ruffling his papers. Perhaps someone hadn't closed the door properly. Before he could sit up, a stronger gust scattered his papers toward the open window.

"Blast." He rolled slowly to his feet and limped over to stabilize the remaining receipts on his desk. The sound of the wind kept him from hearing the man who crept up behind him. The next thing he knew, a long knife was pressed to his throat and his shoulders were jerked back against the foul-smelling intruder.

"Not a sound, if ye value yer life," a coarse accent growled into his ear. The man's breath would wilt a candle.

One, no two, more sets of careful footsteps entered the study. A chill went through Garrett when another harsh voice said, "I sent Graves upstairs, and Ponson to the barn."

"Close the doors," the intruder ordered, drawing Garrett's left arm up roughly behind his back. "And blindfold him."

Were they deserters, or Cromwell's men posing as deserters? Negotiation might work with the former, but if these brigands came at Cromwell's order, he was a dead man.

One of them threw a filthy strip of cloth over his eyes and tied it, leaving only a few tiny gaps of light. Garrett heard the doors shut, then the sound of the key turning in the lock.

He had to think, and think fast. He couldn't let them hurt Bess. A muffled scream sounded upstairs, followed by ominous sounds of a struggle. Garrett reacted instinctively, oblivious to the sting of the blade against his throat as he wrestled with his captor. "Leave her alone! If it's money you want, I can give it to you, but you won't find it without me. Do not harm my family!"

Two more strong arms put an end to his efforts to free himself. "Do not harm my family," a singsong voice mocked.

Breathing heavily from the struggle, his captor tightened his grip and wrenched Garrett's left arm up hard behind his back. "Move!" The man shoved him around the desk, then hurled him into his chair.

Breathless from the brutal treatment, Garrett barely managed to keep from crying out. More hands roughly dragged his wrists behind the chair and tied them, then secured his torso to the chair-back with several coils of tightly cinched rope.

"Gag him."

A foul rag was stuffed into his mouth. Garrett offered no resistance, hoping they would leave him alone long enough for him to work free of his bonds. The fact that they hadn't killed him immediately was a good sign. Maybe they weren't Cromwell's men, after all. Or maybe they were, but were merely waiting until he showed them where the money was to kill him.

Blessedly, the rasping voices retreated. He heard the door unlock, and at least one of the men step out into the main hall. He waited for the sound of the doors closing, but did not hear it.

Garrett tried not to think of what might be happening to Bess and the others upstairs, but his mind conjured vivid, horrific images of abuse. He'd sworn not to let her come to harm again, and here he was, crippled and helpless, while brigands attacked her.

He twisted frantically at the coarse strands binding his wrists. Within seconds, the rope at his wrists slickened with blood, but did not loosen. Then he thought he detected a faint whisper behind him. He stilled, hearing a rustle of movement from across the room, near the study door, and the clink of glass—probably one of the invaders raiding Garrett's decanters. Good, Garrett thought, drink up.

Another gust of wind blew the loose papers toward the open window behind his back. This time, Garrett did hear something.

*"Ease back toward the window, so I can cut the ropes."*

Bess! Thank God, they didn't have her.

He planted his feet firmly on the floor and waited for the next gust of wind to shove the chair back a few inches. Fortunately, the rattling papers covered the sound of his progress. Several more judicious shoves, and he met with welcome resistance.

*"Your wrists . . . they're bleeding."*

Garrett thrust his bloody wrists toward her, signaling for her to cut the ropes, regardless. He felt a dagger slide behind the bindings and begin to saw with almost superhuman strength. To speed things up, he pulled as hard as he could against the motion. It seemed to take forever, but when the rope gave way, he had to tighten his arms abruptly to keep them behind him. He pointed up at the bindings that anchored his torso to the chair.

Bess cleverly cut through the knot first, then tucked the loose ends over the remaining coils. Selecting every other coil, she soon had him bound by only the tucked strands in back, yet to all appearances from the front, still securely tied.

*"Pistols, cocked and loaded. Don't drop them."*

God bless the woman! He felt her press the familiar grips into his hands.

*"There's one man by the door, drinking your whiskey. I don't know where the others are. I saw only four horses down by the stables."*

After brief consideration, Garrett shoved his right-hand pistol back at her. She hesitated before taking it, but when he made a sawing motion, she understood and switched it out for the dagger. Better to dispatch the guard quietly, if he could.

He heard Bess take a deep breath. *"Nod when you're ready, and I'll pull off your blindfold."*

He took a deep breath himself, then nodded. She snatched the blindfold away.

Exploding from his bonds with a burst of primal rage, Garrett spit out the gag and took aim at the lone ruffian across the room. Whiskey in hand, the man turned just as Garrett hurled the dagger with deadly accuracy into his throat. The invader opened his mouth in shock, but made only a brief, gurgling sound before he fell to the carpet.

Garrett loped unevenly across the room, unlocked the doors, and peered out. He saw no sign of the others in the main hall, but heard the sound of destruction from upstairs and hoped their ransacking would keep them busy long enough for him to pick them off. He relocked the doors, then pulled the dagger from the dead man's throat and limped to the window.

He leaned out to find Bess, her eyes squeezed shut and her back pressed to the wall, praying with her hands clenched around the barrel of his carbine, his belted sword and scabbard draped across her bosom, and his shot-bag hanging from her elbow.

"For glory's sake, woman," he whispered, "open your eyes. Some lookout you are." Wincing when he raised his leg over the sill, he climbed out onto the terrace.

When he straightened beside her, Bess propped the carbine against her side and grasped his shoulders, staring wide-eyed at his neck. "Blessed Mother, they've cut your throat."

He swiped at the slick warmth with the back of his pistol

hand. "It isn't deep." Without even thinking about it, he kissed her hard and fast, then limped into the shelter of a huge planter, drawing her with him. "Have you seen any of the others?"

She nodded. "Just a glimpse. I think there were two of them upstairs. They surprised Gwynneth and Stephen in our bedchamber. Fortunately, I had gone alone to your old room, to look at some of your things. Thank God your weapons were still there with your uniform." Her eyes focused rapidly from shadow to shadow in the sunlit garden.

Garrett stuffed the pistol and dagger into his waist, then took the carbine and powder bag from her. "Buckle my sword on me, while I load."

Bess lifted the belt over her head, unbuckled it, threaded it around him as he worked, then buckled it to his hips. Garrett closed his eyes briefly at the weight and pressure so close to his injury, but kept on loading. "Where's the other pistol?"

"Here." She patted a lopsided bulge in her skirt. "In my pocket."

He shoved the ramrod after the wadding. "Well, get it out of there, before it goes off and shoots the baby."

Bess glared at him, but did as he asked. To his surprise, she held the weapon quite comfortably.

"Here." He traded his loaded carbine for her pistol. "Take this; it's more accurate. Ever fired one of these things?"

She answered him with a simple but haughty, "Yes."

"Good. Then you know how." Shouldering his ammunition, Garrett glanced toward the stables. "They sent one of their men to the barn. I'll take care of the two upstairs, first, then worry about him."

"What do you want me to do?"

He laid a blood-streaked hand over her belly, wishing he had done so before this. "Get away from the house and hide." When she started to protest, he cut her off with, "If they take you hostage, they'll hold all the cards. For both our sakes, you *must* stay clear of them, even if something happens to me." She searched his face with such longing his heart twisted in his chest. "Worry about the baby now, not me," he said softly.

She nodded. "All right." She raised up on tiptoe to plant a brief, tender kiss on his lips.

Garrett looked deep into her wide blue eyes and stroked the smooth, silky crown of her golden hair. Until this moment, he had not realized how precious she had become to him. Now he could not imagine life without her. He nodded to the carbine. "Don't hesitate to use that, if you have to." He urged her closer against the shelter of the planter. "Wait here until I've rounded the corner. And be careful."

Keeping close to the side of the house, he watched for any movement from the direction of the barn, but managed to reach the servants' entry without encountering anyone. Once inside, Garrett listened carefully and determined from the distant racket that the raiders were working their way down the rooms of the east wing.

His pain still numbed by the survival response released in the study, he mounted the back stair with surprising ease. He peered through the keyhole and saw Gwynneth, gagged and tied up tighter than a sausage, rolling helplessly on the dressing room floor. Beyond the doorway, Stephen lay motionless on the bedchamber rug. Garrett felt a tingle of dread when he saw the wide, glistening swath of red that streaked the priest's silver hair.

Every nerve on edge, he opened the door and crept inside. Gwynneth made muffled sounds when she saw him, wagging her head toward Stephen, but Garrett signaled for her to be silent. He moved cautiously into the bedchamber to see if Stephen was beyond help. A quick check revealed that the bleeding had stopped and the unconscious man's pulse was strong. Garrett backed into the dressing room and cut Gwynneth loose.

"Get out," he whispered, "as fast as you can, but keep a sharp eye toward the barn. There's another man down there, somewhere. I've sent Bess into the woods to hide. Try to find her."

Gwynneth nodded, her eyes soft with gratitude, then quietly disappeared down the back stair.

Garrett made his way back through the bedchamber to the hall door. When he eased the door open, the sound of splintering wood and breaking glass reached him from the far end of the hall. Advancing from the shelter of one doorway to the next, he worked his way down the corridor, pistols cocked and ready. When he reached the open door to his boyhood room, he flattened himself alongside it and waited.

"Look at his offal!" The brigand's complaint was followed by a crash. "We ain't found nuffin' worth carryin'! Maybe mister high-and-mighty was tellin' the truth about the money."

Garrett judged the man's position in the room from the sound of his voice.

Another voice, slightly fainter, replied, "Could be. Maybe we oughtta go downstairs and do a little carvin' on his fancy face. That usually makes 'em talk."

"Aye," the first man agreed.

Now that he knew where they were, Garrett stepped squarely into the doorway and leveled his left pistol at the closest man. Alerted by the movement, the robber spun and threw his knife, but Garrett held steady and pulled the trigger without flinching. As the knife sailed harmlessly past him, the bullet met its mark square between the eyes. The second intruder hurled the drawer he was holding toward Garrett, then lunged forward, pulling a pistol from his own belt. The drawer fell short, and a hasty aim sent the accomplice's shot wild. Garrett's careful, deadly aim felled his attacker in midstride.

At the sound of someone behind him, he flipped the spent pistol in his left hand and pivoted to strike a blow with the butt, dropping the other pistol in favor of his dagger. When he turned, though, he found himself facing a frightened Stephen.

"Hold!" The priest exclaimed. "It's only me."

Garrett sagged backward. "Faith! You almost met your maker, sir."

Stephen glanced at the two dead men, then focused on Garrett. As he spoke, he waved a haphazard sign of the cross in the general direction of each body. "Lady Elizabeth and Gwynneth . . . are they all right?"

"I hope so." Garrett loaded his pistol, then handed it to the priest. "Here. Cover me, while I arm the other." Noting the reluctance with which Stephen accepted the weapon, he said, "I hope you can use that."

"Not to save my own life." Stephen rolled his eyes to Heaven, repenting in advance. "But to save yours, milord, I might be able to pull the trigger."

"Let's just pray it doesn't come to that." He picked up the second pistol and reloaded, then warily approached the open door. "Let's go."

After making sure the way was clear, he preceded his friend into the hallway. "I sent the women into the woods to hide. There's one more man. He was down by the barn, but he might have heard the shots and gotten curious, so we need to proceed with caution.''

Going down the stairs without his cane was decidedly harder than going up them, but Garrett accomplished the task without help. Then he and Stephen stole out across the terrace and skirted the hedges. Near the stables, they found the horses from the stalls tied to the brigands' mangy mounts. As quietly as they could, the two men separated the horses and hid Garrett's, then set the robbers' agallop across the open fields. Despite the rumble of retreating hoofbeats, they saw no sign of the fourth man.

Garrett led the priest to the back entrance of the stables. Once inside, he motioned to the empty stalls and whispered, ''You take that side. I'll take this one. If you don't find anything, meet me by the hay crib at the far end, and be sure to keep out of sight.'' The far door was wide open to the barnyard.

''Aye.''

Their tense, systematic search yielded nothing, but by the time he rendezvoused with Stephen, Garrett was beginning to feel the effects of his actions. With every step, his knees and hips ached, and he had started to stiffen significantly. He leaned against the hay crib and murmured, ''I don't know how much longer I can keep going.''

The priest frowned. ''Perhaps we should take to the woods, find the women, and head out to warn the others.''

Garrett stepped to the edge of the doorway and squinted into the sunlight. ''Let's check the barn first.'' Just then, a shot rang out in the yard, sending him scrambling for cover.

An unfamiliar male voice sounded from the barn. ''Hold your fire! I've got the woman!''

Both men came instantly alert.

''Blast.'' Garrett looked through a crack and saw the fourth man shove Gwynneth into the open, a cocked pistol jammed against her ribs. The terrified maid gripped something in one of her raised hands. When Garrett looked closer, he saw a familiar leather strap trailing behind her. Calm as you please, Mr. Cromwell trotted out into the sunshine behind hostage and captor.

''A bargain!'' Garrett shouted toward the open doorway. ''Let her go. I give my word, I won't pursue you.''

''I've got a better bargain,'' the intruder shouted. ''I take the woman and the gold. I'll let her go when I'm away, free.''

"Curse the blackguard," Garrett muttered in frustration. After a hasty mental assessment, he whispered to Stephen, "I don't think he's seen you. Leave by the back way, and try to find the countess. I'll deal with this."

"But, milord, I—"

"Go, Stephen. My wife is out there alone. A woman in her condition . . ."

"Very well," the priest agreed, "but if I find her safe and well, I'm coming back for your lordship."

"I can take care of myself. Find my wife."

"I'm coming back," Stephen said quietly, then crept out the far door.

Garrett turned his attention to the unlikely scene in the barnyard.

His firearm still hard against Gwynneth's side, the brigand backed toward the house, Mr. Cromwell in tow. "I said I want gold, sir, or I shoot the woman."

Garrett tucked the pistol against his back, gouging himself slightly with the dagger that was already there. Then he pulled a purse half-filled with cut jewels from his pocket. Holding the purse aloft, he strolled out into the sunlight, grinning. "Here. My gold's in London, but I think you'll like this better. It's all I have left," he lied, tossing the purse to the ground between them.

The gunman tensed, but did not falter. Instead, he shifted the muzzle to Gwynneth's temple, still gripping her arm tightly. "Pick it up and show me," he ordered her, his eyes never leaving Garrett. "And you, keep those hands up!"

Trembling, with Mr. Cromwell's leash still wrapped around her palm, Gwynneth slowly crouched to scoop up the purse. When she poured its contents into her shaking hand, the jewels glinted spectacularly in the sunlight.

The robber gasped aloud. His eyes widened hungrily at the sparkling treasure. "I'll be jiggered." He prodded Gwynneth's temple with the muzzle. "Put em' back and hand 'em over."

"A fair day's wage, I'd say," Garrett offered equably, "and best of all, you won't have to worry about dividing it. You see, your friends won't be joining you."

The man's twisted smile revealed brown, crooked teeth. "They ain't no friends of mine." Once the jewels were safely sealed in the pouch, he let go of Gwynneth's arm to snatch his prize and shove it inside his shirt. "Now tie that strap to me wrist," he growled. "I ain't eat in three days, and I've a taste for pork."

When Gwynneth hesitated, he whacked the side of her head with the muzzle. "Do it!" She unwrapped the leash and tied it loosely to her captor's wrist.

"I heered ye set our horses agallop," the robber told Garrett. "Very clever, but that just means I'll have to keep the woman longer." Dragging her backward, he began to make his escape. "But I'll get somethin' for my trouble out of it." He viciously nipped her cheek, marking her with his teeth. "I ain't had a woman in a while, neither."

Garrett wasn't sure whether Gwynneth's faint was genuine or contrived, but she promptly went limp. As she slithered toward the ground, he went for his pistol and dagger. At first, the robber tried to hold up his human shield between them, but Gwynneth's substantial dead weight was too much for him, so he let her go and scrambled backward, turning his pistol toward Garrett.

Garrett managed to get a shot off, but this time his aim wasn't as good as before. His bullet slammed into the fugitive's shoulder, knocking the man's answering shot wild, but failing to fell him. At the sound of gunfire, Mr. Cromwell let out a terrified squeal and took off, the pig's momentum propelling the robber into instant flight behind her. Garrett gripped his dagger and hobbled after him in pursuit, but by this point, even a wounded man and a pig could easily outrun him.

Then Garrett saw a blur of motion at the corner of his vision.

"He's got Mr. Cromwell!" Bess shouted in outrage, streaking from her hiding place in the hedges. She stepped alongside Garrett and struck a stance that would do a harquebusier proud. Drawing a bead on the robber, she squeezed off a perfect shot.

The robber yelped and went down, grabbing his right buttock. After he fell, he tried to crawl away, but gained only a few feet before he gave up and writhed on the ground while Mr. Cromwell, still tethered, regarded him blandly from a respectful distance.

Bess nodded in satisfaction, stamping the carbine's butt into the dirt. Eyebrow raised, she turned to Garrett. "He had Mr. Cromwell!"

Garrett threw his arms around her and roared, laughing as he'd never thought he would again.

In response, Bess smiled like a little girl, so full of innocence and undiluted joy that he could see how she must have been before life had stolen her wonder and crushed her dreams.

But Bess's practical nature would not be easily routed. "Gwynneth!" she said abruptly. "She may be hurt—"

"Gwynneth is fine." Garrett didn't want to let go of his wife, not even for a second. Holding onto Bess, he glanced down at the maid laid out on the soft earth. "She just fainted. See? She's breathing peaceful as a baby. She'll come around." Glad that Gwynneth was alive, that Bess was alive—that *he* was alive—Garrett pulled his wife even tighter against him.

"Oof. Not so hard, Garrett. There's a baby between us, remember?"

"Aye." Grinning, he rubbed her belly. "And a fine baby it shall be, baseborn or no." Funny, how things could change so quickly. Why had he worried so about rank and wealth? As long as he had his family, he wouldn't lose anything that really mattered, regardless of the Roundheads. Hell, his great-grandfather had amassed a huge fortune, starting with far less than Garrett had squirreled away.

Bess leaned her head against his shoulder. "I don't care whether this baby is baseborn or noble, as long as it's ours and it's healthy."

Garrett tipped up her lovely face and memorized the moment when he knew he loved her and her alone, totally and irrevocably. Then he kissed her, long and lingering. He barely noticed when the baby kicked him, twice.

Their tender embrace was broken by the sound of something crashing through the underbrush from the woods. Both of them turned to see Stephen burst through the hedges, his clothes awry, his blood-streaked hair dotted with leaves, and the pistol waving wildly in his hand. "Milord! I heard shots. Is everything all right?" Spotting Gwynneth, he dropped the gun and bent to render aid.

Garrett grinned. "Everything's more than all right, Stephen." He bussed his wife soundly. "Everything is wonderful!"

Gwynneth moaned, then opened her eyes. "Oh, Mister Stephen! I thought they had killed you!"

The priest helped her to her feet. "Fortunately, they hit me on this thick old skull, where it could do the least harm." He gingerly patted his head.

"Agh!" Bess stiffened in Garrett's arms.

"What is it?" he asked, frightened by the brief flash of pain and shock on her face.

Her eyes widened. "I think it's the baby. It's coming."

# ✖ CHAPTER 25 ✖

*E*very muscle across Elizabeth's distended belly contracted in a wrenching spasm, bending her double. She dropped the musket and bracketed her rock-hard abdomen with her palms. "Garrett!" The pressure tightened to crushing intensity, made worse by an accompanying surge of mindless panic.

She couldn't be in labor yet. It was too soon! The baby wasn't due for at least a fortnight.

Garrett's strong hand closed on her elbow and held her steady. "Stephen," he called, "help me hold her up!"

Stephen instantly abandoned his fuss over Gwynneth's upset. Trailed by the maid, he hurried to Elizabeth's side, but the contraction had begun to ease by the time they got there.

"Whew." Elizabeth straightened, rubbing the small of her back, only to experience a monumental shifting inside her. She looked down and saw the high, hard mound of her belly ripple, then settle lower and lower until the baby was wedged securely into the saddle of her bones. "What's happening?" No sooner were the words out of her mouth than she felt a rush of wet warmth erupt between her legs, spilling to spread into a dark stain that quickly seeped beyond her skirts. "Oh, no." Embarrassed though she was, she thanked God it wasn't blood.

"Nothing to worry about, milady," Gwynneth comforted. "It's just milady's water breaking. Perfectly natural, when the child is on the way."

Garrett's head snapped up, his golden brows drawn together. "Now?"

"Aye." Gwynneth leveled a meaningful look at her master. "Now, my lord. When the water breaks hard that way, the babe is usually in a hurry."

Cold fingers of fear tightened around Elizabeth's heart. "But the midwife isn't here, yet. What if we can't find her?" She looked to her husband. "Oh, Garrett, I'm frightened. It's so soon." And she was so old to be having her first child. Twenty-eight—almost a crone.

Women her age had far more stillbirths and they often died in labor.

"Don't worry, Bess." Garrett's right arm circled behind her and tightened in a protective gesture. "Everything will be all right. Let's just get you inside. Can you walk?"

"Of course I can walk," she said irritably, "but can you?" She could see he was at the end of his endurance. Garrett's eyes were sunken with pain and fatigue, his half smile forced. Elizabeth's tone softened. "You shouldn't be helping me; I should be helping you. Where's your stick?"

"Bother my stick," he said, guiding her toward the house. "Come along."

Elizabeth had taken only a few steps when she felt an ominous tightening in her belly. "Wait." She planted her feet in the hard-packed earth. "Another pain is starting." As it grew, she curled forward, glad for Garrett's firm support on her left and Stephen's on her right. This one was more ferocious than the first, and lasted far longer.

Her eyes squeezed closed involuntarily. Over the sound of her own panting breaths, she heard Gwynneth say, "Her ladyship might have been in silent labor for some time, now. The pains are so close together and so hard, I fear the child is well on its way."

When the contraction subsided, Elizabeth forced herself erect, only to find her husband studying her with a strange mixture of worry and confusion. As they started again for the house, his expression cleared.

"Marry me, Bess," he said, his half smile blooming to a grin.

"Garrett, what in Heaven's name are you talking about?" she said crossly, in no mood for pranks. "We *are* married. You can't have forgotten; you remind me of it every time the subject comes up."

"I haven't forgotten." He cocked his head as if she had just given him an unexpected gift. "But *you* were the one who kept telling me our 'heretic' wedding didn't count. Does this mean you've changed your mind?"

Moving toward the house at all deliberate speed, she laid her hand atop her belly and said, "Well, I'd be in a fine pickle at this point if I *didn't* accept our marriage, now wouldn't I?"

Garrett's pace slowed. "Then you take me as I am, at last?" he asked. Though his eyes were merry, she could see the question was a serious one.

Elizabeth studied him closely and caught a glimpse of the boy within the man—all earnest and vulnerable beneath his banter. Strange, that she had never before thought of Garrett as vulnerable. In a flash of insight, she realized denial would wound him, perhaps irretrievably.

How should she answer? She did not want to wound him. Yet the shadows of her past compelled her to choose safety, to protect herself by hiding her true feelings. But part of her— a part Garrett had awakened—urged her to take a chance and reach out for happiness.

Lady Catherine's voice echoed through her mind: "Give him a chance, and you will love him, too."

There was little use in denying the truth any longer: Elizabeth did love him. For all his flaws, the man had done her nothing but good. He had been her lover, her champion, her protector, her friend. And he had shown fierce courage in fighting to win back his old life after he was wounded.

Anne Murray had said Elizabeth might tame him, but she didn't want to. She wanted him as he was. Before Garrett, her existence had been like a dark and distant dream painted in shades of gray, but since he had come into her life . . . She looked into his face, now, and saw everything that was bright and brilliant—and, yes, even dangerous, and she loved him for it all.

Mary had seen it, even when she, herself, had not.

So, for the first time in her life, Elizabeth opened her guarded heart and chose hope over safety, risk over security. "Yes, Garrett, I accept you as you are," she said softly. "Though it cost me my soul, you are my husband, good and true." When she saw the healing her words worked in him, she had courage to speak the rest. "I would choose no other."

Garrett peered at her in wonder, his stature straightening. Then he halted and turned to the priest. "Stephen, I've finally made up my mind." A fresh resolve firmed his features. "Will you baptize me straightaway into the faith of my ancestors?"

"With greatest joy, my lord," Stephen answered, as calmly

as if Garrett had just asked for another pair of boots.

"Garrett!" Elizabeth's mouth fell open. "You're converting?"

Until that moment, she hadn't realized just how deeply she had despaired of his ever adopting her faith. Ironic, that he offered her the hope of Heaven only after she had chosen to be his wife unconditionally—even at the cost of hell.

"Aye, I'm converting." Garrett's eyes radiated a peace she had not seen there before.

"You would do that for me?" she whispered.

"Yes." The calm assurance in his face confirmed that this was no empty gesture. "And for myself." He turned a grateful smile to Stephen. "Stephen did more than help me learn to walk again. He also helped me find answers to some hard questions."

Elizabeth felt as if she were hovering, weightless, half an inch above the ground—light as a feather, despite her girth. Her fondest desire had been granted! Suddenly, words seemed inadequate. Radiating gratitude from every pore, she murmured inanely, "Garrett, I'm so glad."

Never serious for long, Garrett bent stiffly to one knee before her, his blue eyes alight with humor. "This is the last time I'll ask you, madam: Marry me, in proper Roman fashion, *before* our child is born." His gaze met hers, confirming, "I vow, I shall mean every word."

In the warmth of his promise, Elizabeth felt the cold shell around her heart melt away, leaving the future bright with possibilities. "Very well," she answered in a masterpiece of understatement. "I will marry you, and gladly."

Rapt until now, Gwynneth crossed herself and exclaimed, "Thanks be to the Blessed Mother and all the saints!" She grabbed a startled Stephen and kissed him soundly on both cheeks, then pinned him in a bear hug, exclaiming, "Bless you, Father! Now I can die a happy woman. My lady's soul is safe at last, and her babe will be well-born in the eyes of God and the Church!"

Elizabeth's abdomen tightened again, this time pushing her unborn child against her pelvis so hard, she was afraid the bones would sunder where she stood. She tugged at Garrett's sleeve. "Get up, husband, and help me into the house . . . unless you want our child to be delivered in the barnyard." The crushing pressure intensified, causing her to gasp. "Father, run fetch your missal! I fear you've precious little time for a baptism and a marriage." She added emphatically, "But don't leave out a single word of the wedding ceremony!"

"Not even obey?" Garrett teased as the priest loped ahead of them.

"Not even obey." She met his gaze with a new conviction. "Or love. This time, I, too, shall mean every word."

Two hours later, following an eventful homecoming by the household and an uneventful but productive labor by Elizabeth, Lady Catherine stepped into the hallway where Garrett was waiting. She looked around. "Where are the girls?"

Garrett rose, his heart pounding in fear and anticipation. "I sent them to their rooms. They were driving me mad with their whispers and anxious looks." He leveled worried eyes at his mother. "What's happened?"

His mother looked up at him with a nostalgic smile and brushed the hair from his forehead. It seemed almost a gesture of farewell. "You're a father, Garrett." Her small hand tenderly cupped his cheek, then she reverted to her usual, nononsense self. "Mother and child are doing beautifully."

"Thank God." Breathing a silent prayer of thanksgiving, Garrett turned his forehead to the wall to conceal the happy tears that welled in his eyes. As he struggled to regain his composure, he felt the tension bleed from his knotted neck and shoulders. He had been so afraid for Elizabeth, and for the child. When he could trust himself to speak, he turned back to his mother. "May I see them?"

"Of course. Elizabeth and the baby are all cleaned up and waiting." Lady Catherine opened the door to the master's chamber wide. "Go right in." She motioned him inside, adding firmly, "Keep your voice down, though, and don't make a racket. You'll frighten my grandchild."

Garrett cocked an eyebrow at his mother. "Something tells me I've lost my spot at the center of the universe."

"Don't complain, dear," she said briskly. "You had your turn."

Garrett stepped inside and saw Bess lying under fresh sheets and comforters, her face radiant but her eyes weary. The baby lay swaddled in the crook of her arm, its blankets concealing all but a bit of pink forehead and down-covered scalp.

His child, and Bess's. Together, they had made a new life!

As the reality of it began to sink in, Garrett found himself wishing, with all his heart, that his own father had lived to share this day. He hobbled across the room to Bess's side.

He had never seen her so beautiful. She turned lucent blue eyes up at him, her pale cheeks brightened by a delicate glow. Bess stretched her free hand toward him. ''Come see your son.''

''A son!'' Suddenly weak in the knees, Garrett sank to the side of the bed. ''I was so grateful to hear you and the baby were all right, I forgot to ask if it was a boy or a girl.'' He kissed the back of her hand, then stroked the satiny curls that had worked loose at her temples. Garrett grinned. ''Well, what are you waiting for? Let's see this boy.''

Bess pulled back the blankets to reveal two tiny fists scrubbing at a ruddy little face. The baby frowned and blinked open dark blue eyes, his forehead wrinkling with a serious expression. In that instant, the endless march of generations was no longer a meaningless abstract; it had taken shape and substance in the small, towheaded infant his wife was holding. ''Is he all right?''

''Perfect. Ten fingers, ten toes, and all his parts accounted for.''

Hovering nearby, Garrett's mother couldn't remain silent a moment longer. ''Isn't he wonderful? I do believe he's even more beautiful than you were, Garrett.'' She bent beside Garrett and took the baby's tiny fist into her hand. ''He's Nana's best boy, yes he is. The strongest, most beautiful boy in all of England.'' The baby hiccoughed, to her open admiration. ''That's right, precious boy. Speak up.''

Lady Catherine shifted her admiration to Elizabeth. ''Your wife was made for motherhood, Garrett. I've never seen a quicker, smoother delivery for a first child. The next one will be even easier.'' Reluctantly letting go of the baby's hand, she rose and said with her usual tact and sensitivity, ''Now if you two will excuse me, I'd like to go tell the girls. They'll be so excited to hear that they have a nephew.'' Without waiting for a response, she slipped out into the hall and closed the door behind her, leaving them alone with their child.

More content than she could ever remember being, Elizabeth kissed the top of the baby's head. ''So soft.'' She brushed her lips across the white fuzz that covered his scalp. Then she watched as Garrett wiggled his finger into the baby's fist.

"Look how long his fingers are," he observed in awe. "Do you think that means he'll be tall, like me?"

"Aye," Bess answered. "He came into this world twenty-four inches long—an inch bigger than you were. And he definitely has your hands. Look at his fingernails. They're spatulate, like yours."

"So they are." Garrett's chest puffed with pride. "But the mouth is yours," he observed, leaning closer for a better look.

"Here." Still weak from the strain of delivery, she pushed the precious bundle toward him as best she could. "Hold him. He won't break."

Garrett took his son into his arms and unwrapped the blankets. "Good glory, but you *are* a long drink of water, boy!" Slowly and reverently, he examined every inch of his newborn son. "Such intricate perfection. Look at those toes, and his feet. And his ears. I'm holding a miracle in my hands."

Seeing the joyous wonder in Garrett's face, Elizabeth knew he would be everything to their son that she had wanted in a father, but never had.

The baby began to squirm, prompting Garrett to wrap him back up against the cool evening air. "Sorry, my boy. Didn't mean to give you gooseflesh." He tucked the infant securely into the crook of his arm. "What shall we call him?"

"I thought perhaps Edward, for you and your father, and Blake for my mother's father. What do you think?"

"I think two names aren't nearly enough for such a wonderful child," Garrett said, gently rocking. "He should have at least three. How about Edward *Stephen* Blake?" He considered, then said aloud, "Edward Stephen Blake, Viscount of Chestwick and Earl of Ravenwold. I like it."

Naming the baby after Stephen was a perfect gesture of gratitude and respect. "Earl or not, if our son proves half as good and honorable as those he's named for, he'll need no other titles."

She watched as Garrett held up his free hand to mask all but the child's dark blue eyes. "I do believe he has his aunt Charlotte's eyes."

So moved she could barely speak, Elizabeth whispered, "What a blessing, that you can see it, too."

He grew serious. "Until this moment, I never gave any thought to the past. Heritage, rank, tradition meant nothing to me. But now, holding our son . . ." He looked to Elizabeth.

"He *is* our past—everyone who has gone before us, and everything that has brought us to this moment."

"And our future," she said softly. "I used to fear the future," she confessed, "but not anymore, and not just because of the baby. It's because of you, Garrett. Before we married, I wasted the present, filling my days with endless work so I wouldn't have to admit how empty my life had become." Suddenly shy, she looked down. "But you were so colorful, so alive, so free, so *happy* . . . everything I wasn't." Her eyes lifted to focus on his. "You gave me back my laughter, Garrett. And my anger. And my grief. You brought me back to life." Elizabeth studied her husband's face and saw everything that was bright and brilliant, and, yes, even dangerous, and she loved him for it all. A slow smile formed on her lips. "You've made the present a wonderful place to be, and the future something I can look forward to . . . as long as I have you." She chuckled. "Life will be quite an adventure, I think."

"An adventure we'll face together." Garrett kissed her tenderly on the lips, then handed her the baby, who had begun to squirm and fuss. "I think he wants his mama." He settled back with an expression of absolute peace on his face. "I love you, Bess, but don't let it go to your head."

Her joy overflowing, Elizabeth closed her eyes and sang, her voice as light and clear as a sunbeam:

> Rest well, my love, and calm your weary heart.
> Angels watch and Heaven guards your sleep.
> Nothing more shall harm you or shall part
> The bond of love that constancy doth keep.
> Drift on dreams and ride them to your rest.
> Dreams come true when love is true and blest.

When she opened her eyes, Garrett was staring at her, transfixed. Visibly moved, he barely managed a halting, "That was beautiful, Bess. Beyond beautiful. You sing like an angel." He glanced down into his lap, then back up at her. "Thank you for letting me hear you sing to the baby. It means a lot to me."

She took his hand and pressed it to her cheek. "I wasn't singing to the baby, Garrett. I was singing to you."

Garrett lay beside her, drawing her and the baby close. "Then sing to me again, my love. Tonight, and every night down all the good long years God gives us.''

Basking in the love she saw in his eyes, Elizabeth smiled as easily as she drew breath. Then she closed her eyes and sang her love for him.

And so it was Elizabeth welcomed all the good long nights God gave them with singing . . . and with the sound of laughter.

# Author's Note

$\mathcal{T}$he roots of religious intolerance are as old as mankind. Though not a Roman Catholic, I am appalled and fascinated by the excesses committed in the name of faith by my British ancestors—Protestant and Roman Catholic alike. As in most religious conflicts, great evil and great good were done by both sides.

Following the beheading of Charles I on January 30, 1649, Oliver Cromwell wrestled Britain into a brief, disastrous experiment in republican government. Eleven years of increased religious persecution and retribution against Loyalists followed, during which numerous Loyalists and Roman Catholics sought refuge in America. Ironically, more than a few Roman Catholics who emigrated to Virginia converted to the Church of England, owing to the lack of Roman Catholic churches and the more tolerant attitudes of "frontier" clergy and colonial society.

The fledgling British republic—doomed to failure by continued religious strife and constant infighting among Parliamentary factions and Cromwell's generals—survived Cromwell's death by only two years.

After helping Prince James escape, Joseph Bampfield stuck close to the grateful prince and used his influence to promote his own friends, most notably a former Parliamentarian, Lord Willoughby of Parham. Bampfield convinced James to appoint Lord Willoughby an admiral of the Royalist Fleet, despite the man's complete lack of naval training. Prince Charles arrived at the Hague just in time to prevent Willoughby from launching a premature, and no doubt disastrous, naval strike at England. Charles then quietly, but firmly, banished Joseph Bampfield from his younger brother's retinue.

Seven years later, a financially strapped Anne Murray finagled an audience with Prince Charles and petitioned him for compensation for her role in helping Prince James escape. Prince Charles merely thanked her, granting Anne only a royal smile—owing, no doubt, to his continued suspicions about his younger brother's aspirations to the throne. But one of Charles's Gentlemen of the Bedchamber, Henry Seymour, took pity on Anne and managed to convince the future king to grant Anne a royal gift of fifty gold pieces.

On May 29, 1660 (his thirtieth birthday), Charles II returned to London to succeed his father. As king, Charles II enacted two Acts of Indulgence, promoting religious tolerance, but by 1673, anti-Catholic sentiment in Parliament forced him to agree to the Test Act, which permitted only members of the Church of England to rule the nation. For the next eight years the strong-willed, canny Charles struggled against Parliament, ultimately dissolving it to rule as absolute despot until his death in 1685. Still without a legitimate heir at fifty-four, Charles II died of ''fever'' after receiving the last rites of the Roman Catholic Church.

His brother James II, a Catholic, ruled for only three years before Protestant opposition forced him to flee England in fear of his life, never to return.

Read on for an excerpt of *Damask Rose*, the next enthralling romance by Haywood Smith:

From the first year of his manhood, Tynan's dreams were haunted by the shadow of a woman, her voice as seductive as the first scent of spring on a raw Highland breeze; again and again, she summoned him by name and whispered of his destiny:

> I call the remnant at the root's direction,
> Seed of love from hate in vengeance sworn.
> Blood oath broken by a dark reflection
> Buried with the damask rose's thorn.
> Witch who is no witch works her protection;
> Death from life and life from death is born.

Now he swore he could hear her in the scrape of leather against the rocky shore as he dragged the small boat he had stolen through the fog.

*Tynan . . .*

She was close; he could feel her.

Was it the Isle of Mist that called him, or his own blood hunger? Once he had thought it was the ghost of his mother, long dead and unavenged, but time had convinced him otherwise.

Though he could not see the Isle of Mist for the fog, he'd been told it lay close across the narrows. The Witch, they called the place.

*The witch who is no witch?* he wondered.

After more than a year of searching, all his instincts told Tynan his destiny was waiting there. And his prey.

The fog parted briefly ahead of him, exposing a barren hummock that looked for all the world like the mossy breast of some giant, sleeping earth-goddess. Guided by that one glimpse, he pushed the boat into the cold, fast-moving waters of Caol Rhea and heaved himself inside.

Overburdened by his substantial weight, the little curragh

settled alarmingly low in the swift current. The humble craft had been built for ordinary men, not the likes of Tynan, whose tall, powerful stature sent children scurrying for their mother's skirts and turned heads even among the giants of the Highlands.

Muttering an oath, he shifted cautiously to distribute the burden of his oversized frame. One false move, and he'd end up swimming the half mile to the island—a daunting prospect even for Tynan on this February day. Judging from the whirlpools and eddies all around him, these cold, gray waters would like nothing better than to suck him to a nameless grave. Determined not to oblige them, he moved with agonizing care to lay the oars into their cradles. Tynan gauged the current and the angle of the waves, then rowed with smooth, powerful strokes toward The Witch's breast.

*Tynan . . . Deliverer*, the voice breathed above the rhythmic splash of the oars.

She had never said that before!

His name meant darkness, not deliverer.

Tynan tried to shake off the gathering sense of foreboding that swirled around him like the white oblivion of the mist.

It wasn't easy to maintain his heading through the powerful crosscurrents of these narrows. Despite years of secret training with axe and broadsword, his muscles strained at the oars. There were easier crossings, but he had chosen this one for brevity and stealth. It the fog should clear, he was less likely to be seen here than at An Caol.

Without slacking his pace, he turned in the eerie silence and tried to make out some sign of the shoreline, but saw only fog that seemed to thicken with every stroke of the oars. Despite the westerly currents that tempered these lands even now in February, a sudden chill raised the flesh beneath Tynan's plaid.

Would the place itself betray his coming?

No matter. As he had sworn, he would find Laird Cullum's granddaughter and bring her safe to the old man's feet. The thought of what would follow brought a bitter smile to Tynan's lips. He would do what he must. Only then could he lay down the burden he had borne these twenty years and join his kin. His father and mother were waiting, along with his brothers and sisters. And the rest of his kinsmen, his sept. Only when Tynan had kept his vows would they all have peace.

Strengthened by the prospect, he stroked harder to keep his course amid the whirling eddies of the strait. He would find the girl and bring her back, or die trying.

Haywood Smith's *Damask Rose*—coming from St. Martin's Paperbacks!